LOVELY
WAR

★ *Julie Berry* ★

LOVELY
WAR

VIKING

VIKING
An imprint of Penguin Random House LLC, New York

First published in the United States of America by Viking,
an imprint of Penguin Random House LLC, 2019

Visit us online at penguinrandomhouse.com

LIBRARY OF CONGRESS CATALOGING-IN-PUBLICATION DATA IS AVAILABLE.
ISBN 9780451469939

Printed in the U.S.A.
Book design by Jim Hoover

1   3   5   7   9   10   8   6   4   2

For Cyrena Davison Keith
and Edith Dudley Gardner,
my grandmothers;

for Kendra Levin, forever dear;

and for Phil

························●●···········

And when Hephaestus heard the grievous tale, he went his way to his smithy, pondering evil in the deep of his heart, and set on the anvil block the great anvil and forged bonds which might not be broken or loosed, that the lovers might bide fast where they were.

So they two went to the couch, and lay them down to sleep, and about them clung the cunning bonds of the wise Hephaestus, nor could they in any wise stir their limbs or raise them up. Then at length they learned that there was no more escaping.

—from *The Odyssey*, by Homer

························●●···········

OVERTURE

DECEMBER 1942

I Hear a Rhapsody

IT IS EARLY evening in the lobby of an elegant Manhattan hotel. Crystal prisms dangling from the chandeliers glow with soft electric light. On velvet couches near the fire, couples sit close, the men in officers' uniform, the women in evening wear, resting their heads on their gentlemen's shoulders. Restaurant garçons seat couples at dim tables secluded by faux-Greek marble busts and showy ferns, where urgent kisses may remain unseen.

The orchestra warms up, then begins the strains of "I Hear a Rhapsody." A lady singer fills the glittering stage with her amber-colored voice:

MY DARLING, HOLD ME TIGHT

AND WHISPER TO ME

THEN SOFT THROUGH A STARRY NIGHT

I'LL HEAR A RHAPSODY

She's not Dinah Shore, but she's really something.

A man and woman enter the lobby and approach the front desk. All eyes follow their progress across the Persian rugs. The man, colossal in build and stern of jaw, wears a fedora tipped low over his brow. When he reaches for a billfold from the inside pocket of his double-breasted pin-striped suit, the panicky thought occurs to the desk clerk that perhaps the man is reaching for a pistol. His black-and-white wing-tip shoes don't look jaunty. They look dangerous. He makes half the men nervous, and the other half angry. He's the kind of man who could crush you beneath his feet, and he knows it.

But oh, is he beautiful.

His lady friend, even more so.

She wears a tailored, belted suit of deep blue that fits her better than skin. Her figure is the sort that makes other women give up altogether. From the waves of dark hair, coiffed and coiled under her cocktail hat, to her wide, long-lashed eyes peering out through its coy little veil of black netting, down to the seams of her silk stockings disappearing into her Italian leather pumps, she is arrestingly beautiful. Impossibly perfect. The scent of her perfume spreads its soft fingers across the lobby. Everyone there, man and woman, surrenders to their awareness of her.

The tall man knows this, and he's none too pleased about it.

He riffles a pile of bills under the nose of the stammering clerk and snatches a key out of his unprotesting hand. They make their way through the lobby, with the man urging the woman forward as though time won't keep, while she takes every slow step as though she'd invented the art of walking.

They carry no luggage.

Even so, a stooped and bearded bellhop follows them up the stairs and down the corridor. The violent glares from the tall man would have sent others fleeing, but this bellhop chatters as he lopes along on crooked steps. They ignore him, and he doesn't seem to mind.

They reach their room. Its lock gives way beneath the swift

thrust and twist of the man's key. They disappear into their room, but the persistent bellhop follows them in.

He clicks the light switch back and forth rapidly. "Bulb must be out," he says apologetically. "I'll be right back with maintenance."

"Never mind," says the man.

"Bottle of champagne?" the bellhop suggests.

"Scram," the man tells him. He and his lovely companion disappear down the narrow hallway, past the closet and bath, and into the tastefully decorated suite.

"As you like," the bellhop replies.

They hear the door open and shut. In an instant they are in each other's arms. Shoes are kicked off, hats tossed aside. Jacket buttons are shown no mercy.

One might not trust this man, and one might even envy or condemn this sort of woman, but no one can deny that when they kiss, when these two paragons, these specimens of sculpted perfection collide, well—

Kisses by the billions happen every day, even in a lonely world like ours.

But this is a kiss for the ages. Like a clash of battle and a delicious melding of flesh, rolled together and set on fire.

They're lost in it for a while.

Until a cold metal net falls over them, and the electric lights snap on.

"Evening, Aphrodite," says the stoop-shouldered bellhop.

DECEMBER 1942

The Golden Net

THE PRISONERS, stunned and blinking, have the squashed and deformed look of criminals who pull pantyhose over their heads to rob a bank. The golden mesh of the net, supple and translucent, presses down upon them with the weight of a ship's iron chains. It's a work of exquisite beauty and extraordinary cunning, but neither god appreciates its craftsmanship just then.

Aphrodite's lover tears at the net with savage fingers, but its glittering strands hold firm.

"I'll skewer you, brother," he snarls. "I'll smash your skull like an eggshell."

Most people would flee at the malice in that deep voice. But not Hephaestus. He's not afraid of the massive god.

"Don't waste your breath on him, Ares," says beautiful Aphrodite. She turns a withering gaze on her uniformed husband. "For a hotel this expensive, the service here stinks."

Hephaestus, god of fires, blacksmiths, and volcanoes, ignores the jab. He eases himself into a soft chair and stretches his misshapen feet before him on the carpet, then addresses the battle god, who is indeed his brother. Both are Hera's sons. "Service everywhere has gone down the toilet since your latest war began. All the good men are overseas."

"Where they should be." Ares thrashes again at the golden net. He tries to conjure a weapon from thin air. Normally this would be effortless for him.

"No point," advises Hephaestus. "Might as well be mortal, for all the good your power'll do you. My net blocks you. Can't have you escaping."

Aphrodite, goddess of passion, turns her back upon her husband. He catches her gaze in a long gilt-edged mirror.

"You disgust me," she tells his reflection. "Jealous, cringing dog."

"Jealous?" Hephaestus feigns surprise. "Who, me? With a wife so loyal and devoted?"

If his words sting Aphrodite, she doesn't let it show. She pulls her blue jacket back on over her blouse and knots a fetching little scarf around her neck. "Well, you've caught us," she tells Hephaestus. "Netted like two fish in a stream. What do you plan to do with us?"

"I've done it" is his reply. "Step one, anyway. Put you under arrest."

Ares and Aphrodite look at him like he's mad, which is possible.

"Step two: offer you a plea bargain."

Aphrodite's eyebrows rise. "Offer me a *what*?"

"A deal," he says. "Renounce this chump, and come home with me. Be my faithful wife, and all is forgiven."

The clock on the mantelpiece gets two or three clicks in before Aphrodite begins to snicker. Ares, who has watched for her response, now guffaws with laughter. Too big, too loud, but he's relieved, and he's never been a good actor.

"You think she'll leave *this* for *you*?" He flexes his many (very, *very* many) muscles. They swim like dolphins under his glowing skin. The removal of his shirt has done glorious things.

Hephaestus is drowning inside, but he's come this far and he sticks to his plan. "You reject my offer?" he says. "Then I'm taking you to trial on Olympus."

The net, which had lain over them like a heavy blanket, now encircles and encloses Ares and Aphrodite like a laundry bag, while a chain hoists them upward. Their divine limbs, so impressive in marble statues, jumble every which way uncomfortably. The netting bag rotates slowly through the air, like a ham curing over hot coals.

"What are you *doing*?" Aphrodite cries. "You put us down *at once*."

"Your court date has been moved up," answers the bellhop. "Father Zeus will officiate at the bench, and the other gods will form a jury."

The goddess of beauty has turned a delicate shade of pale green. The spectacle of the entire pantheon of immortals howling and cackling at her mortification! Nobody knows the sting of gods' mockery better than a god. And nobody knows your weak spots better than sisters. Those prissy little virgins, Artemis and Athena, always looking down their smug, goody-goody noses at her.

Bagged like a chicken she might be, but Aphrodite still has her pride. Far better to bargain with her husband in a swanky Manhattan hotel than to quail before her entire family.

"Hephaestus," she says smoothly—and Aphrodite can have a brown velvet voice when she wants to—"is there, perhaps, a third option?" She sees her husband is listening, so she presses her advantage. "Couldn't we just talk this out here? The three of us?" She elbows Ares. "We'll stay in the net and listen. Ares will behave. Surely we don't need to drag others into such a private matter."

Hephaestus hesitates. Privacy is Aphrodite's domain. A hotel room practically gives her a home-court advantage. He smells a trick.

But she does have a point. He, too, has pride to sacrifice upon the altar in hashing this matter out publicly.

"Let me get this straight," he says slowly. "You decline your right to a trial by jury?"

"Oh, come off it," says Ares. "You're a blacksmith, for Pete's sake, not an attorney."

Hephaestus turns to his wife. "All right," he tells her. "We can do it here. A more private trial. I'll be the judge."

"Judge, jury, and executioner?" protests Ares. "This kangaroo court is a sham."

Hephaestus wishes he had a bailiff who could club this unruly spectator on the head. But that's probably not what bailiffs are supposed to do.

"Never mind him," Aphrodite tells her husband. "You're already sitting in judgment upon us, so, yes, be the judge if it suits you."

Ares laughs out loud. "Tell you what, old man," he says. "Fight me for her. May the best god win."

Just how many times Hephaestus has imagined that satisfying prospect, not even his divine mind can count. The devious and cunning weapons he's devised, lying awake and alone at night, plotting a thousand ways to teach his cocky brother a lesson! If only.

But you don't accept a challenge to duel with the god of war. Hephaestus is no fool.

Except, perhaps, where his wife is concerned.

He produces for himself a bench and a gavel. "This court will come to order," he says. "Let the trial begin."

DECEMBER 1942

The Judgment of Manhattan

HEPHAESTUS LOWERS THE net back to the couch and lets it expand so his prisoners can at least sit comfortably. They can stand up, but they can't go far.

"Goddess," he says, "in the matter of *Hephaestus v. Aphrodite*, you are charged with being an unfaithful wife. How do you plead?"

Aphrodite considers. "Amused."

Ares snorts.

"You're in contempt of court," Hephaestus says. "How do you plead?"

"On which charge?" asks the goddess. "Infidelity, or contempt?"

Hephaestus's nostrils flare. This is already off to a terrible start. "Both."

"Ah," she says. "Guilty on both counts. But I don't mean to be contemptible."

Hephaestus pauses. "You plead *guilty*?"

She nods. "Um-hm."

"Oh." He hadn't expected this. The clever lines he'd prepared, the scalding words, they desert him like traitors.

"I've disappointed you." Aphrodite's voice oozes with sympathy anyone would swear is sincere. "Would it make you feel better to present your evidence anyway?"

Who's manipulating whom here?

She's not afraid. No amount of evidence will matter.

But Hephaestus spent months gathering it, so he submits it for the court.

The lights dim. A succession of images appears in the air before them like a Technicolor film in their own hotel room. The goddess of love and the god of war, kissing under a shady bower. On the snowcapped rim of Mount Popocatépetl at sunset. Cuddling on the shoulder of an Easter Island statue. On the white sand beaches beneath the sheer cliffs of Smugglers' Cove, on Greece's own Zakynthos Island.

"Hermes," mutters Aphrodite darkly. "Zeus never should've given him a camera."

If Hephaestus had expected his wife to writhe in embarrassment at this damning proof, he has only disappointment for his efforts. She's shameless. His brother is shameless. He was a fool to think he could shame either of them.

The images fade. Silence falls.

Aphrodite watches her husband.

Hephaestus's thoughts swirl. What had he expected? A tearful apology? A pledge to be true? He should've known this would never work.

But he'd been desperate. Even Olympians, when desperate, can't think straight. Of all the beings in the cosmos, Hephaestus is the only one who can't pray to the goddess of love for help with his marriage troubles. The poor sap hasn't a clue.

"Hephaestus," Aphrodite says gently, "this trial was never to get me to admit something you know I don't mind admitting, was it?"

"You *should* mind."

"Your real question," she says, "if I'm not mistaken, is why don't I love you?"

"It's simple," Ares says. "She loves me."

Something is apparently hilarious to Aphrodite. Ares's huge arms fold across his chest.

She wipes her eyes and speaks. "I don't love either of you."

Ares sits up tall and thrusts out his lower lip.

"Hephaestus," Aphrodite continues. He feels like he's now in the witness stand. "Do *you* love me?"

He's not sure what to say. What's she doing? He wishes his dumb brother weren't here.

"I'll answer for you," she tells him. "Of course you don't."

"I . . . That is . . ." Hephaestus stammers. "I'm here because I want—"

"*No one* can love me," she says. "No one."

"What do you mean?"

"That is the price," she tells him, "of being the goddess of love."

Ares's deep voice breaks the silence. "Don't be ridiculous," he says. "The only reason Father Zeus made you marry him was because all the other gods were fighting tooth and nail for your hand. He stuck you with him to avert a civil war. We *all* wanted you."

She shrugs. "I *know* you all wanted me."

Modesty was never her forte, but then, a humble god is hard to find.

"I'm the source of love," she says, "but no one will ever truly love me. The fountain of passion, but I will never know a true passion of my own."

Ares throws up his hands. "You're nuts! Have you read Homer? Hesiod?"

"Goddess," Hephaestus says quietly, "what can you mean?"

She gazes into his eyes until he squirms. "You male gods are all rapacious pigs," she says dismissively. "I grant you, Husband, you're less horrible than some. You all brag of your exploits. You're no more loving than an anvil is. Fickle and capricious and completely self-centered. You're incapable of love. Just as you're incapable of dying."

"You're calling *us* self-centered?" replies Ares. "You're no Florence Nightingale."

"You have no idea what I am," she tells him, "nor what good I do. I know what you think of my 'silly romances.'"

She turns to Hephaestus. "I might find a mortal to love me," she continues, "but that's worship, not love. I'm perfect. Mortals aren't meant to love perfection. It disillusions and destroys them in the end."

Hephaestus is baffled. Aphrodite has no one to love her? He, the god of fire and forges, has no shortage of ore and fuel. Ares, the god of war, has been enjoying a blood-soaked century like no other in history. Artemis has no shortage of stags to hunt. Poseidon's not low on salt water.

And his wife, the gorgeous goddess of romance, is lonely?

"Do you know what it's like," she says, "to spend eternity embedded in *every single love story*—the fleeting and the true, the trivial and the everlasting? I am elbow deep in love, working in passion the way artists work in watercolors. I feel it *all*." She wraps her arms tightly across her chest, as though the room is cold. "I envy the mortals. It's because they're weak and damaged that they can love." She shakes her head. "We need nothing. They're lucky to need each other."

"Yeah, well, they die," Ares points out.

"Why have you never said this before?" Hephaestus asks her.

"Why should I?" she says. "Why would you care? You think my work is stupid. You never come out of your forge."

She's right. Not stupid, not exactly. But, perhaps, inconsequential. Iron—there's something that lasts. Steel and stone. But human affection? Hephaestus, as any Greek scholar can tell you, wasn't born yesterday.

Aphrodite still looks cold. She couldn't be. But Hephaestus breathes at the fireplace, and the logs laid out there burst into sizzling flame.

Firelight plays across Aphrodite's features. She tilts her head to one side. "Do you want to see what real love looks like?"

Hephaestus looks up. Her eyes are shining.

"Do you want to hear about my favorites? Some of my finest work?"

"Yes." Hephaestus's reply surprises him. "I do."

A groan rises from the couch, but the goddess ignores War.

"I'll tell you the story of an ordinary girl and an ordinary boy. A true story. No, I'll do one better. I'll tell you two."

Ares lifts his head. "Do we know these stories?"

"Barely, if at all," she says. "You never pay attention to girls."

He snickers. "I beg to differ."

"I'm not talking about their bodies." Aphrodite's eyes roll. "You never pay attention to their *lives*."

"Ugh." His head drops back. "I knew this would be boring."

Aphrodite's eyes blaze. "I'll make it easy on you," she says. "My two stories involve soldiers. From the Great War. The First World War. You'll know their names and their rank, at any rate. You may find that you remember bits of their stories."

Aphrodite's dark-lidded eyes gaze out into the skyline of a Manhattan autumn evening. The Big Apple's lights have dimmed, in case of German U-boats in the harbor, or Zeus forbid, Luftwaffe bomber planes from who knows where, but not even a global war can completely snuff out the lights of the City That Never Sleeps.

Ares watches Aphrodite's lovely face, and Hephaestus's grotesque one. For the millionth time, the war god wonders what Zeus intended, forcing these two to marry. What a curse, to be yoked to that monstrosity! All the more tragic for someone so perfectly perfect as she.

Why, then, does Ares find the hairs on his arms prickling with jealousy? Even now, though the golden net divides the blacksmith from the goddess, there's something between them. Something he can neither conquer nor destroy. Impossible though it is, a silver thread binds Hephaestus and Aphrodite together, if only slightly, barring Ares from making Aphrodite completely his own.

But what does he expect? They're married, after all.

"Goddess."

Aphrodite meets her husband's gaze. He points his gavel at her. "Present your evidence."

When she tilts her head slightly, he smiles beneath his whiskers. "Tell your story."

Ares rolls his eyes. "Gods, no," he moans. "Bring out the hot pincers, the smoking brands! Anything but a *love story!*"

Aphrodite glares at him.

"She's always yammering on," Ares says, "trying to tell me about some dumb love letter, some random kiss or other, and how long it lasted, and, by Medusa's hair, *what they were wearing* at the time."

"Goddess?" says Hephaestus.

"Mmm?"

"Leave nothing out," says the god of fire. "Make your tale a long one."

ACT ONE

APHRODITE

Hazel—November 23, 1917

I FIRST SAW Hazel at a parish dance at her London borough church, St. Matthias, in Poplar. It was November 1917.

It was a benefit, with a drive organized for socks and tins of Bovril broth powder to send to the boys in France. But really, it was a fall dance like the one they held every autumn.

While others chatted and flirted, Hazel glued herself to the piano bench and played dance tunes. The chaperones gushed about her generosity, putting others' enjoyment before her own. Hazel was neither fooled nor flattered. She hated performing. But she'd rather stick pins in her eyeballs than make awkward conversation with boys. Anything was better. Even the spotlight.

She thought she was safe. But music draws me like a bee to honey. And not only me.

A young man sat some distance away and watched her play. He could see her hands, and the intent expression on her face. He tried not to stare, with limited success. He closed his eyes and listened to the music. But even as he listened, he saw in his mind's eye the tall, straight form of the piano girl, dressed in pale mauve lace, with her dark-haired head lowered just enough to watch the keys, and her lips parted, ever so slightly, as she breathed in time with the song.

Oh, the minute I saw those two in the same room, I knew it. I knew this could be one of my masterpieces. You don't find two hearts like this every day.

So I sat next to James, while he watched Hazel play, and kissed his cheek. Honestly, in his case, I don't even think I needed to do it. But he had a very nice cheek, and I didn't want to miss my chance. He'd shaved for the party, the little darling.

I was jealous of how he watched Hazel, drinking in her music like water and tasting how she dissolved herself in it like a sugar cube. None of the girls whirling by held anything for him. He was a neat sort of young man, very careful about his clothes, as though he dreaded the thought that his appearance might offend anyone. He shouldn't have worried. He wasn't exactly handsome, not at first glance, but there was something in those dark brown eyes that might cause Hazel to forget Chopin for a moment or two. If she would ever look up.

I slid onto the piano bench beside Hazel. She was so absorbed in her music that she didn't notice my arrival. Of course, almost no one notices me, yet all but the hard-hearted do sense a new mood. Perhaps it's my perfume. Perhaps it's something more. When I pass by, Love is in the air.

Of the young men present, some hadn't yet left for battlefields. Others were home on leave (medical or R & R). To their credit, the girls were wonderful about those with ghastly injuries, and made the wounded feel like princes. A few lads worked war production jobs in weapons factories. Some saw them as cowards shirking the battlefield, but this crowd of girls welcomed them in good humor. They were practical, these Poplar girls, and they preferred local beaux over absent loves. Some enterprising girls hedged their bets and held on to one of each.

The young ladies worked in munitions factories and in private homes as domestic servants. Not long ago they'd all been in school.

And then there was Hazel. She played like the daughter of a duchess, raised under the eye of the finest musical tutors. But she was the daughter of a music hall pianist and a factory seamstress. Hazel's father pounded the keys at night to keep the wolf from the door, but he taught his daughter to love the masters. Beethoven and Schubert and Schumann and Brahms. She played like an angel.

James felt her angel music whoosh through his hair.

Poor James. He was in a predicament. The one girl to whom he'd like to speak carried the party's entertainment in her hands. To interrupt her would be unthinkable; to wait until the party ended would mean she'd disappear into the crowd.

She reached a refrain, and I lifted her chin toward James's watchful face.

She caught his expression in full. Both of them were too startled, at first, to break away.

Hazel kept on playing, but she had seen straight through those brown eyes and into the depths behind them, and felt something of the thrill of being seen, truly seen.

But music won't keep. So Hazel played on. She wouldn't look up at James again. Not until the song was over did she sneak a peek. But he wasn't there. He'd gone.

It's the quiet things I notice. Hazel exhaled her disappointment. She would've liked one more glimpse, to see if she'd imagined something passing between them.

Hazel, my dear, you're an idiot, she told herself.

"Excuse me," said a voice beside her.

APHRODITE

First Dance—November 23, 1917

HAZEL TURNED TO see a forest-green necktie tucked carefully into a gray tweed jacket, and above it all, the face of the young man with the dark brown eyes.

"Oh," said Hazel. She stood up quickly.

"Hello," he said very seriously. Almost as if it were an apology.

His face was grave, his figure slim, his shoes shined, and his dress shirt crisp. Hazel watched his shoes and waited for the heat in her face to subside. Did those shoes contain feet like her father's, she wondered, with hair on top? *Stupid, stupid thought!*

"I'm sorry," the young man said. "I didn't mean to startle you."

"That's all right," Hazel replied. "I mean, you didn't." A fib.

The scent of bay rum aftershave and clean, ironed cloth reached Hazel's face and made it tingle. His cheeks were lean and smooth, and they looked so soft that Hazel's fingers twitched to stroke them. The dread possibility that she might act upon the impulse was so mortifying to Hazel that she very nearly bolted for the door.

"I wanted to tell you," the young man said, "how much I enjoyed your playing tonight."

Now, at least, Hazel had a script. Her parents had coached her over a lifetime of piano recitals in how to respond to compliments.

"Thank you very much," she said. "It's kind of you to say so."

It was a speech, from rote, and the young man knew it. A shadow passed across his face. Of course it did, the poor darling—he only had one chance to interact with her, only one thing he could decently say: that he loved her music, that it took him away from this place, from this night, one week before shipping overseas to the Western Front, where young men like him died in droves, and that she, *she*, had given him this indescribable gift of escape, all the while being so sincere and fascinating in her absorption in the music. Propriety allowed him only to tell her that he enjoyed her playing, when he wanted to say so much more, and the one thing he dared hope was that she would feel how desperately he meant it.

And her eyes, he now discovered, were wide and deep, rimmed with long black lashes.

Poor James.

Hazel knew she'd gotten it wrong. She swallowed her fear and looked into his eyes.

"Truly," she said, "thank you."

The shadow passed. "My name is James." He offered her his hand.

She took it, warm and dry, in hers and wished she didn't have a pianist's wiry, muscular thumb and fingers. Incidentally, that is not at all how James perceived her hands.

"And you?" He smiled. Never mind Hazel; I nearly swooned myself.

She blushed. If she did any more blushing, her cheeks might spontaneously combust. "I'm Hazel," she said. "Hazel Windicott."

"I'm glad to meet you, Miss Windicott." James etched her name into permanent memory. *Hazel Windicott. Hazel Windicott.*

"And you, Mr. James," replied the piano girl.

He smiled again, and this time dimples appeared in his cheeks. "Just James," he said. "My last name is Alderidge."

The stout woman running the entertainment, one Lois Prentiss, came bustling over to see why the music had stopped. An older woman, a favorite of mine named Mabel Kibbey, popped up like a gopher in a hole.

"Miss Windicott has worked hard all evening," she said. "I'm sure she'd like a moment's rest. I'll play for a spell. I think I know some tunes the young folks will like."

Before Hazel could protest, Mabel Kibbey had pried her out from the piano and pushed her toward James. "Go dance," she said. In a blink, James led Hazel to the edge of the dance floor and offered her his arm. Dazzled by the pink spots on James's cheeks, just above the dimples, she placed her left hand upon James's tweed shoulder and rested her right hand in his.

Mabel Kibbey struck up a slow waltz. James pulled Hazel as close as he dared.

"I'm afraid I don't really know how to dance," confessed Hazel. "There's a reason I stay behind the piano."

James stopped immediately. "Would you rather not dance?"

Hazel fixed her gaze on his necktie. "No, I'd like to. But you mustn't laugh at me."

"I wouldn't," he said seriously. He slid back into the music.

"When I trip and fall, then?" She hoped this would come across as a bit of a joke.

He pressed his hand a shade more firmly into her back. "I won't let you fall."

Nor did he.

James, in fact, was a fine dancer, not showy, but graceful. Hazel wasn't, but she was musical enough to find the beat. James supplied the dancing. She only needed to follow along.

I sat next to Mabel Kibbey on the bench and watched. This dance could be a beginning, or an end, depending on a thousand things. Could they speak? Would one speak too much? Or say something stupid? Should I do something?

"They'll be all right," Mabel said, casting a glance my way.

"Why, Mabel Kibbey," I whispered, "can you see me?"

She flipped the page of her music. "I've always seen you," she said. "You're looking especially well tonight."

I gave her a squeeze about the waist. "You're a darling."

She twinkled. "It's nice to know you're still here for the young people," she said. "This dreadful war. How they need you now."

"Not only the young." I nodded in the direction of a spry older gentleman, seated across the room. "Would you like me to make you an introduction tonight?"

Mabel laughed. "No, thank you." She sighed. "I've had my day."

We both saw, then, a faded wedding photograph, an empty chair, and a gravestone.

"Who's to say you can't have another day?" I asked her.

She reached a repeat and flipped her page back. "You go see about Miss Hazel." So I did.

They had covered the basics: She was eighteen. He was nineteen. Hazel, only child, from Poplar, daughter of a music hall pianist and a seamstress. Done with school, practicing full-time and preparing to audition for music conservatories. James, from Chelmsford, older brother to Maggie and Bobby. Son of a mathematics instructor at a secondary school. He, himself, worked for a building firm. Or had, until now. He was in London, staying with an uncle. Here to see about his uniform and kit, before reporting for duty in a week, to be stationed in France.

The war.

You had to walk into the room then, Ares. A final ending, a permanent goodbye.

Yet you were the reason everyone was there. The war was in every sermon, every street sign, every news report, every prayer over every bland and rationed meal.

And so James went from stranger to patriot, hero, bravely shouldering his duty to God, King, and Country.

Hazel went from stranger and pianist to reason why the war mattered at all, symbol of all that was pure and beautiful and worth dying for in a broken world.

When I found them, their heads were nestled together like a pair of mourning doves.

James, the soul of politeness, wouldn't dream of drawing Hazel too close on a first dance. Which was not to say he wouldn't like to. But Hazel, baffled by finding herself so safe and warm in the arms of this beautiful young man, realized, when the song ended, that she'd been resting her forehead against his cheek. That cheek, she had wanted to caress, and now, in a way, she'd done it. She began to be embarrassed, but as the other dancers applauded, James cradled her in his arms, and she knew she didn't need to apologize.

Lois Prentiss began to boom out her thanks for all who'd made the evening a success, but Mabel Kibbey, with a wink at me, cut her off by starting a new song, even more tender than the first. While other couples jockeyed to find partners, Hazel and James found each other wordlessly, having never broken apart, and danced the entire dance, their eyes closed.

If I couldn't knit these two together by the end of a second dance, Zeus might as well make Poseidon the god of love, and I'd go look after the fishes.

I could have watched them forever. By this point many eyes

besides my own were watching Hazel Windicott, a well-known commodity in the parish, as famous for shyness as for music, dancing with the tall young stranger. When the song ended, and she opened her eyes, she saw James's face watching her closely, but over his shoulder there were other faces, whispering, wondering.

"I need to go," she said, pulling away. "People will say . . ."

She flooded with shame. How could she betray this moment to fear of others?

He waited openly, calmly, without suspicion.

What did she owe to other people anyway?

"Thank you," she said. "I had a lovely time."

She looked up nervously into his dark brown eyes. *You're wonderful*, they said.

So are you, her long-lashed eyes replied.

"Miss Windicott—" he began.

"Call me Hazel," she said, then wondered if she ought.

The dimples returned. She might melt. Other people didn't matter. Let them gossip.

"Miss *Hazel* Windicott," he said, "I report for training in a week."

She nodded. "I know." He'd already told her. It was so unspeakably awful. Already lads she'd known had died in the trenches.

James took a step closer. "May I see you again before I go?"

She chewed on this shocking proposal. This was not the way of things. Introductions, chaperones, supervision. Parental permission at each step. Large ladies like naval battleships prowling the seas of church socials, scouting for improper hand-holding and clandestine kisses. The war had relaxed propriety's stranglehold, but only somewhat.

James stewed. He'd said too much. Moved too fast. The thought made him sick. But what choice did he have? He had only one chance to get to know Hazel Windicott, the piano girl.

"May I?" he said again.

Hazel's father appeared in the doorway.

"How soon?" she asked James.

He smiled. "As soon as possible."

"How much?" asked Hazel.

The smile faded, leaving only that intent gaze in its place. "As much as I may."

It was time for Hazel to demur politely, make her excuses, thank him for serving the Crown, and break away from this doomed solider boy. It was definitely time to say no.

"I'd like that."

She smiled, the first time she'd smiled for this stranger. James's poor heart might've stopped beating then and there if he weren't young and healthy.

Hazel give James Alderidge her address. When she felt fairly certain the eyes in the room had moved on from gawking at her, and her father had fallen into chitchat with other arriving parents, she reached up onto her toes and gave James a kiss on the cheek.

James Alderidge didn't know it was the second such kiss he'd received that night. He only knew he was in grave danger of heading off to the Front as a soldier in love.

The thought scared him more than all the German missiles combined. Should he pull back? Should he cut this fantasy short, and not seek out another encounter with the piano girl?

Music. Lashes. Lilac-scented hair. The light grip of her lips in a brief kiss upon his cheek.

And, once more, the music.

What he should do, James decided, and what he *would* do, had no bearing upon each other.

APHRODITE

The Kiss (Part I)—November 23, 1917

IF THAT KISS caused James a night of agonizing wonder, of delicious bafflement, he was not alone. For Hazel's part, the bafflement was wondering what on earth had come over her, and the agony was dreading what James must think of her. She, Hazel Windicott, who never looked at boys! The respectable, serious-minded young lady who spent hours each day practicing piano, who kept her head while other girls did . . . whatever it was that other girls did. Would this James think she was the sort of girl who went about kissing young men upon first acquaintance?

She walked home with her father, buttoning her coat collar close around her neck. The night was unusually cold. Her left arm still remembered resting itself upon James's arm, and her right hand remembered holding James's hand. Her body remembered moving in time with his, and being pulled closer as the last song ended.

"Did some dancing, did we?" observed her father. Hazel was mortified to discover that she was acting it out, holding out her arms toward an imaginary James. So much for secrets.

"Mrs. Kibbey thought I ought to," she said. *Blame it on Mrs. Kibbey, will you? Weak!*

Her father, a tall man with long arms and legs and fingers, and deep grooves carved into his cheeks, put an arm around Hazel's shoulders.

"Mrs. Kibbey's right," he said. "You need to live a bit more, my girl, and have fun. Not just stay cooped up with old folks like your mother and me."

She leaned her head against her father's shoulder. "Don't be silly," she told him. "You aren't 'old folks.'"

"Tell that to Arthur," her father said. "Arthur" was the arthritis that plagued his wrist and knuckle joints. "I mean it, Hazy. You should spend more time with people your age. Just promise me you won't fall in love with a soldier boy. You don't need your heart broken in two."

She nodded. She couldn't exactly look her dad in the eye just then. And she certainly wasn't about to make any promises.

For pity's sake, she scolded herself once more. *You are not in love with that boy. You've only just met him tonight, and danced two dances. People who talk of falling in love after just one meeting have their heads full of pillow down.*

Why, then, had she kissed him on the cheek?

APHRODITE

The Kiss (Part II)—November 23, 1917

WHY *HAD* HAZEL kissed James on the cheek?

This was the question tormenting James as he circled St. Matthias's block. Up Woodstock Terrace, along East India Dock Road, down Hale Street, along High Street, and back. Breezes off the Thames brought the cry of seagulls and the clang of the dockyards. Up ahead, the lights of Poplar twinkled.

Was it a sisterly sort of thing? Surely that was all the kiss meant: *Do not hope for more, you strange stranger. Here is where my view of you begins and ends: platonic goodwill. Patriotic gratitude. Here's a quick little peck to prove it. Now goodbye.*

He groaned. He'd heard of things like that. Girls who went about bestowing kisses on soldiers in their khakis on train platforms, and on new conscripts at recruiting stations.

There was the spot. Right there, upon his cheek. He ran a finger over it.

He passed by a couple that had taken advantage of a deep, dark doorway for some kissing of the type Lois Prentiss would certainly veto. It reminded him of that one smile, lighting up Hazel's lips, making him wonder how kissing them would feel.

What was the *matter* with him?

The war, he decided. The war had addled his senses. The war had driven the whole world to the brink of insanity. Hasty war weddings and fatherless war babies and last-minute love. The whole cheap, flimsy spectacle of it.

But he closed his eyes and remembered, once more, the feeling of holding the piano girl in his arms.

He could still see her father holding her coat for her, and steering her out through the throng. Wild horses couldn't persuade James to shadow their footsteps home. It would be indecent.

Her address. Would she have shared it if she thought of him in a strictly friendly way?

When he'd passed the kissing couple three times, he headed home. He crossed East India Dock Road and came to Kerbey Street, which led to his uncle's flat. He glanced at theatrical playbills and navy recruitment banners. When signposts revealed that Kerbey Street had met Grundy, he stopped.

The corner of Grundy and Bygrove, Hazel had said. Second floor, above the barbershop.

Surely she'd be home by now. Asleep in bed, no doubt. What harm was a little detour? He'd merely note the location. He ought to get a haircut anyway. Perhaps tomorrow he could return for a trim, and while he was there, he might . . . what? Knock on her door?

The utter impossibility of it all hit him.

He could take a look. His motives were pure. He wasn't spying. He only wanted to see the kind of curtains behind which the piano girl lived her luminous life. He would innocently imagine her asleep on a soft pillow, her lashes delicately tangled together, her long hair spread about her, her slim hands playing Chopin in her dreams.

APHRODITE

Sleepless—November 23, 1917

HAZEL WAS FAR from asleep. She'd changed into her nightgown and unpinned her hair. She sat on a low divan beneath her bedroom window, wrapped her arms about her knees, and looked out upon the street. In the upstairs flat, the two spinster Misses Ford played their gramophone recording of "My Heart at Thy Sweet Voice." It was much too late for opera. Hazel didn't mind.

James Alderidge. A nice name. One could certainly do worse.

Had she danced two dances with a stranger, and *kissed him on the cheek?*

She pressed her own burning cheek against the cool, damp windowpane.

Who would've thought, on this utterly normal day, that before bedtime her brain would be scrambled like an egg? She'd only gone to play as a reluctant favor to Mrs. Prentiss, just as she'd gone that afternoon to the Poplar Hospital for Accidents to play for the recuperating soldiers.

James Alderidge. He was heading off to the war. Training, then trenches. That would be an end, not only of their acquaintance, but, very possibly, of his life.

Or, the end of his life as he knew it. Already there were honorably discharged men to be seen, coming and going, in wheelchairs, missing legs. With sleeves tucked into jackets to hide missing hands. With hideous, disfiguring scars where shrapnel had torn their faces.

She knew this, of course. All of Britain knew what a terrible price young men paid each day to stop the wretched Kaiser. That evil, stupid, horrid man who'd unleashed his army like a dark flood across Europe.

The thought of that fearful price carved into the face of the boy with the dark brown eyes filled her own eyes with tears. So she failed to notice the figure on the street corner, gazing up at her bedroom window.

APHRODITE

The King's Whiskers—November 23, 1917

THERE IT WAS. The barbershop. The King's Whiskers. James smiled. Hazel Windicott lived right above the King's Whiskers. Did that make her, perhaps, a nose?

The joke was so bad, it made him snicker.

The dark windows of the second-story flat mirrored, dully, the orb of a streetlamp on the corner. A light on the third floor silhouetted a gramophone. He heard strains of a plaintive opera song. Mezzo-soprano. Very romantic.

But there was no hint of Hazel Windicott. Had she told him the wrong address?

He rounded the corner and stopped. The piano girl leaned against her window, lost in thought. James saw long hair spilling down her back, and the neckline of a white nightgown.

Her reverie rooted his feet to the ground.

By day, this corner would ring with the sound of Hazel's piano playing. That lucky barber, Mr. King's Whiskers, got to hear it all day long, over the sound of mechanical clippers.

James Alderidge, he warned himself, *you only met her once. You don't know her at all. And you're a fool.*

DECEMBER 1942

An Interruption

"HE'S RIGHT ABOUT that," Ares says. "This tale is dull is dirt. Boy meets girl, they dance a bit, and moon about each other. So what? Nothing's happened."

Aphrodite's eyes narrow. "*Everything* has happened."

Ares rolls his eyes. "Get to the real doings," he says. "Get to the Front. The killing fields. That's where war stories happen."

"Who asked you?" inquires Hephaestus, diplomat.

"I'm not telling a war story," says Aphrodite. "This is what I *do*, and how I do it."

"Go on," Hephaestus says. "I'm curious."

"Then you're a sap," the god of war replies. "Here. I know this story. Two sheltered souls meet, boom—they get the hots for each other. They think they've invented romance. They gad about for a few days, then he heads off to war. It's terrible, boo-hoo, he misses his girl, she misses him. They write letters at first, until the trenches turn him from Loverboy into Kid Trying to Keep the Rats from Eating His Face Off. She does some volunteer work"—Ares affects a sneer—"in a *brave* attempt to be like the boys abroad and do her measly bit. She cries into her pillow, wondering why the letters have stopped. Time passes. They both change. Tragedies pop up like boils. They blame me for their problems. Et cetera."

If Ares were mortal, the look Aphrodite aims his way would char the flesh off his bones.

"Are you finished?" asks the goddess of love.

Ares doesn't bother to answer.

"Thirsty, my dear?" asks Hephaestus. He conjures a martini glass filled with ambrosia and causes it to appear in Aphrodite's open hand. She seems surprised, but she takes a sip.

Hephaestus fluffs a pillow from the bed and arranges it behind his stooped shoulders. "I'm not here because I'm dying to hear from you, warmonger," says he. "I want to hear my wife."

Ares laughs. "Are you taking love lessons from mortals now, blacksmith?"

"You could stand a few yourself," says Aphrodite.

APHRODITE

Caught—November 23, 1917

JAMES THOUGHT HE'D get away without Hazel seeing him.

But Hazel saw him.

I may have had a little something to do with that.

As I say, I wasn't interfering, but the whole scene, the street corner, the lamppost, the shadows, the gentle opera spilling down from above, the ruffled nightgown—what was I to do? I'm an artist.

I directed her gaze down to the street. She pulled back from the window when she saw someone standing there. When she saw his head turn away, she leaned in closer.

It was James Alderidge.

Should she mind that he was there? How could she mind something so marvelous?

At the sight of her, his face lit up. He raised his hand in a half wave, then jammed it into his coat pocket and hurried on up the street.

APHRODITE

A Note—November 23, 1917

YOU IDIOT, you idiot, he told himself. *Peeping in windows? She should call the coppers on you.*

A creak behind him made him stop.

He turned to see Hazel's face leaning out the window, with ropes of long hair dangling below her shoulders. "Pssst," she said, and dropped something white onto the pavement. Then she pulled the casement shut and disappeared.

James found the white thing amid the bits and bobs of rubbish littering the street corner. It was a folded piece of paper. James had half expected a lace-trimmed handkerchief. But this wasn't blooming Camelot, and he was no knight.

He stepped farther into the street, closer to the streetlamp, and opened the note.

Eight a.m. tomorrow, it read, in a tall, precise, vertical hand. Letters like the stems of musical notes. *Coffee at the J. Lyons tea shop on Chrisp Street at Guildford.*

James Alderidge looked up at the now-dark window and grinned. Miss Hazel Windicott was no longer in sight. Swallowed by the darkness. Could she see him? He didn't know.

But I knew. You'd better believe she could.

APHRODITE

The Tea Shop—November 24, 1917

SINCE SOME PERSONS, who shall remain nameless, seem impatient with the depth of detail I devote to this pair in their heart-fluttering first hours of finding each other, I'll pass over the drama of James's and Hazel's sleepless nights, their ridiculously early hours of rising, and their anxious dress and grooming, silent to avoid waking uncles and parents on a sleep-in Saturday morning. I will spare my critics the excited nausea that gripped the young darlings' stomachs as they made their way out into a London morning to find J. Lyons tea shop. I will make no mention of the constant rapping of doubt—the fear that this something, which they hoped was something, was actually nothing, that they'd allowed their feelings to fizz and froth for absolutely, positively nothing.

It wasn't their fault that they fizzed and frothed. They could no more scold themselves into indifference than they could will themselves to stop breathing.

It was time for James and Hazel to get properly acquainted. Time to see if the magic of music and moonlight and graceful movement were all that they had shared, or if a grimy gray London dawn and a cheap cup of coffee could make them feel the same way.

J. Lyons tea shops are scattered all about London. James's

illogical dread was going to the wrong one. He arrived well before eight o'clock and, finding Hazel not yet there, paced the street. At eight he entered the shop, sat on a bench, crushed his hat, smoothed it, and crushed it again.

Hazel was late. Not surprising, given that her journey went as follows:

She would walk a block, then turn around and walk back, then retrace her first steps and go a little farther, than panic and scamper back toward home base. By the time she reached J. Lyons tea shop, she was perspiring under her sweater and blouse, even though the morning was chill and damp. So, holding her breath as though that might somehow compel James Alderidge to do the same, lest he notice any body odor, she entered the tea shop.

James leaped to his feet. That looked too eager, he realized, so he stiffened. He hadn't a clue what to do with his face.

Hazel saw him jump up in a spasm of obvious disappointment, then grimace in disgust.

She knew it. She smelled terrible. She looked terrible. She *was* terrible. And inviting him to meet her here was a terrible, terrible idea. She kept her hand on the doorknob and tried to think how to escape. Her parents need never know. It would be as if it had never happened.

James's heart sank as he watched her panicked expression. She was even more adorable by morning light, in everyday clothes. But clearly, she wanted to flee. What could he say to relieve her distress and let her know she was free to leave?

"Good morning." He smiled by reflex. It's what one does when one says "Good morning."

"Good morning." She held out her hand. It was what one did when one said "Good morning" at a tea shop to someone whom one doesn't hug or kiss.

But she *had* kissed him. Oh, mortification!

He pressed her hand between his. He smiled again, and Hazel forgot about fleeing the tea shop. The scent of bay rum may have had something to do with it.

"Table for two?" I said.

They followed me to a secluded corner table. James pulled the chair out for Hazel and hung her coat in the doorway. There was only one free peg, so he placed his own coat over hers. It made him blush. He took his seat opposite Hazel.

I love this boy. In a purely spiritual sense.

"I recommend the lemon cake," I said, and handed them menus.

The serving girls were slow that morning. These two maybe-lovebirds-maybe-not teetered on a knife's edge, and if I didn't get them seated at a table, there was no telling what might happen. So I took shape in the form of a matronly, middle-aged table server. How it pained me to adopt the joyless uniform of the J. Lyons waitresses, I can't begin to express. But I do make sacrifices.

No, I *don't* consider that cheating, interfering, or manipulating. I was only doing what a competent waitstaff ought to have done. Sometimes fates hang in the balance over matters even more trivial than a waitress flirting in the back with a pastry chef.

Hazel and James studied the menus as if their very lives depended on it. Safer than glancing at each other. I sent a little puff of attraction wafting back toward the kitchens, to keep the real waitress chummy a bit longer with Mr. Pastry Chef, who was making roses with a frosting pipe. This forced me to serve a few other customers as well, but I armed myself with a self-replenishing pot of hot Colombian coffee and made everyone's morning that little smidge better. One stout, bald gentleman, in particular. I think he suspected there was more to me than met the eye, the old rascal. He'd been a bit of a Romeo once, several belt sizes ago.

I swept back toward James and Hazel. They'd relaxed into conversation.

"Excuse me," Hazel told me very earnestly. "We don't see lemon cake on this menu."

It was all I could do not to giggle. "It's today's special," I told her.

"I wonder how they got the sugar," Hazel mused. "Rationing's so tight." She turned to him. "Shall we order some, then, James?" Just like that, he became a first-name friend.

"It sounds delicious, Hazel." He turned to me very seriously. "Two slices, please."

My pretty little pets, having a nursery-room tea party for two. The little boy, playing grown-up man for his girl. The girl he hoped would be his girl. You see why I love my work, don't you? Why it's not a career, it's a calling?

I returned to the serving table, conjured giant slabs of cake, and served them. The bald gentleman tapped me on the elbow to order some. Before I was done, I'd served cake to four tables. Compliments of the goddess. With the Great War in its fourth year, Britons *needed* cake.

James and Hazel faced the new predicament—do they eat in front of each other, at the risk of spilling crumbs or blobs of lemon curd? Then again, if they didn't eat, they must talk. How does the old Gaelic ditty go? *O ye'll tak' the high road, and I'll tak' the low road, and I'll be in Scotland a'fore ye?* Hazel took the high road, cake, and James took the low road, speech.

"I'm *so* glad to see you again," he said.

He was in Scotland a'fore her.

Well, there it was. He'd skipped the preliminaries. There was no turning back now.

His words caught Hazel with the tines of her fork still in her mouth, and a very large bite of cake melting on her tongue.

"Mmph" was her elegant reply.

But there he was, all brown eyes and kindness, waiting patiently, watching her face as if he could watch it forever. Her wide eyes drank all this in, and she managed, by a miracle, to swallow the cake without choking.

"Me too." She remembered her napkin. "I mean, you too. Glad to see you."

She was, and there was no hiding it.

APHRODITE

Questions—November 24, 1917

IT'S NOT EASY, overseeing love in its toddler phase. It's a noisy, chattering, babbling thing. Listening closely would turn me old and gray, except that, of course, I don't get old or gray. But it's still an effort, though also a joy, to follow all they say, and all they don't. For example:

What made you go to the dance last night, where you didn't know anyone?

Imagine if you hadn't!

Do you always play piano at dances?

Or do you dance with other lads?

Tell me about Chelmsford.

I'll bet the girls are prettier in Chelmsford.

How long have you studied piano?

How is it that a girl this talented is eating lemon cake in a tea shop with a bloke like me?

What do you do in the building trade?

Do heavy beams ever fall on builders and kill them?

Who's your favorite composer?

Please have one. Don't be a musical ignoramus.

Do you have a gramophone?

Smile again. Just like that. Wish I had a photograph of that to keep in my wallet.

Tell me about your parents.

Look how neat you are. I'm so glad you're not one of those grimy sorts.

Tell me about yours.

Do they know you're here with me? Is that all right?

Do you think you'll ever play at the Royal Albert?

I could talk to you all day.

Why not? I'll bet you could.

I'd be there in the front row.

If you could build any building at all, what would it be?

Oh, why do you have to be heading off to the Front? Why now?

Do you know where you'll be stationed in France?

I'm sorry. Forget I asked you that.

Do you speak any French?

I know you can tell I'm afraid to go. Will you despise me for it?

Do you need to get back home soon? Got anything going on today?

Please, no. Don't leave me yet. We have so little time.

Let's go for a walk, all right?

When do I get to return the kiss you gave me?

DECEMBER 1942

To Forge, to Meld

ARES LOUNGES UPON the couch, underneath the golden net. Aphrodite has a faraway look, and a soft expression.

Her husband watches her. A tear shines in her eye. These mortals do something to Aphrodite. But what? They sound to the blacksmith god like any two mortals among millions.

Until he remembers the surge of awe, of *rightness* he feels when he raises a red-hot sword from his forge. This is what he was born to do. To make, to meld, to master heat and iron with all their power and all their resistance, and bring forth works of usefulness and beauty. If it made him fiery and unbending, how could he not become something like the iron in his forge?

The ecstasies and the wounds of love were Aphrodite's work. Forging passions was what she was born to do. She, too, was a melder, a mistress of fire of a different sort, working in materials more powerful and resistant than carbon and iron. And what did that toil do to her?

If he'd wanted a goddess of hearth and home, of safe domesticity and simple loyalty, Hephaestus could've married Hestia. Maybe he should have. She was single, and by all accounts the cooking was good.

But Hestia could never be . . . *Aphrodite.* There's no going back once you've known the goddess of love. There is no forgetting. No moving on. No letting go.

APHRODITE

A Walk—November 24, 1917

I FELT LIKE a mother watching little Junior toddle off to school for the very first time when those two exited J. Lyons tea shop, huddled together against the cold gray morning.

They took Guilford Street to Upper North Street till it became Bow Common Lane. "This way," Hazel said, "I'll be less likely to run into anyone I know."

James's face fell. "Am I a secret, then?"

Hazel glanced sheepishly at him. "Secrets are fun, aren't they?"

He said nothing, but tipped his hat low over his eyes.

"I'm sorry," Hazel said after a moment. "I'm new to all this. You shan't be a secret." She grinned. "Just last night, Father said I ought to live a little."

James wanted to hug the man. "If I'm not a secret," he said, "what am I?"

Hazel's mind raced. What to say? What words might tumble out in spite of her?

Horses and wagons, noisy motorcars, hawkers, bickering children, haggling shoppers all passed by them on the street, but Hazel and James might as well have been alone on a desert island.

"You're a brand-new piece of sheet music," she said slowly, "for a song which, once played, I'd swear I'd always known."

"Always known" meant something, didn't it? Clever, clever girl.

She turned her face up toward his and waited for proof that she'd said too much. Opened her heart too much. If his heart had wanted to meet hers halfway, surely he would've smiled.

Or had he, only just?

"A piece of sheet music, am I?" he teased. "Makes me rather *flat*, doesn't it?" The joke was so terrible, it was perfect.

"I prefer gentlemen who are *sharp*" was her quick reply.

She got the joke! Of course she did. "There's nothing 'new' about me, Miss Hazel Windicott," he told her. "I've been rolling around Chelmsford for years."

She shook her head. "No, you haven't," she said. "You sprang from the ground."

"No," he said simply. "That was you."

Both of them realized, then, that Hazel's two hands had found their way inside James's. The discovery took them both by surprise. Neither remembered having done it.

They hadn't. That was me. I wasn't about to be idle, now, was I?

And, no, that was *not* interfering. Hazel's hands were cold.

James looked down at the numb fingertips pressed between his own, and instinctively folded the whole bundle under his coat, to the warmth over his heart.

Perhaps, for James, it was his heart, but for Hazel, her hands had just been placed over the muscular chest of a handsome youth who, it seemed, had played an *active* role in the building trade this past summer. A series of little explosions began firing throughout her brain, and spread quickly elsewhere.

She snatched her hands away—I won't deny I was irked by this—and groaned.

He closed the distance between them. "What's the matter?" he cried. "Are you all right?"

She shook her head. "Who *are* you?" she said. "W*hat* are you? I go to a dance, and suddenly I'm sneaking off to meet a young man, and saying things to a perfect stranger that I would never, ever say." She tapped indignantly at her collarbone. "I am a *nice, quiet girl* who plays the piano. Mostly for old ladies. And you've got me—"

"Kissing a chap you just met on the cheek?"

She covered her eyes with a hand. "Did you have to say that?"

He gently pried her hand away. "It's all I've thought of since."

Hazel's innards writhed like Medusa's hairdo.

I whispered in her ear. "Don't be afraid of him, Hazel."

"I'm afraid of you, James Alderidge," she told him, the naughty girl.

He backed away, palms raised in surrender. The look of dismay on his face broke my heart. Hazel's, too.

"No," she said. "You're a perfect gent. I'm afraid of *me* when I'm with you."

"Come with me tomorrow," he said. "To the Sunday concert at the Royal Albert Hall."

"All the way over there?"

He shrugged. "What, is it far?"

She shook her head. "You really don't know London, do you?" She looked up into his dark brown eyes and blinked at all she saw there. She smiled and nodded. "All right, then."

His dimples flashed. He bent and kissed her forehead.

"There," he said. "We're even. Feel better?"

Hazel made her choice. She could be who she ought to be with James. She decided instead to be that terrifying person who she evidently wanted to be.

It was the dimples. Empires have swiveled on less.

APHRODITE

Goodbye—November 24, 1917

JAMES WALKED HER to a corner within sight of the striped barber's pole outside the King's Whiskers. Neither of them knew how to say goodbye.

"Tomorrow," he reminded her. "The concert. We can get some tea after, maybe?"

"When should we meet?" She chewed her lip. *And what do I tell my parents?*

"Let's meet at one o'clock. Right here." He glanced at her. "So I'll get tickets?"

She nodded. "Get tickets."

It was time to part. They both knew it. Neither moved.

"What's your Sunday morning like?" he asked her.

"St. Matthias's. I play for the choir," she told him. "The organist is . . ."

"Overseas?"

She nodded, then shook her head. "He died there," she said. "So he's not there, but he is, because he's buried in Flanders." She couldn't meet his gaze just then.

He understood. He tried to lighten her mood with a spot of poetry.

"'If I should die, think only this of me, that there's some corner of a foreign field . . .'"

"'. . . that is for ever England,'" Hazel muttered. "It's rot." *Don't die.*

"It's all right," he said. "I'm all right. About going." A lie and a truth, becoming every minute more of a lie. "So many have gone, and if I don't . . . Somebody's got to stop the Kaiser."

What could she say? That *she* wasn't all right with him going? Not one bit?

James tried to break the silence. "Was he a good organist?"

"Not especially." She wrinkled her nose. "At his memorial, you'd have thought he was George Frideric Handel himself."

The rest of the day stretched before James as a yawning chasm of Hazel-lessness. He longed to bury his face in her neck. Even if it was wrapped in a scratchy wool muffler.

But that was too soon, too much to ask of a girl he'd known less than twelve hours, a girl with whom he'd shared two dances and a cup of coffee. (*Excellent* coffee, but still.)

So he squeezed her hand. "Guess I'd better be moving along."

She bowed her head. "You've got loads to do, I'm sure."

Would he kiss her? Hazel waited to see. Did she want him to? She tried not to stare at his mouth.

So pretty. She was so, so pretty. At first it was the music, and then her eyes, and her hair, but now he saw how entirely adorable she was. He should be beating off other lads with a stick.

Kiss her, I told him.

With a curled finger he gently, quickly brushed her cheek and the tip of her nose.

Leave now, or you never will, he told himself.

"Till tomorrow," he told her. He turned to go.

No kiss. "One o'clock!" A brave attempt at sounding like she cheerfully didn't mind not being kissed. *I wasn't fooled.*

There was no point in resisting or explaining it away. James wasn't sure what he dared call what he felt, but he knew his happiness belonged to the piano girl. Whether she would take and keep it safe for him, or not.

APHRODITE

In Between—November 24, 1917

HAZEL RETURNED HOME to find her parents had stepped out for an errand, so no awkward confessions were needed. Not yet. She sat at the piano for a good long practice session. Just the solid, practical remedy she needed after twelve hours in the clouds. But she trailed off in the middle of pieces and stared out the window. What was James doing now? She made ridiculous mistakes. She played maudlin, sentimental ballads. She was hopeless.

James was little better. He went with his uncle Charlie to an army supply depot to purchase his uniform and kit. *Pack up your troubles in your old kit-bag and smile, smile, smile.* The constantly sung war ditty spun through his head. An oily old salesman listed all the trench ailments he'd need products to prevent or treat. Trench foot. Lice. Bitter cold. Incessant damp. Rats. Mud. Shrapnel. Hunger. Gangrene. Venereal disease.

James wanted to vomit.

"Never mind," James's uncle said over a cafeteria lunch. "You may end up in one of the colonies. Or you could have domestic duty." Uncle Charlie had seen service in the Second Boer War, but not combat. Supply and transport.

"Besides," he added, "the Americans will be coming over as soon as President Wilson gets 'em recruited and trained and fitted out. Maybe *this* year it'll be over by Christmas."

Unlike 1914. Everyone thought so then.

"How was the dance last night?" his uncle said. "Dance with any pretty girls?"

James looked at the floor. He felt his uncle's eyes on him.

Uncle Charlie chuckled. "Met someone, did you?"

There was no need to answer this, so James didn't.

"Good for you," his uncle said. "You're about to report. You deserve your bit of fun."

James winced at this. Miss Hazel Windicott was no "bit of fun." He finished his food quickly, thanked Uncle Charlie, and left to wander about London. He ended up at the cinema, alone, watching a mediocre film, until it ended and he could go home and go to bed.

Hazel's evening involved a lecture with her mother. An army chaplain, sharing inspirational stories about how God watched over the British faithful at the Front.

Just not our organist, Hazel thought.

Her father was at the Town Hall, which was the name of the Poplar theater and music hall where he played Saturday night. When the lecture ended, Hazel walked her mother home, then stopped in at the Town Hall to pass the evening with her father.

"It's no place for a young lady," her mother protested. "Your dad won't be pleased."

"I'll turn pages for him," Hazel assured her mother. "I'll stay right on the bench."

And she did. It was a cozy night, tucked in next to her father in his bowler hat, striped shirt, and bow tie. His flying fingers embellished "Bicycle Built for Two," "I'm Henery the Eighth, I Am," "Burlington Bertie from Bow," and, of course, "Tipperary."

Hazel knew her father's way of playing would make Monsieur Guillaume, her instructor, queasy, but she still loved watching him. When she was a tiny thing seated on his lap, her daddy had played with his long arms encircling her, as though his curly-headed girlie wasn't blocking his view. The spread of keys seemed flexible under his spell, full of bounce in the sprightly, giddy tunes popular with the stars of the music halls.

And, oh, they were stars. One after another, the performers claimed the stage and the hearts of Poplar. They performed, they bowed, they took an encore, then they dashed offstage to a car waiting in the alley to zip them off to the next nightclub to perform again. The most popular might sing or dance or joke or pantomime a dozen times and more in a night. In garish costumes, in army officers' uniforms, in cutaway coats and gleaming waistcoats, and glittering gowns. And, for some of them, in blackface.

The blackface performers brought down the house. "Look at the crazy coon!" women would shriek. "Sing it again, darkie!"

But Hazel's father didn't like it. When the men painted black performed, his mouth hardened and he stared at the ivories. Normally the man didn't ever seem to need to look at the keys.

"Your father's a coward, Hazy," he told her. "It's wrong, what they're doing. It's disgusting. It's unchristian. If I were a man, I'd quit in protest."

She took his hand in hers. "What would you do then?"

"That's just it," he told her. "I'm a coward. I support this trash to pay my bills. Remember, we're all God's children. Be braver than I've been."

Hazel couldn't fathom a scenario that would require such bravery of her. But she would remember her father's words before long.

DECEMBER 1942

First Witness

"I'D LIKE TO call my first witness," Aphrodite tells the judge.

Ares pulls a pillow over his bare chest. "You're not summoning *mortals* here, are you?"

"Get ahold of yourself," she tells him. "Your Honor? May I?"

Hephaestus wonders what he's agreeing to. An escape plot? A ploy to summon help? But she's come this far with her story. He's curious. He nods.

She glances out the window. A bright streak of light arcs in the sky. Moments later a knock sounds at the hotel room door.

"Come in," calls Aphrodite.

The door opens, and a tall man in a pin-striped blue zoot suit strolls in, lithe and athletic. He sports a wide fuchsia necktie, loose at his collar, brown-and-white Oxford shoes, and a white fedora tipped low over his brow.

There's an awful lot of male perfection in that hotel room all of a sudden. The newcomer is a stunner of a specimen. Greek profile, muscular frame, golden glow. He's got it all.

He surveys the captive pair and snorts with laughter. "I can't *begin* to imagine what's been going on here." He holds up his palms.

"But I don't judge. I do *not* judge." He notices Hephaestus's gavel. "Apparently, you do, though."

He doffs his fedora to Aphrodite. "Evening, sis."

"Good evening, Apollo," she says. "A spectacular sunset tonight."

"Nice of you to notice." He bounces on the bed a few times, testing its springs. "So what's going on, anyway?"

"A jealous husband's tribunal," declares Ares. "His wife chose the better man."

"Go dunk your head," adds Hephaestus.

"She's telling a story," Ares tells Apollo, "to explain to *him* why she's ditching him for me. Why Love loves War, so to speak." He feels clever. A rare occurrence, off the battlefield.

"Have you heard a single word I've said?" snaps Aphrodite.

"'Why does Love love War?'" echoes Apollo.

"That isn't the question at all," Aphrodite protests.

But Apollo is intrigued. "*I'm* crazy about War."

Ares wrinkles his nose. "Well, *this* is awkward—"

"Some other time, perhaps," Apollo says with lazy grace. "I didn't mean *you*."

"There's no coliseum big enough to hold your two egos," mutters Hephaestus.

"Athena's more my style," Apollo explains. "Fierce, fair, fantastic. War, wisdom, and craft. We'd be perfect. Artsy and hip. Bohemian but grounded. Think of the little godlings we could make."

"Forget about it," says Aphrodite. "Athena's not falling for you or anyone. Believe me."

"I'll win her over yet," says Apollo. "But, to your question, what's the attraction of War?"

Hephaestus raps his gavel. "Overruled. Don't care."

Apollo strokes his chin. "There's plague. During the last war, my so-called Spanish influenza was a triumph. Reaped twice as many souls as your 'Great' War, Ares."

"You're proud of that?" demands Hephaestus.

"It's not the body count, Volcano God," says Apollo. "It's the terrible beauty of a massively destructive force. When Poseidon shakes the earth and tsunamis wipe out the coastline, it's something to see. You loved Mount Vesuvius. Admit it. You took pride in Pompeii."

Hephaestus tries to look modest. "They're still talking about it, two thousand years later."

Apollo shrugs. "We're artists." He conjures a platter of grapes, figs, and cheeses, digs in, then addresses Ares. "Don't tell me you didn't glory in the Battle of the Somme. Or Verdun. You were drunk on blood." He offers him the platter. "Snack?"

"You're a fool," says the god of war.

"All I'm saying"—Apollo is still chewing—"is that my little flu virus, in its own microscopic, contagious way, was a thing of beauty." He smacks his lips. "Annihilation has its own je ne sais quoi. We're all guilty of it. So spare me the sermons."

"*I'm* not guilty of it," says Aphrodite. "Destruction has nothing to do with me."

The male gods stare, then explode laughing. Aphrodite turns her back on them all.

"Then there's the poetry," says Apollo. "Another reason to love war. Why, in the Great War . . . Not since the Trojan War has a conflict inspired such verse. Here, let me recite for you—"

"No!" Three divine voices sound together, for once in perfect accord.

Apollo looks genuinely surprised. "You don't want me to?" He plucks a ukulele out of the air. "Well, I'll be darned. Anyway," he says, "there was the music. The Great War lit a musical fire that engulfed the world."

"We were just talking about that," says Aphrodite.

Ares frowns. "No, we weren't."

"We were about to," the goddess says. "Apollo, I summoned you here to tell your part of a particular story."

"Which story?" Aphrodite looks intently at him, and he nods. "Oh. *That* story."

APOLLO

Carnegie Hall—May 2, 1912

COME WITH ME to Carnegie Hall.

It's May 2, 1912. The Great War is still two summers away.

James Reese Europe's Clef Club Orchestra is about to perform, to a sellout crowd, a "Concert of Negro Music." The audience is packed in like well-dressed sardines.

For the first time ever in America, black musicians will perform black music at a major concert hall. An orchestra of over a hundred performers will play brass, winds and strings, banjos and mandolins. The Clef Club Chorus, 150 voices, packs in, as does the Coleridge-Taylor 40 voice choir. Ringing the back of the stage are ten upright grand pianos. *Ten.*

The audience, black and white, waits for the show to begin. They're about to hear a sound so new, so energetic and rhythmic and harmonic, so syncopated, so alive, that music will never be the same. This sound will reverberate around the world—following, though nobody knows it yet, the drums of war.

The ten pianos must be a joke, some people think. What could the Clef Club Orchestra possibly want with ten pianos?

They're no joke to fifteen-year-old Aubrey Edwards, seated behind the third piano from the left. I'd had my eye on him since he was still sucking his thumb. One of the youngest musicians on the stage, Aubrey's got the confidence of ten pianists. Give him enough fingers, and he play all ten of those instruments at once. There's nothing about harmonies Aubrey doesn't understand.

The fathomless darkness of Carnegie Hall gapes at him like a gigantic mouth, waiting to devour him, piano and all. The footlights, lower teeth. The wooden stage, a tongue. Each balcony, another row of fangs.

He hopes his parents and his sister, Kate, are out there somewhere. No telling if they got tickets. When Aubrey arrived, lines were already wrapping around the block. Young as he was, and not carrying an instrument, he had to work to persuade the door guard he was in the band.

The other pianists take their benches. The orchestra's so keyed up with excitement, you can smell it. The air is heavy with cologne and the wood-and-brass-and-oily-velvet smell of instruments.

The conductor, James Reese Europe, takes the stage. A giant of a man in a glittering white tuxedo. The audience bursts with pent-up applause, like a tidal wave rolling through the auditorium and rippling up its balconies. Silence falls. The time is *now*.

Even Aubrey's confidence falters for a moment, then. How does "The Clef Club March" begin? When do they modulate? His fingers freeze. He's going to ruin everything. Jim Europe's going to *kill* him. Uncle Ames, who taught him to play, will kill him *twice*. He'll never play in Harlem again. He wipes the sweat on his palms off onto his gray trouser legs.

Then Aubrey sees sweat shining on Jim Europe's face. He's not the only one nervous. Europe's peculiar eyes bulge behind his thin-rimmed glasses. It always makes his glare intense. Tonight it's ferocious.

Europe raises his baton. The entire room takes one deep breath. *Music* explodes that night in New York.

Nothing, nothing like this has ever echoed off an elite concert hall's carved walls.

The audience includes critics, reviewers, professors, performers. The city's musical elite. They're swept up in the flood like everyone else. They'll talk of this night for years.

Here is a new musical phenomenon. Not songs written for black musicians by white composers. Not humiliating parodies that grope for a laugh, joking at the black singers' expense. Black composers and lyricists, black musicians, excellent in their own right. Not merely excellent, but daring and vibrant and wholly original. J. Rosamond Johnson and Paul Laurence Dunbar. Harry T. Burleigh and Will Marion Cook. Paul C. Bohlen, and of course, James Reese Europe himself.

From the moment the music takes off, Aubrey Edwards never stops grinning. All his jitters peel away. His wrists are limber, his elbows loose. He's fueled by the crowd's excitement.

Attitudes explode, though the evidence would yet be long and slow in coming. Black music would begin to command not only popularity but respect for its originality and power.

For James Reese Europe and his Clef Club Orchestra, the night is a triumph. The orchestra gave and the audience received, and their rapport swelled to a crescendo of its own.

Aubrey Edwards fell in love that night. Not with piano; he'd always loved that. With performing. With audiences. If he could have his wish, he'd play for crowds every night for the rest of his life.

I heard his wish, and I blessed it.

Aubrey Edwards would have his wish at a price, following Jim Europe around the world, performing all the way to the gates of hell, in the killing fields of France.

APOLLO

Spartanburg—October 13, 1917

COME WITH ME now to Spartanburg, South Carolina, five years later. It's October 13, 1917, a hot autumn night. The people of Spartanburg are gathered to hear an outdoor concert. White soldiers from the training camp come in uniform. White civilians come in plaid shirts and flowered skirts, clutching cold beers and glasses of sweet tea to keep cool while they listen to "colored music."

"Colored," of course, isn't the word they use.

The Clef Club Orchestra is no more. In its place is the Army Band of the Army National Guard, 15th New York Infantry Regiment, with Lieutenant James R. Europe conducting a goodwill concert for the people of Spartanburg, home to the army training base Camp Wadsworth. Goodwill indeed.

Moths flutter at streetlights. Silhouetted against a purpling sky, the band tunes their instruments in squawks and scales and riffs. The sound is a discordant mess, but pregnant with anticipation: from this chaos, order and excitement will come.

Aubrey Edwards twiddles drumsticks between his long fingers. He is tense, apprehensive about surviving this concert. The 15th New York goes to bed at night wondering if they'll wake up to morning reveille, or to a midnight lynch mob.

The 15th New York Infantry, an all-black regiment, came to Camp Wadsworth for combat and weapons training after basic training at Camp Dix in New Jersey, where Southern soldiers hung NO COLOREDS ALLOWED and WHITES ONLY signs on buildings.

When Spartanburg learned a black regiment would be stationed at Camp Wadsworth, the governor of South Carolina went to Washington to lobby the government *not* to send black soldiers into their state. Spartanburg's mayor, the son of a Confederate soldier, told a *New York Times* reporter, "With their Northern ideas about race equality, they will probably expect to be treated like white men. I can say right here that they will not be treated as anything except Negroes. We shall treat them exactly as we treat our resident Negroes. This thing is like waving a red flag in the face of a bull. . . . You remember the trouble a couple of weeks ago in Houston."

I know *you* remember Houston, Ares. It was practically a one-night war. A white police officer had entered a black woman's home without a warrant, searching for a suspect. When she protested, he beat and arrested her, dragging her from her home though she wasn't fully dressed. When a black soldier saw this and tried to intervene to defend the woman, the white policeman pistol-whipped the black soldier, seriously injuring him. The men of the beaten soldier's regiment, learning no consequences would befall the white policeman, felt abandoned by white police and army officials. They saw the abuse as a last straw in a long string of injustices. So they marched into the city. Soldiers and civilians died in the shooting that followed.

This concert is trying to prevent another Houston. To prove that black soldiers aren't all mutineers or murderers. Aubrey Edwards and his fellow musicians feel they'd better smile and play like their lives depend upon it.

Private Aubrey Edwards, now twenty, is a few inches taller, a good deal broader, and substantially nimbler on the piano. He wants to take the ragtime world by storm and leave his mark on the new world of American jazz. He already sees his name in lights.

His rhythmic sense is mature for his age as a musician, and his improvisation is crazy-wild. Sometimes too wild, thinks Lieutenant Europe, who became his piano tutor once Aubrey surpassed his uncle Ames, but Europe can see that this wild kid is going somewhere. He doesn't mean the trenches of France.

But that's precisely where Aubrey's going, if General Pershing can figure out what to do with a black regiment. Who'll command them? Who'll fight alongside them? It's a problem.

America has finally joined the Great War. Germany's torpedoing of American ships has awakened the sleeping giant, and the Zimmermann Telegram didn't help matters any. Americans who'd wanted to leave Europeans to their own destruction now sing a different tune.

Aubrey enlisted in the regiment that spring, along with his pal Joey Rice and most of their friends. For music dreams, not dreams of soldier's glory. He'd be *paid* to play ragtime with Jim Europe all over Europe ("they named it after me," as Jim liked to say). Practically a professional musician! Of course, he'd have to shoot a rifle in the bargain, too.

Playing with the soldiers' band sounded better than dressing like a toy soldier every day to operate the elevator at a high-rise office building in Midtown Manhattan. It had been the best job he could find after leaving school. But there are only so many times you can smile and wish "Good morning" to white men in suits who don't answer, nor even look at you, before you start to question your own existence. If he stayed here, he might push elevator buttons for the rest of his life. Coming back as a veteran soldier—maybe even a war hero!—he'd have a future. And if he didn't come back from "Over There . . ." Well, he just would. That was all.

There's only one piano available for the concert on the green in Spartanburg, and Private Luckey Roberts is playing it. So Private Edwards doubles on percussion. Baritone Noble Sissle sings, all swing and eyebrows and charm, and the white ladies melt. He's a handsome devil, but a black one. So they melt, but only up to a point, especially if their husbands are watching.

The 15th Army Band is a smash hit in Spartanburg. They might be insulted by shopkeepers during the day, kicked into gutters by town toughs, even threatened by mob attack from an Alabama regiment, but the 15th New York National Guard band's music is just too good to ignore. Spartanburg can't help clapping its hands and tapping its feet. Younger folks break out dancing, right on the green. They don't want black musicians in hotel lobbies, but blowing a horn to Jim Europe's up-tempo beat is fine and dandy.

Yet danger still hovers like a sparking storm cloud. Aubrey, who could drum blindfolded, sees pretty girls dancing. He's been cooped up with men and only men for weeks, and he'd like to take a second look. In New York, he could, but here? No pretty face is worth swinging from a tree.

His mother's letters are full of urgent warning. She grew up in Mississippi. She knows about lynching. Aubrey wonders if he'll die *in* his country before he ever gets the chance to die *for* his country. Either way, he'd rather not.

The concert ends, and the soldiers march in perfect military form back toward their barracks. The crowd drifts home. Anger's been appeased, but only for tonight. Another week, and tensions will overflow. The army, hoping to prevent a race riot, will decide there's no good place in the States to put them, and no English-speaking outfit anywhere along the Western Front that will serve beside them. So they'll hand them off to the French Army like a goodwill offering. No, toss them like a hot potato.

No, lob them like a hand grenade.

DECEMBER 1942

Intersection

"NOT," ARES SAYS, "that I would ever object to hearing a story about a soldier, but how did we get from a British girl and her soldier boyfriend to this piano-playing American recruit? Did I miss something?"

"Their stories intersect," Apollo explains. "Soon."

Ares shrugs. "I mean, not that it matters to me."

Of course not.

"Want me to stick around, Goddess?" inquires Apollo.

"Certainly," she tells him. "There's so much more to tell. We've only barely begun."

APHRODITE

Royal Albert Hall—November 25, 1917

AT ONE O'CLOCK, Hazel Windicott went down to the street, circled the King's Whiskers, and made for their doorway meet-up. In her stomach lurked a silent fear: James wouldn't be there.

She almost missed him. He leaned against the doorway where they'd spoken before.

"Look at you," he said.

"I can't, unless you've brought a mirror," she told him.

Somehow it was harder, not easier, to meet each other again, this third time together, now that they knew each other a little better. More wonderful, but more unsure; there were no more polite formalities to hide behind. No script at all. The poor darlings.

"Let's get out of here," James proposed, and Hazel seized his hand and dragged him down the street at a run. "Hold a moment." He laughed. "You're in better trim than I am." She wasn't, really, but between laughing and running, James could scarcely draw a proper breath.

He pulled a train schedule and a map from his pocket. "All right, then, Miss You-Don't-Know-London-Do-You," he said. "I'll have you know that I've got matters all figured out."

"Oh?"

"S'right. We'll head up to the train station at Bow. From there, we'll take the District Railway to Gloucester Road"—he squinted at his notes—"and we'll take the Piccadilly Line one stop up, to Kensington High Street. From there, we walk to Hyde Park."

"Impressive, my Man About Town," said Hazel.

"None of that, now." Dimples again.

They reached the station, bought tickets, boarded the train, then collapsed into seats. The train pulled out, and London slid by. James watched the skyline. It was the more gentlemanly option than staring at Hazel.

"You notice every grand building, don't you?"

"Do I?"

"What sorts of buildings do you favor?"

No one had asked him that before. He looked to see if she was merely struggling to make polite conversation, but she watched his face with open curiosity. She really wanted to know.

"Of course I like the grand old buildings. The guildhalls and churches and government palaces." He turned toward her. "But what really interests me is less, oh, showy, and more useful. Take hospitals. Ever since the war, we haven't had near enough. They could be bigger, too, and more modern. Better plumbing and wiring. I've been reading about it."

"Will we need such hospitals after the war ends?" asked Hazel.

"You mean, if it ever does." He immediately regretted it.

She laid her hand on his arm. "Don't say that. It must."

He risked a look into her eyes. "I was a kid when it began," he said. "I have to remind myself life was normal once. Cousins gathering over Easter holidays. Summer visits to my gran on the coast. Playing at the beach. Making castles in the sand."

Hazel, with neither siblings nor young cousins, saw this rosy picture wistfully.

"One older cousin died in the fighting at the Somme," he said. "The other lost a leg."

Hazel leaned against his shoulder. "What were they like?"

He stared out the window. "Footballers." He smiled sadly. "Will was light on his feet. Mike was *quick*. You should've seen them."

"The war must end before long," said Hazel. "They can't be insane enough to let it last forever. Besides, the Americans are coming. I expect the Germans are terrified of them."

He laughed ruefully. "I suppose a German's at least as tough as an American. But the Americans will have the numbers on their side, once enough of them get here." He sighed. "I wish a couple million would arrive this week. If the war ended Saturday, I wouldn't have to go."

Hazel threaded her arm through his elbow.

"Let's hope they will come," she said. "Millions on Monday. Millions on Tuesday. Extra millions on Wednesday."

He smiled, but his eyes were sad. "I'm a coward, aren't I?" he said. "Now you know."

She reached up and pulled his chin to face her. "Not a coward," she said firmly. "You'd like to live, and who wouldn't?" She smiled. "I'd like you to live, too."

Her face was so near, and her eyes so warm. It took all of James's self-command not to kiss her, there on the train. *Not like this*, he told himself. *Not here.*

"All right, then." He managed a smile. "For your sake, I will live. Since you want me to."

Why wouldn't he kiss her? Hazel tried not to mind. Her gaze kept sliding down to his inescapable lips.

"I do want you to live," she said. "Hurry on back, and build those hospitals."

"Not only hospitals," he said. "Factories. Warehouses. Apartments. With the train lines expanding, there'll be a need for more homes, schools, more communities along the routes. The building magazines all say so. If, after the war, I could study architecture . . ." He caught himself. Surely he was putting the piano girl into a coma of boredom. "Sorry. Listen to me nattering on!"

"I *am* listening," she said. "I think it's marvelous. You *should* have an ambition." She frowned. "I wish I had a clearer one myself." She gazed out the window at drab buildings abutting the tracks. "In Poplar there are awful slums, down near the docks. St. Matthias's runs charities for dockworkers' families. But I suppose selling jam at bazaars and old books at jumble sales won't fix anything, will it?"

"Not unless you've got an awful lot of books and jam."

They only just barely caught the conductor's announcement that they'd reached Gloucester Road. After changing for the Piccadilly Line, they got off at Kensington High Street and followed the press of bodies into the slanting afternoon light. Grayish, wintry-green Hyde Park led them to the Royal Albert Hall, which loomed like an ocean voyager. They joined streaming throngs of concertgoers at the entry doors, then climbed flight after flight of stairs, to the level just below the gallery at the very top.

Hazel marveled at the drop beneath them, past two tiers of balconies, to the stage below.

"I'm sorry these were the best seats I could get," James said.

"Don't be silly," she said. "This is breathtaking." She peeped over the rail. She swallowed. "How high up are we?"

"Best not to think of it."

James helped Hazel out of her coat, then eased out of his and sat. Spectators up at this level were fewer and scattered, so they were, for all intents, alone. With four thousand other people. He felt all arms and hands, with no place to put them, and a terrible dread that he might wrap them around Hazel and not let go. He jammed his hands under his thighs.

Hazel watched the flood of humanity streaming in. She commented on the size of the grand piano and the number of seats for the orchestra. She was never dull, never bored. Always alert and interested. He thought of all he'd said on the train. He'd never spoken at such length to a girl who wasn't a relative. He could talk to Hazel all day, all year, for a lifetime, forever.

Hazel gestured to the music hall. "How would you like to have built this little place?"

"Little!" He looked about the vast room. "Designing it would've been fun," he said. "All that weight to support, and no columns to block the view. But I wouldn't be one of the chaps on the scaffolding, plastering ceilings. Not for the Crown Jewels."

She laughed. "I don't like heights much, either," she said, "but for the Crown Jewels, I think I'd give ceiling plastering a try."

"You're braver than I am." He grinned. "You should be the one going off to the war."

She sat up at this. "Do you know? Sometimes I wish I were." She saw his surprised face. "I don't mean fight in the trenches. I don't think I'd be cut out for that." She smiled. "I knew some girls in school who would give Jerry an awfully stout whack in the shins, given the chance. But not me. And I'd make a terrible nurse. All that blood! I'd be sick on the operating table."

James tried not to laugh.

"But I do wish I could do something to help. Not just sit at home practicing audition pieces while the boys are over there, dying."

The lights dimmed. The roar of the crowd settled to something like a rumbling purr.

James leaned in closer and spoke into her ear. "Keeping the world safe for people to practice their audition pieces seems like the one good reason to fight this war. If music stops, and art ceases, and beauty fades, what have we then?"

He watched her long lashes open and shut. This beauty before him would never fade.

(It's one of my most useful little lies.)

In the dim hall, lit only by stage lights, their copper-colored faces searched each other.

Kiss her. Do it.

The musicians began tuning their instruments. The spell broke. A master of ceremonies welcomed everyone and announced the program. Then the conductor, a Mr. Landon Ronald, took the stage, and the orchestra rose. Applause filled the Royal Albert. Mr. Ronald bowed, the orchestra sat, and the great hall sank into silence.

Then, the music began.

James and Hazel closed their eyes and let the music wash over them. Sonorous brass in slow, solemn chords. Woodwinds chasing one another in lilting ribbons of sound, swirling around the balconies. Then brass and winds together. A marcher and a dancer. A soldier and a piano girl.

Hazel pulled pulsing sound into her lungs. Beside her, a grave-eyed young man made the air crackle around him. She made a wish. *Let tonight never end. Let the music play on and on.*

James had attended concerts but nothing like this. The sound, surrounding him, passing through his body. Each tone, so alive, so pure, so mighty.

Hazel glanced sidelong at him, and saw him breathe in time with the music. She saw tears well at the rims of his dark eyes.

This one, she decided. *This lad, for me.*

And it was done.

APHRODITE

Concert, Continued—November 25, 1917

THE PIANO SOLOIST, a Miss Adela Verne, played her first solo, a Hungarian fantasy by Liszt. To James's mind, Miss Verne played as masterfully as any man might. He'd hoped Hazel would be especially interested to see a woman pianist in the solo role.

Catching Hazel's eye, he pointed down to the stage. "How would you like to perform for this crowd on that piano?"

She smiled. "There you are with that question again."

He leaned closer. "What color gown would you wear?"

She gave him a funny look. "Black, of course. Pianists aren't opera singers."

"So you'd do it, then?"

"I'm nowhere near as talented as you seem to think." She smiled. "I'm just a girl, like countless others, who plays the piano."

James watched her long, slender fingers on her lap. "But after conservatory studies?"

She shrugged. "If I want to end up on that stage, a conservatory is essential." The statement was very much an if. "My parents work so hard, and sacrifice so much, for me to have lessons we really shouldn't be able to afford." She gazed at the grand piano onstage.

"They have such hopes for me. I owe them everything."

He couldn't pinpoint the source of her reluctance, so he said nothing.

She thought a moment. "If I could come here alone in the middle of the night," she said, "and shine just one spotlight on that piano, and play for the darkness, I'd like that very much."

James watched her curiously. "Alone?"

She nodded. "Think how romantic, to play in the dark, with only this great hall, that has heard so much, for an audience." She rubbed her arms. "It gives me goose bumps."

"Why no people?"

Mr. Landon Ronald made yet another entrance to loud applause.

"People get in the way."

He lowered his voice as the conductor raised his baton.

"I'm not people, then," he said, "because I'd be there. I wouldn't miss it."

She took his hand and gave it a squeeze. "We'll see."

Piece after exquisite piece of music peeled away. Dvořák and Alkan and Paderewski and Saint-Saëns. Some concertgoers might have felt the performance was long, but not James. Not Hazel. They applauded at the finale, lingered as long as they dared, then made their way through the throng and out into the cold twilit air. They turned toward the train station.

"Stop for tea, then?" James asked.

Hazel shook her head sadly. "I'd better not. I . . . er . . . I didn't tell my parents where I was going this afternoon."

His mouth hung open. "You *what?*"

She looked at the ground. "I *will* tell them," she said. "I just didn't see a way to do it." She glanced up at him. "My folks, they're lovely. I can't believe I'm doing this. I do think they'll like you, once they get to know you."

"Thanks." James laughed. "I'm an acquired taste, then? Takes a bit of patience?"

She flushed, and elbowed him lightly in the ribs. "Stop that!"

"Stop what?"

"Teasing me."

He stopped walking and turned to face her. She shivered a little in the cold, and he instinctively reached his hands up to cradle her face and keep it warm.

KISS HER.

Hazel held her breath. His brown eyes were so beautiful. Surely he would kiss her now.

He didn't. Maybe, Hazel realized with awkward horror, he was waiting for an explanation about her parents. So she gave him one.

"My dad is very protective of his 'little girl,'" she explained, "and my mum is terrified of life in general. She's always telling me horror stories about what happened to so-and-so's daughter who fell in with a worthless, no-good chap, and on and on."

"Worthless and no-good," James echoed.

Hazel held up a firm hand. "Now, you stop right there," she said. "You know that's not what I'm saying."

He grinned and admitted that he did know that.

"Dad's always warning me against soldier boys, too," she said. "And . . . I can understand why he would. He doesn't want me getting hurt."

James stroked the pads of his thumbs softly across her cheekbones.

"I will never hurt you, Hazel Windicott."

She came very close then to kissing him herself.

"I know," she whispered. "Not if you could help it."

Neither could find words for all they didn't dare say.

Finally she mumbled something about the cold, and he

mentioned their train. They broke apart and resumed walking, then reached the station and boarded their train.

"Anyway," she said, resurrecting an abandoned conversation, "I knew if I told my parents about you, they'd insist on meeting you, and on chaperoning our time, and on limiting it to whatever they felt was proper. Which wouldn't be anywhere near enough." She looked earnestly into his dark eyes. "We only have one week. I don't want to waste any of it."

If it weren't for the prying eyes of a plump older woman across the aisle, James would've enfolded Hazel in his arms then and there.

"I feel I could tell you anything," he told her. "Sometimes I think I already have."

True, and false. He couldn't tell her what he really felt.

"Then why," she said, "haven't you kissed me yet?"

All her limbs clenched, as if, maybe, by sheer muscular will, she could pull back those words and unsay them. But James let the nosy older woman be hanged and slipped his arms around Hazel and drew her close.

"Oh, don't worry," he told her. "I have every intention of kissing you."

His face was an inch from hers.

She took a deep breath.

Nothing happened.

If he was trying to kill her through kiss deprivation, it was working.

She tried to sound nonchalant. "Every intention, eh?"

He nodded, very seriously, but with a twinkle in his eye.

"I'm planning it carefully," he said. "Can't rush these things."

"Actually," she said, "one can. If one wants to."

She saw the texture of his skin and the dark stubble forming on his chin. She saw his teeth—quite nice teeth—and the adorable dimples, when he smiled.

"I will kiss you, if I may, Miss Windicott," he told her, "on the train platform at Charing Cross next Saturday. Before I set off overseas."

I don't like delays. I was not amused.

Hazel, however, was. She began to laugh, and the shape of her smile nearly made James abandon his plan of waiting. He pressed his cheek against hers. Just like when they'd danced.

"I appreciate the advance notice," she said. "I can dress for the occasion."

"It'll be a kiss to remember," he told her. "I'll make sure of that."

Hazel laughed in his ear. "You'd best *remember* to do it, then."

"I won't forget."

She pulled back, with difficulty, and met his eyes.

"Out of curiosity," she said, "why then? To be like the photos in the papers, of soldiers and sweethearts kissing goodbye at the station?"

He shook his head.

"I need a reason," he said, "to go to the train station. Something to look forward to about that day."

She didn't know it, but she felt it; Ares, you were the man seated in the row behind them. The War and all its finality prying its cold fingers in between them.

"Besides," he said, "if I kiss you before then, I may never get on that train."

APHRODITE

Torture—November 25–26, 1917

THEY SAID GOODBYE. It was torture.

Hazel went inside and faced her parents. It was torture.

She returned home, not to anger, but worse, to betrayal and disappointment.

James returned home to a telegram.

James and Hazel had made plans to see each other at lunch the next day. Waiting all night and all morning for luncheon was torture.

But it was nothing compared to her torture, the next day, waiting at the café where they said they'd meet, for James not to appear.

Nothing, compared to James's torture, watching the gray sky out the window of a morning train bound for Calais, there to board a ship for Boulogne, and from there, a train to Étaples for training at the British Expeditionary Force base camp.

Nothing compared to the torture for Hazel of receiving a letter, that afternoon at her flat, explaining he'd been summoned to report days earlier than expected. Prime Minister Lloyd George and Field Marshal Haig had an urgent need for new men to replace casualties at the Front. Private James Alderidge, someone in a war bureau had decided, would do as well as any.

APHRODITE

First Night—November 26, 1917

THE CHANNEL STRETCHED between James and Hazel that night. It looks narrow on a globe, but when it divides two hearts, it might as well be the mighty Atlantic.

Hazel paced her bedroom. Her flannel robe, she clutched tightly across her ribs. Her nightgown couldn't keep her warm. A bitter cold wind blew in from the Continent, from France. Cold enough to chill a girl in her bedroom; how much more a soldier on a boat or in a tent?

She'd seen pictures, films even, of British soldiers, row upon row, marching. An impressive sight, majestic in size and discipline and uniformity. It made her tremble to realize that now, out there, one of those immobile faces would belong to her James. His dear mind and heart, trapped inside that khaki cage. His warm body, tall and graceful, the target of a speeding lump of German steel.

It would be nice, at a time like this, if she could cry. Get it all out in a big rain of tears and finally drift off to sleep. Tears were better by far than the tightness in her throat and the lead weight in her stomach.

She paced the room.

Friday, Saturday, Sunday. One weekend. Only that. A lifetime, crammed into three days.

Monday, Tuesday, Wednesday, Thursday, Friday, and a Saturday kiss, stolen away.

If her heart could entwine so completely around his in three days, what would have happened after a week? What words would've passed between them? What memories created? What promises exchanged?

Was all of this nothing more than a dream one gradually forgets upon waking?

She sank upon her bed. *Stop this, my girl*, she told herself. *You'll drive yourself mad.*

She closed her eyes and wrapped her arms around herself. She took herself back, back to the Royal Albert, to the train, to the walk, the other walk, the tea shop, the dance. Bay rum and wool, a clean shave and soft, steady brown eyes. Dark hair and dimples. Warmth rushed upward from her belly to her head, and tingles shivered down her spine.

It was real and true. However new, however young.

The war was hers now. It was inside her. No more a matter of headlines and jargon.

"God, keep him safe," she whispered. But it was out of my hands.

Poor lamb.

James had had the day's travels to distract his thoughts, but they failed him. He couldn't bring himself to make conversation with fellow soldiers. All around him, on train and ship, young men talked and laughed as if they were all bound on holiday. A grand game of playing soldier.

James wasn't going anyplace. He was only leaving Hazel. Leaving her, and leaving her, and leaving her still some more.

They arrived at night at a base camp, drank lukewarm beef broth, then followed a commander to a field of tents. They were barely warmer than the bitter night, but canvas flaps kept the wind out, and eighteen men sleeping three deep in bunks added some body heat.

He slid out of his pack, kicked off his boots, and climbed into bed. It felt like hours before he generated any warmth under his blankets. He couldn't have slept anyway.

He tried to remember what it felt like, holding Hazel in his arms.

Fool, he told himself. *You should've kissed her while you had the chance.*

Precisely what I was thinking, but I'm not one to say I told you so.

Could it even have been possible for this lovely, lovely girl to decide to favor him, James Alderidge from nowhere, with her laughter, her company, and the way she ate lemon cake? That he should be the one to hold her hands and watch her lashes sweep each time she blinked?

Now that he'd found her, how could he let himself be carried away from her?

He'd never have met her, if it wasn't for the war. And now the war had torn them apart.

"The War giveth, and the War taketh away. Blessed be the name of the War."

His vicar back home would've had a swift comment on such blasphemy. James still remembered his cousin Will's funeral. Vividly. Ashes to ashes, dust to dust. The Lord giveth, the Lord taketh away. . . .

"God, bring me home to her," he whispered. "Please."

You may ask me, as others have done before, whether it was kindness or cruelty to allow them to meet, so soon before his departure, with so little time to discover each other. Whether the pangs of loss do not invalidate the bliss of love. Especially where war is concerned, and Death runs rampant with his bloody scythe. You may say that it was wicked of me to allow James to find Hazel, and Hazel, James, if three days were all they would have.

I don't call it cruelty.

I do not apologize.

ENTR'ACTE

December 5, 1917

Dear Miss Windicott,

I hope you'll excuse my writing to you without permission. There's so much I've wanted to tell you. Nothing short of a court-martial could've made me board that train. If I hadn't gone to war, I wouldn't have met you. If I hadn't met you, I wouldn't now be missing you so terribly.

I had hoped, with my experience in building, that I'd be selected for the Royal Engineers, but I've been assigned to an infantry division. I've been here nearly a week. Training isn't as bad as I feared. The testing occupies my mind, and marching keeps a body warm. Sleeping in tents is miserable. We're miles from the Front, but the guns echo night and day. One bright spot is making comrades of my squadron. I expect some will come to be good friends.

Our days are mostly drilling and marching in the bull pen. Watching the convoys arriving with wounded men from the Front is hard. Some kind of sickness is spreading, and trainees do go down with coughs and fevers from time to time. So far, I am hale and hearty.

Write, if you will, and tell me about ordinary life. It will help me to picture a world outside this dirty camp. Tell me about you, your growing-up years, your parents, your adventures at school, your pastimes. I feel I know you so well and yet hardly know you at all, so please, help me fill in the missing bits. Tell me what you like for breakfast, and what you would name a dog.

Your friend,

James

◇───◆◇◆───◇

December 11, 1917

Dear James,

I would name a dog Pepper. I always wished for a dog. When I was young, I read storybooks about a boy named Willie and his splendid dog, Scout. I used to imagine myself on those adventures, and Scout sleeping at the foot of my bed. Most of my childhood, when I wasn't practicing scales, was spent curled up with a book. I always wished for siblings.

For breakfast, I like a poached egg on toast, and an orange, when we can get them. They're harder to come by nowadays. Were groceries as restricted in Chelmsford?

Ordinary life is fairly well summed up in Christmas choir rehearsals. There's a great deal of singing to be done in the parish, and I'm the one they call. I don't mind accompanying as much as soloing. I need a distraction. I'm not rehearsing audition pieces as I ought. I shouldn't complain about piano when you're sleeping in a tent, marching through mud, and waiting to head to the Front. But you've asked for normal life, so you shall have it.

Dad and Mum have gotten over being so upset with me for not telling them about you. I'm determined that you shall become acquainted. Do you have a photograph you could send?

My dad, as you know, plays piano in a music hall, and wishes he had more chances to go fishing. He's crazy about chestnuts. My mum writes sentimental poems and keeps so many perfumed sachets in her bedroom drawers that just going in there makes my father cough. Her hands are rough from the thousand needle pricks one gets sewing shirts and trousers for a living. Every year I buy her a bottle of lotion for Christmas. Scented.

They're both dears, and I adore them. They put me first always. It makes me all the worse a person for feeling so restless, for wishing to do something outrageous on my own for a change.

How about you? What would you name a dog? What do you prefer for breakfast? How do you feel about cats? Also, what's the best book you've ever read? Where, if you could go anywhere in the world, would you plan a picnic? Tell me about your siblings. And about the most foolish thing you've ever done.

Yours,

Hazel

December 16, 1917

Dear Hazel,

Asking you to dance was the most foolish thing I've ever done. Look what it did to me.

I'd never call it great literature, but I enjoyed <u>Tarzan of the Apes</u>. And Kipling's <u>Jungle Book</u>. In school, I was partial to <u>Macbeth</u> over <u>Julius Caesar</u>.

Pepper is a fine name for a dog. A second dog could be named Salt. As for cats, I have no objection, and Ginger and Nutmeg would do nicely. I draw the line at Mustard.

My siblings: Maggie is fifteen, still in school, and keen to become a typist. The typewriter noise gives our dad headaches. Maggie frets about her frizzy hair, but she's just the girl you want around in a pinch. Bob, age thirteen, is wildly enthusiastic, and devoted, body and soul, to Boy Scouting. He spends every spare moment tracking around meadows and woods with a compass and field glasses. It's good there aren't wolves in Britain, or he'd be eaten by one.

I'd eat a picnic someplace wild and hot. The Congo, perhaps, or the Amazon rain forest. But perhaps that's just a French December talking. If Congolese or Amazonian ants invaded the meal, they might eat the picnickers and not just the cold chicken.

My turn for questions: What's your favorite book? Tell me about your friends, and your piano tutor. If you had a little cottage with a garden, what would you plant in it? And, if you were going to do something absolutely shocking and outrageous, what would it be?

Your letters bring more cheer than I can express. Don't stop.

Yours,

James

December 23, 1917

Dear James,

Thank you for the photograph. My mother took quite a shine to it. Dad said, "Humph."

Books: <u>Evelina</u> by Fanny Burney. <u>North and South</u> by Elizabeth Gaskell. <u>Wuthering Heights</u> by Emily Brontë.

My dearest friends are Georgia Fake and Olivia Jenkins. I went to school with them both, and we've been chums since we were small. They live here in Poplar. Georgia is quite hilarious, tough as nails, and smart as anything. She's volunteering at a soldiers' hospital here in London, with *plans to become a trained nurse. Olivia's just the opposite. Soft and tenderhearted. It's odd that Georgia is the nurse and not she, for Olivia is so thoughtful and kind. She'd bring such comfort to the ill. Georgia, on the other hand, can keep a level head while someone's arm is being sawn off. Perhaps she's learned to be tough after a lifetime of people ragging her about her name, Fake. Olivia's already engaged to a lad at the Front. It's hard to comprehend. It seems only a moment ago that we were wearing our first fancy dresses to school teas.*

My piano tutor is tyrannical and marvelous. Monsieur Guillaume. He's in his sixties. He's been my tutor since I was eleven, once I outgrew my first instructor. I know he loves me, as the best teachers love their pupils, and I love him. It makes it all the harder to sense his disappointment in me. I can't ever live up to his hopes. The war has been terrible for him. To see France teeter on the brink of losing to the Huns has torn him apart.

In my cottage garden I would plant daffodils. Tulips in every color, and heavenly narcissus. And, when spring is gone, geraniums for cheer, and irises and lupines to sway in the breeze. Oh, now you've got me picturing it so clearly, and how can I be content if I don't get my cottage garden someday? Such a spot would cost a mint in London. Even in Poplar.

My most outrageous scheme? I've already put it into motion. Soon after you left, I submitted my application to be an entertainment secretary in a YMCA relief hut in France. I shall play piano night and day for homesick soldiers. My parents are fit to be tied. They begged me to request a London hut, but I am determined to go where the soldiers are in greater need of diversion to get their minds off the war. I dread performing, but I can't possibly fear it as much as soldiers dread the battlefield. I might as well divert the woes of actual soldiers as the woes of church ladies. I'll be there soon after the first of the year. My parents are certain this will derail my path to conservatory. But if Europe is about to fall to the Germans, does that matter?

I'm sure you're itching to finish your training, but I'm so glad you're away from the German guns. Be safe and stay warm. Write and tell me about your comrades. And whether or not you enjoy fishing. It will mean a lot to Dad if you do.

Have a very happy Christmas. It breaks my heart to think of you spending it at a cold army base. May it be a festive one anyhow.

Yours affectionately,

Hazel

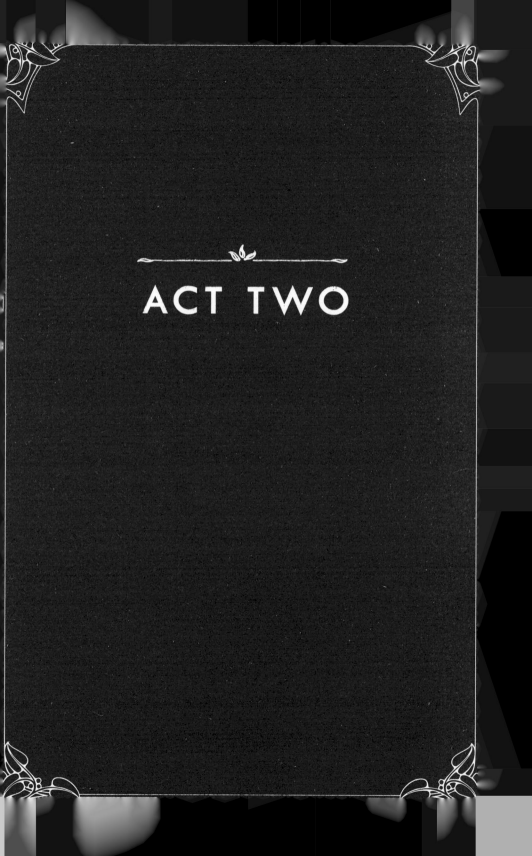

ACT TWO

APOLLO

"I Want to Be Ready"—January 3, 1918

JANUARY 3, 1918, two A.M. Thirty degrees below zero.

Aubrey Edwards and some forty other soldiers from the 15th New York huddled for warmth in straw strewn about the floor of a cattle car. They'd boarded the train in Brest, on the coast of France, an hour after disembarking from the USS *Pocahontas*, and now rattled, *chuh-chuh-chuh-chuh*, through the starlit dark over snow-covered countryside.

Cold, weary, and famished, they thought they were heading to the Front, and might see German combat by morning. Combat might have been better than where they were bound.

Locomotive wheels sang along the frigid metal rails. The rhythm was steady and would've been soothing, if the air weren't so bitter, bitter cold. No whistles sounded and no horns blew. Even trains kept secrets during a war.

Harlem and home were so far away. Would he ever see his parents again? Taste his mother's chicken pie? Smell the sweet tobacco of his father's pipe? He'd give a lot to hear Kate squawk about him playing piano when her sleepy old boyfriend, Lester, came calling.

His father came home early from the paint factory, the day the

Pocahontas sailed for France, to meet Aubrey at the docks and tell his only son goodbye.

"You conduct yourself with dignity and pride, young man, you hear me?" he'd said. "Nobody can take that away from you."

Was that really true? Aubrey remembered Spartanburg. Hadn't those vicious shopkeepers and farmers worked like the devil to do exactly that?

"And stay alert," his father continued. "Anything can happen in a war, but it's less likely to happen to the man who keeps his eyes open." He held out his arms wide and crushed Aubrey in a hug. "Whip those Germans and hurry back to us." Aubrey could still feel his dad's whiskers and smell the chemical-clean scent of paint in his father's collar.

He pulled his hands from his pockets and blew on them. His breath turned to ice before it could do any good. He shoved them under his shirt. A pianist couldn't risk his hands.

Was he even a pianist anymore? Everyone else in the band could pack their instrument in a case and bring it with them. Not Aubrey. A pianist's got to play, or his fingers lose their tunes. And Luckey Roberts, darn him, usually got the lead.

The band had played on board ship for two weeks. Hymns and Christmas carols, old plantation tunes, and hours of rehearsing jazzified versions of patriotic melodies. "La Marseillaise" and "Tipperary" and "Pack Up Your Troubles" and "Over There." But only by day. As soon as the sun set at around four p.m., it was lights-out for the entire ship, lest German vessels spot them. And anyway, the old ship *Pocahontas* had no piano. So Aubrey, as third drummer, clashed the cymbals now and then, while the Wright twins (who weren't even brothers) on percussion rapped out Europe's syncopated rhythms. When they disembarked in Brest, they performed an impromptu concert in the square. Aubrey played castanets.

The French gave the 15th New York a hero's welcome, and applauded their jazz wildly. Then the regiment boarded the train and set off, exhausted and hungry, for their next stop.

In the cattle car, a soldier began to sing in the darkness, softly, slowly, in time with the engine, in a plaintive, resonant baritone:

I WANT TO BE READY, I WANT TO BE READY . . .

Heads rose and ears turned to locate the voice.

I WANT TO BE READY, LORD . . .

Another voice joined in. A tenor, doubling the melody an octave higher.

TO WALK IN JERUSALEM, JUST LIKE JOHN.

"Aw, go to sleep," someone said in a rear corner.

But there was too much momentum now. A deep bass joined the group, and then a high tenor, singing the alto part. They repeated the refrain. By the time they reached "Jerusalem," someone had added a rat-a-tat rhythm by knocking on the steel walls of the car with the heel of his hands. Murmured laughter rippled through the tired heads, and the quartet sailed into the first verse at a driving double tempo.

OH, JOHN, OH, JOHN, OH, WHAT DID YOU SAY?
WALKING IN JERUSALEM, JUST LIKE JOHN.
I'LL MEET YOU THERE ON THE CROWNING DAY.
WALKING IN JERUSALEM, JUST LIKE JOHN.
OH, I WANT TO BE READY, I WANT TO BE READY . . .

The whole car sang now. Freezing cold, stiff as oak, heading off to war, and terribly far from home, Aubrey felt his cheeks smile and his belly warm. He had his boys with him, and they'd been through a lot already. No matter what happened, they'd keep on singing.

APHRODITE

Relief Huts—January 4, 1918

HAZEL ARRIVED IN Saint-Nazaire, France, on the morning of January 4, 1918, after a cold Channel crossing and an overnight train ride.

She couldn't believe this was really happening. Her entire life, she'd sailed upon the quiet ripple of her parents' lives. But here she was now, watching the sun rise over the frozen fields and frosty hedges of coastal France. The sky was pink, flush with promise, and golden sun glistened off filaments of ice webbing the world. It was hard to comprehend that this glorious morning, this fairyland view, shone over a country ravaged by years of war, and that she was hurtling her way toward thousands of soldiers in need of comfort.

Hazel'd never even comforted a dog. Perhaps she'd made a very grave mistake.

The train pulled into the Saint-Nazaire station. Hazel rose and collected her things.

When the train left, four other persons stood on the platform. A young woman with thick blonde curls, and three middle-aged men. She caught a glimpse of the young woman's uniform jacket under her coat and ventured a question.

"Pardon me," she said. "Are you a YMCA relief volunteer?"

The blonde girl's face lit up. "I am," she said. "You as well?"

Hazel nodded.

"I am also," said one of the men, "if you'll excuse my interrupting your conversation."

"And I," the others said in turn.

"Greetings. Welcome to Saint-Nazaire." A brisk older woman in half-moon glasses dismounted from a wagon and greeted the arrivals. "All here for the YMCA, then?" She gestured to a pair of soldiers to load up luggage into the wagon. "I'm Mrs. Davies. I work with Mr. Wallace, the head Y secretary here. Come, you must be ravenous."

After brief introductions, the five arrivals climbed into the wagon and sat upon their bags. Mrs. Davies twitched the reins, and the horses plodded down the hill toward camp. Chickens waddled across the road, nearly perishing under the horses' hooves before scuttling off in an indignant spray of feathers.

As the camp rolled into view, Hazel's heart sank. It was all so gray and dirty. *What did you expect?* Not this. She'd volunteered to bring cheer to a cheerless wasteland.

Numberless soldiers marched in razor-straight rows across frozen training grounds, their rifles slung over their shoulders. Most stared straight ahead, but a few curious faces turned as the wagon passed. Some eyes found hers, cocky and saucy; others made her gulp at the loneliness there. Commanders' voices lashed out, and all eyes turned away.

James. She would write him another letter tonight. Was that too many, too often?

"These aren't British soldiers," the blonde girl wondered aloud. "Wrong uniform."

"British! Good heavens!" Mrs. Davies turned sharply toward

where the two girls sat. "Didn't they tell you where you were going?"

Hazel shrank back on her travel bag. "To the training base at Saint-Nazaire."

"To the *American* army's training base at Saint-Nazaire," cried Mrs. Davies. "Headquarters will get a letter about this. Not informing the volunteers whom they'd serve! It's a crime!"

"Figures they're Americans." The blonde girl craned her neck. "They're giants."

"The Yanks are tall," admitted Mrs. Davies, "and as they've spent the last four years enjoying Mother's home cooking instead of slogging in trenches, of course they're robust."

She resumed her role as tour guide. "Those buildings in rows are barracks," she indicated, "and over there are mess halls. These are stables and pens for livestock—that's pig you're smelling—and there, hospitals. Straight ahead is our relief hut."

The word "hut" had left Hazel picturing something small and primitive. This was vast. With tens of thousands of soldiers at the camp, the huts would have to be.

Mrs. Davies steered them inside to a table with tea laid out. "Do tell me your names once more," she said, through a large bite of roll in her mouth. "In cold such as this, I can barely think straight."

"I'm Reverend Scottsbridge, and this gentleman is Father McKnight, of the Roman Catholic profession," explained the stout clergyman. "We're here to provide spiritual consolation, eh, Father?"

"God willing," answered the priest.

A small, slim man in a faded tweed suit polished his glasses with a pocket kerchief. "I'm Horace Henry," he said. "Professor, retired. St. John's College."

"Ah! Cambridge!" exclaimed Reverend Scottsbridge. "Nothing but the best for our boys." He winked. "Even if they come from the colonies."

The professor took a gulp of tea. "They're all our boys," he said. "Even the Americans. I'll provide lectures in the evenings. I thought I'd begin with a course in English history."

"I wonder how interested American doughboys are in that," mused the blonde girl.

"We'll soon find out," Professor Henry said mildly.

"Believe me," Mrs. Davies said, "after rotating through the training circuits, never mind the trenches, these soldiers would be glad to listen to lectures on how to boil an egg."

The professor chuckled. "I hope I can do better than that."

Father McKnight's eyes twinkled. "I doubt we'll be as popular as these young ladies."

Hazel smiled. "I'm Hazel Windicott," she said. "Entertainment volunteer. I play piano."

Mrs. Davies eyed her sternly. "Do you play well?"

"I . . . believe so," she said. "I suppose it depends on your notion of playing well."

The other girl laughed. "Ellen Francis," she said. "Lacking any discernible talent, other than being chatty and amusing." She winked at Hazel. "You'll play piano; I'll play checkers."

Mrs. Davies gathered her tea things. "Gentlemen, we have a house in the village, not far from here, with rooms fitted out for you. You young ladies, for safety's sake, will occupy the spare room here in my hut. Miss Ruthers and I are nearby. The nurses' dormitories are full, so we'll make do in this way. We don't need you walking to and from camp after dark."

"How many huts are there?" Ellen Francis asked.

"Two," said Mrs. Davies. "And the Negro hut, at Camp Lusitania. You won't go there."

Mrs. Davies became aware of an awkward silence. "They have their own colored volunteers," she explained. "So it's all right. They've got plenty to amuse themselves with."

Father McKnight's balding head tilted. "What is the concern, Mrs. Davies?"

She waved the inconvenient question aside. "The girls' safety, naturally. In a camp filled with thousands of hot-blooded soldiers, strict rules must be followed. The last thing the YMCA needs is a scandal, when we're engaged in such important work."

Hazel remembered her father's words. *Be braver than I have been.* "I wouldn't mind playing in *all* the huts," she said. "I'm sure black soldiers enjoy music."

Mrs. Davies peered over the rims of her spectacles at Hazel. "There is simply no need." She attempted a conciliatory smile. "These American Negro soldiers supply their own music. It's natural to them. Instinctual. In fact, their band is performing here tomorrow. But as for you going there, your more refined musical sensibilities won't be to their liking."

Hazel's pulse thrummed in her ear. "I thought all the troops needed entertainment."

Mrs. Davies sighed and rolled her eyes heavenward. "Young idealists," she muttered. "They're all the war cause seems to attract." She faced Hazel resignedly. "I don't like using language of this sort, Miss Windicott, but you leave me no choice; Negroes can't be trusted to behave like gentlemen toward young ladies."

Hazel was about as comfortable challenging authority as she was deep-sea diving. To make Mrs. Davies dislike her on her first day seemed foolish in the extreme. But she had to.

"That may be true for a few," she said, "as I'm sure it's true for a few in any large group of soldiers. But I'm sure most are as much gentlemen as anyone else."

Reverend Scottsbridge's cough made little effort to conceal a chuckle. "My dear," he said, "you haven't seen enough of the world to know its dangers." He gave a knowing nod to Mrs. Davies. "You'll have more than enough soldiers to entertain, and handsome ones at that."

Hazel thought she might be sick. Black soldiers were *less handsome*? So that should appease her concerns—because she wasn't truly concerned on principle; the reverend knew best. She was only here for *handsome* boys. Her mind roiled.

Father McKnight gave Hazel a sorrowful look, then closed his eyes as if in prayer.

Mrs. Davies had clearly had enough with delays. "This way, please, girls, to your rooms."

DECEMBER 1942

Second Witness

APHRODITE ADDRESSES the bench. "Your Honor, I'd like to call my second witness."

"Not again," groans Ares. "How many immortals are you dragging in here? We should've gone to Olympus. Besides, I thought the whole 'court' thing had fizzled out."

"Overruled," Hephaestus tells Ares. "The defense may proceed."

"I call," Aphrodite says, with courtly theatrics, "Ares, God of War."

Ares sits up straighter, and shoves his arms into his shirtsleeves. No point in buttoning the shirt; his magnificent chest would be hidden. He feels he'd better keep his attractions on full display. But a court appearance demands decorum.

Lacking a court officer, Hephaestus administers the oath. "Do you solemnly swear to limit boasting, tell the facts and only the facts, and otherwise keep your great yap shut?"

"Hey," Ares protests, "you didn't swear in Apollo."

"I grew up with you," says Hephaestus darkly.

"Ares," Aphrodite says soothingly, "he's piqued, is all. Won't you tell us the story now, from your point of view?"

Ares rises and addresses the court. "Not for his sake, I won't," he says, "but if you want me to, I'll tell it. Just to set this sappy record straight."

ARES

Bayonet Practice—January 4, 1918

PRIVATE JAMES ALDERIDGE lined up with his squadron in the training grounds at the Front to practice using a bayonet. They were a few miles behind the trenches. James still hadn't gotten used to the constant roar of artillery guns.

"Bayonets on!" barked the commander. James screwed a blade onto his Lee-Enfield rifle.

"Guard position!" He snapped his gun upward with his left arm and braced it against his side with his right. He aimed the point at an imaginary German's throat.

"Alderidge," someone said. "Spread your feet wider." It was Private Frank Mason, a fisherman from Lowestoft. He was retraining after recovering at home from a combat leg wound.

The training commander strolled down the line, correcting men's imperfect form.

"Rest position!"

Down went the rifles, and up went everyone's backs.

"I didn't say take a nap, soldier!" At six foot two and seventeen stone, Private Billy Nutley, a Shropshire farm lad, should've been a deadly fighter but seemed more like a large target.

"Guard!"

Up snapped the bayoneted rifles.

"Aim for their throats, ladies!" The trainer's face was red. "When you're down in Jerry's trench, it's kill them before they kill you. Germans show no mercy. Points at the throat!"

James licked his lips and pointed for the unseen throat.

"Long thrust!"

Rear legs lunged forward. Blades jabbed and sliced upward.

"Thrust and twist! Screw their guts out!"

James thrust and twisted. Nutley puffed away. Beyond him, Chad Browning, a wiry Welsh ginger, jabbed at the air. Young, nimble, and talkative, but barely nine stone soaking wet.

"Throat and armpits, vulnerable!" their trainer said. "Face, chest, and gut! At their rear, go for the kidneys. Or have you geniuses forgotten where kidneys are? Rest position!"

Rest position.

The trainer paraded up and down the line. "Now, find your dummy."

They moved closer to the line of rickety wooden gallows from which hung straw dummies—pillow-like stuffed effigies of Germans.

"The German soldier is a ruthless killing machine," said he. "A lethal weapon in the Kaiser's hands. A fraction of a second is the difference between your throat cut, or his."

James's fingertips brushed against his Adam's apple.

"Survival at the Front," the trainer cried, "requires the will to kill. Guard!"

Bayonets low and at the ready.

"High port!"

Rifles snapped up over the shoulders.

"Guard!"

Ready.

"Long thrust!"

Lunge and jab, right at the dummy. It swayed at the impact.

"Guard!"

Back to the beginning.

"Long thrust! Twist! Kill, kill, kill! You say it!"

James gulped. "Kill, kill, kill!"

"Not like that, you pathetic sops! They'll wipe the floor with you!"

"Kill, kill, kill!"

Just say it, James told himself. Just do what they want you to do. He lunged at straw-filled Fritz like a ruthless killing machine. Like a lethal weapon in King George's hands.

"Rest position. Bayonets off. Tomorrow we'll spar and engage in hand-to-hand."

They headed back to their barracks. Ambiguous smells wafted from mess kitchens. James was hungry enough today to eat bully beef.

Private Chad Browning began to sing in a high-pitched, nasal, comical voice.

OH, OH, OH, IT'S A LOVELY WAR,

WHO WOULDN'T BE A SOLDIER, EH?

OH, IT'S A SHAME TO TAKE THE PAY. . . .

"What pay?" muttered Nutley. "When do we ever see that?"

UP TO YOUR WAIST IN WATER,

UP TO YOUR EYES IN SLUSH,

USING THE KIND OF LANGUAGE,

THAT MAKES THE SERGEANT BLUSH.

OH, WHO WOULDN'T JOIN THE ARMY?
THAT'S WHAT WE ALL INQUIRE!
DON'T WE PITY THE POOR CIVILIAN,
SITTING AROUND THE FIRE.

"Someone's gonna hear you, Browning," warned bowlegged Private Mick Webber, a bricklayer from Rutland. "If the wrong sergeant does, you'll spend a night in the chokey."

OH, OH, OH, IT'S A LOVELY WAR,
WHAT DO WE WANT WITH EGGS AND HAM,
WHEN WE'VE GOT PLUM AND APPLE JAM?

"I don't mind the plum jam so much," admitted Billy Nutley.

"You will," muttered Mason, "when it's the only sweet thing you've had in six weeks."

"Mason," James said. "Is it really as bad as they say out there?"

Mason took in the lot of them. "You'll soon see for yourselves."

"This war was supposed to end before I got old enough for it." Everything Browning said came out as a joke. "Who do I submit my complaints to in writing, is what I'd like to know."

"Sorry we were slacking on the job, sonny boy."

"How about the food?" Nutley asked the old campaigner. "Is it as bad in the trenches as here?"

"Worse." Mason elbowed Nutley. "But you'll be lucky if food's your main problem."

Webber chimed in. "I want a nice Blighty one like you got, Mason," he said. "An injury bad enough to send me home to my girl, but not so bad she won't love me anymore." He grinned. "How'd you manage it, getting pelted in the leg?"

James tried not to picture the horribly disfigured faces he'd seen near base hospitals. He pictured Hazel's sweet face. How many scars would it take to change the way she looked at him?

Thrust, twist, kill.

"How often, Mason, do soldiers use their bayonets?" he asked.

At this, Mason smiled. "They make good can openers, and candleholders when you stick 'em into the trench walls. And there's nothing like a bayonet for toasting bread over a little fire."

DECEMBER 1942

Third Witness

"IF I MAY," Aphrodite asks, "summon one more witness?"

"Do we need to move down to a ballroom?" asks Hephaestus.

"Ooh, get one with a grand piano," says Apollo. "I'll sing."

"That won't be necessary," says the goddess smoothly. "I summon my third witness."

Outside the window, clouds obscure the moon and stars. The earth rumbles and shakes beneath them. It feels as though a subway train is hurtling by, the size of an ocean liner and traveling at the speed of sound.

A single knock sounds at the door of the hotel room. It opens, and a figure enters.

"That's all right," calls Hephaestus to the shadowed figure. "Just let yourself right in."

"I always do."

At the sound of the voice, Apollo and Ares freeze.

The new arrival glides down the corridor as noiselessly as a cat. His dark clothing calls to mind an undertaker. But when he removes his coat, they see a long black cassock stretching to his ankles. The square in a clerical collar forms his only speck of white.

They gape at him.

"A priest?" bleats Ares. "The god of the Underworld is a *Roman Catholic priest?*"

"Good evening, Uncle." Aphrodite makes a deep bow.

Hephaestus sinks down onto one knee, and Apollo, sliding off the bed, follows his lead. Ares, muttering, genuflects as well, after a kick from Aphrodite.

"I thought you played professor when you visit mortals," says Apollo. "My lord Hades."

"IRS auditor," says Hephaestus. "'The only things certain are death and taxes.'"

Hades smiles. "I dress in the role that suits me."

He surveys the room and finds no seat to his liking, so he produces one. A black leather chair, rather Spartan in appearance. He sits, crosses one leg atop another, and interlaces his fingers over his knee. His face is clean-shaven. His nails, manicured. His glossy black hair, sleekly combed straight back from his forehead.

Like Ares and Apollo, Hades, Lord of the Underworld, is a man of striking beauty, though serious and grim, with a bloodless precision to his aquiline features. Handsome, though you'd more likely stamp his face on a coin than hope he asks you for a dance.

"Why are you a priest?" demands Ares. "Your, er, Holiness?"

"Good evening, my nephews, my niece." Hades's voice, like the rest of him, is smooth.

"But why a Catholic priest?" War is persistent. As always.

Hephaestus coughs. "Doesn't this create, for you, some, er, theological difficulties?"

Hades looks thoughtful. "I don't think so," he says slowly. "I enjoy being a rabbi just as well, possibly more. I honor the mortals' worldview, and I speak from within their frame of reference." He looks slightly injured. "The life of a cleric suits me. I spent the better part of a happy century as an abbot. I think I make quite a good priest, actually."

"Nothing has ever been quite so spiritually motivating as Death," says Aphrodite.

Hades smiles. "The work of the priesthood, preparing souls to cross the river to my domain without undue fear, is a great help to me." He grimaces slightly. "Unprepared souls are *sticky*. Most inconvenient."

Hades produces for himself a tin of mints and selects one carefully. "Mortals are so very fleshy. Ruled by appetites. They gurgle. Bulging with fluids. You, Love, and you, War, find these quite useful in your work, but my interest in humans is entirely spiritual." He shudders. "Bodies don't interest me in the slightest."

"Bet that's not what you told Persephone." Ares laughs like a boy in a locker room.

"And who was that nymph again . . . ?" Apollo scratches his head.

Hades favors them with a wan smile. "Boys, boys." He can indulgently say, "Boys, boys," in a tone that also says, *I could disintegrate you if I wanted to.*

He studies the room.

"Oh dear," he murmurs. "Have I wandered into an unfortunate marital moment?" He fingers the golden net enclosing the cheating lovers between two fingers. "As a man of the cloth, Hephaestus, I can't condone your methods, much as I admire your handiwork. 'If you love something, you must set it free.'"

"Bet that's not what you told Persephone." Ares thinks he's even funnier the second time.

Aphrodite intervenes to save Ares from an untimely end.

"My lord Hades," she says sweetly, "I've been telling these gods a tale of love. To demonstrate, among other things, the vital role death plays in making true love possible. We've always understood each other, you and I. Would you share your part when the moment comes? The story is"—she nods to him—"this one."

Hades smiles regally. "You honor me, fair Aphrodite," he says. "It will be my pleasure."

Colette Fournier—July–August 1914

APHRODITE

I'LL BEGIN WITH a girl and a boy climbing an extremely tall set of stairs.

It was a hot summer day in July 1914. The air was still; only bees were at work. Everyone else had the good sense to find a shady spot to avoid working.

But not Colette Fournier, and not her companion, Stéphane. Colette was determined to reach the top despite the heat. Stéphane was determined to stay within arm's reach of Colette, and his master at the docks, taking a midday nap, had given him just that chance.

The stairs, cut into rock, mounted a dizzying ascent up the high stone outcropping overlooking the town of Dinant, Belgium. At the top stood a medieval citadel, a fortress of hewn stone that for centuries had protected the town. The view from the citadel plateau was breathtaking, showing a broad curve of the peaceful Meuse River winding through bright-green farmland, now bursting with the yield of high summer.

The girl's sweaty hair stuck to her forehead, and her blouse clung to her damp body. She didn't care, and neither, I might add, did Stéphane.

The carillon of bells in the tower of Notre Dame de Dinant, directly below them, played a bright melody. Just part of the color of Dinant, that jewel hugging the Meuse, its rainbow of homes reflecting like crystals on the surface of the river's smooth waters.

Colette was sixteen, Stéphane eighteen. Stéphane lived near Colette's family and had been underfoot forever. Colette knew Stéphane like she knew her brother, Alexandre, and her cousin, Gabriel. Stéphane was always there, like a stray dog one makes the mistake of feeding.

There was nothing unusual in Stéphane challenging Colette to climb the citadel stairs. They'd dueled in footraces and boat races and breath-holding contests since they were small.

But there was something unusual about the way Colette had caught Stéphane watching her lately. Quietly, slowly, in the midst of the usual clamor, as if he'd never seen her before.

Which was ridiculous.

Also curious were the sensations Colette had begun to recognize whenever Stéphane appeared. When she realized that she missed him when he didn't show up as expected, and that when he did appear, she had no idea what to say to a boy as familiar as an old sock, she knew she was in some kind of trouble. When she began studying Stéphane, noticing how his dark hair curled at his temples, and how new things were happening to his cheekbones, his collarbones, his neck, she knew she was in grave danger.

Which was even more ridiculous.

So when Stéphane appeared, this hot summer day, and teased her into climbing to the citadel, she left a sinkful of dirty dishes and accepted the challenge. Maybe, once they reached the top, she could confront him about what on earth was going on, and put a stop to it.

Stéphane also intended to confront Colette at the top. If he could find the nerve.

The stairs would've exhausted athletes, but Colette was young and strong and resolute. Even so, muscling her way to the very top left her breathless and boiling, so rather than enjoy the view, the first thing she did upon arrival was pass through the stone courtyard and flop down into the tall, cool grasses, beyond it, stretch out, roll up her sleeves, and fan her face.

I hovered at Stéphane's side.

Now? he wondered

Why not now?

"Colette . . ." he began.

Not that way.

"Yeah?"

He gulped and scrambled for something else to say.

"Your song," he said. "At the beer festival. It sounded good."

It sounded good. What a clod. What a pathetic way to pay a compliment.

"Thanks," she said. She saw his silhouette against the afternoon sky and wondered how Stéphane had grown so tall so quickly, and what business he had acquiring such muscles. He'd been such a *lump* of a boy. Loading and unloading ships all day would do it, she supposed, but in that hazy, damp moment, the *why* of Stéphane's changes became less important than their reality.

He sank into the grasses beside her. Her cheeks were red, and her eyes bright, and there she was, unbuttoning her top button and fanning herself.

Poor Stéphane. It's a terrible thing, risking a lifetime of friendship for a dream that has suddenly spiraled into something too big to contain. He'd offend her, he was certain, and she'd reject him, and shun him, no doubt, and then what would he do?

He couldn't make it through a day without at least seeing Colette half a dozen times. But if she never wished to see his face again, there'd be no place in Dinant to hide from her disgust.

And what could he say? Words weren't his particular forte.

She sat up in the grass. Bits of grass and dirt clung to her blouse and her hair.

"I'm a mess," she said.

"No, you're not."

"*You're* a mess," she told him, "so you're not qualified to judge."

Stéphane gazed up into the clouds and grinned. Lying on the grass, tired and peaceful, with Colette nearby, and scolding—that was all right with him.

"If it's just us two up here," he said, "what does it matter if we're a mess?"

She turned her gaze toward the panoramic view, leaving him free to study her back. So graceful, the curve of her spine. He could run his fingers along her back, right now, if she wouldn't chop his hands off for trying. He'd have to be content with imagining.

Colette turned back to see his eyes closed. It left her free to do some studying of her own.

"Sleeping?" she said. "Some company you are. Did you drag me up here to take a nap?"

Don't be content with imagining, I told him.

He held out a hand to her. "Let's do that," he said. "Let's just take a nap."

She took his hand, wondering why she was doing so, and felt a jolt of—of what? What *was* it she felt when silly old Stéphane took her hand?

She lay back down on her side. He wasn't silly old Stéphane anymore.

Attack first and analyze later. "What's gotten into you?" she asked him.

He propped himself up on his side, and they were face-to-face. Only centimeters apart. It might as well be a river of lava between them.

He braved it anyway. He leaned forward and kissed her.

And missed her lips and got her nose.

Colette's eyes fluttered shut. She couldn't think. *Of course Stéphane wants to kiss you, I told her. You want to kiss him, too.* It was true. I wasn't "putting words" into her mind.

Poor Stéphane's heartbeat clanged in his throat. It would be a long descent back to town with Colette if he'd just ruined all. But she hadn't run. She hadn't kicked, nor squawked, nor bolted, nor scolded. He almost wished she would.

One more try, I whispered to Stéphane.

Colette's eyes opened again. She saw Stéphane's lips part and felt her own do the same. Before she quite knew what had happened, she'd leaned toward him, and he'd pulled her close, and she kissed his lips. Or he kissed hers. Either. Yes.

Some moments later, Colette broke away, gasping for air. Stéphane slipped an arm around her and pulled her close. He lay smiling. She gazed at him in wonder.

Thought wasn't easy, between the havoc in her rib cage, and the electricity skittering across her skin.

Stéphane?

Who else?

Remember this moment when you think of Stéphane. Remember Colette, once upon a time, standing atop the citadel mount, leaning over the rampart looking at tiny rooftops below, for one last look before climbing down, with her old friend standing close beside her, now strange and new.

ARES

The kids had that first kiss in July of 1914. In the weeks following, Colette and Stéphane were too drunk on love to pay attention to the talk of war that began to fill the newspapers.

Until, on August 4, ignoring it was impossible. German armies invaded neutral Belgium and conquered Liège. Rumors flew of civilians mown down, and towns razed to the ground.

On August 15, a German division captured the citadel. French armies met them there in battle and recaptured the citadel a few hours later. (Incidentally, one of the French fighters injured there that day was Charles de Gaulle, today the leader of the underground French Resistance against the Nazi occupation of France. War, you see, gives birth to heroes.)

On the night of April 21 to the 22, carloads of German soldiers rolled into Dinant. They set some twenty houses on fire and killed thirty civilians. They reported later that the civilians had opened fire on them. All survivors denied that this was so.

On August 23, the Germans returned in force. They set fire to hundreds of homes. They blamed the civilians for all German losses thus far in Dinant, and pulled men from workplaces and homes and hiding places, and executed them in the streets. Women, children, and babies were executed too. As old as eighty-eight. As young as three weeks. Nearly seven hundred in total.

Dinant's flames raged for days. Only smoking rubble remained. The old church, Notre Dame de Dinant, caught fire. The carillon in the bell tower burned, silencing the town.

HADES

Among the dead were Colette's papa; her uncles Paul and Charles; her cousin, Gabriel; and her brother, Alexandre. The carpentry workshop where the Fournier men built wooden furniture was one of the workplaces raided. Colette and her mother lost everyone.

When shots first rang out, Stéphane ran through the streets, searching for Colette. The Germans caught him and shot him too.

The slaughtered died in excruciating fear, less for themselves than for those they left behind in the grip of German soldiers. It's the most pitiable state in which to enter my realm.

Stéphane entered my realm, bleeding from his very soul, for all the dreamed-of weeks and years of love ripped away from him by the firing line. He paced the citadel for years afterward, searching for what could not be found.

Colette took shelter in the abbey, le Couvent de Bethléem, across the river from the Germans, when the first shouts and cries began. She crouched in a dark cell, rocking and praying, begging her god to spare those she loved.

She emerged to a town on fire, to learn she'd lost everyone she loved except her mother.

Her mother died a few days later. Technically, a stroke, but it was grief that killed her.

Colette the child died that day.

The Dinant she loved was gone. She spent weeks trying to help the survivors clean up the rubble. She held motherless infants and tried to shush their wailing. She took fatherless children into the fields to pick flowers so their mothers could drink and sob.

She pictured, over and over, Alexandre crumpling to the ground. Papa doubling over. Oncle Paul and Oncle Charles, clutching vainly at their shattered chests.

She could not bring herself to picture Stéphane.

She worked to offer comfort, but it tormented her that she'd had no way to comfort those she loved best, who needed comfort most at the gates of death.

So one moonless, cloud-covered night in early fall, she wrapped her few remaining belongings in a rag, stole a boat, and rowed all night against the Meuse's slow current, making her way south into France, and hiking across the countryside until she reached Paris and her aunt, Solange. She made her way to the YMCA headquarters, lied about her age, and volunteered.

She couldn't face the Red Cross and the dying and the blood. But she could try to help where she could, to listen to somebody else's Alexandre, and somebody else's Stéphane, as if she were listening to the conversations she'd never be allowed to have with her own dear ones.

For the next four years she grew into young womanhood surrounded by soldiers and weapons and war. She politely deflected declarations of love and poured thousands of cups of coffee. She worked tirelessly to provide comfort to others who would face the German guns.

She believed if she could comfort them, then she might one day receive comfort, too.

APHRODITE

Entertaining the Yanks—January 4, 1918

AFTER SUPPER, SOLDIERS began filtering into the vast YMCA re-lief hut, bound for games tables, a library, the chapel, and a coffee station where Hazel waited to make cheerful conversation.

There were so many of them. They were so very *male*.

Hazel, in her freshly brushed Y uniform, poured hot drinks and dreaded talking to young men. But the Yanks, with their harsh Rs and their wide smiles, soon won her over.

"Howdy, ma'am! You ready for us to wallop those Germans?"

"Ain't you two a sight for sore eyes!"

Then Ellen let it slip that Hazel played piano, and a general uproar demanded that she perform. Here it was. Playing was what she'd come to do. But she didn't know their music.

"Play 'For Me and My Gal'!"

"Got any Irving Berlin?"

"How about 'Cleopatra Had a Jazz Band'? Do you know that?"

"'Carry Me Back to Old Virginny'?"

One mortifying no after another. Mrs. Davies, watching, shook her head.

Hazel's hands shook and notes swam before her eyes.

Fortunately, she'd memorized "La Marseillaise" and "God Save the King" and "Rule, Britannia!" so she played those.

European anthems. They failed to rouse the troops. Her terror turned to paralysis.

She didn't know the American anthem. Something about their flag? In desperation, she played familiar pieces. Brahms, Schubert, and Schumann, and Chopin. The Yanks cheered.

Hazel played until Professor Henry's lecture was to begin. The Americans stomped and whistled. This would take much getting used to. Sure enough, the chairs were packed for the professor's first lecture on British history, starting with the early Iron Age.

A doughboy swaggered over to talk to golden-haired Ellen, leaving Hazel to herself.

"*Pardon.*" A soft voice spoke in her ear. "You are the new pianist?"

She turned to see a young woman in a YMCA uniform. Her accent was French, and her hair jet-black, bobbed short, in sleek curls closely coiling around her face. Hazel had never seen such a look outside the more daring fashion magazines.

"Wow," she whispered, "you look just like Irene Castle."

The stranger smiled. "I can't dance like her. Too bad for these soldiers."

Hazel felt embarrassed at her reaction. "I'm sorry," she said. "That was rude of me."

The other girl pursed her lips. "Rude, how?" She paused. "You don't like Irene Castle?"

Hazel laughed. "Don't I, though!" She held out her hand. "Hazel Windicott."

The girl's smile transformed her expression. "I'm Colette Fournier. *Bienvenue à Saint-Nazaire.*"

Hazel smiled. "*Merci beaucoup.*"

Colette nodded appraisingly. "Not the worst accent I've heard from *une anglaise.*" She nodded toward the soldiers. "The Americans with their tourist's phrase book French are unbearable. They think they'll sweep me off my feet. *Parles-tu français?*"

"Umm . . ." Hazel laughed. "Not really, no."

"No matter." Colette pulled open her pocketbook. "Want some chocolate?"

I always say, chocolate makes all the difference. And friendliness, of course.

"How long have you been with the YMCA?" Hazel asked Colette.

Colette gestured toward a low couch under the building's eaves, and they both sat.

"Four years." She smiled ruefully. "They've been an education. I volunteered early on in the war, because I desperately needed something useful to do."

"What did your parents say?" Hazel asked. "Mine weren't thrilled about me going."

Colette hesitated. People treated her differently once they knew. *Trust Hazel,* I told her.

"My parents and all my family are dead," Colette said simply. "I volunteered soon after my village was destroyed by the Germans."

Hazel gasped. The girl's matter-of-factness astonished her.

Then something Colette had said caught her attention. "Your village destroyed, early in the war . . . Then that must mean you are . . ."

"That's right. *Je suis belge.*"

Not French. Belgian. Even worse battle scars. The better part of Belgium had fallen to the lightning aggression of Germany's August 1914 invasion. The Rape of Belgium, they called it. The stories of women raped, children crucified, nailed to doors, of old men executed . . .

Hazel's breath caught in her throat. "Oh, I am so sorry!"

Colette looked amused. "It's not such a terrible thing, you know, being Belgian."

Hazel flushed. "I don't mean that. I mean, all that Belgium has suffered!"

Colette wondered why she was telling this English girl so much. "My father, my brother, my two uncles. My cousin, and many friends from my childhood. All gone. My home, everything."

"Oh, no." Hazel pictured her own father, and boys from her neighborhood. Even James. Tears ran down her cheeks. "I'm sorry I'm such an idiot." She wiped her eyes. "For years I heard about all the atrocities in Belgium, and about the need to help the refugees, but . . ."

"But they didn't seem real to you?"

Hazel hung her head. "I suppose not." She wiped her eyes. "Which is your village?"

"Dinant," Colette said. "What's left of it, that is."

"How did you survive?" Hazel asked.

Colette paused. The first wrinkle in her steady calm. Hazel's heart broke for her.

"I hid," she said. "While those I loved were murdered, I hid in a convent."

And there was the grief, and guilt, overflowing the dam that had held it in.

"That is exactly what all those who loved you would have wanted you to do," Hazel said.

Colette had been through these memories a thousand times, yet at Hazel's words, Alexandre and Papa and cousin Gabriel and oncles Paul and Charles appeared. And Stéphane.

When Colette's eyes met hers, Hazel saw a glimmer of gratitude there.

"Where is home for you now?" asked Hazel.

"I have an aunt in Paris," Colette explained. "My mother's sister. She took me in, after. I had nowhere else to go. I volunteered for the Y so I wouldn't be too much of a burden to her. But come," Colette said, sitting up. "I didn't introduce myself to tell you my sad story."

"That's quite all right," Hazel said.

"I came to ask if you would accompany me," Colette went on. "I'm a singer, or so I tell myself. I was hoping you and I could practice together. At night, after lights-out."

"Won't we wake Mrs. Davies and Miss Ruthers?"

Colette laughed. "I think not. We'll play softly. They sleep with cotton in their ears. And they snore enough to sleep through a bombing. Meet me tomorrow night?"

Hazel nodded. "I look forward to it."

APOLLO

Wake-Up Call—January 3, 1918

REVEILLE SOUNDED.

"Somebody hit that alarm clock," moaned a soldier in the 15th New York's K Company.

"You mean, strangle that bugler," replied another voice from across the room.

Aubrey opened his eyes and shut them quickly. It was still dark. Hadn't they just arrived? He rolled over in his bunk and offered his backside as a general comment on the day.

Somebody lit a lantern. His mates sat up and stretched. The heartless chirpy bugle tune squiggled into Aubrey's ear. He rolled back over, flat, and listened to the wake-up call.

Listen, I told him. *What would happen if you turned the reveille on its head?*

How?

A minor key.

He hummed it to himself.

That's right. It's got a whole different color to it. Now swing it.

He cut the tempo in half and swung the rhythm.

Ooh. That's something.

You're good at this.

"Get your bones out of that bed, Aub," his buddy Joey Rice told him. "Or Captain Fish's gonna come in here and knock you one."

Aubrey slithered out of bed and into his boots. "Joey," he said, "where's your horn?"

Joey Rice pulled a cornet mouthpiece from his pocket and waggled it. "Right here." He used it to mimic the reveille. Without the horn attached, the mouthpiece made a tinny sound.

"Geez, my tongue's gonna fall out," Joey said. "Too early in the morning to play."

"Morning's the whole point of it, *tonto*," said Jesús Hernandez, clarinetist. He was one of the horn players Lieutenant Europe recruited from Puerto Rico for the band.

"Make it minor," Aubrey told Joey. "Drop the top note half a step."

Joey Rice changed the note. A spooky tone emerged.

"Now slow it down," Aubrey said. "*Sliiiide* the second tone— that's the third note. Scoop it too, then pop the next three, coming down, *pop-pop-pop*, staccato."

"*Tu amigo es loco*," Jesús whispered to Joey.

Joey stretched the second note like taffy and cracked the next three like peanut shells.

"That's it," Joey said. "Bum-ba-*daaaaah*-da-bum-ba-da."

Joey caught what Aubrey meant and started improvising.

"What's going on in here?"

The soldiers all stiffened to a salute. "Sir, Captain, sir!"

Captain Hamilton Fish III strode in. "Quit horsing around. You'll miss your grub."

The captain's eyes smiled, even if his stiff military bearing did not. One of the founding officers of the 15th New York, Fish was the scion of a wealthy New York family and a Harvard football star.

He was an imposing figure, but the regiment liked him. They found him fair, reasonable, and unprejudiced. Mostly. For a rich white man, he was all right.

"At ease, and go eat!"

"Just a minute, Captain."

Another tall figure entered the room.

"Sir, Lieutenant, sir!" barked the soldiers, saluting once more. It was First Lieutenant Jim Europe, head of the machine gun company, and leader of the 15th New York band.

"Morning, Lieutenant Europe," Fish said. "What can I do for you?"

"What was that I was hearing out of this barrack?"

Several of the men snickered.

"Just a little musical fooling around," said Fish.

Europe peered through his glasses. "Was that you, Rice? Clowning on your mouthpiece?"

"Edwards made me do it," Joey said. "Jazz up the morning bugle call."

Lieutenant Europe sized him up. "Aub-rey Edwards." Look-what-the-cat-dragged-in.

Aubrey snapped to a salute. "Morning, sir, Lieutenant, sir!"

"I should've known it," Lieutenant Europe said. "While other soldiers are getting ready to make the world safe for democracy, you're inventing the 'Reveille Blues.'"

"Yes, sir, Lieutenant, sir!" It took all the muscles in Aubrey's face to keep from grinning.

Europe folded his arms. "You know how to write that out in musical notation?"

Of course he knew it. Jim Europe knew he knew it, too. He'd been Aubrey's teacher.

"Yes, sir, Lieutenant, sir!"

"Got paper? Staff-lined paper?"

He shook his head. "No, sir, Lieutenant, sir."

"This is gonna get old in a hurry," Europe muttered to Captain Fish. "Edwards. Stop by my quarters tonight, and I'll give you paper. You can show me your 'Reveille Blues.'" He glanced up at the rest of the barrack. "An announcement, for those of you in the band. We've been invited to give an opening concert, two nights from now, at one of the YMCA relief huts. Hut One." He smiled. "Our reputation precedes us."

Joey scratched his head. "A concert in a *hut?*"

Captain Fish smiled. "They're huge. Wait till you see. They're recreation spots for the soldiers, after hours. Games and shows, coffee and books, lectures, music, that sort of thing."

Smiles and nods welcomed this bit of news. They hadn't anticipated recreation.

Lieutenant Europe and Captain Fish exchanged a look. "The Negro Y hut," Lieutenant Europe said, "is in Camp Lusitania. We'll rehearse there tonight at seven."

Segregated recreation.

"Now clear out of here," Captain Fish said, "and get some food."

Aubrey decided to risk a question. "Sir, Captain, sir!"

"Yes, Private?"

"When do we fight the Germans, sir?"

Captain Fish cast a quick glance at Lieutenant Europe. "Not for a while. We're pretty far from the Front. This is Saint-Nazaire, the American military training base on the coast of France."

"When do we meet French girls? *Ooh là là!*" said Joey. The others laughed.

"None of that," ordered Fish.

A grumble rose from the men. They were already bitter about

a US Army rule forbidding black soldiers from having contact with white women overseas.

"Now, look," Fish said. "I'm not talking about *that*. They've got no right to tell you whose company you can keep, or what color it can be. But none of you has time for girls. And we can't have you sick. I want no disease in this company! Now, we've got a full day ahead of us. We're going to be digging a dam while we're here and laying miles of railroad track."

They all froze.

Jesús Hernandez, clarinet, couldn't hide his disappointment. "Labor work?" He wasn't alone. "I mean, sir, Captain, sir?"

"We came here to fight the Huns, Captain Fish," said Herb Simpson, vocals. "Just like Lieutenant Europe said. To keep the world safe for democracy."

Aubrey's mother always said he never knew when to keep his big mouth shut.

"You said, sir," he said, "that this regiment wasn't gonna be like the other colored ones. Hauling freight, and digging roads, and cooking, and that sort of thing."

Joey made a slashing motion at his throat. Asking a question was one thing, but challenging an officer could mean discipline. Or court-martial.

But Aubrey was too far gone. "We could've done digging and hauling work back in New York. You said this regiment would get its chance to fight for America, and make the nation proud of its black soldiers. Change the way they see us back in the States."

Now he'd done it. He held his chin high and thrust out his chest. *Dignity and pride.*

"You're right, Private. I did say that." Captain Fish's voice was calm but firm. "This regiment will accomplish great things for our nation and your race. You've all shown remarkable discipline at Camp Wadsworth and Camp Dix, in the face of shameful prejudice. I'm confident your courage and discipline will carry you far when we get to the Front." He scrubbed a weary hand across his forehead. "Now go eat breakfast before they feed what's left to the pigs."

Aubrey exhaled at last. He wasn't in trouble. Hallelujah.

"We'll get to that Front before long," Herbert Simpson said.

The captain replied in a low voice, more to himself than anyone else. "We will," he said, "if I have anything to say about it." He left, and the other soldiers filed out behind him.

Aubrey felt a tug at his elbow. Lieutenant Europe pulled him out of line and around the corner of the building and fixed him with his penetrating stare.

"You're a smart one," Europe said, "and if you want to last in the military, you'd best learn to be smart about how you use that smart mouth of yours."

Aubrey's face burned, even in the cold.

"Smart means knowing when to talk and when to shut up." His mouth twitched. "Even if you're right."

Aubrey tried not to smile. "Yes, sir, Lieutenant, sir."

Europe clapped a hand on Aubrey's shoulder. "You come get paper tonight, you hear?"

Aubrey smiled.

"Let's go eat, Private," Europe said. "You can't dig a dam on blues alone."

Aubrey laughed. "You shouldn't swear like that, sir."

They followed their comrades' footprints in the snow to the mess hall, then waded through a haze of coffee-and-burnt-egg steam to where Aubrey's K Company stood in line for oatmeal.

"Well, if it ain't the Coon Platoon." A slow Southern voice spoke behind them.

They turned to see two soldiers watching them with folded arms and narrowed eyes. Aubrey curled his fingers tightly around the empty bowl in his hand. The nerves in his shoulders twanged. A vein in Joey's temple throbbed.

"Maybe the French don't know a coon when they see one, but you can't fool an Alabama boy," said a red-haired soldier. "An ape's an ape, no matter what uniform you put on him."

Lieutenant Europe's body stiffened. His eyes somehow found each member of 15th New York's K Company and silently ordered them not to respond. Aubrey felt rage swell in each breath—his, and his comrades'. It was as if they breathed as one body. As if he could feel their flexed, coiled pain as keenly as his own.

"Soldier! State your name and rank."

A white mess sergeant had emerged from the kitchen, addressing Mr. Alabama.

"Private William Cowans, sir," the soldier answered, saluting as if he didn't care one way or the other. "Army One Hundred Sixty-Seventh Infantry, Forty-Second Division."

The mess sergeant frowned. "Rainbow Division? They left for the Front weeks ago."

The pair looked like they'd pulled a fast one. "We stayed back," Cowans said. "Measles."

The sergeant turned to the aproned cook serving oatmeal, standing with wide eyes and an outstretched spoon. His face was more pimple than not. "Don't let these soldiers' food get any colder, Durfee." Private Durfee began scooping porridge while the sergeant turned toward the Alabamans. "You. Measle-mouth. General Pershing's ordered me to feed soldiers, not cowards and pigs. Your commanding officer will hear about this."

Cowans and his hanger-on slunk away and left the mess, muttering to themselves. When the door had banged shut behind them, the sergeant saluted briskly to the black soldiers.

"Welcome to France," he told them. "Mess Sergeant Charles Murphy. Sunnyside, Queens."

APHRODITE

Pathétique—January 8, 1918

EARLY MORNING, Hazel found, was a time when she could have the entire Y hut to herself. Ellen, her roommate, slept in late, and Colette, next door, did the same. The older women, Mrs. Davies and a middle-aged Miss Ruthers, woke abysmally early and went to a secretaries' planning meeting most days with the head secretary for all of Saint-Nazaire, a Mr. Wallace. (They coiffed their hair specially for him.) This left Hazel with an hour to play without bothering anyone.

This day, a Tuesday, she began by sight-reading through the more-requested titles from a book of popular songs she'd found in the piano bench. They were light pieces, lots of military march tunes, and humorous songs like those her father played at the Town Hall. She turned to a bright rondo by Mozart that made her smile, and then the second movement of Beethoven's eighth piano sonata, the "Adagio cantabile" especially. "Pathétique." A tender, romantic piece, filled with longing.

She played it for James.

Come back to me. Come safely home. Let no harm find you at the Front.

She was back at the parish dance. Back in his arms. Back in the flood of nerves and terror and bliss and heat and wool and bay rum. And a smooth cheek resting against her forehead. The memories were still as sharp and clear as when they were new.

Her hands sank to her lap. A dangling chord echoed across the empty stage.

"Don't stop."

Hazel jumped. The piano bench legs scraped the floor. She couldn't spot the speaker.

"I'm sorry." A figure stepped from the shadows. "I didn't mean to scare you."

He was a young soldier, black, and tall.

"You didn't scare me," she told him. "I just thought I was alone."

"You're British," he observed with some surprise.

"And you're not." She held out her hand. "I'm Hazel Windicott. I'm from East London."

The young man shook her outstretched hand. "Pleased to meet you, Miss Windicott. I'm Aubrey Edwards, from Upper Manhattan. And you should *never* feel stage fright."

She smiled. "That's very kind of you."

Now that he had stepped out of the shadows into the patch of pale sunlight near the stage, she got a good look at him. He carried himself with a soldier's upright bearing, but not a soldier's stiffness. His eyes drifted hungrily, over and over again, to the piano.

"Do you play?" she asked him.

His face lit up. "I do." He started inching toward the instrument. "I'm in the Fifteenth New York Band."

"How wonderful!" Hazel clapped her hands. "Your concert here last week was marvelous. Your sound! Incredible! Soldiers talked about it for days afterward."

"We try to keep your toes tapping." He grinned. "When we're

not sweating away at laying tracks by day, we're sweating away at rehearsals and shows by night," he said. "A soldier in a military band does double duty. But that's what I enlisted to do."

"Please, come sit." Hazel offered him the piano bench. "Relief hut pianos take a beating. There's only so many times you can play 'Over There' before the hammers break. And 'Chopsticks'! Twenty times a day, someone sits down to play 'Chopsticks.'"

He slid himself behind the keys and explored them, playing a quick chromatic scale. "Not bad," he said, "for an army piano." He immediately played "Chopsticks."

Hazel folded her arms. "Oh, very funny."

"There's no piano in the Negro Y hut at Lusitania," he said. "There was, but it's busted."

He began to play the melody line to Hazel's romantic Beethoven sonata, tentatively, experimentally. "That's right?"

She nodded. "You've got a good ear."

"That's not all I've got that's good."

He picked up the tempo, adding bouncing chord chops with his left and high octave frills with his right between the melody notes. Partway through, he added a driving bass line wherever the left-hand accompaniment found a pause.

Hazel watched in wonder. "Did you just do that, just now?"

His eyebrows rose. "You saw me, didn't you?"

She shook her head. "I mean, have you done that before? With Beethoven's 'Pathétique'?"

He made a wry face. "Not if that's French for 'pathetic.'"

She laughed. "Not 'pathetic.' Wistful. Sad. Like missing the one you love."

"All righty, then," he said. "No, I've never played Mr. Beethoven's 'pathetic' before. I've gone ahead and fixed up his mistakes."

Hazel's jaw dropped. "His *what*?"

"Who wants a sad song? Who's got time for that? *That's* pathetic, if you ask me."

Hazel sat beside him and watched his hands closely. Seeing he had an appreciative audience, Aubrey let loose, owning the keyboard. Even Hazel, a pianist herself, couldn't comprehend the loose agility and lightning speed of his hands.

"You're not Aubrey Edwards," she declared. "You're Scott Joplin. The King of American Ragtime!"

"Hunh." He snorted. "Don't kid yourself. I'm Aubrey Edwards. Scott Joplin *wishes* he were me. Or he would. But he's dead. So he's probably wishing hard that he could be me. Or just about anybody, come to think of it."

"You must be his reincarnation, then," said Hazel. "Show me how you did that."

"Nothing to it," he said. "You play your tune, find its key, fill in the chord progressions, and the rest is applesauce." Aubrey's fingers roved across the keyboard. "If I'm Joplin's reincarnation," he went on, "I'd have had to grow up quick. He died last spring." He shrugged. "My mama always said I was a big baby, though. So maybe."

Hazel laughed. "You're quite a character, Mr. Edwards."

"Please," he said, "if we're going to be friends, I insist you call me 'Your Majesty.'"

Hazel hooted with laughter.

"You said I was the King of Ragtime." He waggled his eyebrows at her. "Actually, I'm the Emperor of Jazz."

"You're its jester," Hazel said. "I've never met anyone like you before, Your Majesty."

He switched tunes, playing something she didn't recognize.

"Like that?" he asked her. She nodded. "That's 'The Memphis Blues.'"

"Something you wrote?" she asked.

He laughed. "I wish. Gentleman by the name of Mr. W. C. Handy. Also from Harlem."

"Harlem?"

"The part of Upper Manhattan where I live. Where a lot of black folks live."

She watched in fascination as he played. The fluidity of his style puzzled her. He looped through phrases and refrains. It was as if he understood how the music was built, and could build it again, re-creating it differently if he wished. Not playing it, but playing *with* it.

"When you say, Miss Windicott—"

"Hazel, please."

"Her Ladyship, Hazel de la Windicott." He glanced sideways at her. "When you say you've never met anyone like me before, do you mean that you've never met a black fella?"

Hazel leaned on the piano and looked at him earnestly.

"Oh, no," she said. "I only meant that I'd never met anyone with your humor. And confidence." She pursed her lips in anxious thought. "I'm certain that's all I meant. Wasn't it?"

He watched her for many seconds with the music marching on uninterrupted.

"I can't know the answer to that," he said. "*Have* you ever met a black fella before?"

"Well, of course I have," she said. "London has people from all over the world. The Caribbean, and Somalia, and Nigeria, Gold Coast, South Africa, Kenya, and oh, lots of other places in Africa."

"Places Great Britain has colonies?"

She nodded. "And where I live, in East London, there are loads of black dockworkers."

"Know any of them well?"

"No," she admitted. "Though I don't know any white dockwork-ers either."

He gave her a quizzical look. "Live in an ivory tower?"

She felt she deserved it. "If I did," she said, "I came here to climb down out of it."

Aubrey switched to another tune. Familiar, but with a dark thread woven through it.

Hazel recognized it. "That's the wake-up call," she said. "What's it called? 'Reveille.'"

"That's what it *was*," he said loftily. "I'm fixing its mistakes."

She laughed. "I'm glad to know you, Your Majesty."

He nodded grandly. "You as well, Your Ladyship."

"But you must take it back," she said. "About Beethoven making mistakes."

He gave her a pointed look. "*Everybody* makes mistakes."

"I suppose, but—"

"Except me."

She gasped. "You're unbelievable!"

He winked. "You've got that right."

Hazel smiled. Already she'd begun to mentally compose a letter to James about this outrageous young pianist. She doubted she could capture the humor of his jokes.

"You'll come back and play more, won't you?"

He nodded, jiggering with the reveille until a sleepy voice with a lovely accent spoke.

"Isn't once a day more than enough to be dragged out of bed by that bugle song?"

It was a tousle-headed Colette, coming out of her bedroom. A wide-open robe was all that covered her very short silk nightgown and her long-legged frame.

The music stopped.

King Aubrey Edwards blinked.

Colette squeaked and clutched her robe around her.

Hazel jumped up, feeling she ought to do something, but it was hard to think, just then, which new friend of hers was more in need of rescue.

Colette stifled a giggle with a hand over her mouth. Her eyes sparkled.

Aubrey held out a hand for Hazel to shake without taking his eyes off Colette. "Pleased to make your acquaintance, Miss Windicott," he said. "I will most definitely be back." He tipped his hat toward Colette on his way out. "Ma'am."

"And I," Colette said between gasps, "will most definitely be dressed."

"That's all right," said the unrepentant Emperor of Jazz. "I'll still come back."

APHRODITE

Midday Mail—January 9, 1918

ELLEN FRANCIS BURST through the hut door with a bang, waving a packet of letters. "Mail's here!"

Hazel tried not to pounce. Surely, today, there'd be a letter from James.

Ellen passed them around. Four letters for Colette—her aunt in Paris, and three doughboys. Two for Ellen. Several for Mrs. Davies.

Two letters for Hazel. One from Georgia Fake. One from her mother.

It was treasonous to feel disappointed at that.

Hazel curled up on a corner couch and read her mother's letter. It contained more questions than news. Pleas for Hazel to dress warmly, watch out for pushy Americans, be safe, and come home soon. Bits of parish gossip and news of Dad's "old Arthur" flaring in winter, of the opera-loving spinster sisters in the flat above, and of the boisterous barber below. Hazel pulled a leaf of letter paper from her writing box and tried to form a reply.

"May I?"

She looked to see Colette. Hazel patted the seat beside her.

"Bad news?" Colette watched Hazel's face. "Or . . . no news?"

Hazel couldn't answer.

"Sometimes no news is worse," said the Belgian girl. "At least, when bad news comes, there is no more wondering if it will. Is there someone special you hope to hear from?"

Hazel considered this delicious, dreadful thought. To tell someone about James! Telling her parents had been more of an apology than a revelation. Would Colette think she was silly?

I squeezed in between them on the couch. I didn't want to miss a word.

"I met a young man," Hazel said hesitantly, "right after he'd enlisted. Right before he had to leave for France."

Colette, like the best of listeners, waited.

"He was lovely." She found herself whispering. "We met, and we had such a good time together." She gulped her embarrassment. "I only knew him for a few days before he left."

"But you felt like you'd always known him."

Hazel nodded.

"That's how it should be."

"It doesn't even make sense to me," Hazel confided, "how much I miss him. How constantly I think of him." She blushed. "Feels like I've got no right."

"What is your soldier's name?"

"James Alderidge."

"Do you have a photograph?"

She pulled it from her writing box. Might as well hand Colette her own beating heart.

Colette studied the picture. "Ah, *Jacques*," she said. "*Vous êtes très beau. Et très gentil.*"

Hazel beamed. "Do you really think so?"

"But of course," replied her friend. "He looks handsome. And kind."

"Oh, he is." Hazel sank back into the couch cushions. "The picture doesn't half do him justice. He loves music and dancing, and he makes me laugh all the time. He's thoughtful, and *good*, and ambitious, but in the right sort of way, and he wants to build safer homes and hospitals and . . ." She was rambling. Idealizing him. She couldn't help it.

"He sounds like a dream come true." I was ready to put Colette on my payroll.

"I just hope the war doesn't . . . change him, you know?"

Colette watched her thoughtfully. "It's unavoidable that the war will change him."

Hazel's heart sank.

"But that doesn't have to change how you care for him. Nor how he cares for you."

Hazel tried to imagine what the future might bring. She saw nothing but fog and smoke.

"His last letter was three weeks ago," Hazel admitted. "I get so worried. That he has . . ."

"That he is hurt, that something has happened to him, *non?*"

Hazel couldn't acknowledge the question, that it was even a possibility.

"Of course you do." Colette answered her own question. "But cheer up. There are many reasons why letters are slow. Soldiers catch colds. Letters are misplaced. Misdirected. And you just arrived here, yes? Maybe his letters are going to your old address."

"Colette," Hazel said cautiously. "Have you ever been"—*oh dear, say something else instead*—"in love?" *Too late.*

My favorite question.

Colette hesitated. "Yes," she said quietly, "I was."

Sweet Stéphane. What a man he would have made. What I could've done with them.

"What happened?"

Colette was surprised Hazel hadn't realized. "The Germans shot him."

"Oh, God." A sob burst from Hazel's throat, and she clutched Colette's wrist. The pain of this death, of this boy she never even knew, crashed down upon her like a tidal wave. "Oh, Colette, how can you bear it?"

Colette found a handkerchief and some chocolate. Hazel accepted both in good humility.

"How ridiculous is it," she said between sobs, "that you sit there, calmly comforting me, while I bawl over *your* old beau?"

"Not ridiculous at all," said Colette. "Your tears are for your Jacques. You pray that the worst will never happen, and then you meet someone to whom it has."

The storm passed, leaving Hazel puffy and spent.

"How have you gone on, Colette?" she asked. "You haven't shriveled up with grief."

"Who says I haven't?" She smiled, then her face sobered. "I light a candle each year for my poor Stéphane," she said. "And my family." She held up the photograph of James. "By day, I keep busy. But I don't really sleep much. It's at night when they come back to me."

Hazel looked up in surprise.

Colette smiled sadly. "I don't mean ghosts," she said. "Unless ghosts are memories."

Hazel wished she hadn't dragged her friend into such a painful conversation.

"The Americans are wild about you. Why hasn't one of them swept you off your feet?"

"The 'Yanks'?" Colette aped the accent. "*Non, merci.* They are only passing through."

"Maybe one of them will come back for you, one day."

She shrugged. "He'd be wasting his time." She handed back the photograph. "You asked me how I have survived." She looked around at the stage, the coffee station, the shelves of books and games. "It's the work that has helped. Just having something to do each day. It's very powerful. It requires me to help others with their troubles." Colette paused. "To make them smile a little bit. It is a better cure than anything the doctor gives."

Hazel waited.

"I think about the soldiers," Colette said. "The war, it did not kill me. But it might kill them. So, I am the lucky one. I try to give a little kindness. A little patience." She wagged her finger. "No patience, though, for when they get . . . what is your word . . . frisky." She winked.

Hazel shuddered. So far, she'd been spared such unpleasantness. But Ellen had stories to tell nearly every night of some soldier more confident in his charms than he ought to be.

And I thought the soldiers wanted piano music, Hazel thought. *I am so naïve.*

Hazel unrolled the wrapper off her chocolate and popped it in her mouth. Colette took another piece and did the same. They sat there, sucking on the bonbons, and thinking. Each pictured a different face. Hazel's was far away. Colette's was gone forever.

"And then, of course, there's the music," Colette said, still at odds with a glob of caramel.

Hazel nodded. The music.

ARES

Target Practice—January 7, 1918

GUNS, GUNS, EVERYWHERE GUNS.

Guns slung against the sides of corrugated steel Nissen huts like rows of baseball bats.

Heavy guns at the Front booming, missiles shrieking.

The *crack* of Webley revolvers, and the *bang* of Lee-Enfield rifles.

Guns in the arms of not-so-new recruits, all lined up for target practice.

A gun in James's hands.

His Lee-Enfield Mk III. A heavy wooden beauty, smooth and silky. He cradled it against his shoulder and peered through the aperture to the square that aligned his sights.

How many soldiers held you before? he asked it. *Are they now dead? In hospital?*

How many Germans have you shot? Did they die quickly, or suffer?

The weapon kept her secrets.

"Your rifle is your life," the trainer said. "When you go on a raid. When Jerry raids you. In no-man's-land. Keep her clean and loaded. Your speed with the rifle will determine whether Jerry gets to die for his country, or you. Let Jerry be the hero, and you go home to kiss your gal!"

Hazel's face appeared. Gone was the neat young man who'd caught her eye. In his place, a filthy brute caked with dirt. Chapped hands, blackened nails, a grimy face, a scraggly beard.

His comrades had changed. Billy Nutley was leaner, more brawn than bulk. His rifle lay in his huge arms like a toy. Chad Browning, the skinny ginger, was still wiry but with a commanding stance. He knew what his gun was for. Mick Webber, bricklayer, had been strong, but now he was quick and agile, the first to finish each obstacle course.

Frank Mason was still Frank Mason. That was reassuring.

It was nothing now to throw the bolt, clear the chamber, shove the bolt back to load the new bullet and cock the hammer, take aim, and shoot. The bolt-action maneuver that had been so stiff and clumsy at first was now effortless, automatic. Less than a second on the clock. It turned British soldiers into ruthless killing machines. Lethal weapons in Field Marshal Haig's hands.

It's them or you.

"Load!"

He pulled strippers from his pocket and loaded them into the chamber.

"Take your sights!"

He peered through the aperture at his target. Some clever Tommy had painted "Wee Willie Winkie" on the rough wooden human cutout. One of many names for Kaiser Wilhelm.

"Take aim, fire, and note where the bullet goes. The difference between where you aimed and where it went is how much you adjust, each time. There's no wind today, so the distance and direction gives you the tolerance you'll need in the future, at this range."

Soldiers looked to see if it was okay to reveal that they had no idea what he meant.

"Look. It's simple. If you aim for the middle of the chest, but the bullet goes through his brain, your rifle shoots a foot higher than you think. It's twenty-five yards. It'd be different farther out. So if you want to hit his heart, aim for his crotch. If you plug him in the crotch, that's fine too! Rifles up! Cock position!"

James deflated his lungs and cocked the rifle.

"Aim!"

He centered the finder in the view hole, and steadied it on the two Ls in "Willie." His finger brushed the curved steel trigger.

"Fire!"

Whump went the rifle butt against his shoulder. The bullet punched the wooden heart.

Webber, to his left, whistled. "Lookit you, Alderidge! Willie Winkie's a dead man."

James couldn't believe his eyes. "Dumb luck."

"Nah," said Webber. "Good eye."

Frank Mason shaded his face against the wintry sun. "Good gun."

"Now, calculate what your tolerance should be," the trainer cried. "Ready? Clear!"

Ka-chunk. Dozens of soldiers, in mechanized, deadly symmetry, threw back their bolts and shoved them in. Chambers spat out the last bullets' empty casings. They fell into the slush.

"Calculate . . . aim . . . fire!"

Another perfect shot.

"Clear!" *Ka-chunk.* "Take this new margin into consideration. Average the two. Aim!"

James emptied himself of air. Straight at the heart.

"Fire!"

Two inches off. Still fatal.

"Clear!"

Ka-chunk.

"Aim!"

Out went the air.

"Fire!"

"Clear!"

"Aim!"

"Fire!"

"That'll do. Rifles down!"

Spent casings lay scattered like birdseed at his feet. It felt like a horse had kicked his shoulder. But his pulse thrummed. He *liked* shooting.

Too bad, he thought, Germans couldn't be made of wood.

"Off to dinner with you now," the trainer said. He beckoned another officer and pulled him toward James's target. They pointed to his results. A little flush of pride didn't hurt on a cold day. Could he tell Hazel about it without sounding like a braggart?

He gathered his stuff and started to head for the mess hall with the others, when a call from the trainer stopped him.

"Hold up there, Private . . ."

"Alderidge," said James. He stood at attention.

The trainer reached his side, along with the other officer. "You a hunter, Alderidge?"

James shook his head. "No, sir."

"Shoot clay pigeons?"

"No, sir."

"Really." The trainer stroked his chin and glanced significantly at the other officer. "Impressive shooting, there. We'll note that on your file." He nodded to James. "At ease, Private. Off to mess with you."

APHRODITE

Girl Singer—January 12, 1918

ANOTHER EVENING, a few days later, found Hazel and Colette at the piano, rehearsing.

Colette's gravelly voice, sultry and low, was mesmerizing. Hazel couldn't believe her talent. Her voice crackled with longing. Maybe, Hazel thought, one must suffer much to sing like that. She felt the power tingling down her spine.

Aubrey heard the siren's song, even before he chucked a handful of pebbles against the windows. Who sang like that? He had to know. Singing foreign, but with that voice, so what?

He tossed the pebbles, then waited. Nothing. He chucked another handful.

Hazel unbolted the door and peeked around the corner of the building. "Who's there?"

"It is I," said Aubrey, with a bow. "The King of Ragtime and the Emperor of Jazz."

"Aubrey! You came back!" She beckoned him in. "It took you long enough."

He leaned against the door. "Been too busy with concerts to get here sooner."

"What fun! Aren't you coming in?"

"I'm not allowed," he said. "I tried to come this afternoon, but a lady turned me away."

"Oh, Aubrey. I am so sorry." Hazel felt sick about it. "Say, why don't you come in now?"

Aubrey hesitated. "Won't we get in trouble?"

"Who's to know? Mrs. Davies has gone to bed." What a rule breaker she was becoming! But some rules demanded it. "It's revenge. She won't let me play at the Negro hut."

Aubrey followed Hazel inside. "Because you wouldn't be safe there," he said bitterly.

They reached the stage, where Colette sorted her music pages and hummed snatches of a song. Aubrey swept his cap off his head and made a deep bow. Colette was dressed, this time around, in her uniform blouse and skirt, but Aubrey was in no way disappointed.

"Aubrey Edwards, at your service," he told her. "Pleased to make your acquaintance."

"You haven't, yet," she told him.

"Then I will be even more pleased," said the unsinkable Aubrey, "when you acquaint me." He glanced at Hazel and back at Colette. "Was that you I heard just now, singing?"

Hazel watched Aubrey unleash his charm on Colette. *This ought to be fun.* She could be cool as ice. When doughboys tried to catch her eye, she just smiled and poured them lemonade.

The king glanced in Hazel's direction. She could see his eyes sparkling. "Your Ladyship," he said in a stage whisper, "are you gonna introduce me to this lovely friend of yours, or do I have to guess her name?"

"It would be fun to see you try," she said. "This is my friend Colette Fournier. Singer extraordinaire. Colette, this is Aubrey Edwards, King of Ragtime and Emperor of Jazz."

Colette held out her hand to shake, but Aubrey kissed it.

"What is 'jazz'?" Colette asked. "Is that what you call the music the band played here last week? *C'était fantastique!*"

He swelled up like a bullfrog. "That's jazz, or something like it," he said. "We're not just the best band in the US Army. We're the best band in the whole dang war. We'll set you free, then we'll set you on fire with our jazz beat."

"Watch what he can do, Colette." Hazel gestured Aubrey toward the piano bench.

He found the melody to her song and explored chords until he'd shaped it into a rag.

To him, it was child's play, but to Colette, Aubrey had musically parted the Red Sea.

"Do that again," Colette demanded.

Aubrey was glad to oblige her. Soon they were ragging her other sheet music.

Apollo, you remember what this felt like, for musicians first experiencing the baptism of fire that was jazz. Ragtime seized Colette. Her mind fizzed, her hips swayed. Gone were the old swoony, melodramatic refrains and hackneyed, chirpy tunes. This was oil lamps becoming electric lights. It was dynamite. Voodoo. Sorcery.

It was *sexy*. And so was its athletic high priest at the piano bench. He played for Colette with a there's-more-where-that-came-from gleam in his eye. She found her gaze returning to him oftener than it should. And lingering there.

Non, Colette told herself. *Non, non, non.*

But there was something about the King of Ragtime that wasn't just the music.

Aubrey had never encountered Rococo perfume, straight from Paris, and short, sleek curls pinned up like that, so glamorous and daring. And her figure! But it was her voice that hooked him. She knew where he'd take the music; when he improvised, she followed, and sometimes even steered him to modulate to a new key.

Hazel began to yawn. It was getting late. The time had come.

Aubrey made himself stand up. "I'd better go." The hardest words he'd said in a while.

Colette offered him her hand. "*Enchantée.*"

"Good night, Aubrey," Hazel said.

He made his way to the door. *They didn't invite you back,* his mother's voice told him.

He grinned into the cold night air. *Who needs an invitation?*

APOLLO

The Next Morning—January 13, 1918

"WHERE WERE *YOU* last night?"

Joey Rice jabbed Aubrey in the ribs. They shivered in line, waiting for the latrine.

"You look like a dead body," Joey said. "I heard you come in. What was it, midnight?"

Aubrey rubbed his eyes. "S'matter, Rice? Did I disturb your beauty rest?"

Joey poked Aubrey in the chest. "I had to lie to Lieutenant Europe and say you were at the infirmary last night at lights-out."

That got Aubrey's attention. "He was looking for me?"

"You're lucky it wasn't Captain Fish. I told him you'd got the runs."

"Gee, thanks." He hopped on one foot. "Move it along there, fellas! I gotta go!"

"Seriously," Joey said, "where'd you go?"

Aubrey hesitated, then gave in. "You've gotta keep it secret." He spoke into Joey's ear. "I met someone."

"Here?" Joey's eyes grew wide. "She pretty?"

Aubrey's eyes rolled heavenward. "Oh man. You don't even know."

Joey's eyebrows rose. "Did you . . . ?"

Aubrey shoved him in the shoulder. "Shut it, Rice," he said. "It's not like that."

"Well, don't get sore at me. I'm only asking." He rubbed his shoulder. "So, is she at the Y hut in Camp Lusitania? They've got some lookers. Strictly business, most of 'em."

Aubrey remembered Colette's perfume. "Nah," he said. "The girl I met is Belgian."

Joey's mouth hung open.

"You look like a codfish," Aubrey told him. "Relax. That officer's watching us funny."

Joey shut his mouth. After a minute, he whispered once more to Aubrey.

"So you found yourself a Belgian hooker," he said. "Did you go into town alone?"

Aubrey dug two knuckles between a pair of Joey's ribs.

"Ow!"

"Say that again," Aubrey hissed, "and I'll knock you over. I told you it wasn't like that."

Joey elbowed Aubrey away. "Cut it out," he said. "I'm the reason you're not in the clink this morning. So I'd cool it if I were you."

Aubrey considered. He might need an ally again. He was definitely going back.

"Well," Joey said, "what's she like? Besides pretty."

Aubrey sighed. "You should hear her sing," he said. "In the States, she could be a star."

"What, they don't have stars here in Europe?"

Another soldier vacated the latrine.

"Speaking of Europe," he said, "What did Lieutenant Europe want with me last night?"

Rice pretended to play his cornet. "Something about band practice tonight."

Aubrey clapped his hand on his forehead. "Tonight? Shoot!"

"What's the matter?"

Aubrey shook his head. "I was gonna go see her tonight."

"Look," Joey said. "Captain Fish doesn't want us getting tangled up with girls, period." He lowered his voice. "And if you mess with a white girl, there'll be trouble."

Aubrey was in no mood for a lecture. He began to wish he hadn't opened his mouth. "Forget it," he told Joey. "I only just met her, all right? I didn't propose."

Joey ignored him and went full throttle. "It was hard enough getting here. Don't screw it up. Our job is to work hard, play great music, and smile big no matter what. You get tangled up with some nice white gal, not a hooker, I mean, and you'll get yourself killed." He lowered his voice. "I heard guys talking. About a regiment of marines. Lotta Southerners've been making threats."

Aubrey shook it off. "Relax, Rice," he said. "You worry like my mom." He clapped Joey on the shoulder. "You'll see. I'll be fine. Nothing bad's gonna happen to Aubrey Edwards, King of Ragtime and Emperor of Jazz."

"Except I'm gonna knock that big head of yours off those skinny shoulders."

"I'd like to see you try."

"You're the King of Stupid, is what you are."

"Then you're my loyal subject. Who're you calling skinny?"

Finally they were next for the latrine. A soldier exited it, pinching his nose.

"Lemme in," Joey said. "I'm gonna explode."

"No way." Aubrey darted ahead and beat him to it. "You said I had the runs. Wouldn't be right to make you a liar."

APOLLO

At Band Practice—January 13, 1918

I FOLLOWED AUBREY to band practice that night to remind him of his goals. Here, I thought, Aphrodite wouldn't have her claws in him. No offense, Goddess.

"I said, listen up! You clarinets, shut your mouths and listen up!"

Lieutenant Europe's spectacled eyes glared at the 15th Army Band.

Aubrey thought a crash of the cymbals would quiet everyone down, so he produced one. Drum Major Noble Sissle, the band's baritone vocalist, flicked the back of Aubrey's head.

"Ow!"

Half a minute of Europe's evil eye finally shamed the rest of the band into silence.

"All right, all right!" said Europe. "We've got a lot of work to-night. Two more performances this week. One at Hut Two, and one at the Camp Lusitania Y. We're a huge hit, fellas, with all the troops. Officers, too! You've done great."

Europe allowed himself a smile as the band whooped and cheered.

Aubrey rubbed the back of his head. Next time, he'd wear his helmet to rehearsal.

"Not only that," the band director went on, "but there's talk of us being sent on the road, all around France. A goodwill tour to boost morale until the American army's here in force."

Aubrey should've been excited. This was just the break I needed for him. More exposure! He once dreamed of playing around France. Now he had nothing but a pretty face on his mind.

"It's like I told you," Europe said. "We're saving lives, one *rag* at a *time.*"

Yuk, yuk.

"One *trunk* at a time," said Alex Jackson, tuba. Murmurs rippled through the band.

"Look, I know you're sick of unloading trunks and boxes," Lieutenant Europe said. "We came to France to fight, so we'll fight. Colonel Hayward's figuring it out. But we also came to play jazz. So let's get to it. Sis, pass this new music around, will you? It's labeled by instrument."

Noble Sissle took the pile of pages and began distributing them to the band.

Lieutenant Europe consulted his notes. "Now, let's see. Oh yes. You piccolos, you were dragging two nights ago on 'Stars and Stripes Forever.' What do I always say? Without you, it's just a bunch of blatting horns. If you don't get those trills on time, and on pitch, so help me God, I'll take a flute and trill you over the tops of your heads, you hear me?"

Muttering and elbowing among the woodwinds.

The bandmaster returned to his notes. "Oh. Get this, boys: the army has taken over a luxury resort for American troops on leave," he said. "Place called Aix-les-Bains. It's got baths and a spa, mountains and a lake. Casinos, theaters, you name it. Quite the hot spot.

J. P. Morgan and Queen Victoria used to vacation there. We'll go at the end of our tour. We're the opening act."

"Sending us there to relax?" asked Pinkhead Parker, saxophone.

"To play music, not roulette," Europe replied. "Maybe, in free time, you could, but . . ."

"But what?" demanded Pinkhead.

Europe paused. "We're the entertainment," he said. "The resort's not for black soldiers."

Silence, that rare commodity, fell over the band.

"Just like back in New York, playing for the swells," said Pinkhead. "Use the servant's entrance, and eat your soup in the kitchen."

Jim Europe sighed. "We'll figure something out, all right?" The band was full of flat expressions. "It's a big place. I'll do what I can to make sure you fellas get some fun."

Drum Major Sissle handed Aubrey his music. He took it without much interest. Leave Saint-Nazaire? Go play Dixieland at some fancy resort?

Come on, Aubrey. This kind of chance is the reason you enlisted. Seize it!

But all he thought of was that girl. Not, at that moment, what a fine musician she was, nor how they could duo their way to fame. This was your dirty work, Goddess.

"Edwards . . . Edwards!"

Aubrey blinked. Lieutenant Europe had his fists on his hips and was glaring at him.

"You with us today, or what, Private?"

Aubrey stood up straight and held his drumsticks at the ready.

"Perhaps you'd care to take a glance at your music, once in a while?"

Any idiot could read a drumbeat if they understood rhythm. Aubrey was made of rhythm.

"I see it, sir, Lieutenant, sir!"

"Do you, now."

Snickers ran through the woodwinds.

Aubrey looked around. Behind Lieutenant Europe, off to one side, stood Noble Sissle, all eyebrows and exclamation points, holding up a sheet of music and pointing hard at the top.

"Reveille Blues," it read. By A. Edwards. Orchestration by Jas. R. Europe.

"Oh," said Aubrey.

You're on your way, I told him. Barely twenty, and Jim Europe's scoring and performing your music! The future's yours! This is your moment. You're at a fork in the road. One fork leads to certain heartache. The other, immortality. Choose your music!

But all he could think of was what it would sound like if Colette sang along.

Goddess, I tell you, you do not fight fair.

ARES

In the Trenches—January 9, 1918

NOTHING IN THIS world had prepared James Alderidge for life in the trenches.

The message came. Replacement troops needed in the trenches. Forming a new section. Get your packs ready, and wait to meet your commanding officer.

They ate, mailed letters home in case they might be their last, said a prayer if they were that sort, and strapped on their seventy pounds of gear. Six new conscripts: James Alderidge, Billy Nutley, Mick Webber, Chad Browning. An Alph Gilchrist and a Vince Rowan. Two returning soldiers: Frank Mason, whom they knew, and Samuel Selkirk, whom they didn't.

An officer appeared. "Morning, lads," he said. "I'm Sergeant McKendrick. This section is under my command. You're the Third Section, First Platoon, D Company, Thirty-Ninth Division."

3rd, 1st, D, 39th. Stationed outside the town of Gouzeaucourt. James tried to file that where he could remember it.

"Button that top button, soldier," the sergeant told Billy. "Slovenly dress is punishable."

He worked his way down the line. "Who taught you to wrap

your puttees like that, Private?" The cloth strips wrapped around Chad Browning's chicken legs drooped. "We're soldiers, not mummies, for God's sake."

This emergency addressed, the sergeant ordered them to open their packs for inspection. They slung them off their backs and opened them. When satisfied, he led them on their march.

They wove through artillery mounds, field kitchens, and wound clearing stations, past live horses and dead horses and trucks and motorcycles. From time to time, in a lazy sort of way, artillery shells sailed over from the German lines and exploded, sending up geysers of dirt.

One landed close enough for them to feel its impact, and a few of the new men screamed.

"That's nothing," the sergeant said. "Just a bump. Didn't even knock you over." He pointed. "See that black smoke? That's a Jack Johnson. Like the American prizefighter, you know. Big black chappie. You'll learn how to spot 'em from the noise they make."

Soon walls of earth rose around them. As a boy, James had visited grand old country estates, where for a penny you could wander through a garden maze of high hedges. He'd hated them, though they, at least, were made of flowering bushes, and country gardeners never shot trench mortars.

This labyrinth wound on and on. The dark corridors turned at right angles every couple of yards, so you never knew if you were in step with the others unless you ran into them, or they collided with you. The narrow passageways couldn't fit two people abreast, so they flattened against the wall to let stretcher-bearers pass by.

"What's the matter, soldier?" Sergeant McKendrick watched James stare at a groaning man on a stretcher with blood seeping through his shirt. "This is a quiet sector. You wait."

"Try not to look shocked," Mason told him quietly. "It doesn't help to look green here."

James lost all sense of direction. He tried to picture the diagrams he'd seen in training at Étaples. Zigzag front firing lines, then support lines, then reserve lines, all more or less parallel, with communication trenches running between them like filaments in a spider's web. Behind the reserve trenches, a row of heavy guns, manned by artillery gunners. The little shoots that ran off the front firing line trenches into no-man's-land to spy on Jerry were called saps. What did it matter what name you called it? A trench by any other name would smell as sweet, right?

These smelled like rotting human flesh, urine, and feces. And cheap cigarettes.

The path opened up to a right turn, revealing a wider trench. It felt less like a passageway and more like a chairless waiting room where grubby men stood in an endless queue to see a dentist. Some soldiers had stretched themselves out on their packs or on sandbags to sleep.

Here Sergeant McKendrick addressed them. "Home sweet home, lads," he said. "You'll spend ten days here in reserve, then move up to the support lines. Ten days there, and you'll move up to the Front. After that, if all goes well, you'll get a few days' rest."

Thirty days in the trenches. Could rest mean leave and seeing Hazel?

"Of course," added the sergeant, "if the Germans attack, the whole plan goes bugger up." He looked around. "Well, lads, make yourselves at home. The old-timers here can fill you in. They're Thirty-Ninth Division, just like you. Second Section. Now, take a load off your feet until lunchtime, and after that we'll have gas mask training." And he was gone.

The other soldiers peeled themselves off the trench walls where they'd been leaning and came over to sniff out the new additions to the wolf pack.

"Welcome home, me darlings," said one, a lanky, wiry fellow. "What'd you bring me?"

Billy, Chad, and Mick eyed one another. James looked at Frank Mason for some hint.

Mason pulled a cigarette tin from his pocket. "Box open." Billy, Chad, Mick, and James stared. Five or six experienced soldiers, standing by, wasted no time crowding in around Mason and grabbing at his Woodbines, with calls of "Thanks, mate" and "There's a chum."

"Box shut." Mason pocketed the tin. The soldiers who didn't get any weren't bitter.

Chad whispered in James's ear. "Nobody told us we were supposed to bring a bribe."

"I'm Frank Mason," Frank told the 2nd Section lads. "What's it like up there?"

"Pretty quiet," said a stocky, broad-faced soldier. "Benji Packer. We don't hear much from Fritz except at stand-down and stand-to, and even then, his heart's not in it."

James was puzzled. "But then, what've we been hearing all day?"

The 2nd Section men laughed. "What's your name, kid?"

"James Alderidge," he said. "From Essex."

"It's German artillery," Packer said. "But that's just Fritz having a sneeze now and then."

Another soldier took a drag on his cigarette. "You wait till he really catches cold."

"Tell you what, though," said the taller, wiry fellow. "Something's cooking. I overheard the adjutant talking to Feetham—"

James interrupted. "Feetham?"

Several heads turned his way, as if this were an embarrassing question. "Brigadier General Feetham," said a heavily freckled soldier. "CO of the Thirty-Ninth."

Adjutant: a captain and aide to the CO, commanding officer. Brigadier general: head of a brigade, or in this case, a division. So, the adjutant was aide to Brigadier General Feetham.

At least, James was fairly sure that was how it worked.

"The Fifth Army's line keeps spreading," said the chap in the know. "They've given us too many miles to cover. We're stretched too thin. Don't have enough soldiers to defend it. That's why they hurried you boys into the army and up to the Front."

Sam Selkirk, who had seen service before, spoke. "What's on the other side? How many divisions has Jerry got?" Selkirk had a face like a basset hound's. It was tricky not to stare.

"Who're you?" asked the wiry 2nd Section chap.

"Sam Selkirk," said the basset hound.

The other nodded in greeting. "Clive Mooradian. Good to meet you." He blew smoke into the inside of his coat pocket.

This got Chad Browning curious. "Here, why d'you do that?"

"And you are?"

"Browning. Chad Browning."

"Well, Private Browning," said Clive Mooradian, "there's half a dozen of us here smoking. What d'you think will happen next if we let the smoke rise up, easy as you please?"

Chad scratched his head. "Er . . . I dunno."

"Fritz'll know just where we are, won't he?"

Chad looked like he must be daft. "You telling me Fritz doesn't know we're here?"

Second Section thought this was hilarious. "Course he knows we're in the trenches, dippy. If they can tell by the smoke that a handful of us are lolling here, smoking, here's what'll happen. His bombers will lob an egg grenade right into our laps. Or his snipers will train their sights on this spot, waiting for one of us to poke our heads up." He glanced up at Billy Nutley. "You'd best find a way to get shorter, mate, if you want to make it through the week."

Billy slumped as best he could. His back would soon hurt like the devil.

Frank Mason blew smoke through his coat. "Mooradian," he said quietly. "You said you heard the adjutant talking to Feetham. Is that all you heard? About the thinning of the line?"

Clive Mooradian tapped the ash off the end of his cigarette. "No, it ain't," he said. He looked around to make sure no officers or NCOs (noncommissioned officers) were near enough to hear them. "Russia's pulling out of the war, see? They've gone communistic over there, and the new government wants to be out of the war before the Germans kill every last starving Cossack."

"So what?" chirped Chad. "What's a bunch of Russkies got to do with us?"

Clive gave him a scornful look. "Think, dumb-arse. The Germans and Russians are in peace talks, right? And when they sign an armistice, where d'you think all those German armies from the Eastern Front are gonna go? Back home to kiss Ursula and Hildegard?"

"If they won't," said an older man from 2nd Section, waggling his eyebrows, "I will."

"Go ahead, Casanova," said Benji. "Tell ol' Fritz to bring his sisters to the Front for you."

"Shut up, shut up," drawled Clive casually. "You're wrecking my story."

"They'll come here," said James. "That's what you mean, isn't it, Mooradian?"

"That's right, genius." Mooradian pointed his cigarette at James. "Who's this bright young lad? Oh. Right. You're Jimmy. So, Jimmy, how long d'you think the Eastern Front is?"

James shrugged. "I don't know. A lot longer."

"You're not half right. A *lot* longer. We'll have double, triple the German soldiers, all their artillery and planes. Facing our thin line of Fifth Army. How long d'you think we'll last?"

Frank Mason spoke up. "What about the Oise River?" he said. "They said it's so wet and soupy, it's a natural defense, so a thinner line's okay. The Germans can't cross it easily."

"Better hope so." Benji took a drag on his cigarette. "Sounds like betting on a puddle."

"But the Americans are coming," Mick Webber said.

"Seen any sign of 'em?" replied Mooradian. "At this rate, they'll get here in time to toast the Germans' victory."

Sam Selkirk, basset hound, shook his head. "It'll be Wipers all over again."

Frank Mason, seeing his comrades' bewilderment, translated. "Ypres. Belgium."

"What he means," said Private Mooradian, "is that it'll be suicide."

APHRODITE

Caught—January 15, 1918

AUBREY CAME TO the Y hut on his next free evening.

They sat at the piano. Hazel on the bench, and Aubrey to her right. When Colette sat by Aubrey, Hazel found herself sliding off the edge, so she got herself a chair.

Aubrey played, reminding himself not to stare at Colette. He had to hear her sing. Watch her move. She wore a dark blue dress tonight. No stiff uniform. One dark curl escaped her hairpins and dangled beside her ear.

He pointed to a French war tune. "What would you think of doing it like this?" He began to play it with a slow, sleepy, take-it-easy beat.

"What do you call that?" demanded Colette.

"Syncopation," Aubrey said. God, she was gorgeous. So intense, like she wanted to pry answers out of him. *Pry away, mademoiselle.*

"How does it do that?" she asked. "It . . . turns the song on its head. It protests the, how do I say, the proper, the stuffy . . . Hazel, what do I mean?"

Hazel chewed on her lip. "It subverts it," she said slowly. "It makes the song a rebellion."

"A rebellion," Aubrey said. "I like that, Lady Hazel de la Wind-icott."

Colette handed Aubrey an old French goodbye song. He played it slowly, darkly. Colette immediately understood. She sang, knowing exactly what color to add to give it the blues.

"Where, Miss Fournier . . ." Aubrey began.

"Colette, please," said she.

First-name basis! "Where, Colette, does that anger come from?"

Colette felt suddenly exposed. "Anger?"

Aubrey nodded. "To look at you, you're this sophisticated lady without a care in the world. But when you sing, *whew!*"

Whew, what? Colette feared she was blushing. That hadn't happened in a long time.

"There's a whole lotta something bottled up in there. Emotion. Intensity. Anger's not quite the word, but it's the closest I can find."

Colette glanced down into her lap. "Maybe it's just that I sing loud," she said. "My choir director used to scold me for that."

"Anybody'd be nuts to scold you for the way you sing," Aubrey said. "I want to take a voice like that on the road with me and make it famous around the world."

Colette watched Aubrey's face. Was he just flattering her? His dark eyes met her gaze unapologetically.

Mon Dieu, was she staring at him? She was *staring at him.* Quickly, she looked away. She should leave. Now.

Hazel, watching them, wished she could tiptoe away silently without them noticing.

Aubrey was just playing the introduction to a new song when Hazel snapped her fingers. She'd heard something. An opening door. From one of the bedrooms near the front door.

Aubrey's hands froze over the keyboard.

"Down," hissed Colette. She pushed Aubrey's head toward the

ivories, out of sight of anyone below the stage. She stood quickly, gesturing for Hazel to stand also.

"What's going on here?"

Mrs. Davies appeared in a robe and a frilly cap perched over the curlers in her gray hair.

Hazel rose, her heart pounding and her face flushing. She was the worst liar in the world.

"I'm sorry, Mrs. Davies," Colette said calmly. "We didn't mean to disturb you."

"We were practicing," Hazel said. Was the tremor in her voice as obvious as it felt?

Aubrey, bent behind the wooden piano cabinet, tried not to breathe. He was free to ogle Colette from the shoulders down just at that moment, and he took advantage of it.

If the girls were caught, they'd be dismissed in disgrace from the YMCA. They likely wouldn't be allowed to work for a relief organization again. But if Aubrey were caught? Military disobedience had terrible consequences. Sometimes fatal, to make an example of the guilty.

The enormity of their crimes became agonizingly real.

"There's no call for you to practice when decent people are asleep," said Mrs. Davies. "Off to bed with you, now."

"We will go, right away," Colette said.

Mrs. Davies scowled, as if to say, she wasn't one to be put off by such flimflammery.

"Well?" the secretary demanded. "I'm waiting."

"Oh," Colette said smoothly, "you wish to see us off to bed before you go yourself." As though this was entirely reasonable, and not in the least insulting to two young women old enough to be away from home on their own. Calmly, slowly, even leisurely, she collected and straightened her music. Hazel attempted to do the same with shaking hands.

Colette left the stage as if without a care in the world, and Hazel followed after her.

"*Bonsoir,* Mrs. Davies," said Colette. "See you in the morning."

"Good night, Mrs. Davies," Hazel mumbled, fearing the words might accidentally tumble out as, "Good night, Mrs. Davies, we are hiding a soldier behind the piano."

She eased her bedroom door shut, then waited, listening for an eternity for any sound.

Colette prepared herself for bed and lay down to read. The night grew quiet. Aubrey must've snuck out, and from the seesawing sounds coming through the partition, Mrs. Davies had fallen asleep too.

The book couldn't hold her attention, so she switched off the light and began her nighttime ritual of visiting her dead. She'd discovered a trick, years back: if she thought of her parents, her brother, her cousin, her uncles, every night, if she summoned their faces and thought of them, one by one, she was less likely to dream, and see blood—less likely to dream, and drown in anguish.

But for the first time in ages, her thoughts wouldn't stay trained on those dear faces. Try as she would, her thoughts kept drifting back to Aubrey Edwards.

She wasn't quite sure what had happened that night. She hadn't seen this storm brewing on the horizon. The King of Ragtime was a hurricane, and somehow she'd forgotten to close one of her windows.

She'd have to be more careful, next time.

APOLLO

Half an Hour—January 15, 1918

HALF AN HOUR'S a long time to sit behind a piano in the dark and wait for some old biddy to go to sleep. Aubrey stayed awake by dreaming of Colette. There she lay, in her bed, fifteen feet away.

Oh lordy. In her bed. In that silky nightgown. Purple. It was purple.

Nothing stood between them but a thin partition wall. What he'd give . . .

Nothing but a thin partition wall, and the United States Army.

What if he tiptoed in there, and put his arms around her, and kissed her?

Aubrey Edwards—he heard his mother's voice—*she never said she wanted to kiss you. She just likes your music.*

"Give me time, Mama, and I'll play my way into her heart," he whispered.

Never mind girls, I told him. Play your way into the life you dream of. Play your way into legend.

But he had other things on his mind.

When Aubrey couldn't take the waiting anymore, he pulled off his boots and tiptoed across the stage, feeling his way to the stairs. He climbed down and went out the door.

He stuffed his feet back into his boots and struck out for his own barracks.

Then he heard it. A click. He froze.

The unmistakable cocking click of a pistol.

Military police. He should've known. But whoever it was said nothing.

Finally he couldn't bear waiting. "Who's there?"

A footstep. Aubrey turned to face it.

"Who's there?" he repeated. He couldn't see anything in the darkness. But he felt someone there. More than one? He crouched, coiling his muscles, ready.

"I saw you go in there," said a soft Southern voice.

Not the military police. They'd be direct.

"I was just playing some music," Aubrey said. "Lady in there says I can." It made him sick, needing to invoke some white person's permission.

"We say you can't."

"Who's we?" He strained his ear to hear if anyone else was there. He tried to think. It was dark. If he couldn't see them, maybe they couldn't see him. He got ready to spring.

Aubrey knew his mom's stories. She knew, growing up in Mississippi, what could happen to black folks who put a foot outside of the line. Her brother, Audrey's uncle Ames, had never been the same after the night a gang of white drunks beat him up. He'd played Dixieland at a Biloxi club, and he smiled, they said, at some white ladies.

Right now, far as Aubrey could tell, it was just one soldier. A kid, looking for a fight. If it was a fight he wanted, Aubrey'd give him one. He just had to get that gun out of the mix.

"You Negroes"—*Negras* on his tongue—"you got a hut of your own. If you want to fool around with your own black girls, that's between you and Uncle Sam."

Carefully, Aubrey lifted one foot.

"Where you going, Negro?"

"Nowhere."

"That's right."

Aubrey's head spun. This could *not* be happening. This stupid kid was going to kill him.

"What are you planning to do?" Keep him talking. It was Aubrey's only plan.

"Tell you what we ain't gonna do." He came closer. "We ain't gonna let you Negroes get a taste for white women. That's why you was all in such a hurry to get to France."

Aubrey wanted to retch. *A taste.* As if they'd risk their lives, leave home, and put up with all this redneck prejudiced shit in the army, just to lay hands on white girls.

Dignity and pride. They can't take that away from you.

They could come pretty close.

"Can't have y'all getting spoiled, now, can we? You'll want our white girls, and think that uniform give you the right."

Never mind guns. Rage would kill Aubrey Edwards. Explode his veins. Send fire shooting from his hands. The vicious insult to every black man, woman, and girl! His feisty mother, his classy sister. He'd go for the throat, and with his own bare hands, he'd . . .

. . . do the last thing he ever did in this world.

Aubrey had a few other things he'd like to do with his hands before his life was over.

"Ever been with a black girl?" Aubrey asked.

A low laugh was his reply. Aubrey owed that boy a thrashing

for that poor girl's sake. He had no illusions about her being a willing participant.

"Why would you stoop so low," Aubrey asked, "if white girls are so much better? Or can't you get one of your own?"

A snort of anger. "Shut your mouth."

Aubrey swayed on his feet. Was there a loaded gun? How badly did he want to find out?

He'd been in fights before. Upper Manhattan was no Sunday picnic.

He crouched down. The white guy made no move. Aubrey picked up a chunk of ice.

He waited. His fingers became icicles. He just needed to break the other guy's focus.

Far away, down the path, one of the barracks switched on a light. The shadow puppet of the Southern soldier turned. Aubrey heaved the chunk of snow to land near his feet. The soldier jumped toward the sound. Aubrey tackled him, knocking him hard into the ice.

The Southern boy fought back, but was unprepared for Aubrey's rage and momentum, and his skill in a fight. Aubrey soon had his pistol, with the guy pinned underneath him, facedown in the snow. He pressed the cold nuzzle of the revolver against his victim's temple.

"Let me tell you something," he hissed. "You don't know what you're wandering into, messing with the Harlem boys of New York 15th." He felt the guy's panicked breath underneath his knees. "We bite back."

He nodded frantically.

Aubrey stood up, uncocked the pistol, and slid it into his pocket.

"Tell it to the rest of the bigots," he said. "Harlem boys won't put up with your shit." He kicked at the body lying in the snow. Not too hard. But maybe a little harder than was needed. "Get out of here. Don't let me see your ugly face again."

The body scrambled upright and skidded away until the darkness swallowed him.

Aubrey patted the gun at his side and disappeared into the darkness himself. Too bad, he thought, that he'd never actually seen the kid's ugly mug a first time. He'd like to be able to recognize his new friend if he saw him out and about.

The wine of victory was on his tongue. *Just try to get in my way again, white-trash boy.*

He glanced back once at the Y hut before leaving and breathed in the Rococo-scented thought of purple sleep.

Still worth it. He might wait an extra day or two, just to be smart, but no Southern coward would keep him from coming back to try to win Colette's heart. Noway, nohow.

ARES

Under the Moons of Mars—January 9, 1918

THE SOLDIERS IN James's 3rd Section ate lunch on their feet with 2nd Section—fried bully beef with cheese—then gathered in the reserve trench for gas mask training.

"The most important thing, with any kind of gas," said Sergeant McKendrick, "is to stay calm. Folks want to panic and run, but you suck in a lot more air. Stay calm. Yes, soldier?"

Chad Browning gulped. "Don't these gases, sir, destroy your lungs? And your eyes?"

Sergeant McKendrick nodded matter-of-factly. "If they don't kill you first," he said.

"But"—Browning looked pale—"how do you stay calm for that?"

"Put your mask on," McKendrick said. "If you've lost your mask, you still stay calm. If all else fails, piss on a hankie and breathe through that."

The 3rd Section recruits glanced around. Was it a joke? Apparently not.

"Now, the Germans are mostly using mustard gas," the sergeant went on. "With a mask on, your lungs'll be all right, but it'll make your skin break out in sores. It gets into your clothes, and you'll have to strip as soon as you can, or you'll break out in damnable sores everywhere."

He seemed to enjoy their stunned faces.

"But, pip-pip," he said. "The sores hurt like hell, but you recover eventually. Now. These," he said, passing out small haversacks, "are your box respirators. Put them on."

James opened the kit and pulled out a rubberized mask. It felt grotesque in his hands, like a freshly killed thing from a swamp. Mick Webber got his on first. Tinted lenses goggled out, and the breathing tube looked like some sinister, groping proboscis. Like a human insect out of a nightmare. No, from a space story he'd read in a serial magazine: "Under the Moons of Mars."

"Something holding you up, soldier?"

The sergeant eyed him expectantly.

James fumbled to put on his mask. Breathing through the tube was suffocating.

"Take it easy," warned the sergeant. "You're lucky you've got masks that work. Those poor buggers in the first gas attacks drowned in their own blood."

The sergeant covered how to distinguish a gas shell from a regular artillery shell, and what the different forms of gas looked and smelled like, and how to spot which way the wind was blowing. At last the 3rd Section folded their masks and trudged back to their traverse of the trenches.

James sat on his pack. So many ways to die, and all they required was the least instant's neglect of one of two thousand rules for survival. Blow smoke out through your coat. Don't ever light a third man's cigarette with the same match; by the time you've gotten to the third fellow, a sniper will have spotted your match and taken aim at you.

Even if he followed every rule, a trench mortar or a grenade or—what was it?—Jack Johnson could drop in his lap one day for pure spite and blow him to smithereens.

Goodbye, Life; goodbye, Future; goodbye, Mum, Dad, Maggie, Bob; goodbye, Hazel. Some other lad would someday give her the kiss he'd stupidly postponed.

He had to see her again. He had to get leave time to go see her, somehow. Wherever she was. If she was here in France, there must be a way.

Frank Mason decided to join him.

"You'd best get some sleep now, while you can," Mason said. "At dark it'll be stand-to, and then the night work begins."

James gulped. "You mean, trench raids? Going over to attack the Germans?"

Mason smiled. "Nah. Not yet. Not for you new lads, back here in reserve. But there'll be plenty of work for us to do. Sandbagging, maybe, or repairing trenches, or digging new ones. We'll see what fatigue the sergeant assigns us." He tipped his helmet low over his eyes.

"Mason," James whispered.

"Yeah?"

"What are the chances of someone like me getting permission to go on leave?"

Mason burst out laughing. "You just got here!"

"I mean, once our rotation is through," he said. "Thirty days, he said. Ten in each trench, and then some rest. What would the odds be of me getting a couple days' leave then?"

Frank Mason lifted the brim of his helmet. "You're nuts," he said. "Most soldiers don't see leave until after months of service. And if the fighting picks up, nobody's going anywhere."

James persisted. "But if everything were to work out, then

what? Would I just ask McKendrick? Or would he be furious?"

The fisherman-turned-soldier shrugged. "Who can say? Yeah, you'd ask him. No telling what his answer would be."

All right, then.

"But I tell you what," his friend cautioned. "Don't even think of asking him if you haven't been a model soldier between now and then. First up at stand-to. Clean and sharp always. Working hard. First to volunteer for everything."

James nodded. "Makes sense." He paused. "Mason," he said. "D'you miss your wife and kid?"

Frank Mason regarded him curiously. As if to say, *What kind of a question is that?*

"Every minute of every day."

James listened.

"I figure I'm lucky to have somebody to miss," said Frank.

"Got a picture?"

Mason opened his personal haversack and pulled out a small prayer book. From its pages he pulled a faded photograph. The woman sitting there with a chubby baby on her lap looked like someone who always got the joke. The infant looked lusty and strong, ready to give even his soldier father a poke in the eye if it suited his fancy.

"You're right," James told his friend. "You are lucky."

APOLLO

Colt M1910—January 16, 1918

IT'S A CURIOUS thing, sweating to death in subfreezing temperatures, but that's what all five companies of the 15th New York's Third Battalion did, hauling wooden railroad ties. They lined them up like the teeth of a miles-long comb and pounded in the spikes that held the iron track in place. Aubrey Edwards, K Company, filled his piano hands with splinters. I wasn't happy about that.

They'd peeled off their coats and were working in their shirtsleeves, despite bitter breezes blowing off the Atlantic. Their backs ached and their hands were raw. Even so, it felt amazing, drinking all that cold air into a burning-up body. Like bellows to a forge, Hephaestus would've said.

Their captains were concerned, though. Sickness had spread throughout Saint-Nazaire. Fevers had laid up hundreds of soldiers in their beds, and some had died. Captain Hamilton Fish III, K Company, worried that sweating in such cold could sicken his soldiers. First Lieutenant James Europe told his Maker that he'd better not lose any more band members to the ague.

I heard his prayer and duly considered it.

This illness was, as I've said, my own handiwork, but I do not boast. You can stop giving me that look, Goddess; even then I was busy, inspiring scientists to take a second look at mold, and nowadays penicillin is the miracle of modern science, but I am humble; I seek no praise.

The field kitchen cart arrived with pork-and-bean soup for their lunch. The mess detail ladled everyone's food and passed out chunks of bread. It wasn't scrumptious, but it wasn't terrible, and there was plenty of it. The wind froze them through their sweaty tunics as they ate.

"That's it," Joey declared. "I'm getting my coat."

"Get me mine, too, will you?"

Joey nodded and trudged to where they'd left their belongings. When he returned, carrying Aubrey's coat and wearing his own, his face wore a worried look.

"What's this, man?" Joey handed Aubrey his coat, patting the interior pocket.

Aubrey led Joey away from the rest of the Company, and pulled from his hidden pocket the handgun he'd wrestled away from the stranger the night before.

Joey's mouth hung open. "That ain't army issue. Where'd you get it?"

Aubrey looked left and right to make sure no one could hear.

"Last night," he said. "I was leaving the Y hut—"

Joey groaned. "You were out seeing that Belgian girl again, weren't you?"

"Shh!" Aubrey's eyes bugged out at Joey. "Can it!"

Joey folded his arms across his chest. *Make me.*

"I was leaving the hut," Aubrey said, "and some guy stopped me. Held me up."

Joey's eyes grew wide.

"Said we black soldiers better not think we can *help ourselves to white women.*"

"He *what?*" Joey's hands curled into fists.

"Said he wasn't gonna let us get *spoiled*, and then go back to the States with an *appetite* for white women there. Said we'd never go back to black girls once we'd tried white ones."

"Just let me catch him saying that," Joey fumed. "I'll teach him! Southern?"

Aubrey nodded. "Sure sounded like it."

Joey began to pace back and forth. "I don't know where to punch first."

Aubrey nodded. "I know."

Joey looked up. "You could've been killed." He stopped. "How many were there?"

"Just the one."

"Did you get a good look at him?"

Aubrey shook his head. "Way too dark last night. Barely saw him at all."

"But you knocked his head off, right?" Joey said. "Tell me you knocked his head off."

"Last call for more," cried the mess soldier with the ladle.

"Dang, I wanted more," said Joey. "Never mind that. What'd you do?"

Aubrey shrugged. "Took him out, man. What'd you think?" He wiped the dirt off his hands. "Had no weapon, but I laid him out on the ground. He'll be feeling it for a while."

As I say, *I* do not boast, but Aubrey isn't me.

Joey took a sloppy bite of soup, then pulled out the handgun once more.

"That's not army issue," he repeated. "That's a Colt. The 1910 model."

"Since when are you the gun expert?" demanded Aubrey.

"Since I went off to war, dummy." He ran a finger across the pistol's rough texture. The Smith & Wesson revolvers they'd been issued felt graceful and old-fashioned, with sleek silvery curves and wooden handles. This weapon felt cruel and ugly.

"These are the handguns they give the marines," Joey said.

Aubrey didn't much care which branch of the armed forces they were. The 15th New York had already had enough run-ins with bigots in the army.

"What're you going to do with that Colt?"

Aubrey turned it over in his hand. "An extra pistol might come in handy."

Joey gave him a penetrating look. "You're gonna tell Captain Fish about it, aren't you?"

Aubrey thumped him in the arm. "Are you kidding me? I'd get thrown out on my ear. Court-martialed, maybe, for being out after hours. And with a white girl? No way."

"Listen, man, you can't just ignore this. You gotta figure out some way to report it." He leaned in closer. "I was talking just this morning to a couple of those guys from M Company."

Aubrey nodded. "So?"

"They've got a funeral to go to tonight for one of their men," Joey whispered. "Geoff Somebody. A Brooklyn boy. They're saying he died of the flu. That's what their captain's saying, I mean. But the M Company men don't believe it. He was perfectly healthy, and the next thing you know, he disappears. And one of them, they're saying, says he was sworn to secrecy by the captain, but he found his body. Strangled. And they think it's the marines that did it.'

Aubrey's mouth went dry. "That can't be. There's no way."

"You know there's a way," Joey said. "Weren't you at Camp Wadsworth? Or Camp Dix? Or were you busy chasing some girl then, too?"

"K Company! Attention!" barked Captain Fish. "Back to work. These tracks won't lay themselves, and we've got a lot more to lay down before we head in for the day."

They scraped up the last bites of stew and buttoned up their coats. Until they got heated up again from work, they'd need the warmth.

Joey pulled Aubrey's elbow and spoke directly into his ear.

"Aub, those Company M boys are saying a group of them is gonna take revenge. An eye for an eye. A marine for one of ours."

We bite back. Aubrey gulped.

"I came to fight a war with the Germans," whispered Joey. "For democracy. But they're gonna start a war right here at Saint-Nazaire. For stupidity."

APHRODITE

Two Letters Arrive—January 19, 1918

THE BROWN ENVELOPE read, YMCA *Interdepartmental Correspondence*. It looked highly official. *Miss Hazel Windicott, Y Relief Huts, US Army Training Camp, Saint-Nazaire.*

Hazel opened it to find a thick envelope addressed to her, from her mother, care of the Y headquarters in Paris. It contained a letter and two more envelopes from James, sent to Poplar.

I would do Hazel an injustice if I didn't report that she read her mother's letter first. I would do the truth an injustice if I didn't report that she could barely see what she read.

She opened the two letters from James, compared dates, and started reading the first.

December 30, 1917

Dear Hazel,

I like fishing well enough, and if your father loves it, I will love it too.

After Christmas, we received orders to leave Étaples for the Front. We came by train and then a long march through the snow. I've traded the call of seagulls for the roar of shells, but they're still far away. You do see craters, though, and the ruins of old farmhouses. The war is felt everywhere.

We joined up with the Fifth Army just outside the ███████ ██████████████ two days ago. I'm not in the trenches yet. The training officer says we new recruits still have a good deal more to learn.

Are you in France? I like thinking of you on the same side of the sea. It's grand that you volunteered. I visited our Y huts often at Étaples. The Germans may kill us, but only if boredom doesn't get us first. I envy the lads who will hear you play. What I wouldn't give to trade places.

I think of you every day. Can't believe it's over a month since we were together. Do write to me so I know how to reach you. Be safe, stay well.

Yours,

James

January 7, 1918

Dear Hazel,

In case my last letter got lost, I've been at ███████████ for a week and a half. You must be in France now. Where did you end up?

The weather's cold, but the sun is pleasant at midday and it warms things up considerably. Apparently I'm not half bad at target shooting.

I don't know when my turn for leave will come around, but when it does, I could take a train to Paris and meet you there. Is Paris within your reach? Let's meet there.

I wish I were the sort with words to express what the thought of you brings me.

Say you'll come, do. I owe you something.

Yours,

James

Hazel burst into Colette's room, waving the letters. She found her friend pinning up her dark curls with the help of a small travel mirror.

"A letter?" asked Colette. "From your Jacques?"

Hazel cast herself down upon Colette's cot, nearly crumpling it. "Two letters. He's gone to the Front." Hazel scanned the lines again. "With the Fifth Army. But he's not in the trenches yet. He's still training in reserve. Colette," she said breathlessly, "he wants me to go see him! In Paris!"

Colette pinned up another sleek curl. "How marvelous!"

"How can I go?" Hazel moaned. "I have to go! I must go!"

"I agree," said Colette blandly. "Have you ever been to Paris?"

Hazel shook her head.

"*Sacre bleu!* Then, it is fixed. You *will* go."

Hazel sat bolt upright. "I couldn't possibly!" She gasped. "It's unthinkable."

Colette looked at her curiously. "Why not go?" She dabbed small drops of lotion around her face. "Because of Mrs. Davies? It can all be arranged. Volunteers take leave, now and again."

Hazel shook her head. "You don't understand," she said. "I'm eighteen. I know no one in Paris. Where would I stay? I can't just go there, all by myself. And especially not to spend time with a *young man*. What if—" She snatched the pillow from Colette's cot and hid her face in it.

Colette sat next to Hazel on the bed. "Oh, you English." She sighed. "More afraid of yourselves than of all the Kaiser's armies combined."

Hazel lowered the pillow. "How's that?"

"Are you afraid," asked Colette, "that your Jacques will take advantage of you?"

Hazel shook her head. "No. Not in the least."

"Then what is there to be afraid of?"

Hazel sank her chin into her palm. What to say? What was it, exactly! "Myself!"

Colette's eyebrows rose. "You are afraid *you* will take advantage of him?"

Hazel fell sideways on the bunk and shrieked into her pillow.

"Aha," Colette declared. "I have hit the hammer on the nail."

"I could no more take advantage of James than I could . . . Never mind."

"Then what are you afraid of?" asked *la belge*. "You two will spend a riotous weekend in Paris, eating bread-and-butter sandwiches, drinking milk, and quoting Psalms to each other."

Hazel puffed out her cheeks. Her *petite passion* wasn't quite so tepid as that.

"We could go to a symphony," she said.

"Ah." Colette nodded very seriously. "Perhaps you *would* need a chaperone, after all."

"Oh, stop!" Hazel biffed her friend with the pillow. "We never had a chaperone. I always snuck out to see him."

Colette gasped. "Mademoiselle Windicott! You shock me!"

Hazel rolled over. "You see," she said, "I'm not quite so innocent as you think."

"I see," said her friend, "that you are exactly as I think, and more so." Colette watched Hazel turn lavender and wanted to squeeze her on the spot.

"If anyone found out, there'd be such a scandal," Hazel said. "When I'm around James, I do the most outrageous things."

Colette smiled. "Then I would like to meet this James. It is settled," she said. "I'll come, too. I'll be your chaperone when you need one, and I will disappear when you don't."

Hazel took a deep breath. The idea was even more frightening now that it took on a whiff of actual possibility.

"But where will we stay?" said she. "How do we—"

"Never mind that," ordered Colette. "My aunt Solange will be delighted to have us, and will provide all the respectability your English heart could wish for."

With each word, this terrifying, tingling possibility grew more and more real. She'd have two, maybe three, days to spend with James. As much time as she'd ever had with him thus far. What might happen? With James Alderidge, anything was possible.

She remembered the end of his letter. *I owe you something.*

She seized her friend's wrist.

"Colette," she whispered. "What if I do something dreadful?"

Colette laughed. "I'll hold the flowers. And the priest will be the one to read a Psalm."

Hazel decided to turn the spotlight off herself for a spell.

"What about you, Colette?" Hazel said. "I think Aubrey likes you."

Colette busied herself with arranging her toiletries. "I don't think so," she said. "He's just very friendly."

Hazel sat up and took notice. Colette was avoiding looking at her. Interesting.

"I don't know," Hazel said slowly. "I don't think you saw how he was looking at you. He likes you, Colette."

Colette frowned at her reflection and bunched up her nose. "Looking at this? Pah." She turned and smiled at Hazel. "Let's say, for the sake of argument, that he was looking at me. That he does like me, which I doubt." She shrugged. "A soldier, looking for love on the eve of war? It's as old as the hills. I've heard that song before."

Hazel knew when not to push a point. "Speaking of songs," she said, "how about his piano playing?"

Colette allowed herself a smile. "Now that," she said, "is really something."

ARES

Moving Up the Line—January 20, 1918

"PRIVATE ALDERIDGE."

James woke in a dugout to a pair of boots in front of his face.

He crawled out of the dugout, and stood in the shelter of the trench's eastern wall, and saluted. "Sergeant McKendrick, sir!"

"At ease, Alderidge."

The sergeant scrutinized him. Was he in trouble?

It was his third day in the support lines. After a ten-day stint in reserve, his section had hiked through two miles of zigzagging communication trenches to the second line, support.

"You've been working hard, Alderidge."

James held his head high. "Thank you, sir." Should he ask about Paris leave?

"I have a report on you from your training sergeant," McKendrick said, looking at a clipboard. "Seems you acquitted yourself well."

James rocked on his toes and waited. A report?

"I also see you were a crack shot in target practice."

This was all becoming a bit much.

"Are you a gamesman?"

"No, sir, Sergeant. I've never done much in the way of hunting."

McKendrick's brow furrowed. "Is that so? Interesting." He sized James up. "We need a new sniper at the front," the sergeant said. "Lost a man at dawn. A German sniper identified our hidden loophole and took him out. Some mighty fine shooting there."

The sergeant admired the German shooter more than he mourned the British one. Not a comforting thought.

James didn't want to be a sniper. A cold-blooded killer. The enemy's number-one target. But he did need to curry favor with the sergeant. His goodwill was James's Paris ticket.

"I'm putting you into sharpshooter training," the sergeant said. "There's a pay increase." A pay increase for murder.

James seized hold of *training*. A trainee wouldn't shoot people. Not just yet. He'd probably head back behind the reserve line, to open country, where it was easier to take long aim. He could do poorly enough in training that he'd be moved back into the regular infantry.

"May I ask a question, sir?"

"You may."

James had no idea how to approach this. "Sir, when our rotation through the trenches is up, and we get some rest time . . ." he began.

The sergeant's eyebrows rose. James was already doomed.

"Yes?"

He swallowed. "I have a girl, Sergeant, and she can meet me in Paris for a day."

Sergeant McKendrick's expression hardened.

"You're hoping after *one* tour through the trenches, you'll be eligible for leave, to spend a day in Paris with your girl? As a new recruit? After likely seeing no combat to speak of?"

No retreat and no surrender. "That would be," he said, "what I was hoping. Sir."

Sergeant McKendrick studied James's face, as if waiting for

something to buckle or crack. For James to beg forgiveness and say, "Never mind."

"This girl of yours," the sergeant said. "She pretty?"

James gulped. "She is, sir. Very pretty."

"I see." The sergeant began to pace back and forth. "And why would she be in Paris?"

"Volunteer service, sir. With the YMCA." Close enough to true.

"Ah. They do good work."

James nodded. *If you say so. If it helps my case.*

"Let me hear a good report of you, soldier," the sergeant said, "and I'll consider that request for leave."

James wanted to shake his hand. He stood tall. "Yes, sir!"

The sergeant turned to go, then paused. "Redhead? Brunette? Blonde? What's she like?"

James didn't want to pull Hazel out of his pocket to show to anyone. But he needed this.

"Brunette, sir," he said. "She plays the piano beautifully."

"A talented young lady of some quality."

"Yes, sir."

"That's grand. Make sure you write to her often. Right then. In half an hour I'll have someone lead you up to the fire trench, to the snipers' lookout post."

James's mouth went dry. "The fire trench? Lookout?"

"Precisely." As if to say, *What is your point?*

"That's where training will take place?"

The sergeant nodded. "Simulations are never adequate," he said. "There's nothing like training on the job."

APHRODITE

A Headache—January 26, 1918

PEBBLES ONCE MORE, and this time, Colette opened the door. Aubrey plucked off his cap.

Her smile was all Aubrey needed. He'd face an entire marine company for that smile.

"*Bonsoir, monsieur,*" she said.

Aubrey hadn't particularly cared for high school French class—lordy, if he could go back!—but he knew a welcome when he heard one.

"Evening, mademoiselle," he said, with a pronunciation he hoped wasn't too awful. (It was awful.) "Safe for me to come in?"

She drew back the door.

"Where's our friend tonight?" he asked.

"Hazel had a headache," Colette said. "She went to bed early."

Whump went Aubrey's heart in his chest. Only Colette tonight.

Whump went Colette's heart. She was all alone with Aubrey.

"That's a shame," Aubrey said. "I hope she feels better. There's sickness going around."

Colette agreed. "I'm sure it's nothing," she said.

It was, indeed, nothing I hadn't caused to bring Aubrey and Colette together alone.

Oh, for pity's sake. It was a *mild* headache. The dear girl needed rest.

"Do we play piano, then?" asked Aubrey.

Colette laughed. "The senior secretaries know Hazel went to bed. If they should hear you playing, I can't pretend it was me."

"Oh. Right." Aubrey clutched his hat. "Suppose I ought to be moving along."

Oui. Go. Please. It is best, no?

Stay, I told him. *Invite him to stay,* I told Colette.

"We can sit and talk awhile," Colette said. *Mon Dieu,* she'd said it. *Idiot!*

Aubrey was out of his coat and on the couch in record time.

She sat a cushion away. Her short hair drew his eyes to her graceful neck, and to the turquoise sheen of her dress, made of drapey silk. Like something worn by a goddess.

That was all him. I didn't even plant the thought. But I *did* visit her Paris dressmaker later on.

"We've missed you," Colette said.

"You have?"

"Hazel and I."

Oh. Safer waters. "That Lady Hazel," Aubrey said. "She's a great gal."

Colette smiled. "I adore her," she said. "I'm so glad we met. She is sunshine."

"She feels the same for you," Aubrey said. "You're a good friend."

"*Moi?*" Colette looked thoughtful. "I just enjoy her, that's all. I can't help it."

I planted an idea, and Aubrey ran with it. "Has Hazel got a boyfriend?"

Colette tried not to smile. "That's not for me to say."

"She does!" Aubrey chuckled. "What do you know? Lady Hazel's got a beau!"

Well, the damage was done. "She's extremely fond of her soldier," Colette admitted. "His name is James. He seems to feel the same for her."

"He'd better," declared Aubrey, "and he'd better treat her right, or he and my fist are going to have a conversation."

"You sound like a big brother." Without warning, her face contorted with pain. *Alexandre.* He'd never learned about Stéphane. She would've fought him if he'd tried to play protector, but now, oh, what she'd give if Alexandre would walk through that door!

The sorrow. It came in waves. Just when she thought the storm had subsided, it ambushed her all over again.

Aubrey pulled back. Colette seemed on the verge of tears. Had he said something wrong?

"I'm a little brother, as it happens," he said at length. "My sister, Kate, doesn't need my help with protection. She's got the most boring boyfriend in the world. Ol' sleepy Lester."

"Poor Lester." Colette smiled, grateful for a change in the subject. "If your sister likes him, he can't be so bad."

She still seemed fragile, somehow. Aubrey tried to think of a safer topic of conversation.

"Anyway," he said, "Hazel's terrific. I'm glad I met her." *Extremely* glad.

Colette smiled again. "There is something ... How do I mean? Pure about her. The war is so ugly, and humanity has gone mad, but then, there's Hazel."

He took a chance. "And there's you."

Colette's eyebrows rose. "I'm not pure. The war has wiped her dirty boots all over me."

How could she say such a thing? She, so lovely, in every way, and not just to look at, though she sure was that.

"What do you mean?" he asked. "Has somebody hurt you?"

She hesitated.

He actually cared. She could see it in his eyes, in the concern written on his face. It would be easier if he didn't.

"Kaiser Wilhelm has," she said.

She was covered in nails, all of a sudden. A brittle eggshell in broken, jagged pieces.

"What happened?"

Colette's skin prickled. "Oh, you know," she said. "The war's awful. Life's unfair."

Aubrey could write a book about unfair, but there was something she wasn't telling him.

Get close to him, Colette, and you will lose him, she warned herself. *If your bleeding soul doesn't drive him away, the war will snatch him from you.*

Colette took a deep breath. She was better now. Herself again. Music was what they had in common. Music. They could be musical friends.

"What are you working on lately?" she asked. "Any new compositions? Jazz arrangements?" She paused. "That march you transformed into blues last time? *Fantastique!*"

He knew she was steering him away. Changing the subject. But it gave him an opening.

"The way you sing, Colette. It's like nothing I know."

"Oh?"

"I don't just mean your voice."

It drove him wild, the cool amusement with which she took everything he said.

"I am afraid to ask," she said, "what else besides my voice affects the way I sing."

He turned as much toward her as he could without actually putting his feet on her lap.

How had he drifted here? When what he really wanted to do was tell her how he thought of her all day, every day, with every swing of the pick and every crash of his hammer; how he'd filled notebook pages with ideas for songs that would be perfect for her voice, ideal for her register? Sultry, smoky, dark. Emotional.

That was what she was. Colette was *emotion*.

"You've changed how I think about music," he said. "I've got some new songs in the works. I don't know what the words would be, yet, but I've got the tunes, and maybe . . ."

"*I've* changed how *you* think about music?" She shook her head in wonder. "I'm just a girl who sings French songs. You're the one whose music is electric."

"That's just it," he said. "Man, I wish I could show you what I mean at the piano. Up till now, I was all about speed. Tricky harmonies. A show-off, you know? I was aiming for glitz."

"Glitz" was not a word Colette had ever learned, but she was too polite to say so.

Aubrey knew he was boring her. "You've got me thinking more," he said, "about how to pull the feeling out of a melody. Make it something you can sing with your whole *life*. Not just the body. That's how you do it, every time."

I could see you there, Apollo. Waving in the window like a nosy neighbor. Go away.

Aubrey Edwards, I told him, *you're not here to talk music theory or vocal technique.*

"You're a mystery, Colette Fournier," he told her. "That deep, dark place you sing from."

Colette didn't know what to say. She didn't think her singing sprang from some inner truth, some prior pain. Of course she was angry about Dinant. Anger didn't even begin to describe it. She'd carry the rage to her grave. But every Belgian was angry. Aubrey, she feared, was swirling some fantasy around her in his mind because he liked her voice.

"What *did* happen to you?" he said softly.

Why must he persist? *Run, Aubrey, run. I am too broken to be loved. All I love, I lose.*

And yet, here he was, this American with electric fingers and dancing limbs, sitting in a small cloud of orange lamplight. Speaking low, asking her about her life, her actual life, and waiting to hear the answer.

They were all alone in the dark. There was no one to hear them. There were dozens of ways a young man could try to take advantage of this situation. But he didn't.

So she told her story, about growing up in Dinant. About the magical village reflected like glass on the smooth waters of the Meuse River, about her happy childhood there, in the lilacs by the citadel, about her mama and papa and Alexandre; her oncles Paul and Charles; and her cousin, Gabriel. About the Rape of Belgium, and the annihilation of Dinant, about the convent, and about Stéphane.

And when she sobbed until her eyes were bloodshot and her nose ran, he gave her a handkerchief and took advantage of nothing. Nothing but the chance to say, wordlessly, *Here; you've been carrying that alone for a long time. Let me carry it with you awhile.*

Colette's story broke Aubrey's heart. Without one ounce of push from me, he opened his arms to her, and she enfolded herself in his embrace. His tears fell into her hair.

He ached to comfort her, but what could he say? "I'm here," he told her. "I've got you."

He *did* have her. For the first time in years, Colette did not feel alone.

Aubrey held her close. *Who could hurt this girl?* What devils would destroy the precious life of this lovely person—dash the happiness of this vibrant, kind, strong, funny girl?

Now he understood, as he hadn't, as deeply, before, why they needed to stop the Germans and win this war. Now he also understood that when his time came to leave Saint-Nazaire and face the trenches, it would be impossible to tell Colette goodbye, and go.

It was hard enough to say goodbye that night. The brief kiss she gave him at the door was filled with neither passion nor desire, but sweetness, affection, gratitude.

Aubrey returned a kiss to match and quietly slipped out the door.

APHRODITE

Stéphane—January 26, 1918

THAT NIGHT, COLETTE dreamed of Stéphane.

It was a simple dream. Just Stéphane, walking along with her in the grasses beside the citadel. He didn't say anything. Just smiled and held her hand, and looked at her with eyes filled with love. All that she felt in his presence—*he's alive! All those horrors were only a terrible dream!*—filled her limbs with joy and light. She knew it was real. As real as she herself.

Together they watched birds fly over the green valley and the winding river. When she turned to look at him again, he was gone.

She woke up sobbing.

Hazel heard the sound and hurried to Colette's room and lay down beside her. "It's all right," her friend said soothingly. "It's all right."

But it wasn't.

Let this soldier boy go, the Colette of yesterday told herself. *He'll soon be gone, but you'll have Stéphane forever, and that's enough. You don't need the pain of another goodbye.*

She lay there, remembering her evening with Aubrey. All the

things she couldn't believe she'd told him. All the other things she hadn't yet shared.

I don't need goodbyes, she realized, *but I need Aubrey Edwards. After tonight, I can't be a girl who doesn't have the King of Ragtime to tell everything to. I can't not be close to him. Not if he's anywhere to be found.*

ARES

Don't Shoot the Dummy—January 30, 1918

"THERE. SEE THAT?" Private Pete Yawkey spoke in a whisper, lest the Germans hear.

James swiveled his scope half an inch. "I see it."

Between a gap in the top two sandbags of the German lines, a helmet rose slightly.

James's tongue stuck to the roof of his mouth. Were they about to kill that Jerry?

"Let's see now," Yawkey said softly, talking to his target. "Are you real, or not?"

"Real?" James whispered. "How do you mean?"

"What do you see, Alderidge?"

If this was a trick question, James would fail the test. "It's a head."

"Is it? Look closer."

"A helmet," said James.

"What's under it? Quick, what's there?"

He swallowed his impatience. "A face."

"And what's it doing?"

"Nothing."

"That's right."

James had little patience for games. "It's a face," he said. "Brown-haired chap."

"I don't care about hair color," said Yawkey. "Ever see a human being hold so still?"

James looked again. "He's moving a little."

"How?"

Count to ten. "Sort of bobbing up and down. Side to side a little."

Yawkey nodded significantly. "What does that tell you?"

James looked again. "His face, itself, doesn't move," he said slowly. "He's like a statue."

"That's because he is one," Yawkey explained. "A dummy. A plaster head jammed onto the end of a bayonet with a helmet on top. They're trying to lure us into taking a shot."

James blinked and rubbed his eyes. "For spite, you mean?"

"To find us. To study the bullet angle. They'll point their artillery right at us. *Kaboom!*"

Not so funny. But most seasoned soldiers he'd met were like this. Laughing at their own destruction, casual about carnage. Maybe laughing was the only way to survive it all.

Yawkey pressed the heels of both hands into his eyes. He was a lanky, bony bird with protruding ears and a large Adam's apple. Every word of his training made James's flesh crawl.

Pete Yawkey didn't invent sniping. It wasn't his fault that James hated his every word. Everyone had their job to do. Survival depended on doing it. And the only way to end this war was to win it.

"Only shoot when you're sure," Pete said. "Don't shoot the dummy. A sniper has zero shots to waste. Every one's got to hit its target. Because it tells the enemy where you are."

He took up his rifle and peered through the scope. James watched the German lines.

At night, he and Pete were relieved by another sniper-and-spotter pair, and they got a decent amount of sleep, compared to what James had grown accustomed to. One perk, at any rate, to playing assassin.

He'd memorized each tangle of barbed wire, each crater in shell-blasted dirt, each clod and stone and bump. Each corpse. It was a colorless wasteland. Only scavenger birds moved. Yet at any moment, there could be an attack.

Their dugout was a marvel. Army tunneling engineers had dug from the fire trench into a slight rise of land. By night, a fatigue party crept into no-man's-land, cut away the covering sod, and completed the nest. They replaced the sod over a wooden frame and carefully concealed the holes the snipers used for rifles and scopes. Next morning Jerry saw nothing different.

"Hsst," Yawkey said. "See that? Three hundred yards back."

James saw what might be a tree trunk, or a gray German uniform. An officer, probably.

"Lot of activity back there lately," Pete said. "They're getting shipments of heavy ammo. They must have something planned." He flexed his fingers. "Should I take him?"

James's stomach roiled. *Don't ask me. Don't put this on me.*

The man, the gray smudge—did he have a wife? A sweetheart? Sons, daughters? Whether the rest of their lives would be joyful, or tragic, suddenly rested in James's choice.

Stall. "Can you make the shot from that far?" he asked.

"Sure." Pete's mouth hung open. He kept his open eye on the target. "Well, should I?"

Do not ask me. "That's up to you," James said. "You've got him in your crosshairs."

"I sure do." Yawkey pulled the trigger.

Of course James couldn't see the bullet spiraling across the gulf between them. But it felt like he could. Of course the German officer couldn't know that the *crack* ringing in James's ears was his own death knell. The bullet would reach him before the sound.

"Did I get him, Alderidge?" asked Yawkey.

"Yes," said James. "You did."

APOLLO

Vampire Squad—February 3, 1918

THAT SUNDAY MORNING, with a pocket of free time on his hands, Aubrey decided to walk past Hut One to see if, perhaps, a certain young relief volunteer might be on her way somewhere. She wasn't. So he circled around again, and a third time. At length even he admitted defeat and settled for a long walk into the village of Saint-Nazaire, off the base. Stretching his legs would do him good. And so would the illusion, however temporary, of freedom from others' commands.

On his way back, at a crossroads, he saw an officer approach the intersection to the right from a distance. He saluted, just in case, and moved on.

"Edwards!" A voice pulled him back to the corner.

Uh-oh. "Good morning, Captain Fish."

"At ease, Private," said Captain Hamilton Fish III. "Walk with me?"

"Yes, sir." This was unexpected.

"What were you up to this morning?"

"Just a walk, Captain, sir," he said. "A little exercise."

Captain Fish grunted. "I should think you got enough of that during the week."

Aubrey conceded. He had a point.

"Edwards," Captain Fish said, "next time you go off base, take a pal, all right?"

This hardly sounded like an order. "Sir?"

Captain Fish was slow to respond. "There have been . . . threats."

Aubrey's interest piqued. "Southern soldiers, sir?"

Fish nodded. "Well, yes. Though bigotry is hardly so simple as North versus South." He shook his head. "I've spent enough time in the officers' lounge to see that."

Aubrey suppressed a sly smile. It was good of Fish to explain bigotry to him. White *folks*.

"There are some fine, unprejudiced men too," Captain Fish added earnestly. "I've had many compliments on the discipline of our men, from officers from all over the country. I am certain that once this war is done, your courageous example will help redress that inequality."

These rich, white Harvard types. Everything they said sounded like a speech from a candidate for Congress. It was a nice thought, but if so many Americans were already angry at the sight of a black man in uniform, standing tall and proud with a gun in his hand, Aubrey doubted whether a chest full of medals would make a difference.

They'd reached the outskirts of the base.

"Still, Edwards," Captain Fish said. "You will be careful, won't you?"

"I will, but—"

"Yes, Private?"

Aubrey didn't want to seem disrespectful. "It's just, I hear you, but we're from the city, you know, Captain? We can look out for ourselves." His hand went to the Colt in his pocket.

Captain Fish clapped a hand on his shoulder. "All the same," he said firmly, "take a pal with you. Some of these boys making the threats are—well, I don't like saying it of any soldier of Uncle Sam, but—they're the scum of the earth, and that's God's truth."

There was no safe answer for Aubrey to make to this statement, so he made none.

"You're a good soldier and a fine musician," Fish said. "Don't want to lose you."

And a human being, Fish. "I'll be careful, sir," he said. "I promise."

"Good day, soldier." Captain Fish saluted.

Aubrey matched the salute. "Good day, Captain."

Captain Fish strode off another way, and Aubrey finished the journey, sauntering extra slowly past Hut One. He made his way to Camp Lusitania and the Y hut for black soldiers. There was still some time to kill before duty called him anywhere, and since being in the mood for love didn't matter one way or the other, he decided he was in the mood for ping-pong.

Joey Rice spotted him when he came in and pulled him aside into a corner.

"Did you hear?" Joey whispered. "Our boys. The ones taking revenge for the killed soldier. Calling themselves the Vampire Squad." His grip on Aubrey's elbow was tight. "They killed a marine last night."

ARES

Rotating Out—February 8, 1918

THEY WEREN'T THE same lads when they emerged from the trenches. The morning after their thirty days were finished, they stumbled out, bone-tired. They spoke a new language. Understood survival as never before and cared about it less. They were used to cold and mud, to the sounds of shells and the sight of blood. They'd gone on raids, bombing several traverses of German trench. They hadn't lost any men.

James hadn't gone on the raids. He and Private Pete Yawkey had been rotated to overnight detail, so they stayed in the snipers' nest. When, the next night, a company of Germans crept through a hole to enact revenge, James saw them. Shadows in the brief glow of a flare.

Perhaps it was because they were only shadows in the dark that James could do it. Perhaps it was because he knew they were on their way to murder his own best lads. Perhaps he could see, in his mind's eye, bowlegged Mick Webber blown against a trench wall by a grenade, or Chad Browning's singing throat slashed open by a serrated German bayonet.

He saw them, trained his scope on the shadows, and fired. Twice.

Yawkey, glued to his scope, gave him a thumbs-up. "I think you got 'em both."

James already knew he had. Somehow he had felt each bullet find its German, as if it were still connected to him by a fishing line, and he could feel the tug of impact.

The Germans came no farther. They spent the night dragging back their fallen.

"I think one's dead," Yawkey said. "From the other one's screams, I give him fifty-fifty."

James wasn't listening. He had backed away from the rifle toward the rear wall of their dugout. He knew he was breathing, but no air came in.

"I don't blame you," Yawkey said, "for not picking off the stretcher-bearers. It doesn't feel cricket. God knows the first kill is the hardest. We've all been there."

James didn't answer. He stared at his shaking hands.

"Go on," Pete said. "Find some food, and rest. Chew the fat with your mates. All right?"

"There's supposed to be two of us," said James.

Pete swatted the objection away. "Get lost. Not much for a spotter to do in the dark."

It was a lie. James didn't care. He collapsed into a dugout and slept. When he woke up, Sergeant McKendrick saluted him and shook his hand. His shooting had saved British lives. The shrewd eye to see Fritz in the dark, and the presence of mind to take out two of his raiders, halting the raid—these were the sterling qualities of a true British soldier, so proudly represented this morning by Private James Alderidge. A written commendation would be attached to his file.

So when James requested two days' leave in Paris, then and there, it was granted, provided all remained quiet at the Front. Two Germans, two days. A curious calculus. They weren't the last he'd kill before rotating out.

APHRODITE

Two Days' Leave—February 8, 1918

February 8, 1918

My dearest Hazel,

My sergeant has given me his word. I can take two days' leave to travel to Paris. I can arrive late in the afternoon of Wednesday, February 13. The trains could well be slow, but I think I could get to Gare du Nord by about four o'clock in the afternoon. Can you join me there? If you wait for me, I promise I will find you.

I hope you'll come. I need to reassure myself that you aren't a dream. I'll find a place to wash the grime off me before I see you, so that I'll be someone you won't mind being with.

Please come. Prove that you exist, and allow me to prove how much you mean to me.

Yours affectionately,

James

Hazel's answer was short. More telegram than letter.

Four o'clock, Wednesday the thirteenth, Gare du Nord, it read. I'll be there.

APHRODITE

Concert Night—February 11, 1918

ON THE EVE of their departure for the tour that would lead them to Aix-les-Bains, the 15th New York Band threw a farewell concert for Saint-Nazaire. Everyone who could finagle a seat went.

Aubrey wasn't going to Aix-les-Bains. Not after Colette had shared so much with him. He'd already told Lieutenant Europe. With Luckey Roberts at the piano, Europe could spare him. He'd rejoin the band later when their division reported to the Front. So there was no need for him to play that night's show.

Someday, he told himself, *I'll headline any band I'm in.*

He decided to go to the concert anyway, for kicks, and took the long way there, conveniently passing by Hut One on his way. If anyone in his Company had been counting how often Private Edwards took this detour, he'd have some explaining to do.

Hut One's door opened. He ducked behind a Nissen hut to see who it was.

Shoot. It was the wrinkled bat who'd shooed him away and some other old biddy beside her. He smiled. There was Lady Hazel de la Windicott. The three women left without Colette.

But where was she? Why wasn't she going to the concert? Time to find out.

"We're closed," Colette's voice called through the door when he knocked.

"It's me," he called back.

The door flew open. Pink cheeks and sparkling eyes stood before him.

"*Bonsoir, mademoiselle,*" he said. He'd been practicing that for days.

Colette laughed. His pronunciation! It was too much. "Howdy, mister."

"I want to show you something." Aubrey held out a hand. "Mind if we go to the piano?"

She took his hand. So new, and yet so familiar. She wanted to explore it, study each line in the palm, and the shape of each fingernail.

What is the matter with you?

"Come on," he teased. "To the piano."

She'd been rooted to the floor. If Colette's face were any more red, she'd be a tomato. They reached the bench.

"I need my hand back," he said.

She surrendered it unwillingly. He winked and began to play. A plaintive melody, sweet and slow, growing more melancholy until its mournful ending trailed away, leaving silence ringing through the hut.

She took a deep breath.

"I'm calling that one 'Dinant,'" he told her.

She swallowed. She already knew that.

"Thank you," she managed to say. "Was this something you'd written before?"

He shook his head. "I wrote it since I saw you last."

She shook her head. *"Formidable,"* she whispered. "Would you play it for me again?"

So he did. And now that she knew, really knew, who it was for, and what it all meant, she could absorb it, slowly, phrase by phrase.

Yes. Dinant deserved a requiem like that.

"I'm going to Paris tomorrow," she told him, after he'd played a while longer. "Hazel and I. To see her beau, Jacques. That is to say, James."

"Really?" Aubrey's face fell. "How long will you be gone?"

She pursed her lips, considering. "Four or five days, I imagine." She forced a smile. "But you're leaving tomorrow with the band, aren't you? The soldiers have been complaining about your departure for days."

He turned to face her. "I'm not going on the trip."

Her eyebrows rose. "Oh, I'm sorry!"

He smiled ruefully. "Sorry I won't be gone?"

"Of course not," she said. "Sorry for you to miss out on the opportunity to perform." She smiled. "You were born to perform."

"I sure hope so." *Now,* he thought. *Now's the time.* "I asked to be taken off the list for Aix-les-Bains," he told her.

"Why would you do that?" Her quickening pulse already knew the answer.

He gazed into her eyes, desperate to learn anything they might reveal. "I didn't want to be so far from you." *Not after all you told me. Not after that kiss.*

Hope washed over her. It hadn't only been kindness that night. Not just sympathy.

Sounds and voices from outside the hut burst my little bubble and reminded them that people would soon return from the concert to the Y hut.

"I guess I'd better go," said Aubrey.

"No," Colette said quickly. "There's something I need to tell you."

Good or bad? "Come outside, then?"

They put on their coats and went outside, while the way was still clear, and found a spot behind a shed where they could talk just a little more before the cold drove them back indoors.

The sky stretched above them, riddled with stars. Ocean breezes blew more stars ashore. It was so cold that the only sensible thing was to stand close. She stared at Aubrey's collar and tie.

"What was it you wanted to tell me?" he said gently.

"I want to thank you," she said, "for the other night. For listening."

His brown eyes studied hers. "There's nothing to thank me for," he said. "I wanted to."

Her glance darted away. *She's nervous,* Aubrey realized. He took her gloved hands in his.

"You are kind," she told him. "You were so good to listen, and to care. I—" She hesitated. "I didn't plan to burden you with all of that. It's too much."

"Much too much," he replied, "for one person to bear all alone."

She didn't trust herself to answer that. "Anyway, I wanted to thank you."

Was that what this was? A polite thank-you note? Not if Aubrey could help it.

Gently, he lifted her chin toward his. "They tell you all the time that you're beautiful, don't they?" Colette's eyes grew wide. "All these Yanks?"

Puffs of frozen breath escaped her lips. "They are not very original," she conceded.

He grinned. "Then I'm going to have to do better. Do they tell you that you sing like a goddess?"

She shook her head. "Most have never heard me sing."

"That makes me the lucky one."

Colette had all but forgotten how to breathe. But she saw where Aubrey was going, and for his sake, felt she ought to warn him.

"You see a girl who sings," she told him. "You like my voice. You might not, always. You don't hear how I wake up screaming. How I see them all in my dreams. By day I hold it together. At night. I fall apart."

It took all he had not to pull her close and hold her tight. "I wish, when it happens, I could be there to comfort you."

He realized what he'd just said. *I wish I could be there with you in the middle of the night. When and where you sleep.*

Good one, Aubrey, his mother's voice said.

Love you too, Ma.

He tried again. "I wish I could be the one to help. If I can."

The sweetness of it was too much. That purity. That hopeful innocence, to think taking on a raging mess like her would be worth it. To tantalize her into building a dream of somebody beautiful and wonderful, somebody like *him*, only to see the dream die when the ugly truth of grief and trauma took off its clothes and stood naked before him.

"There is no helping this," she told him. "That's what I'm trying to tell you."

"Mademoiselle Fournier," he said, "you've got me confused. First you won't let go of my hand, and now you're telling me to run away."

Aubrey tried to think. She was leaving tomorrow. Would she return? Would he be here when she did? No knowing. There was only now, and he was determined to make the most of it.

"I don't want you to let go of my hand," he told her. "I don't want you to push me away."

Her eyes fell shut. When she spoke, it was in a whisper. "I don't want to push you away."

"Colette," he told her. "I can love Stéphane. I can honor his memory. I can love your parents, and your brother, your uncles, your cousin. I can love them beside you, and I will, if you let me."

He wished he could say it now with music instead of words. The best words he could find just then didn't feel like much.

"Please," he told her. "Be with me. Be you, with me. All of you."

With a quiet breath, she let her fear float away upon the night, and leaned against his chest. He pulled her close and pressed his cheek against hers. *Shoot.* He should've shaved.

"When I'm with you," she told him, "it doesn't hurt as much."

He kissed her hair. "Then here is where I plan to stay."

More voices, and louder ones, clanged most unwelcomely upon them.

"Come on," he said at last, "we'd better get you indoors."

They made their way as far as they dared toward the door. Impulsively, she wrapped her arms around him.

"I'll be back soon," she told him.

He grinned. "I'll be here, waiting."

She kissed him.

Not a thank-you kiss. A kiss that said, *There's more where that came from.*

APOLLO

Trouble with Joey—February 11, 1918

AUBREY HAD WALKED in the shadows for an hour before deciding it was safe to sneak into his barracks. If his feet were cold, his brain didn't notice. He wanted to shout it from the rooftops. He, Aubrey Edwards, the King of Ragtime, the Emperor of Jazz, was the luckiest dog in the world. The heavenly Colette Fournier had kissed him tonight! Kissed him like she meant it.

When the lights in the barrack windows had been out for a while, Aubrey used the latrine, then crept to his quarters. Quiet as a cat, he jimmied the flimsy lock and let himself in. He relocked the door, untied his boots, and tiptoed to his bunk. No point taking off his coat, so he crawled under the blanket.

The bed above him creaked. Joey Rice hung his head down over the edge.

"You got a death wish, Edwards? Is that what you've got?"

"Shh!"

"You're gonna get your butt kicked all the way back to Harlem, if they don't send you home in a box."

"G'night, Joey."

"Don't think they're not onto you. The officers know."

Aubrey sat up at that. "Why, were you wagging your tongue about it?"

"That's right. Blame me."

The sounds of other soldiers stirring in their sleep made them pause.

"You think you're so smart," Joey went on, when it seemed safe. "These other boys ain't blind and dumb, jackass. They know you're stepping out. I sure hope you're getting something good out of it, for the price it's gonna cost you."

"Good *night*, Joey. And you watch your mouth."

"Defending his lady's honor. Ain't that sweet."

"Mind your business," Aubrey told him.

"You make it my business, every time you're stupid, which is *all* the time."

Aubrey snuggled down under his blanket. Maybe if he ever thawed out, he could get some sleep. If sleep was even possible on a night like tonight.

"Now you got me wide-awake," complained Joey. "I gotta take a leak or I'll never sleep." He swung himself off the top bunk, stuffed his feet into his boots, and made his way to the door.

"Don't fall in," Aubrey said.

Warmth had begun, and his eyes closed. He couldn't possibly sleep, but maybe, maybe he could remember Colette, and compose a perfect dream.

HADES

Vertigo—February 11, 1918

AUBREY WOKE. It was still dark. Had he slept through a whole day? No, it was still night.

He dangled in time. The sounds of sleeping soldiers all around him pulled him back to earth like a tether, while the horrid vertigo of wrenching from dreaming to consciousness made his head spin.

He'd heard something. It must have been a dream.

No, he'd heard something. And now he didn't hear anything. Something was wrong.

He lay there, waiting for up and down to stabilize.

What was missing?

He leaned an arm over the edge of his bunk and groped at the floor. There were his boots. He sat up, almost whacking his head on Joey's bunk.

Joey.

He reached upward and poked at the coils underneath Joey's bunk. The mattress bounced easily. Joey wasn't in his bed.

His boots weren't on the floor.

Aubrey rubbed his eyes and climbed out from the under the blankets. Must be he'd only been asleep a couple of minutes, and

Joey was still using the latrine. Sleep was misleading. A little could feel like a lot, and a lot could feel like a little.

Aubrey pushed his feet back into his boots and edged toward the door. His brain seemed to slosh in his skull. The night had the crawling-through-molasses unreality of a hallucination.

He was outside. All about him was darkness and trodden snow. The stars overhead felt sterile now. He followed his nose toward the latrine.

What little light there was painted the ground a deep shade of blue. The outhouse rose up before him like a foul-smelling mountain.

"Joey?" he called softly. "Joey, man, where are you?"

But there was no sound except the distant bark of a village dog.

He knocked on the door. No one answered. He pulled the door open.

A figure came out. Fell out. Toppled into Aubrey's arms.

His foot slipped out from beneath him, and he landed in the snow with the other man on top of him. Warm, and still, and dripping something wet onto Aubrey's cheek.

"Joey?" Aubrey said. "Joey?"

HADES

Torchlight—February 11, 1918

AUBREY PELTED THROUGH the snow. His arms windmilled. His feet slipped. He reached the door to Lieutenant Europe's quarters and pounded.

A voice inside muttered. Let Jim curse him to the skies, but he had to *come, now.*

The door opened. An electric torch blasted his face.

"Aubrey?" Jim Europe's voice was thick with sleep. "What the hell are you doing here?"

"You gotta come, Jim," Aubrey said. "It's Joey."

"What's the matter with him?" Lieutenant Europe fumbled in the pocket of his robe for his spectacles. "Shouldn't you call Captain Fish?"

Aubrey seized Europe's wrist. "You gotta come, Jim," he begged. "Please!"

"Is Joey hurt?" Europe demanded. "What's happened?"

"Shh!"

Europe grabbed his coat. "C'mon. Show me."

Lieutenant Europe's torchlight swung wildly across the ice as they ran. Until it found Joey lying in the snow.

"Oh no."

Europe's light searched Joey from head to toe. He'd been—maybe—please, God—sick? Drunk? A little roughed up?

But that was blood on the snow.

His head. His face. His bloated, blackened face.

Aubrey fell to his knees. His body jackknifed, and he vomited.

Europe knelt beside Joey. He felt his wrist and then his neck.

"Bastards strangled him." His voice was deep with grief. "Beat his face in with their rifles. You almost wouldn't know it's him."

Hope.

"Maybe it isn't," Aubrey said. "Maybe it's somebody else!"

"Aubrey. Don't do this."

False hope.

"This is my fault," Aubrey told the night. "This is all my fault."

"We've got to get him out of here," Europe said. "Clean this up. Leave no trace."

"My fault," Aubrey repeated. "I'm the one who did it."

Jim Europe shone his torch directly at Aubrey's face. He squinted.

"Are you telling me, son, that you strangled Joey, then clubbed him with your rifle butt?"

Joey. Joey. Knucklehead Joe.

"*Are* you?"

Aubrey had already forgotten the question.

"If I hadn't gone out, Joey wouldn't have . . . It was me they were following. . . ."

The crack of a large leather hand across his cheek jolted him awake.

"Pull yourself together, soldier," Europe barked. "That's an order."

Europe did what he could for Joey. Wiped the blood off his face.

Gently closed his gaping lower lip to hide the horribly broken jaw.

"'Death, where is thy sting?'" Bitter irony laced itself through Jim Europe's recitation. "'Grave, where is thy victory?' Right here. That's where."

He waved his torch at Aubrey. "Grab his feet. We'll get him back to my quarters." Aubrey nodded dumbly. They'd just been talking. Only just. Messing around like usual. To carry his feet and touch that hardening, chilling thing that used to be Joey Rice? How?

"Look, kid, we're in danger too, all right? Grab his feet and let's get outta here."

Aubrey picked up Joey's ankles and pinned them under his elbows. Lieutenant Europe hefted up the upper body. They staggered back to Europe's quarters. Joey Rice's body drooped like wet laundry.

Lieutenant Europe switched on the light. Fumbling with the weight, he managed to spread a towel over his bed before they laid Joey down upon it.

Aubrey backed away from the bed. "Should I get a doctor, Jim?"

Europe's always-intense gaze searched Aubrey's face. "It's a bit late for that now."

"But what if we're wrong about that?" Aubrey panted. "What if there's something we don't see, and they can fix him up?"

Europe pulled up a stool from a writing desk in one corner.

"Sit down, son," he ordered. "Put your head between your knees."

Aubrey darted for the door. "I can't do that; I gotta get help."

Europe blocked Aubrey's exit like a cinder-block wall. "Sit *down*." He took a flask and poured him an inch of something. "Drink this." He handed him the glass.

Aubrey stared into the swirling resin-colored liquid. "I don't really drink," he mumbled. "Not much of one for—"

"Drink it."

It burned and stung his already wounded throat.

Europe found a sheet and draped it over Joey. Then he sat at the foot of the bed.

"Now," he said slowly, "tell me exactly what you mean when you say this is all your fault, and you're the one who did it."

Aubrey didn't know it, but he was beginning to shake.

Lieutenant Europe, with some effort, pulled a blanket out from under Joey's body. He wrapped it around Aubrey. He fished a chocolate bar from his desk and thrust it at him. "Eat this."

When Aubrey finally became still, Europe tried again.

"Aubrey," he said gently. "I've known you for a long time, all right? You can trust me. I need you to tell me what happened. Unless you yourself choked and clubbed my cornet player to death, you've got nothing to fear from me. Tell me everything. All right?"

The sheet, covering Joey's feet. Just as if he were asleep in bed.

He owed it to Joey to tell the truth. No matter what they did to him. They could do the worst, and it'd be nothing he didn't deserve.

"I was out after lights-out," Aubrey whispered. "Seeing a girl."

Europe kept quiet.

"I've gone there before," he said. "Once, a white soldier stopped me. A marine, I think. Pulled a gun. Threatened to teach me a lesson about laying my hands on white women."

Whatever Europe thought of this, Aubrey was not to know.

"I got the guy's gun away from him," Aubrey said. "And I didn't stop going out to see my girl. Joey always warned me that I shouldn't. Sometimes he covered for me."

"You didn't think your attacker would come back?"

Aubrey looked up. "He was a coward. Figured I'd shown him we weren't gonna put up with that. Whatever he was used to down South."

Europe's voice was low. "Go on."

"I was out tonight, with my girl," Aubrey said. "I think they followed me home. Must've been a bunch of them. I stopped to use the latrine, then went to my barrack. When I came in, Joey went out to use the latrine. See, I'd woken him up."

"And that's where you found him?"

Aubrey nodded. "I must've fallen asleep," he said. "But I woke up all of a sudden. Something wasn't right. When I realized Joey wasn't in his bed, I went looking for him."

Jim Europe allowed his head to droop. "Poor kid," he murmured. "Poor kid."

Aubrey clutched the blanket. Grief hit him like a sledgehammer, and he began to cry. Lieutenant Europe handed him a clean handkerchief. The kindness only made Aubrey cry harder.

"It's my fault," he said again. "I'm the one who should've got it."

"Listen up, Aubrey Edwards," Europe said, "and listen good."

Aubrey blinked. His nose was inches from Europe's.

"Going out at night was against the rules, and you *ought* to get in trouble for that."

Aubrey nodded. Consequences were coming. It was only fair.

"Going out at night when you knew killers were hunting for you wasn't your best idea."

Aubrey nodded. God, if only he hadn't be so damnably stupid.

"Some of you city boys have no idea what we who grew up down South understand."

He sounded just like Aubrey's dad.

"But let's get this straight. You're not the one who should've gotten killed. Joey shouldn't have gotten killed. Nobody should've been killed. A black man's got as much right to live, and see a girl, and go to the toilet, for Chrissake, as anyone else."

Europe's words crashed down like a wave, and then, like a wave, they slipped back out to sea. If Aubrey was supposed to find any comfort in them, it didn't last.

Jim Europe paced back and forth, thinking. Aubrey watched the still form of Joey, under the draped sheet. How odd it was that not the slightest breath or movement stirred the sheet. Because he was dead. Over and over, the surprise of it clawed at him.

"What happens now?" Aubrey asked.

Jim Europe took off his robe and began changing into his uniform. "First thing," he said, "you're telling nobody what happened. Understand?"

Aubrey sat up. "You think people aren't going to notice him missing?"

Jim fed a leg into his trousers. "He's sick," he said. "You helped him to the infirmary."

"You mean, you're going to hush this up and let those bastards get away with it?"

Jim Europe's look reminded Aubrey that he was speaking to a superior officer. It was harder to remember that when the superior officer was buttoning his trousers over his union suit.

"I'm letting nobody get away with anything," Europe said in a heavy tone, "but I'll handle it my way. I'm not going to add to this Hatfield–McCoy devilry. 'An eye for an eye' doesn't get us to the Front, and we didn't come here to play soldier with marines." He fastened his socks to his garters. "As for you, you're getting on that train this morning for Aix-les-Bains."

Leaving? He wasn't supposed to. Colette. "I wasn't on the roster."

"You are now."

Colette stood, a silhouette in the light at the end of a long, long corridor. Small, like a statuette. As he watched, the hallway stretched longer and longer until she disappeared.

Joey should be alive right now. If someone had to die, it should be the reckless one who ignored the rules and brought destruction down on an innocent man. A guy who would sacrifice his friend's life so he could sneak out to see a girl didn't deserve to live.

"Send your girl a letter when we arrive, but I'm getting you out of this mess."

He knew it. Before he even found the body or discovered Joey missing. That disorienting feeling in his sleep. This was the message it had been trying to send.

Of course it was. I sent it to him. It was no boon, but I needed to prepare him. Wrapping him in confusion was more merciful than leaving him with full faculties to face the stark truth.

He had stumbled upon my gates. I am gracious to my guests.

Lieutenant Europe poured Aubrey a refill. "I've got a lot to do before sunup, and you'd best not be around for any of it. Get back to bed, and sleep if you can. We leave at seven." He handed Aubrey the glass. "Drink that. You'll need it."

Aubrey drank the burning cup and followed his feet out into the snow, back to his barracks. Last time he'd returned to this door, Colette's kiss still hung on his lips. That aliveness, that joy that he felt beside her, the music, the possibilities—they all slipped down beneath the undertow pulling Aubrey Edwards to Aix-les-Bains and far away from his own soul.

HADES

Homecoming

ACUTE TRAUMA TO the head swells the brain, choking off those parts that control breathing and heartbeat. Before the brutes had quite finished killing Joey Rice, he slid from terror into insensibility. His body, realizing no recovery was possible, swiftly implemented its self-destruct procedure, releasing it host, the soul, from any further fear or pain.

Untethered, unbound, and still unconscious, the soul of Joseph Rice winged its way across the portals of earth and eternity, and arrived at my doors.

He opened his eyes, his true eyes, and found himself in a grassy field dotted with small white flowers. Bigger by far than Central Park. Birds sang. A warm breeze wrapped itself around him and rustled the boughs of nearby trees.

He found his feet on a path that led to a familiar door. He opened it and went inside.

It was his home in Harlem. His parents' flat. There was his mother at the table, doing her nightly crossword puzzle. Beside her sat his father, replacing a guitar string. They shared a bowl of popcorn between them on the table. A photograph of Joey in a jacket and tie stood on the mantel.

"Mom," he called. "Dad. How're you doing?"

They didn't look up.

He stood by the table. "Mom, Dad! It's me, Joe!"

I joined him. No footsteps, but he knew I was there. He didn't look. "What's going on?"

It's better, I find, to let liberated souls figure things out at their own pace.

"Am I dead?"

He turned toward me. I'd taken the form of his dead grandfather, but Joey wasn't fooled.

"Does it feel like you are?" I asked him.

"No," he said. "What was that grassy place?"

"Asphodel," I told him. "Do you like it?"

He seemed unwilling to admit that there is anything to like about being dead. This is common and does not offend me.

"Tell me straight. I'm dead, aren't I?"

"You are."

"Then why am I here?"

"It's where you wanted to be."

He turned back to his folks. He knelt beside his mother and stroked her hair.

"I'm sorry, Ma," he told her. "I'm so sorry. I said I'd always look after you."

She didn't notice a thing. She did, however, decipher a tricky clue.

Joey's father got the new string tested and tuned. He fingered a few experimental chords to make sure the strings were in agreement. Joey squeezed his father's shoulders.

"Dad," he whispered. "I didn't make it."

His father began a song in earnest. "*I looked over Jordan, and what did I see, coming for to carry me home . . . ?*"

Joey turned to me once more. "It's going to kill them when they get the news," he said. "Especially if they hear how it happened. Dad's heart might not hold up. And Ma—"

He began to cry. I am so often moved by souls whose first concern is not for their own lost years, but for the grief their passing will cause to those they love. It's more common than you might think. The most ordinary mortal bodies are housed by spectacular souls.

"*Swing low, sweet chariot, comin' for to carry me home,*" sang Joey's father.

Joey knelt beside his father and rested his head on his knee.

"Somebody's got to warn them," he insisted, "so the news doesn't destroy them."

"It sounds good in theory," I told him, "but in practice, where death is concerned, it's quite tricky to pull off."

"Somebody's got to look after them," Joey said. "It'll be hard for them for years to come."

"Why not you?"

He stopped and looked at me. "Could it be me?"

I nodded. "Of course."

"Don't I have "—he gestured broadly—"things I'm supposed to be doing?"

I smiled. "Not strumming harps, or stoking fires, if that's what you mean."

I liked Joey Rice.

"What else happens here?" he asked. "In Heaven, or the afterlife, or whatever?"

I rose to leave. "The options," I told him, "are practically infinite. And you have all the time you could wish for to explore them. But anytime you like, you can rest in Asphodel."

Joey sat in a chair between his mother and father. "I think I'll stay here awhile."

"Stay as long as you like," I told him. "I should warn you: it won't be easy."

"Wait," he said. "Am I supposed to be judged? Have my soul weighed, or whatever it is? Good or bad? Should I be worried about that?"

I shook his hand before leaving the room. "It was a very brief examination," I told him. "You've already passed."

ENTR'ACTE

Three Trains—February 12–13, 1918

APOLLO

ONE TRAIN TOOK the 15th New York Band to Nantes, where they kicked off their tour with a standing-room only concert in the opera house. They played French military marches, "Stars and Stripes Forever," and plantation melodies.

"Then came the fireworks," drum major Noble Sissle recorded. "'The Memphis Blues.'

"Colonel Hayward has brought this band over here and started ragtimitis in France; ain't this an awful thing to visit upon a nation with so many burdens?" wrote Sissle. But when "The Memphis Blues" was over, the audience roared, and Sissle made a discovery. "This," he wrote, "is just what France needs."

Which is precisely why I had brought them there.

Aubrey Edwards, however, missed the whole show. He lay curled like a cocoon in the backseat of an empty car on the train.

APHRODITE

Hazel and Colette boarded a noon train from Saint-Nazaire, bound for Paris, with nothing but excitement and fun on their minds. It would be midnight before they reached Paris.

They passed the time with a game Colette invented. "What's Your Secret?" As passengers, porters, conductors, and waiters passed by, Colette and Hazel spied on them and then proposed to each other what each stranger's secret might be. A stout, stern woman, Colette declared, suffered an unrequited passion for her dentist. A miserly looking old man, Hazel decided, wept nightly over the grave of his childhood goldfish. A blue-eyed soldier was a German spy. A forlorn young woman in a fine but faded coat was a Russian Romanov princess in exile.

Laughter was just what Hazel needed. She was a mass of nerves and butterflies, but they only added to the thrill of anticipation. Mortals curse me for the jitters of love, but I overlook it. Such delightful terror proved to Hazel that she was alive.

It's what I do best.

ARES

At dawn, James took a supply line from a few miles behind the lines to a depot in Bapaume. From there, a southbound train took him to Paris. It was a ride of about five hours.

He watched the signs of war slip away behind him until all that was left was countryside. Even frost-covered, it was painted with rich colors. He marveled that color still existed, that there was anyplace left on the planet not scarred by shell holes.

He wished he could peel off the war like a scab. All he wanted now was to be was a chap with a lovely girl at his side. Even if his uniform was all he had to wear.

(They never just send me soldiers. They send me heartaches.)

The warmth of the train car, its lulling rhythms, and a month of sleep deprivation pulled James under. He didn't even realize he'd fallen asleep until the conductor jolted him awake by declaring they had reached Paris.

ACT THREE

APHRODITE

Gare du Nord—February 13, 1918

I'D WAITED MONTHS for this. I was not about to leave anything to chance.

In all that vast metropolis, Hazel and James approached each other. Two needles in an enormous haystack. How easily they might have missed each other! But I was the magnet at the center. The nearer they drew, the stronger my hold upon them.

I flitted back and forth between them like a sparrow. Find the restroom, James; your face needs washing. Hurry along, Hazel, but not too fast; James needs to clean his face. Colette, buy that poor girl a flower. She's as gray as her coat. Find some water, James. It's been a long ride. Perhaps a mint while you're at it. Breathe, Hazel. This is no time to pass out. Smile, James; you're about to see Hazel. Don't worry, Hazel. It'll all be fine.

I like to keep a little bit of nervousness simmering. It keeps mortals alert at crucial moments. Sensitive to every detail. It imprints lasting memories. These moments belong to forever.

Everything now depended on *this* moment. When they saw each other, would they see their heart's desire? Or a stranger they'd imagined they were fond of in a brief moment of loneliness?

At four p.m., by the clock over the door to the terminal, Hazel approached the grand stone façade of Gare du Nord, the largest and busiest train station in Europe. It was *enormous*. It made her feel like a mouse, going in. Small, insignificant, and about as attractive.

She'd slept and bathed at Colette's aunt's flat. Colette made all decisions involving clothing and hair, as Hazel was, herself, completely incapable of thought. On their way, Colette bought a pink rose from a street vendor and pinned it onto her friend's gray coat. When they reached the plaza outside Gare du Nord, Colette kissed both of Hazel's cheeks.

"I'll be in this café across the street with a book," she explained. "If he hasn't come in an hour, come find me. If you don't find me, I'll see you back at Tante Solange's this evening."

Hazel took a deep breath and went inside.

The grand entryway was dim in the late afternoon. Up ahead, the glass-and-iron train shed glowed with golden sunlight reflecting off the mist from steam engines. Train after train lined up in the shed, while thousands of disgorged people poured around her like water around a stone.

It's so big, she thought. *I'll never find him.*

French soldiers in their gray-blue uniforms and British soldiers in khaki were everywhere. Tradesmen and laborers, porters and conductors and engineers, businessmen and politicians, and mothers and children. James could walk right by her and never see her.

Where was the best place to see and be seen? Did she look pathetic and conspicuously desperate, standing right in the center of the station?

That's not what James thought when he saw her.

He emerged from a second trip to the lavatory, rechecking his tie. It was 4:02. The terminal swarmed with people, but her stillness at the center drew his eye. There she was.

He stood a moment, watching her. That was her. That was the shape of her nose; he'd forgotten. Her hair was a bit different; her coat and hat were the same. She'd traded her dark blue wool muffler for a thinner, finer scarf of rose-colored silk (*merci*, Colette), and pink certainly was her color. Against the teeming backdrop of the vast station, she shone like an angel. Her cheeks were flushed, her face anxious, adorable, and dear as she watched for him to appear. For *him*.

He should go to her. He shouldn't prolong her waiting. But he couldn't move.

That there were females in the world! After weeks at the Front, they were a forgotten miracle, these beings who smelled clean and pleasant, and wore bright colors, and did not go about killing one another!

It wasn't sex on his mind. Not lust. More of a baffled reverence. Like a child's first sight of a Christmas tree. But give me time, and I'd supply whatever was lacking.

This girl had traveled all the way across France to spend a day and a half with him.

That he should be the reason this lovely girl was here felt like an outrage, a lie, an offense against nature. He had fleabites all along his ankles. The skin of his feet, where he hadn't removed boots for weeks, looked like cheese. He should take the duffel bag he'd borrowed from Frank Mason, turn around, and get right back on the next train north to Bapaume.

Enough, James. Enough.

All right, Hazel. Look to your right.

She turned. She saw him.

What is it about uniforms? What magic spell do they cast? The service dress hat, the trench coat, the tunic with its brass buttons—to see it all draped over her boy from the parish dance, from J. Lyons tea shop, and the Royal Albert Hall—prepare herself how she might, she was slain by the uniform. She wasn't the first. (The current war's getup has much more sex appeal if you ask me, and you should.)

Even before Hazel dared to smile, her face lit up, and she took a step toward him. James knew then that, outrage or no, he was *not* getting back on that train. Ever, if he could help it.

APHRODITE

Archimedes—February 13, 1918

IT WAS ARCHIMEDES of Syracuse who first said that the shortest distance between two points was the straight line connecting them. Far be it from me to ever cast a shadow upon the wisdom of a Golden Age Greek, but Archimedes had it wrong. The length of the straight line between two people who don't dare admit they're in love is infinite. Especially after months apart.

But they got there eventually.

They stood, face-to-face. Still young, still whole, still beautiful.

And yet, changed—each a little leaner. More experienced. More complicated.

Neither of them could remember a word of English.

That Hazel. You see why I am so very fond of her. She got past that problem in a trice and flung her arms around James. She left him no choice but to wrap his arms around her and hold her close. Hesitation is not an option in a full-body tackle. Her hatpins and hairpins gave way, and he buried his face in her unraveling hair. After weeks of her being an idea, a memory, a dream, and some bits of paper, here she was, warm and real, holding on to him as if she was afraid to let go.

In truth, she was. But all hugs must end, so they pulled apart, just a little. That hurt too much, so he rested his forehead and nose upon hers. Sometimes happiness is just about more than a body can bear.

Was this the moment? Would there be a kiss? All three of us were thinking it.

Not yet.

Fine. I'd waited this long; I could wait a little longer. At this rate, James's entire Paris leave would be spent standing in this very spot.

"Are you hungry?" Hazel asked him. "Tired? You must want to lie down."

James was a gentleman, and his thoughts were pure.

"Not even," he said. "I want to do everything. See everything. With you." He pressed a hand over his belly. "Eat everything too."

"Come on, then." Hazel threaded her fingers through his. "Let's get started."

He set off to keep pace with her, then halted and drew her close.

"You came," he whispered. "You really came."

What does a girl say in response to so much feeling? The wrong thing, of course.

"Well, you asked me to." Her eyes sparkled.

There was no wrong thing she could say.

"Hello, Hazel."

She blushed. "Right. Hello, James." She grinned. "I got it a bit out of order, didn't I?"

"No." James couldn't help smiling. He'd almost forgotten how. "Not at all."

"*Food,*" she said. "Time won't keep."

We'd see about that.

APHRODITE

Café du Nord—February 13, 1918

AT A TABLE near the window of La Café du Nord, directly across Rue de Dunkerque from the train station, sat Colette. A server brought her a cup of *chocolat*, set it next to her unopened book, and asked what she was doing later on. She answered with a vague smile and took a sip. Not bad.

She watched the train station. It was too soon, no doubt, for Hazel to have found her beau yet. Trains had become wildly unpredictable ever since the war had begun. She should start reading.

Et voilà. There, exiting the station, were Hazel and a young man, arm in arm. He was tall, dressed in a British soldier's uniform, and he had no eyes whatsoever for the charms of Paris, even as it began to light its evening lamps. He focused entirely upon Hazel.

Bon, she thought. *Hazel a trouvé son Jacques.*

She finished her chocolate, read a page, and found her attention refused to comply. So she left a few coins and headed for her aunt's flat.

If only Aubrey were here with her tonight, she thought. Even a citizen of the grand New York metropolis would find much to enjoy in la Ville Lumière. Paris was made for two.

Almost, Colette Fournier envied her charming English friend that night. But, she considered, tomorrow Hazel would need to bid her Jacques goodbye, whereas in a few day's time she could return to Aubrey. She would need to offer Hazel comfort when the time came.

APHRODITE

Saint-Vincent-de-Paul—February 13, 1918

GREETINGS ACCOMPLISHED, love and longing gave way to the awkward business of making a plan.

They exited the train station, and James got his first glimpse of Paris. Even after four years of war, its hardships, its labor shortages, the city was a sight to see.

People were everywhere. Soldiers and officers in uniform. Buses full of wounded, headed to hospitals. Couples arm in arm, and older men smoking in doorways. Everywhere, lights twinkled. Music could be heard wafting from somewhere.

"Do you want to go walking?" asked James. "See a show? Maybe there's a concert?"

"We need to feed you," Hazel said.

James glanced back at the train station clock. "Supper? Now? It's not even five o'clock."

She steered him across the street. "There's a covered market," she said. "Let's get something and call it tea. Later we'll find a restaurant. Colette's aunt made a list."

"So, you're staying with Colette and her aunt?"

Hazel nodded. "You are too." She gave him a nudge. "I'm a guest, but you'll have to pay rent."

The same place as Hazel! "Are you sure? I figured on a hotel."

"I had to assure Colette's aunt that you were a gentleman," Hazel teased, "so you'd better not prove me wrong."

They reached the food market, Marché Couvert Saint-Quentin, and explored the stalls. They settled on warm rolls and a bag of roasted nuts. Poor James didn't realize, quite, how eagerly he inhaled his food. Manners died in the trenches. But Hazel was glad to see him eat.

She studied the map. When she looked up, he presented her with a bouquet of pink roses.

"What's this?" she cried. Behind him, a flower cart with signs reminded *les hommes* not to forget *la Saint-Valentin*. A stout, aproned vendor was grinning at her.

"Will you be my valentine, Miss Hazel Windicott?"

She inhaled the perfume of the roses. "Well," she said, "only because no one else appears willing to take the post."

This girl. James wanted to laugh out loud. He'd been so worried, that somehow the easiness he'd felt with her in London couldn't survive their time apart. He couldn't get enough of her.

Would she feel the same, when she knew his deeds of war?

At least, he thought, he could enjoy these moments now.

The sun had set by the time they headed northwest on Boulevard de Magenta. James carried his duffel bag and the sack of rolls. Hazel cradled her roses like a kitten in her arms.

They turned onto Rue la Fayette and soon came to a square containing a grand church. It dwarfed the buildings around it. Situated on a rise of ground, the gray stone basilica was flanked by two grand clock towers. Carved saints, beggars, and angels looked down upon them. In terraced gardens, the stalks of last year's weeds shivered in the wind. The war. Everything nonessential was neglected.

Hazel watched James thoughtfully. "You need to come back to Paris," she said, "and spend a year looking at buildings, don't you?"

The thought of becoming an architect seemed buried in the trenches with the war dead.

"That'd be brilliant," he said. "But it wouldn't be any fun if you weren't there too."

That caught my notice. When Forever Talk enters into the conversation, I'm all ears. Or even Long-Term Talk. Things were moving along swimmingly.

Two blushing young people climbed the steps up to l'Église Saint-Vincent-de-Paul.

"Colette says," said Hazel, feeling a change in subject might be needed, "this church is well worth seeing. Some fine artwork inside, and a splendid organ."

"Will you play the organ?"

She gave him a look. "You don't just waltz in and play the organ anytime you please."

They passed through the portico and entered the sanctuary.

"Oh my," whispered Hazel.

By the soft light of hanging lamps, they beheld the grandeur of l'Église de Saint-Vincent-de-Paul.

Two rows of grand columns ran on either side of the length of the vast sanctuary, and a second level of columns from an upper gallery extended to the beautifully carved ceiling. Gorgeous paintings adorned the walls and the domed apse. The paintings, heavily gilded, gleamed in the lamplight, suffusing the space with a somber glow.

They strolled along the corridor that led behind the nave to a secluded chapel. Chapelle de la Vierge. The Virgin Mary's chapel. A private place one might go to pray.

James dropped his duffel bag and sat. He watched Hazel curiously examine the sculptures and stained glass, and smiled. Then she realized he'd sat down and returned to sit beside him.

"It's really something, isn't it?"

He nodded. "Magnificent."

She watched his face earnestly. "I thought, maybe, after your time at the Front, in all that dirt and smoke, that something very beautiful might be just what you needed to see."

He wrapped his arm around her and pulled her close. "You were right."

"I wasn't fishing for a compliment," she said indignantly.

"You'll have to take it, all the same."

"Hmph."

The windows darkened as night settled over Paris. It made the lamplight both brighter and smaller, as the upper echelon of the sanctuary slid into darkness.

"It's good to see something that was lovingly and carefully made," he said at length. "The war makes it feel as though all humans have ever done is destroy."

She leaned against his shoulder. "Is it quite terrible?"

All he wanted to think about was her. Not the trenches.

"It is," he said. "But I don't think I've seen the worst of it yet."

She turned to look him in the eye. "I hope you have."

"Tell you what," he said. "Let's you not go back to Saint-Nazaire, and me not go back to the Front. Let's just stay here, looking at things. All right? Let's not let this end."

She smiled. "All right."

He laughed. "You only say that because you know I don't mean it."

"You can't mean it," she said. "But you would if you could."

She understood him so quickly, so completely, so naturally. It almost frightened him. If she understood all that he felt for her, would it frighten her?

"Do you know," he said, his words tumbling out, "I was afraid to come see you."

She watched him with eyes brimming with concern.

"I didn't know how it would be," he said quickly. "I didn't know if what we felt—what you felt—what I hoped you had—could survive. If it had even been real, or if I'd imagined it."

She nodded. "I understand."

"But here you are. It's as if we've been together every day."

Something, Hazel knew, pressed heavily upon him.

"There hasn't been a day," she said, "when I haven't thought of you."

His eyes searched her face. The time was now. Please, God, not now, but it was now.

"Hazel," he said. "I'm a sharpshooter."

Those wide eyes, with their long, dark lashes, swept open and shut, open and shut.

Concealment was past. He'd ripped a hole in her picture of him. She would leave. She might as well know all the reasons why.

"I've killed six Germans," he said. "That I know of for certain. Shot them in cold blood."

Now she would recoil in horror.

Might as well hurry her along the path she must unavoidably follow. "Left wives widowed," he said quickly. "Children orphaned. Parents brokenhearted. Shot them as they mended fences or cooked their dinner."

Speak. Tell me you never want to see me again. But say it quickly.

This wasn't how he had intended to tell her. He knew he must, but at least, he could've enjoyed a bit more of her company, selfishly and unapologetically, before ruining everything.

And Hazel?

What did she see?

Her beautiful James, more beautiful than ever in the golden light, grief-stricken by what duty demanded of him. What war demanded. *Should* war or duty have such power? The war, she saw, killed more than those whose families received telegrams.

Six lives taken. Nothing, she knew, that she could do or say to offer comfort would erase that pain. It would never leave him. And he, so young.

She rose and walked slowly back toward the corridor leading toward the church offices, leaving her roses behind.

There she goes. James closed his eyes. Then opened them again, because he would rather hurt than *not* watch her walk away.

But she didn't leave, not yet. She stopped near an office door and spoke to a black-robed cleric. She took some coins from her pocketbook and gave one to the cleric. A donation on the way out. But then the cleric gave her something, and she returned to James.

Hope and despair choked him. He didn't know how to look at her.

She held out her hand. "Come with me."

He took her hand and followed her. She led him toward a rack of glass votive jars at the front of Mary's chapel. The glass jars were red, and candles flickered in a few of them. She opened her parcel and a book of matches. From the parcel she took one candle, which she handed to James.

"For the first German." She gave him the matches. He hesitated, and she nudged him. "Light it."

With shaking hands he struck the paper match. It took two or three tries before orange flame overtook its woven threads. He carefully lowered the candle into an empty jar and placed it on the rack. As the little flame grew more self-assured, the red glass began to glow.

Hazel handed him another candle. "For the second German."

He struck another match and lit the candle. Hazel stayed by him. He placed his second candle beside the first, already burning brightly, its filament of smoke rising like a soul to God.

The rack of candles swam before his eyes, a sea of bobbing golden lights in a field of red.

"For the third German."

He scrubbed the tears off his cheeks with his fingers, and they ruined the next match. He had to try another. He lit the third candle and set it beside its brothers.

He lit the fourth candle, and the fifth. For each, a life. For each, a light. He filled an entire shelf in the candle rack with flickering flame. He saw his hands strike the matches and remembered: these hands pulled the trigger. He knew he was openly weeping now, and that Hazel saw him, but it didn't matter; nothing mattered; he didn't matter.

He covered his eyes with his hands.

"There will be more," he whispered, "before I'm through. How many candles will I need to light, if I ever make it home?"

She took the book of matches from his pocket, struck one, and lit the last candle, then gently peeled his right hand off his face and placed the candle in his palm.

"For the sixth German."

He placed the candle in a jar, set it on the rack, and watched them all burn. Slow currents of air bent the flames to the left, to the right. Gracefully, like a flock of starlings in flight.

APHRODITE

Le Bouillon Chartier—February 13, 1918

POOR MORTALS. I feel for them. That evening in Paris couldn't be described in its full richness, its second-by-split-second splendor, not if they spent decades trying to tell it. And that's just *one* of their nights. They rack them up by the thousands, yet they still get up each morning and tie their shoes. You have to admire them. They are so very brave to keep on living.

Take a kiss, for instance—

But wait; I'm getting ahead of myself.

Hazel managed to lead James, with her map, on a long ramble through the city. Eventually they arrived at le Bouillon Chartier, a restaurant Colette's aunt had recommended. Red tablecloths, warm light, ample food, no royal pedigree required, and generous patience for *les anglais*. The waiter situated them in a corner booth in the upper deck, took their order, and left them, knowingly, in peace. I rarely need to intervene with French waitstaff. They're my people.

Hazel scooted over next to James and sat close to him. He was left with no choice but to drape his arm over her shoulder, and of course he didn't mind.

"It wasn't you," she said. "You didn't kill those poor soldiers any more than I did."

How could he be plucked from the trenches and whisked to this warm Paris restaurant with the dearest, kindest girl close beside him, offering balm for his wounds?

"The world's gone mad," she said. "It's as if the nations of Europe are . . . I don't know . . . lions, or dragons, savage beasts with cruel intentions of their own. It's not you, and it's not me. It's the dragon, locked in combat with the other dragons. And all we can do is watch, and try not to be stepped on or burned."

"I'm not merely watching," he said.

"This analogy is pretty shabby, come to think of it," she admitted. "I was never good at metaphors in composition." She tapped her chin. "You are the, um, you are one of the dragon's claws. Which you have to be, or else they will throw you in jail for not being a claw. . . ." She sighed. "Maybe you'd have to be a fire-breathing nostril. I give up. But it's still not your fault."

"A nostril," he said. "I've been called worse."

"If you had to be a nostril," she said, "I think a dragon's would have a certain clout."

"A certain snout?"

She made a face at him. "Did you know your jokes are terrible?"

He nodded. "That's how I like them."

She laughed. "Me too."

Oh, but he wanted to hold this girl and never let go.

A couple caught James's eye. They kissed in their booth as though they had the room to themselves. He gulped.

"You say what the chaplains say," he said. "'It's not you. Don't take it personally.' You'd have to be a monster not to take it personally. But that's what you become out there. A monster.

Someone who laughs at dead bodies. Or you don't survive."

She took his face in her hands. He'd had a shave in her honor, and she'd been dying to feel his cheeks ever since she first saw him in the train station.

"Then be a monster," she said. "Do you must to survive, so you can come back to me."

He took her hands and kissed them. "Hazel Windicott," he said, "if there's anything left of me after the war, nothing would keep it from finding its way back to you."

The words Hazel had wondered and fretted about fell down so naturally, she wondered what she'd been afraid of. They were true, and the truth should never make you afraid.

"You have to come back," she said. "I love you, you know that?"

All the knots melted from James's weary body and mind. "I do know that," he said, marveling in the discovery. He did know. So this was how it felt, being loved.

As for himself, he'd known for a long time. "I love you too."

There's no telling what might've happened next if the waiter hadn't appeared just then with two steaming plates of duck confit and potatoes. The first course. He had waited a moment, discreetly, sensing that important words were being spoken, but when a pause occurred, he seized it. If they have a deep understanding of love, the French have an even deeper understanding of food and when it is to be eaten. That is precisely when it's ready and not a moment later.

James and Hazel, both stunned and bashful, welcomed the food as a way to busy themselves with something other than words, after the avalanche that had just landed upon them.

As for myself, well, I don't mind telling you, I was a complete mess. I had to borrow a cloth napkin to dry my eyes. I knew from the start that these two belonged together. But that doesn't make it any less wondrous when I'm proven right.

Let them start their dreadful wars, let destruction rain down, and let plague sweep through, but I will still be here, doing my work, holding humankind together with love like this.

DECEMBER 1942

A Kiss Is Just a Kiss

"SO HELP ME," thunders Ares, "if that boy doesn't kiss that girl and soon, I'll—"

"You'll what, Ares?" asks Hades.

Ares fumes. "I'll kiss her myself."

Aphrodite begins to laugh. "Not for nothing am I the Goddess of Love," she purrs. "I can make the God of War himself woozy for a girl he's only heard about in a story."

Apollo produces for himself a sumptuous piano, trains a light on its gleaming surface, and begins to play.

"*You must remember this,*" he sings. "*A kiss is just a kiss. A sigh is just a sigh. . . .*"

"Would you stop that noise?" Ares has never particularly appreciated music.

"Hephaestus's net may hold you, Goddess, but your story holds us all captive," says gallant Apollo. "I can understand Ares. Your Hazel does seem to cry out to be kissed. Metaphorically speaking."

"What was that about a dragon?" asks Ares. "Was she calling *me* a dragon?"

"Never mind, Ares." Aphrodite actually pats him on the head. "Just listen to the silly little love story."

APHRODITE

About Time—February 13, 1918

THEY ATE. They gazed into each other's eyes. They fed each other bites of their dinner. They did all the adorable things a young couple does together in public, when they imagine they are subtle and discreet. In fact, they brought a great deal of warmhearted amusement to many at the restaurant, who loved seeing a young British soldier and his *petite amie*. The lovebirds were blithely oblivious.

But it was *time*. Ares, Apollo, I know how you feel; I felt the same way. James and Hazel both felt it.

But where? Once upon a time James had wanted to plan something perfectly romantic.

Paris, I told him, is romantic enough. Get on with it.

So when the genial server finally brought their bill—he had not charged them for the profiteroles for dessert—James paid the tab, and they ventured out into the cold. Ostensibly they were walking home, toward Colette's aunt's home, but in reality, they were both looking for the right spot.

They found it. A tiny park, just a corner, really, with a few naked trees, and an empty fishpond, and a statue of my own dear

Cupid, bless the darling child. Made to order, and in fact it was, though I do not like to tip my hand. It was dark, but I parted the clouds overhead and painted the sky with stars. It was cold, but I sent the wind rushing past on either side of the park and left a comfortable bubble of stillness there.

The duffel bag and the flowers found their way to a park bench while the two sweethearts strolled a bit about, arm in arm. Dried leaves crunched under their feet when they left the cobblestone paths. They both knew what came next. They would not allow hurry or urgency to get in their way.

"Hazel?"

"Yes, James?"

"Dance with me."

So they danced in the park to Hazel humming a tune. And when she forgot how the next bit went, and the silliness of what they were doing caught up to them, and they began to laugh, nothing could be easier than folding themselves into each other's arms.

"Oh, you," he whispered. "How can you be real?"

"When I'm with you," she said, "I'm not sure that I am."

And before he knew it, he had slid his hands behind her ears, and threaded his fingers through her hair. He kissed her forehead, there, and there, and found her cheek and kissed it, there, and her nose. Then slowly, slowly, he brought his mouth to hers, and gently, reverently, kissed her.

DECEMBER 1942

An Answered Prayer

"THANK GOD," sighs Ares.

Aphrodite says: "You're welcome."

APHRODITE

When We Were Young—February 13, 1918

WAS THERE EVER a time when we were young?

We'll never grow old, of course; we have eternal beauty and passion and vigor, but was there ever a moment when we were *new*? When had we any firsts?

Can you recall your first real kiss? All that rushed upward from your feet to your face, all that awoke in you that you hadn't realized was sleeping?

There's nothing like the rightness of it. Nothing like its wonder. If I see it a trillion more times before this world spirals into the sun, I'll still be an awed spectator, right to the last, drinking in its nectar in holy jealousy.

How shall I waltz you through the next twenty-four hours?

I don't want to embarrass James and Hazel, yet I don't want to miss any of it.

James had kissed a girl or two before. They were statues, in a way; they held their breath, they allowed themselves to be kissed, passively, coolly, without response. Perhaps it was a feminine fad.

Some fellows even seemed to like it. This ice maiden, they seemed to feel, could be melted; it was a challenge that could be conquered by dint of manly effort.

Not so, Hazel. She kissed him back. Any other girl he'd ever kissed eroded into dust.

Well.

A good time was had by all.

They eventually found their way back to Colette's aunt's home. There were many, many stops along the way, but I leave these to your imagination. Colette and her aunt Solange had stayed up, keeping themselves awake with violet-flavored candies and endless rounds of *Le Tourn'oie*, a board game Hazel knew as the Game of the Goose. It would be the hospitable thing, Tante Solange insisted, to wait up to greet them, no matter how late.

"Pah," was Colette's reply. "You want to see how handsome is Hazel's British soldier."

Tante Solange shrugged. *"Bien sûr,"* she said, without a speck of apology.

When Hazel and James finally rang the bell, Tante Solange availed herself of that dubious privilege of older Continental women to comment upon his height, kiss his cheeks, pinch them, admire his shoulders, and generally mortify her guest till he was redder than a tomato. When he produced francs to pay for his lodgings, Tante Solange waved them away and showed him his room. That matter settled, she retired to bed. Colette followed her lead.

The kitchen was the farthest from the bedrooms, so James and Hazel found their way there. Left to their own devices, they discovered that kisses sans overcoats were an entirely new pleasure to be explored, and they might be in that kitchen still, had Tante Solange not emerged for an urgently needed pair of nail scissors kept, naturally, in the utensil drawer. So they bid each other adieu for the night, each certain that sleep would be utterly impossible

But James hadn't slept in a proper bed in months, and Hazel had spent most of the prior night sitting up on a train. So it wasn't many moments after each found their way between lavender-scented sheets before they succumbed to a sleep that was deep and nearly dreamless, save for one lovely image that filled the hours between "good night" and seeing each other again.

HADES

Midnight Train—February 13, 1918

AUBREY EDWARDS'S MOTHER always said nothing could keep that boy down for long. He was buoyant, like his music. He was flexible, like his piano-playing hands. Whatever pushed him under, he popped to the surface like a rubber ball.

She worried about damage that would push him back down. That it would come was certain; Aubrey was a confident young black man growing up in a segregated America.

Not that New York wasn't better than Mississippi. Lord, yes. In New York, you had a chance. You got jobs with better pay. Not great, but better. You could vote. You could get a government job. You might even get a fair trial, or at any rate, a real trial in a courtroom with a judge who'd listen. You could usually buy groceries where whites bought theirs. You didn't have to call whites sir and ma'am and pretend to like it when they groped you or kicked you or spat at you in the street.

But make no mistake: Theaters were segregated. Public pools were segregated. Restaurants, clubs. Schools, neighborhoods, churches. The military. The police force. There was prejudice, there was discrimination, there was hateful language, there was brutality.

There was, at least, in New York, the possibility of building a life for oneself in Harlem or Brooklyn. There was schooling to be had. Art, poetry, and music. Thriving entrepreneurs and entertainers, newspapers. There was *energy*. There was Jim Europe and his band. And in spite of everything, there was hope and faith that in God's own time, justice would prevail, and a better day would come.

Even so, there was no way to steer her Aubrey toward adulthood without his outrageous confidence being battered and scarred by hostility. She only prayed they'd be the kinds of scars he could survive. The kind where getting up and walking away was at least possible.

If she could see her boy now, leaning against the window of a midnight train, watching dark France roll by in the light of a waxing crescent moon—if she could know how muffled and silent was his soul, cycling between memories of Joey alive and Joey dead, her heart would break. If she knew what violence he'd witnessed firsthand, she'd be shattered. If she knew that Aubrey'd been the intended target of that violence, she would fall to her knees, thanking God he was spared. And lie awake nights, trembling with fear for the next time, when he might not be.

APHRODITE

Valentine's Day—February 14, 1918

THEY WERE UP before you were, Apollo, when morning was only a murmur along the cobblestone streets of the city. Neither wanted to lose another moment to sleep.

Tante Solange's guest bedroom had its own *salle de bains*, so James bathed, a luxury he no longer took for granted. He shaved and dressed in record time and ventured out into the flat. Hazel surprised him in the kitchen.

"Good morning," she told him.

He took his time returning the wish. Who knew "good mornings" were so heavenly?

They heard the sound of stirring coming from the direction of their hostess's bedroom and were both seized with the desire to be alone. They found their coats and scarves, and James grabbed his pack, leaving a pile of francs on the little stand beside his bed.

They crept down the stairs and out into the streets to an awakening city. A brisk walk back to Gare du Nord warmed their bodies but dampened their spirits. They would have to come back before this day was done. For now, they checked James's bag at the claim counter and scanned the schedules. The last northbound train left at midnight. James purchased a ticket. Only one day, and one day wasn't anything like enough, but they'd squeeze as much into it as they could.

They found a patisserie and ate a breakfast of decadent pastries, each as elegant as it was delicious. Did you know food is infinitely more scrumptious when you're in love? And Paris is a good place to be hungry. Even with wartime rationing, there was cream and butter to be had if you could pay a premium for it, and for this one day together, James and Hazel could afford it.

They wandered around the streets of the city, admiring the sights, the showy buildings, the carvings, the stylish curves and contours of the Capital of the World.

They passed by a women's boutique where a pink spring coat, displayed in the front window, caught Hazel's eye. She didn't say a word about it, but James noticed, took her by the hand, and led her into the shop. Before she could even protest, James and a very knowing shop woman had gotten Hazel out of her gray coat and into a perfectly fitting pink one. James slipped the woman the money while Hazel studied the coat in the mirror.

What was three months' worth of army pay for, if not for moments like this?

"You look like a tulip," James told her.

"I feel like one," she said. "You shouldn't have." Her smile clearly said otherwise.

They came upon a photographer's studio where the gentleman was about his business early, preparing for a Valentine's Day wedding, and had him take their portrait together, and mail prints to the addresses provided. Feeling quite hilarious, they posed beside a plaster model of a statue of my precious Cupid.

Don't scoff at them. Young lovers may be ludicrous creatures, but I'll have no sarcasm at their expense. Anyone who's never been where they are is only to be pitied. The photographer kept any opinions to himself. He made his living off the love business and was paid up front.

I made sure the sun was as warm as it could be in mid-February. I didn't want cold to rain on their day. Though it hardly needs my help to do so, I wanted Paris to shine.

They wended their way toward the Eiffel Tower. James gaped at its towering height. "Now that's something I'd have liked to see being built."

Hazel threaded her arm through his. "Can you imagine what it was like for the workers?"

Her nearness immediately eclipsed the steel monument. "You're not volunteering to paint the top of the tower, are you?" he asked.

"I already told you," she said. "My price is the Crown Jewels."

James smiled. She'd remembered.

They purchased tickets and stood in a long queue. The colossal tower, looming beside them, made them feel very small indeed. The use of riveted steel felt so wonderfully modern. To James, it signaled change, new materials, new vistas, new possibilities for building a cleaner, stronger world. If there was anything left with which to build one in years to come.

There is something wonderful about being in love in a city where you know no one. Public opinion of your behavior isn't worth a trifle. So, if you want to kiss your girl at the esplanade of the Eiffel Tower, you do.

And at the first-floor observation level, which might as well be the moon.

And at the second floor, from which all of Paris stretches before you in spectacular detail.

Then you board the hydraulic elevators that carry you all the way to the tower's dizzying top, and you kiss like there's no tomorrow.

From the top, you can see forever. The River Seine, winding about the city. The beautiful Trocadéro palace across the river from the tower. The gaudy dome of Napoleon's tomb. The long, elegant green spaces of the Champ de Mars reaching away in the other direction.

Champ de Mars. Field of Ares.

They descended in the elevators, then found a café for lunch.

They strolled arm in arm along the banks of the Seine, an absolute requirement.

As they ate and walked they talked of their parents and families. Stories of Maggie and Bob, and Georgia Fake and Olivia Jenkins. About childhood summers spent at the seashore with grandparents, and year-round childhood in Poplar with no living grandparents. A great deal about Colette and Aubrey and their music, and about Frank Mason, Chad Browning, Billy Nutley, and Mick Webber. About Pete Yawkey, and the more battle-seasoned lads from 2nd Section. About American soldiers and American accents, and Mrs. Davies. About sniping, and life in the trenches, about artillery fire and the flowing river of wounded men, and the shell-blasted wasteland of no-man's-land.

It helped so much to talk about it all. It helped James to have someone to tell.

They came upon chocolate shops draped in Valentine pomp and made the most of them. If James were a couple of decades older, he would've regained all the weight lost in the war that day alone. They decided to get in out of the cold by catching an afternoon film at a cinema. Neither one of them could tell you one thing that happened in the movie. Any language barrier had nothing to do with that.

They found their way to an elegant restaurant for supper. Might as well go out with a bang, James thought. He'd barely spent a farthing on himself since leaving London, and today was worth any cost. They surrendered their coats and found a table. A waiter greeted them, took care of the essentials, then left them to their solitude.

"There's so much of Paris left to see." Hazel sank her chin into her hands.

"We'll come back." He slipped his arm around her waist. "I promise."

She buried her face in his neck. They'd had such a lovely day, and so much fun, but now, as darkness settled over the city, Hazel found it hard to keep sadness at bay. For his sake, she thought, she ought to stay cheerful and hopeful. She failed.

"Don't go," she whispered.

"All right," he said. "Let's run away together, shall we?"

She sat up. "In a hot-air balloon?"

"With a poodle for company."

"A poodle?"

"Why not a poodle?"

She could think of no reason why not. "All right. A poodle."

"We'll pack chocolates for food," said James.

"And roses for beauty," said Hazel.

James shook his head. "We'll have you. You're all the beauty we need."

She gave him a pointed look. If she hoped he'd believe she was irked, he was smarter than that.

"Otherwise," he explained, "the hot-air balloon would be too heavy to fly."

"With all that chocolate."

He nodded. "Exactly."

She remained unconvinced. "Then I suppose I won't be able to bring a piano."

"Oh, absolutely bring the piano," said James. "We will need music, where we're going."

How she loved this boy who kept her laughing!

"And where, exactly, are we going?" she asked.

He considered this question. "The moon."

"That sounds cold," she said.

James made excellent use of his eyebrows. "I'll keep you warm."

Delighted though she was, Hazel thought she'd better steer the conversation elsewhere.

She made a proposal. "How about a tropical island?"

He grinned. "Even better." The naughty boy! I knew what *he* was thinking.

"I suppose the chocolate would melt there," she said.

"We'll live on coconuts."

She offered a hand to shake. "It's settled, then."

He took her hand and held it a moment, and they both realized, at the same time, what they'd actually promised. What offering a hand meant.

She tapped her cheekbone with a finger. "You know," she said, "we might run out of things to talk about. With just us two."

He suppressed a grin. "We'll talk to the children on the island."

"Oh?" Hazel was intrigued. "What children?"

He shrugged as if the answer should be obvious. "The children who live there."

She pursed her lips. "We're going to an island full of children?"

"Not at first," he explained. "It'll get that way eventually."

Hazel suddenly felt a great need to hide behind a sip from her water glass.

James kissed the back of Hazel's hand.

Her shining eyes met his.

With impeccable timing, the server brought the soup course.

APHRODITE

Letting Go—February 14, 1918

"I CAN'T LET you go," Hazel told James as they departed the restaurant at about nine thirty.

"I'm not really leaving," he said. "I'm just going away for a little while."

Hazel studied signs. "This is the wrong way. This leads toward Colette's aunt's place."

"That's where I'm taking you."

She stopped in her tracks. "I want to come with you to the train station," she protested.

"And walk home alone at midnight, through the streets of Paris?"

"I can take care of myself," Hazel said.

The concern in his brown eyes made her melt. "I know you can," he said. "But it's a long way. I couldn't bear the thought of anything happening to you."

Says the boy heading back to the trenches. "All right."

Their steps led them past a door from which music spilled. "What do you say, Miss Windicott?" he asked. "Valentine's Day isn't quite over yet. Go dancing with me?"

She smiled. "I'll probably trip and fall."

"I won't let you."

I did all I could to make that hour last. Almost, James could imagine that he was back in that parish hall, at the benefit dance, dancing with Hazel for the first time. Perhaps he'd never gone to war. Perhaps that was all a strange reverie; perhaps they were dancing in Poplar still.

"What if you hadn't agreed to dance with me, back at that church dance?"

Perish the thought! "What if Mabel Kibbey hadn't made me do it?"

James chuckled. "Is that her name? I'll have to thank her."

The music wound on.

"You will write to me often, won't you?" she asked.

Nobody was watching, so he answered her with a kiss. "Every day, if you like."

"I do like."

"Me too."

I did all I could, but the moment came all the same. They had to leave the dance hall. Slow steps still led to Tante Solange's door. The last moments they dared to stall were used up. Their lips were sore and their eyes stung. Hazel meant to be cheerful, but she couldn't.

"Be careful," she said, over and over again. "Be safe."

"And you," he said. "Be healthy. Be safe."

It's not what's said at times like these. We don't give prizes for rhetoric to the best goodbye. To thank each other for a wonderful time; to separate with a smile, or tears; to part with a final kiss or a final word—no one knows what to do. Even I look away and give couples their privacy.

When I look back, I see a girl on a doorstep, watching a uniformed soldier's back as he hurries away, lest he give in to the unendurable temptation to turn around. I see a friend on the stairs, waiting to catch a brokenhearted girl in her arms after the girl has waited outside, long past reason, in the slim chance that he might.

Three Trains Again—February 15, 1918

HADES

A TRAIN DISGORGED Aubrey Edwards and the rest of the 15th New York National Guard's band, the K Company Quartet, and a small troupe of dancing infantrymen at Aix-les-Bains.

It was the oddest place: a sumptuous, luxurious resort town nestled in the French Alps, with a crystal-blue lake and stunning mountain peaks, a glittering casino, an opulent theater, premium hotels and restaurants. All but empty. A desolate ghost town.

An army staff sergeant met them at the station and led them to the one hotel that could plausibly be called the lower-rent option for Aix-les-Bains. Even so, they were nice rooms and the general mood among the band was upbeat.

Lieutenant James Reese Europe directed his band members to find rooms, eat, and meet for a first rehearsal on the theater stage in two hours. Before he could disperse along with the others, Lieutenant Europe pulled Aubrey aside.

"You," he said. "Get some food, then find yourself a piano somewhere. The casino, or a hotel. I want you playing ragtime piano until sundown. Do you hear me?"

Aubrey's head drooped. "That's okay, Jim," he said. "I'll just go to sleep—"

"That's an order, Private," Europe replied. "You're gonna play with the band eventually, but you'd better get your sorry hands moving first. I want you so solid on the 'St. Louis Blues' that you could solo it backward for me. Understood?"

Aubrey saluted. *Understood.* Then went straight to bed.

ARES

Private James Alderidge rejoined his regiment outside Gouzeaucourt early in the morning of February 15, 1918, after riding north all night to Bapaume and hitching a ride east on a supply train on to the stop closest to his combat sector. He was exhausted after a sleepless night of swinging between bliss and torment. But he was ready, by the time he rejoined his comrades, to answer their questions about his Valentine's outing with "his girl."

"Yeah," he said at least dozen times that morning, "we had a grand time of it."

APHRODITE

Tante Solange was more than a little put out that she hadn't had another chance to lay her eyes, and presumably, her hands, on the handsome British soldier before he left. It took several board games to appease her. But by midafternoon on Friday, Hazel and Colette had stowed their bags and boarded a slow train headed toward Saint-Nazaire, riding straight into the setting sun.

APHRODITE

Waiting for Letters—February 19–28, 1918

IT TOOK A few days for James's letters to begin arriving at Hut One in Saint-Nazaire. They followed in a steady stream.

Colette returned to Saint-Nazaire eager to rehearse songs each night. She checked the door at the slightest sound.

Days passed, and Colette grew anxious. Had something changed Aubrey's mind about her? She visited the commissary and finagled excuses to pass by the parade grounds. No Private Edwards had been in the infirmary's colored soldiers' wing.

She asked other members of the 15th New York if they knew where Aubrey was. With nearly two thousand soldiers in the regiments, most didn't know him. Finally she found one who did.

"Haven't seen him in a while, miss," he told her. "He must've traveled with the band."

Better gone than faithless. But why go? And why not write to her?

Weeks passed without word. Surely if he'd sent a letter, she'd have it by now.

She dispatched a letter to Private Aubrey Edwards, 15th New York National Guard, Aix-les-Bains, US Army HQ, and waited.

Nothing came back.

HADES

Hideaway—March 1–12, 1918

TRAINLOADS OF AMERICAN soldiers began pouring into Aix-les-Bains. First Lieutenant James Reese Europe's 15th New York Infantry Band was the most popular feature there. Their engagement was upgraded, by popular demand, from two weeks to four.

Finishing the winter under blue skies, beside a crystal glacial lake, certainly could have been worse. It was warmer here, and when the soldiers weren't rehearsing or performing, they hiked the foothills surrounding the town. They could almost forget *la Grande Guerre* was going on.

Aubrey sat by the shores of Lac du Bourget. He watched the water and saw Joey's swollen face. He didn't hear birdsong, but Joey ragging on him for staying out late. Joey giving Aubrey a hard time, Joey rescuing his sorry hide.

He tried to play piano, but it only brought back Colette.

It slashed his heart to hurt her, after all she'd lost.

Maybe it had only been a beginning. But he loved her. With a girl like Colette, it didn't take long to be sure. But where could it lead? He had nothing to offer her now.

He loved her, and Joey had died because of it.

In a better world, the war wouldn't have started. Colette Fournier would be in Dinant, in the arms of her old beau, Stéphane.

The only honorable choice was for Aubrey to let her find a new Stéphane.

So when her letter reached him, asking if he could let her know he was safe, he did the hardest thing possible. He put it away without answering it.

APOLLO

Three Million Notes—March 13, 1918

"SO, HAVE YOU written much to your girl since you got here?"

Aubrey Edwards looked up from the desk in Lieutenant Europe's hotel room. It was after midnight, and his eyes were tired from the painstaking work of transcribing musical notation, scoring new pieces for the band.

"No," Aubrey said slowly. "I haven't."

Jim Europe peered over Aubrey's shoulder.

"You're not writing it in B-flat." He pointed at an offending measure.

Dang. How did Europe spot that so fast? He'd forgotten he was writing for horns, not piano. He needed sleep. He reached for a fresh sheet of staff paper. Some soldiers stayed up all night digging trenches or manning lookout posts. Some stayed up all night setting ditties to jazz accompaniment.

"You left without a word?" Europe asked. "She's got no idea what happened to you?"

Aubrey looked up. "Wasn't that the point?"

Europe filled in note heads and stems and flags with astonishing speed. "I wasn't trying to break apart your love affair," he said.

"Just wanted to get you out of a bad mess." He blew on the wet notes. "You know Saint-Nazaire wasn't safe for you." He yawned.

"You should get some sleep," Aubrey said. "Sir."

The lieutenant sat up and stretched. "Not finished," he said. "I told the fellas I was up all night, copying out three million notes." He grinned. "Didn't tell 'em I've got a secret helper."

"Gee, thanks."

Europe resumed his scribbling. "It seemed to me," he said, "that you thought that girl was worth an awful lot of risk and trouble." He hummed a snatch of the tune, his fingers tapping it out on an imaginary piano. "Didn't you care for her much?"

The fastest way to get Europe to drop the subject would be to lie, to say, No, he hadn't cared for her all that much, not really.

He thought of Colette's tragedies at the hands of the Germans. She'd lost so much. Just when she'd begun to have hope again, Aubrey had abandoned her without a word.

"I guess, if she wasn't much more to you than some laughs," Europe said, "you're better off just letting it die. It's painful, no doubt, but maybe it's for the best."

Aubrey leaned onto the stack of musical staff paper.

"Edwards," Europe said, "you're not doing Joey any favors by staying miserable."

Aubrey lowered his eyes. "Yes, sir."

Lieutenant Europe didn't seem satisfied. He waited until Aubrey looked him in the eye.

"If she was worth it then, she's worth it still," he said. "Don't be a dope."

"No, sir," Private Aubrey Edwards replied. "I mean, yes, sir. I won't be."

APHRODITE

Note for Note—March 16, 1918

Dear Colette.

On his final night in Aix-les-Bains, Aubrey pulled out his own musical staff paper.

Some Romeo I am, Aubrey thought. *Writing to Colette because a commanding officer ordered me to.*

He tried to think of what to say. *Sorry I disappeared? I know we said a lot of things to each other, but, you know, I've been busy?*

He never should've kept her waiting. It was selfish. Stupid. You don't throw aside a girl like Colette Fournier.

It would be so much easier if he could tell her about Joey, but Lieutenant Europe had warned him, repeatedly, to say nothing to anyone. The truth would devastate her. No need for yet another heart to be racked with guilt. He already had that job covered.

The thin lines of musical staff stared up at him.

He knelt down by the side of his bed and fished underneath it for his knapsack. At the bottom, he found his notebook, and in it, the songs he'd begun to write for Colette.

He chose the first song, and copied it out, note for note. At the end he wrote, *Love, Aubrey.*

APHRODITE

Digging—March 18, 1918

THE SEA BREEZE in Hazel's face brought a whiff of spring as she made the trek to Camp Lusitania and its YMCA relief hut. Hope hung in the air. Saint-Nazaire was on the move.

New shipments—what a word!—of American soldiers poured into Saint-Nazaire almost daily. There was barely a place to put them. Daily, trained divisions shipped out toward the Front. The moment would soon come when the American impact on the war, if there was to be any, would be fully felt. *Let it be swift,* Hazel prayed, *and let it be decisive.*

Hazel entered the hut. It was quiet inside at midday, though there were soldiers and YMCA volunteers about. Hazel noted the young ladies with some surprise. Their uniforms were just like hers. Why hadn't she met them when she'd been introduced to the other Y volunteers at Saint-Nazaire?

Because they were black.

A young woman approached her. "Can I help you?" she asked. "Are you bringing a message from Y headquarters?"

Hazel shook her head. "No," she said. "I'm here with a question of a, er, more personal nature. About a soldier from the Fifteenth New York."

The young woman eyed her sideways. "Come with me." She ushered Hazel toward a pair of low chairs in one corner.

"My name is Jennie," she told Hazel.

"Pleased to meet you," Hazel told her. "I'm Hazel."

"You're British, aren't you?"

Hazel nodded. "Guilty as charged. Do you know a Private Aubrey Edwards?"

Jennie blinked. "Have you seen him?" she whispered urgently.

Hazel was taken aback. "Do you mean, have I seen him play the piano?"

Jennie shook her head. "No. I mean, have you seen him lately?"

Hazel's heart sank. This young woman didn't know either.

"You know him, then," Hazel said. "No, I don't know where he is. I came hoping someone here might."

Jennie drew back a bit, as if a new caution had occurred to her. "Has there been trouble?" she asked. "Why are you looking for him?"

"No trouble," Hazel said quickly. "No, none whatsoever."

Jennie's face relaxed. "Aubrey Edwards is well-liked around here."

"It's plain to see why," said Hazel. "But you, also, think he's missing?"

Jennie's brow furrowed. She nodded.

"He and my friend had grown . . . close," Hazel said, "and even the night before the band left on its tour, they spent time together. He assured her that he wasn't going."

Jennie's expression was unreadable.

"After that, he disappeared," Hazel said. "He hasn't been around, and no one has seen him. My friend sent him a letter at Aix-les-

Bains, and heard no reply." She realized how this must sound. "Of course, sometimes friendships do, er, end. But there was no indication that this one would. Quite the contrary, in fact. And my poor friend is quite distraught."

She saw Jennie's eyes scan the room nearby, as if to make sure they were really alone.

"I was hoping," Hazel went on, "you might know someone to whom we could write a letter, to ask if Aubrey made the trip? We just want to know he's all right." Her words spilled out. "Even if he'd rather break things off."

Jennie was silent for a time. "Nobody knows where he is," she finally said. "He wasn't on the list of soldiers to travel."

Hazel nodded. Jennie seemed to be holding something back, but whatever it was, she finally laid it aside.

"Here's what I do know." Jennie leaned closer. "Some soldiers here are grave-diggers."

Hazel blanched. "Grave-diggers?"

"Between the sickness and casualties, there are hundreds of graves here at Saint-Nazaire."

Hazel feared what Jennie would say next.

"The day the band left, one of our soldiers, who's a grave digger, told us, in confidence, that he'd been given a hush-hush assignment to bury a young black soldier."

Hazel's brain began to whir. She would not allow this idea in.

"He'd been murdered," Jennie said. "Clubbed to death. Beyond recognition."

"But . . . there are thousands of black soldiers here," Hazel protested.

"Shh." Jennie held a warning finger over her lips. "I know. When I first heard about it, I felt terrible, of course, but I had no reason to connect it to anyone I knew." She looked around the room once more. "Aubrey stopped coming around when the band left. But he'd told a lot of folks that he wasn't going on the tour." She sighed. "So when he was nowhere to be seen, I asked his friends in K Company. Nobody knew anything." She dropped her voice even lower. "The grave-digger told me that the body was brought in on a stretcher by Lieutenant Europe and Captain Fish."

"The bandmaster? *That* Lieutenant Europe?"

Jennie nodded. "Captain Fish was Aubrey's CO."

Hazel pressed her hands into her temples. It couldn't be. Aubrey was more alive than ten people combined. Killing him should be impossible. He should have more lives than a cat.

Poor Colette!

"This still isn't proof," Hazel said. "We might be wrong."

Jennie said nothing. She seemed like someone who'd tried and failed to convince herself of the same thing.

"Would it be worthwhile to write to someone stationed with the band?"

Jennie pressed her lips together. "I can't get my grave-digger friend in trouble by divulging what he said." She looked sadly at Hazel. "I'm sorry I couldn't be of more help."

Hazel took her hand briefly. "I'm glad I met you," she told Jennie, "though your tale is terrible to hear. But it's clear that you care about Aubrey too."

The young woman stiffened slightly. "He was a good friend."

Possibly, Hazel thought, Jennie had hoped he could be more. Who could blame her?

Hazel nodded, thanked her once more, and took her leave.

APHRODITE

Treason—March 18, 1918

WHAT IS WORSE? A lover's heart growing cold? Or losing a love to death, having doubted them?

Worst of all is being caught unknowing in the clutches of both agonies. Too many sweethearts found themselves in this nightmare during the war. When letters stopped, were they killed or captured? Dead, or drifting away? If you are humane, and Colette was, you hope they're still alive to love again, God willing. An agonizing treason of the heart against itself.

When Hazel shared her report, the color drained from Colette, leaving her waxen. She rocked back and forth, shivering. Hazel took her hands in her own. They were cold to the touch.

"Aubrey?" Colette whispered. "You can't be gone."

"I'm sure he isn't," protested Hazel. "That could've been anyone."

"His whole life before him," Colette said faintly. "His music. His friends. His family." Her face contorted. "It can't be true."

"I'm sure it isn't," protested Hazel.

"Some cruel Fate hates me," Colette whispered. "It enjoys watching me suffer."

Hazel's heart bled. "We don't *know*," she said "I pray it wasn't him."

"I'm less than a pawn." Colette's eyes were hollow. All light had left her. "I'm a plaything to a vindictive god." She gazed at the ceiling. "Where have I sinned?"

Hazel wrapped her arms around Colette and tried to still her shaking. "It can't be that."

"But it can." Colette broke free. Her eyes were wild. "A loving god would never allow this. And if there was no god at all, surely chance would occasionally favor me, *non*? Probability alone might sometimes spare me?" She laughed bitterly. "But no. There is a god, a malicious one, and it despises me. My tears are its favorite sport."

Hazel rubbed Colette's back, and brought a cold cloth for her burning forehead.

Colette did subdue in time, but that, Hazel found, was worse. She seemed almost lifeless.

"Oh, Aubrey," Colette whispered. "What did they *do* to you?"

Hazel brought her blankets and a pillow, and her camp mattress, and slept in Colette's room that night. After Hazel had drifted off, Colette roamed Hut One in the dark, dressed in her nightgown and robe. She sat at the piano bench. She sat upon the couch.

She had sharp words for me, but I'm not offended by the bitterness of heartache. I would be unfaithful indeed if I abandoned my own when love slips through their grasp.

The Goddess of Passion understands. It is no blasphemy to blame me when a love is lost. Only to surround a heart in hatred, prejudice, greed, or pride until I can no longer find it at all.

APHRODITE

Do You Deny It?—March 19, 1918

AT SOME POINT before dawn, Colette slept. I helped; the poor child needed oblivion. Her rest was brief. A sharp knock at her bedroom door woke both Colette and Hazel. The door pushed open.

"Ah. Miss Windicott. Miss Fournier. Please report to my office."

They dressed quickly, smoothed their hair, and went to Mrs. Davies's study.

She wore the look of a woman who has prepared her remarks in advance.

"It has come to my attention," she said, "that many evenings, after I had gone to bed, you entertained male soldiers *in this very hut*." Mrs. Davies's lips quivered. "Do you deny it?"

Cold water closed over Hazel's body. She had no experience, none, with serious defiance or rebellion. Not an inkling of how to respond.

Colette wanted to laugh. She was going insane. This British busybody, on top of all else.

"It seems you believe the reports you have heard, Madame Davies," she replied coolly.

Hazel wanted to bow to Colette. Where did she find such strength, such control?

But Mrs. Davies was having none of it. "Brazen girl!" She turned to Hazel. "What have you to say, Miss Windicott?"

Be Colette. "I say," Hazel began, "that in light of your fixed opinion, it appears Miss Fournier and I should pack our things." She rose.

Mrs. Davies hurried toward the door, as if she to block them from leaving.

"The Young Men's Christian Association was formed to *improve* the moral character of young people. Not to corrupt it!"

"Mrs. Davies," Hazel said, "please excuse us." Boldness was intoxicating.

"I do *not* excuse you!"

"We resign," said Colette.

"You are dismissed in disgrace," cried Mrs. Davies. "Your families will receive letters describing your conduct. You'll be barred from any future association with the YMCA, and you will receive no reference. Other charitable organizations will be warned not to engage you."

Hazel yearned to tell her what she could do with her nasty blacklist letters. "Good day, Mrs. Davies," Hazel said. "We will gather our things and go."

They left the office. Hazel felt a pang as she looked around at the great room, the stage, the piano. So many memories here. She retrieved her music from the piano bench, then returned to the room she and Ellen shared to pack. Perhaps, Hazel thought, she could find Father Knightsbridge before she left. She wasn't a Catholic, but at the rate she was going, she probably needed a priest to take her confession. Before she was struck by lightning and cast down to hell.

Ellen sat up in bed and watched Hazel pack through sleepy, bewildered eyes.

"What's most shocking," cried Mrs. Davies, who had followed them, "is that you mingled romantically with *Negro soldiers.*"

Rage filled Hazel. Aubrey Edwards was worth ten of Mrs. Davies. Twenty. Fifty.

"Have you no shame? No pride in your race?"

"None at the moment," Hazel said, "but I do take pride in my friendship with a brilliant young man who was always decent, kind, and a perfect gentleman. Which is more than can be said for plenty of my own *race* that have passed through these doors."

Colette had already finished her packing and emerged into the corridor. "Madame Davies," she said sweetly, "our final pay."

Mrs. Davies had anticipated this. "This way, and sign for it."

"What's going on?" Ellen whispered.

"Goodbye, Ellen," Hazel whispered. "Colette and I are resigning. Whatever Mrs. Davies tells you, we did break a rule or two, but we did nothing wrong."

"You're *leaving*?" Ellen stumbled out of bed and gave Hazel a hug. "Must you go?"

Hazel returned the embrace. Ellen shook her head in dazed wonder. "I don't understand. Write to me when you get home, will you?"

Home? Hazel gulped. What, exactly, would her next step be? She had no plan.

"I will." She blew her roommate a kiss, buckled her carpetbag, grabbed her coat, signed for her pay, and, with Colette at her side, she left.

ARES

Preparations—February 20–March 20, 1918

THERE IS A SAMENESS to life during wartime. Days blur together when combat isn't active. A raid here and there, the daily dose of shelling. Casualties, but not enough to write home about. Unless the British Army does it for you, and they sent telegrams. Very brief telegrams.

"Regret to inform you that your son, Private Such-and-Such, is reported killed in action during heavy bombardment" or "has died of wounds at a casualty clearing station." Followed by a letter from a CO reporting, in every instance, that they passed bravely, swiftly, without much pain. They never said, "hung for hours on a barbed wire fence with his bowels hanging out, pleading for rescue, but nobody dared go for fear of hostile fire."

The first casualty of war is the truth.

If James and his comrades in 3rd Section and 2nd Section weren't working, they were sleeping. They slept on the ground. They slept on mounds of artillery. They slept standing up. They slept while marching. You don't believe me. Half an hour was a long night's rest.

When the sun went down, their supply fatigue began. Slogging through miles of narrow, congested, twisting tunnels carrying cases of food rations, water, bullets, grenades, sandbags, and wound dressings. Bales of barbed wire that cut their hands to ribbons.

The days grew longer, the nights shorter. Combat activity was quiet. Yet there they were, hauling heavy shells, hauling bales of rifles up and bales of damaged weapons back for repair. Clearly, they were gearing up. The Germans, too. Supply trains, troop trains, and spy planes. Gearing up for a massive onslaught, pointed at the Fifth Army. James's army. The Germans would outnumber the British forces by something like three to one.

They saw it, they lived with it, they put it out of their minds. Nothing they could do about it until something happened.

The constant grist for the rumor mill, and the source of a lively small-change betting operation, was when the Big One would start. All kinds of dates were thrown into the hat. March 1. The Ides of March. St. Patrick's Day.

When word spread of a new date, the troops were jaded. Third Section scoffed at March 21. The vernal equinox. The first day of spring. It seemed arbitrary. Superstitious, even. But captured Germans, taken in trench raids, swore that would be the day.

James wrote letters to his parents, to Maggie, and to Bob. So much he'd like to say, but how? Well, he reasoned, if you might die, you don't worry about what others think.

On the night of March 20, James wrote Hazel a long letter full of things he'd never dared say. Hopes for the future. Hopes that included her. If he never came back from the coming battle, would her heart be more broken, or less, knowing he would've given his forever to her?

If it was his lot in life to die for King and Country, if that was his price to pay, it seemed not too much a recompense to ask of Fate that the girl he loved, and would have loved forever, be asked to bear to her grave the burden of knowing how he'd felt.

On the night of March 20, 1918, James Alderidge posted the letter at sunset from his position with his comrades in the support trenches, then found a dugout to lie down in and went to sleep while he still could.

APHRODITE

Regrouping—March 20, 1918

ON THE MORNING of March 20, 1918, Hazel and Colette arrived back in Paris. Colette crawled straight into bed and stayed there.

It had been a quiet train ride, but at one point Colette spoke.

"When the Germans killed my family," she said, "nobody let me see their bodies."

Hazel waited, heartsick.

"I asked, but they all said, 'Non, mon enfant, you mustn't see; the sight would kill you.'"

Hazel closed her eyes. Her own parents, slaughtered. James, lying on the ground.

"Hazel," Colette finally said, "do you think Aubrey is dead?"

The words hit Hazel with a pang. What *did* she believe?

"I think," she said slowly, "it's too soon for that conclusion."

Colette's red-rimmed eyes watched for the truth. She would not be lulled by false faith, or lies dressed as encouragement.

"I think," Hazel said, "we should hold on tightly to hope."

Colette went back to watching farmland slide by.

ARES

Operation Michael—March 21, 1918

JAMES WOKE WITH a start. It was dark, the air thick and heavy. Noise thundered in his ears.

Shelling, but no ordinary shelling. The Germans were launching artillery shells so fast, James couldn't make out the space between one explosion and the next. Just one continuous roar of destruction. A bombardment like a wild beast's howl.

He groped for his helmet. The air tasted of smoke and dirt, and the faint onion smell of mustard gas. Officers ran, shouting orders. Soldiers crawled out of dugouts and found their rifles.

The ground heaved and shook like a ship in a storm. Explosion, scream. Explosion, scream. The slap of dirt raining down. They were back in the support lines, but the big guns knew it. No line in the trench network was safe from such a massive shell attack.

Third Section gathered around him in the dark. He knew them by sound, smell, height.

"You owe me two bob, Nutley," shouted Chad Browning's shrill voice. "I said today would be the day, but did you believe me? Nah, and it's gonna cost you."

"Shut it." Billy had to shout to be heard.

"Not on your granny's grave," protested Browning. "Pay up. Dunno if any of us will be alive tonight, and I wouldn't feel right picking the pockets of a dead chum, now would I?"

Mick Webber's voice originated well below Billy Nutley's. "Where's McKendrick?"

"*Whizz-bang!*" cried Mason. They ducked. The shell exploded ten feet away.

They spread out, so one shot couldn't get them all, and crouched low. Shells overhead shrieked. Finally their own artillery guns roared to life and belched out retaliation at the enemy.

"Lots of luck," Mason said. "Fritz'll be way out of range. They planned all this."

"Is it just me," yelled James, "or are the explosions getting closer? Pushing our way?"

"Creeping barrage," answered Mason. "They make a canopy of shellfire, and their infantry creeps out underneath it to invade our trenches under safe cover while we're hiding from their shells. They push it forward while their men advance. Course, if they bungle it, their guns take out their own men."

"I wish," muttered James. "Should I get to the snipers' nest?"

"Wait for orders," Mason advised. "In all this smoke and blackness, there'd be nothing to see. You're safer here."

Explosions and screams grew nearer. Only the occasional spurt of flame gave any light. They crouched over their knees with their hands clamped hard over their ears.

But screams wiggled between James's fingers. Were they lads from 3rd Section? Billy, Chad, Mick, Sam, Vincent, Alph?

Where was Sergeant McKendrick? Had something happened? If nobody led them to safety, they'd die out here like sitting ducks. They couldn't abandon a post without orders.

The assaulting wall of sound overwhelmed their ears. Their

rifles, as useful as toothpicks, lay slung across their thighs where they crouched. If they hid in dugouts, a shell blast could turn that dugout into a tomb. At least, in a trench, there was a chance of being dragged away.

They took each smoke-filled breath as if it was their last, and waited to be proven right.

APHRODITE

From Paris—March 21, 1918

THE BEDROOM WINDOWS rattled.

Hazel woke in the darkness in the bedroom she shared with Colette at Tante Solange's.

The windows kept on rattling.

The clock on the bedside table said 4:45 a.m.

Her bare feet landed on the cold wooden floor. She went to the window and pulled back the blinds. Unlatching the casement, she swung it open and leaned into the early morning cold.

The whole city thrummed with a pulse felt in the bones. The earth rumbled, and its buildings rattled. A dog barked in the street below, and another answered from afar.

An earthquake?

Cold prickled on her skin. Other windows swung open too. She heard Colette stir in bed.

The sound came from the north. On and on it went, a sound like distant boulders tumbling against one another, or, like the clashing of a vast drum brigade.

Guns at the Front, she realized. Guns without letup. Guns to the north. Where James was.

ARES

Handed to the French—March 21, 1918

FINALLY THE MOMENT had come.

By Thursday, March 21, the 15th New York National Guard arrived by train in Connantre, in the region of Givry-en-Argonne, and met up with the rest of their division, which had gone straight there from Saint-Nazaire.

They were given a new name. No longer were they the 15th New York National Guard. They were now the 369th United States Infantry. Or rather, the *369e Régiment d'Infanterie US (RIUS)*. They'd been handed over to the French Army to fight with them.

The French and British Armies had begged the United States to send supporting reinforcements, but General Pershing had refused to relinquish command of any US troops. They were his responsibility to lead and, as much as possible, to safeguard. He didn't want Americans used as expendable cannon fodder by non-American generals.

But he could spare a black regiment, to be used as needed.

ARES

Fog—March 21, 1918

THE HEAVY GUNS droned on for hours. Howitzers and field guns, searching for James.

There was nothing to do but wait. No place to go any more safe, nor any less.

Through the smoke and dirt and confusion, the risen sun barely showed itself, until well after seven in the morning, when a lull fell over the battle. The guns stopped. The sky was lighter, wreathed in fog. It hung, cold and damp and heavy, over the trenches. James couldn't even see Frank Mason, a yard or two away.

The silence, after the guns, was deafening. The fog muffled and muted everything. The air was so wet that breath became a slow drowning.

Low voices began calling out to one another. Cries of "Medic!" and "Stretcher!" pierced the cloud, but they seemed to die before reaching the ears of anyone who could help.

"Mason," James whispered.

Mason was in his ear. "Quiet," he hissed. "They're coming."

James stripped the clammy dewdrops clinging to his rifle and screwed on the bayonet.

A grenade exploded down the line. Chad and Billy. They'd gone that way. Were they all right? His pulse raced. How could he warn them, without drawing danger down on them all?

They landed softly, when they stormed the trenches. Like the *plash* of an ice cube dropped in a drink. Dreamlike figures in gray, loaded down with grenades, rifles, and ammo. Their coal-scuttle helmets were painted in camouflage.

Storm troopers. Elite soldiers, heavily armed. They took no prisoners. They only killed.

Two of them. He saw them, but they hadn't seen him. They swam in and out of view, both carrying pistols ready.

James raised his rifle. They were only a few yards away.

A step sounded. They turned. It was Mason, his back turned. He didn't see them.

James pulled the trigger.

One German down.

The other turning,

James clearing and cocking,

the pistol clicking,

his own rifle rising,

crack,

the butt of Mason's gun knocks the German's gun arm,

if James shoots, he could kill Mason,

guard,

aim,

long thrust,

twist,

kill,

kill,

kill.

A mouth flies open,

blue eyes gaze up into his,

the surprise of robin's-egg-blue eyes

as a red throat pours blood down a gray uniform.

He'd shot the first storm trooper in the neck. Storm troopers wore armor. Neck and armpits, vulnerable.

"Thanks, mate," Mason says.

He takes their pistols, Mason does, one for each. Spoils of war. He straps on a sling of grenades. James takes the gun he hands him, still hot, uncocks it, and sticks it in his belt.

They hear it now: the firing lines, under siege. Of course they are, if storm troops are invading the support line.

Chad and Billy run into their traverse.

"You guys all right?" says Chad Browning.

"Where's McKendrick?" says Billy Nutley.

Another footstep. A smell, a sound.

"Down!" screams Mason.

The jet of flame arcs across the trench. A storm trooper with a flamethrower. *Flammenwerfer.* Liquid fire strapped to his back, shooting yards from a hose in his hand.

James crouches, his rifle still in his hands. No time for sights. He aims for the face.

The German's headless body tumbles forward, still spraying fire. Chad screams.

"Fall back!" comes a cry from somewhere. "Fall back!"

Chad writhes on the duckboards. Mason and Nutley dive on top of him. They beat him to quench the flame. The smell of flesh on fire reminds James of food, of cooking meat.

"We need a stretcher." Billy is pale and panting.

Mason shakes his head. "Never gonna get one here."

James slings his rifle behind him. "Put him on my back," he says. "Get him on me, then you fall back. I'll be right behind you."

"I'll do it," Billy says.

"So you can both get killed?" says James. "You're too big. Stay low, and get out of here. Billy, you carry my pack. Cover me, all right?"

"He's right, Bill," says Mason. "You can't do it."

"Put him on me," James tells Mason, "and get out of here."

Chad Browning has stopped his screaming. His clothing is half melted away, half fused to his skin. Mason peels off his trench coat, and they wrap Browning in it, then drape him over James's back. His limp arms flop over James's shoulders, and his head bumps against his own. His body is light. He seems to weigh no more than a pack.

"Third Section," calls Frank Mason, its new, undisputed commander. Other familiar forms materialize from the mist.

"Where's Alph?" asks Mason. "Where's Sam?"

Vince Rowan shakes his head. "Grenade."

No more basset hound. *It'll be Wipers all over again. Suicide.*

"Dead?" Mason watches their faces. "Right." He points northward. "Communication trench, this way. Bill, you first, and Mick, then James. Watch for Germans up top. You next, Vince, and I'll follow behind."

Billy Nutley, bayonet ready, makes for their retreat. His large back disappears into the mist. Mick Webber, James and cargo, Vince Rowan, and Frank Mason follow. Back toward the east, toward the fog-veiled sunrise, the German guns roar back to life.

ARES

Jesse James—March 21, 1918

THE COMMUNICATIONS TRENCHES were a nightmare. Choked in fog, slick with blood. Stretcher-bearers pushing back to field-dressing stations, jostling with reserves running up to the Front. German storm troopers swarmed over the top. British troops with pistols watched the rim and took out anything that moved through the fog. But they couldn't spot grenade-throwers.

Chad Browning was all James could think about. Flopping along on his back. He must be in agony. Feisty, funny Chad. *Who wouldn't be a soldier, eh? Oh, it's a shame to take the pay!*

They reached a Red Cross team and handed Chad over. His body burned through the trench coat as though the *Flammenwerfer* still had him alight. He was alive. Nothing more they could do.

"Third Section. Is that you?"

Clive Mooradian and stocky Benji Packer swam into view.

"Come on, me darlings," said Clive. "German infantry are following the storm troopers, following the barrage. They've taken a section of the firing line, and we're going to take it back."

"Firing line?" said Mick. "Storm troops just kicked us out of the support line!"

Private Mooradian shrugged. "Storm troops don't stick around," he said. "Let's get back there before Fritz gets too comfortable and starts rearranging the furniture."

"Do you chaps know what happened to Sergeant McKendrick?" asked James.

"Wounded, this morning, somebody said," said Benji Packer. "Badly concussed by a shell blast to the officers' quarters. He may pull through."

They followed 2nd Section back toward the front line, through the choking maze of the crowded communication lines. Another grenade dropped into the line, just behind where they'd been.

"That's it," Mason declared. "You lads go on. I'm going up top to take out the bastard shooting those grenades. Gimme a boost, Alderidge."

James froze. "You'll be a sitting duck up there, Frank."

"Come on," cried Benji. "You're gumming up the line."

"Let me," said James. "I'm a better shot, and I don't have a wife and kid at home."

"Quit bragging, Jimmy," snapped Clive. "Who's it gonna be?"

"We'll both go," said Mason. "Jesse James here can take out the Jerries. I'll cover him."

"Catch up to us, then, "said Mooradian. "Got ammo? Right. Up you go."

Billy laced his fingers together and heaved James over the parapet. He landed and flattened himself. He still had fog for cover, but without trench walls beside him, he felt naked and exposed. Once he'd hated the trenches. Now he was lost without them.

Frank Mason sailed up over the top and landed smack on James's rump.

"Sorry, chappie," said Frank. "Nothing personal."

They peered through their rifle sights into the swirling fog.

ARES

Sniper in the Snow—March 21, 1918

WHAT'S IT LIKE, being a sniper in the snow?

The fog was a wall of snow. Such pure whiteness. Like a terrible joke. It blanketed the sounds of death and destruction.

James had fought against being a sniper. But he was one now, like it or not. Snipers need their blinds. Their covers. Their protective plates to shield them while they quietly watch, wait, kill. But now battle engulfed him.

James and Frank inched forward, crawling on their bellies.

"Come on, Fritz, where are you?" whispered Mason.

James held up a hand to silence him. There was so much noise and commotion from heavy guns and swarming soldiers that he couldn't pick out a footstep or a cracked twig like he could on a midnight watch. But, maybe . . .

There. In the distance. A gray form, creeping. Taking aim with an enormous gun. A rifle grenade launcher.

James aimed for the heart. Down went the shooter.

"*Move move move*," hissed Mason. "Now they know we're here."

They clutched their rifles and rolled sideways a few yards.

Sure enough, a storm trooper crept through where they'd just been, searching.

Crack went Mason's pistol. The German's head snapped sideways. Blood sprouted from his temples.

"Great shot," murmured James.

"You're not the only one who knows what to do with a gun."

They rolled and waited. "They know there's a trap, now," Mason whispered.

Nothing moved. But someone was out there. James felt it.

In pantomime, he told Mason: *You stay here. Watch. I'll go this way. You cover me.*

Mason nodded.

Inch by inch, James slid to the right until he was three yards from Mason. The fog thinned as the morning sun burned it away. He could see Mason, watching him.

Then he saw what Mason couldn't see. Looming up behind him. A storm trooper with a rifle trained right on his friend.

No time to swing his own rifle around. With his free left hand, he pulled the German pistol from his belt. Could he shoot with his left?

In one fluid movement, he cocked the pistol and blasted it into the German's chest.

The fog reclaimed the falling Jerry. But Mason, startled, jumped up on hands and knees, and stood upright.

An incoming whine.

A silver flash.

An explosion, up. A column of dirt and smoke. A bang of percussive air shoving James back, blasting dirt in his face.

When the smoke lifted, and James scrubbed the grit from his eyes, Frank Mason wasn't there anymore. Just a fire, a helmet, a torn pair of boots, and a little charred prayer book.

DECEMBER 1942

Telegram

THE HEAVY QUIET of night falls over the hotel room.

The fire has died, and the room is nearly black. Only the subtle sheen of the gods offers any challenge to the night.

"Adelaide Sutton Mason," Aphrodite says. "I remember her. She'd had a hard time of it, growing up. A rough father, who drank. She seemed in great danger of ending up with the wrong sort of man, before Frank came along." She wiped her eye. "They had three very happy years together. And, of course, two children."

"Two?" Ares looks up. "Mason's photograph only had—"

"She'd written to tell him," says Aphrodite. "She'd fallen pregnant. Remember? His injury? He was home for a while?"

All the male gods present are fathers. Possibly not the best of fathers—the subject is open to debate—but they are not without feeling.

Before their eyes, a scene appears. A doorbell rings. A skinny youth, his bicycle propped against a hitching post at the curb, stands on the front step. An envelope wobbles between his finger and thumb. The young wife whose eyes always get the joke peers around the slowly opening door.

HADES

At the Beach

PRIVATE FRANK MASON tumbled rather abruptly into my realm.

"What happened?" he said aloud. "Where's James?"

The fog was still thick around him, but the air no longer reeked of smoke and gunpowder. It smelled damp and green. He clambered to his feet and took a step forward.

"James?" he called. "You there?"

There was no sound of shells, no rifle shots ringing. Just the quiet of nature, that isn't quiet at all, when you listen. Singing birds, buzzing insects, swaying branches.

The fog lifted. He saw himself in a field of dark grasses sprinkled with delicate white flowers. Up ahead he smelled the sea. After so many landlocked, trench-locked months, it beckoned to him.

He began to run.

He reached the sand and looked down to find that his feet were bare, his body loosely dressed in the lightweight trousers and shirt he used to wear, summers, on fishing boats. Damp sand squeezed between his toes, and salty spray blew in his face.

"I'm home," he said.

The beach was mostly empty. It was early evening, when late

afternoon leans toward twilight. A woman slowly walked along the water's edge, holding a toddler by the hand.

"Oh no," Frank said. "No, no, no!"

I appeared, then. An old sailor he used to know, ages ago, when he'd first joined a crew.

My presence didn't surprise him. It rarely does; I'm the one each soul knows will find them in the end.

"I'm dead, aren't I?" He turned to me then. "They got me, the bloody bastards!"

I nodded. "In a sense, yes. They did. But now you've got you."

He sank into the sand and wept. "My poor wife, all alone," he sobbed. "My little son, never knowing his daddy. And the baby!" He turned to me imploringly. "Who's going to look after them?"

"They'll get very good at looking after each other."

That wasn't much comfort. "It'll be brutal on them," he said. "You can't pretend it won't."

"It will be brutal on them," I told him. "You'll need to send comfort and help. What you would do for them, if you could."

He looked up. "Can it be done?"

"It can," I told him, "when desire is strong."

Frank Mason gazed dejectedly at his approaching family. His son sat down and began shaping a castle out of the sand.

"Take comfort," I told him. "Remember: sleep brings them closer to you."

He looked up hopefully.

"So does childhood," I added. "Little ones see everything."

Frank Mason Jr. turned toward his father and smiled a drooly smile. In a bound, his father was at his side.

"And watch out for cats," I told him, by way of goodbye, though I don't believe he heard me.

HADES

Identity Discs—March 21, 1918

WHEN THEY FOUND James, it was dark.

He was in the relief trenches, hundreds of yards from the place where he'd gone up top to take out the storm troopers. He didn't know how he got there.

It was clear to the medics, when they finally examined him, that he'd neither eaten nor drunk water at all that day. He lay curled in a dugout, and wouldn't come out.

But he had to. The Germans had taken their lines. They were pressing hard against the BEF's Fifth Army. British troops were in full retreat. He'd be a prisoner of war if they didn't get him out.

He trained a rifle on anyone who tried to make him come out of his dugout. He was lucky not to be shot on the spot by an officer for that. They couldn't allow their retreat to be slowed, and they couldn't allow soldiers to fall prisoner and be tortured, maybe give up secrets.

Private James Alderidge had no secrets.

"Where's Mason?" is all he would say. "Has anybody seen Mason?"

The officer tasked with luring him out was more humane than

some. He coaxed the hiding man to hand out his identity discs, so they could find someone he knew. He complied. The discs, formerly strung about his neck, gave his name as Private J. Alderidge, Fifth Army, 7th Corps, 39th Division, D Company. With some hollering, they found another soldier who knew him: Private William Nutley.

Billy tried to talk in him into coming out. When coaxing wouldn't work, Billy crawled in after him. He yielded up his guns to his comrade without resistance, and Billy scooped up James, all six feet of him, and carried him out of the dugout.

Clamped against Billy's chest, James began to shake. Nighttime bombardment shot little bursts of orange light that were almost festive, like fireworks.

"It's all right, Jim," Billy told his comrade. "It's all right."

"Have you seen Mason?"

"I haven't," said Billy.

He almost added, "I'm sure he's fine." But I cautioned him against it. Lies are worse than no comfort at all. Especially to a mind already scorched by the truth.

Billy brought him to the Red Cross tent. James lay there, twitching, shivering under a thin sheet and blanket. When a nurse approached his cot, he sat up and took her by the arms and said, "Have you seen Frank Mason?"

"Sedative," called the nurse. An orderly appeared. He plunged a steel syringe and needle into a bottle and drew up a dose of something. James felt a sharp pinch in his arm, and remembered no more.

ENTR'ACTE

APHRODITE

The Fates of Certain Letters

WHEN A LETTER arrived at YMCA Relief Hut One, addressed to Colette Fournier, sent from Aix-les-Bains, Mrs. Celestine Davies reasoned with herself. This letter could be from any American serviceman. But most likely, it came from one of the Negro soldiers in that traveling army band that had gone there to perform.

So instead of sending the letter to the address she kept on file for Miss Fournier—some female relative in Paris—she forwarded the letter, with a note of complaint, to a staff sergeant at the US Army HQ in Saint-Nazaire. Negro soldiers were behaving wantonly toward white YMCA volunteers. American army leadership needed to take responsibility for its Negro problem.

The staff sergeant, to his credit, opening the letter and, finding it contained nothing more provocative than a wordless snatch of music, rolled his eyes and tossed it into the trash.

A letter from a Private J. Alderidge, serving in the Fifth Army, north of Paris, arrived at Hut One addressed to Miss Hazel Windicott. Mrs. Davies's patriotic heart bled for the poor young man. J. Alderidge, serving King and Country, deserved far better than to waste his affections on an object such as Hazel. She may be faintly pretty, and she may play piano in a nice sort of way (though Celestine had heard better), but she wasn't worthy.

So Mrs. Davies returned his letter to him, care of the Fifth Army, and enclosed within it a note explaining that Miss Windicott had been dismissed in disgrace from the YMCA for entertaining men of ill repute after hours. She omitted mentioning that at least one had been a Negro, seeing no reason to wound Private Alderidge's natural manly pride. She had left, Mrs. Davies said, no forwarding address.

One other breakdown of mail communication to note had nothing to do with Mrs. Celestine Davies.

As the sounds of shelling and dire news reports poured into Paris, Hazel sent letter after letter to James, letting him know where she could now be reached and begging him to write to let her know that he was safe. They were addressed to his attention, in care of the Fifth Army, but in their present state of chaos and retreat, and in light of events that followed, most of Hazel's letters never reached James. Thousands of letters were mislaid at this time. When eventually the dust settled, and overlooked mail bags were distributed, there was no Private James Alderidge to give letters to.

ACT FOUR

ARES

Chocolate—March 24–April 5, 1918

WITHIN DAYS, PARIS newspapers were full of the horrible news. The British Fifth Army, stationed from Gouzeaucourt to the Oise River, had suffered a devastating defeat. Spring offensive hostilities, centered around Saint-Quentin, dubbed "Operation Michael" by the Germans, had all but annihilated the Fifth Army. The Germans had pushed the front line some sixty miles back.

Sixty miles lost! After years of virtual stalemate!

Worse than miles, tens of thousands of lives were lost on both sides, in just a few days' fighting. The defeat was so bad, the Fifth Army was being disbanded.

Hazel, reading Paris papers with her sketchy schoolgirl French, went numb with shock. An entire army, dissolved due to failure and massive losses. Was James among them? She refused to believe it. Yet with an entire army disbanded, what else could she think?

Were the Germans actually going to win this war, after so much British bravery and sacrifice, and with the Americans lining up at the doorstep?

If any silver lining was to be found, it was this: The Allies *had* stopped the Germans eventually. The Jerrys had failed to take the city of Amiens, or reach the Channel ports. Britain's vital command of the seas remained in force. That, the Allies felt, was more crucial. Paris was still as safe as it could be when the Germans had long-range guns pointed straight at it.

Costly and disheartening though it was to retreat sixty miles before the German onslaught, the land lost wasn't of any particular strategic value to the Germans. Their storm troops and infantry pushed forward faster than supply routes could keep up. And the British line hadn't moved everywhere. Soon the advancing Germans found themselves stranded, surrounded, and hungry.

Raiding through the supplies left behind in haste by the British, they found beef, chocolate, cigarettes, even champagne among their provisions. Fritz had been led to believe that the Allies were as poor and starving as they were. After four years of the war, here they were, enjoying the finer things of life, while Fritz's family, back home, starved.

Whatever boost sixty captured miles might have brought to German morale was erased by the chocolate in the BEF's packs.

War is morale. War is supply. War is chocolate.

Try as the German propaganda machine might to reassure Fritz that they were winning their glorious war, Fritz wasn't fooled. If the British drank bubbly and ate chocolate, while the Germans drank ersatz coffee brewed from nutshells and coal tar, it was over. Nine months and four million more casualties from over, but over all the same.

HADES

Disappearing—March 22–25, 1918

THE SYRINGE APPEARED many more times in the days to come.

James would wake in searing daylight, or confusing dark, wondering where he was. Dreams crossed the threshold between sleep and waking: the blue-eyed German. The German with the flamethrower, engulfing James. No, engulfing Hazel.

Hazel. Where was she? Gone, gone. Here, standing before him, then, *boom*, gone.

No, that was Frank. Thank God, it wasn't Hazel, but oh God, oh God, it was Frank.

Then, the ringing. His ears rang with a missile's shrill, incoming whine. But it never hit, never landed. It kept coming for him. Ringing and ringing in his skull. He thrashed between sweaty sheets, but his wrists were tied to the bed. He was clad in a thin hospital gown, so thin, it would never stop the missiles. Where were his clothes?

He had to get away. He had to take cover. Anything could hit him here.

No, no. He was in a hospital. He was safe in a hospital.

Then there was an explosion. Doctors and nurses running, patients screaming.

Figures rushed to his bed, lifted it, and carried him, bed and all, to a truck. The truck rattled, and he cried out. Someone came with the silver syringe, and the pinch that burned, and his field of vision, already shallow and dark, blurred at the edges, and James disappeared.

HADES

Horse-Race Gambling—March–April 1918

MR. AND MRS. WINDICOTT of Grundy Street and Bygrove, Poplar, London, had thanked their stars, when the Great War broke out, that their only child would never face battle's danger. She, a quiet girl devoted to piano, would pass through this ordeal unscathed.

Then she'd begun to act secretively, and suddenly she'd fallen in love with a soldier, dropped her piano lessons, and run off to France to volunteer at a huge base of American servicemen. The horrors that could befall her there kept Mrs. Windicott up at night.

Her letters were full of love for them, and anxiety for her poor soldier boy.

In time they began purchasing, from a bookseller, the Weekly Casualty List. (The *London Times* had stopped printing it with the daily paper. It had grown so long, there was no room for any other news.)

Others in Britain studied this list with hearts in more dread than the Windicotts'. But each week they pored over the list with a magnifying glass, searching for Alderidge, J. (Chelmsford). He was a name to them, but he mattered to Hazel. They came to love him for her sake.

Pick any name, and watch for it long enough, and send up a silent prayer of thanks when you don't find it on a death list, and pretty soon, if what you feel isn't love, what is it?

A horse-race gambler who follows with avid interest the winnings, times and injuries of Bachelor's Button (1906 Ascot Gold Cup) or Apothecary (1915) knows what I mean. Those whose lot it was to raise the generation fed to this war were horse-race gamblers, one and all.

APOLLO

Émile—March 22–April 13, 1918

MAYBE, AUBREY FIGURED, a letter to Colette after so much silence, containing nothing more than music, was too confusing. So he wrote another. And still there was no answer.

Reaching the Front had been good for Aubrey, oddly enough. His French trainer, Émile Segal, was fun. He was a true *poilu* ("hairy one"), covered head to neck in thick, matted brown curls. And the faces he made! How he mimicked the Boche Germans, and the mannerisms of French officers. And the soldiers of the 369e ("Sammies," to Émile, after Uncle Sam), who were knocked on their backs by the routine daily allotment of wine for French soldiers. Sammies couldn't handle so much potent French wine.

Aubrey didn't need to be tipsy for Émile to get him laughing.

That was a miracle, in its own way. Weeks went by, then months. The ache of Joey's absence, and Aubrey's terrible guilt, never faded. But after two months had passed, time, work, and friendship brought Aubrey to a place where it was possible to hurt, and to laugh, in the same day. He never would've guessed he could.

Aubrey and Émile quickly developed a language of their own, of parroted French and borrowed English phrases. They knew enough of the other's language to be thoroughly confusing, such as when Aubrey misused the French for wind, *vent*, for the word for wine, *vin*, and told Émile he'd like some more wind after dinner, *s'il vous plait*. Émile obliged him with an award-winning fart. If they could've lit the fart, it would've made a *Flammenwerfer*.

Beans for dinner. Good times.

Émile taught Aubrey how to survive at the Front. How to tell shells apart, and explosives from gas. How to creep quietly, and discern *vent* sighing in the trees from a tiptoeing Boche raiding party. How to heat a tin can lid over a tiny flame and fling caught lice pinched from clothing down onto the red-hot tin till they sizzled and popped like popcorn.

In Maffrécourt, where they were billeted, Aubrey found a piano in a bombed-out tavern. It wasn't in the best condition, but Aubrey gave Émile a show that brought others from K Company for an impromptu performance.

After that, Émile Segal trotted out his pianist comrade every chance he got, claiming all bragging rights. The way those *poilus* danced to the first jazz they'd ever heard made Aubrey want to shove his fist into his mouth to keep from cackling out loud. Aubrey taught them the fox-trot, lest they die and go before the pearly gates dancing like a pack of clowns with arthritis.

Until they entered the trenches in earnest on April 13, 1918, Aubrey performed every night. Émile should be a booking agent after the war, Aubrey thought. He sure knew how to draw a crowd. And Aubrey sure liked having one.

The Champagne sector was quiet, and they counted themselves lucky. They could hear the drums of war thundering along the line to the north. But here, not much was being shot besides wild boar. And the only pain in his heart, besides the loss of Joey, was the fact that day after day, no letter came from Colette.

APHRODITE

Any Work Will Do—March 29, 1918

AFTER A WEEK of roaming, silent, arm in arm, through the streets of Paris, mourning, Hazel and Colette managed to face mundane reality and find war work. Any kind. Just something.

It was hard. Everyone wanted to know what they were doing in Paris, a Belgian girl and a British girl. They must've been doing war work already, and what was it? How did it end? Were there letters of reference? Had there been any problems?

Colette was too mute with sorrow to talk their way into a position, and Hazel wasn't prepared with smooth, confident, not-too-terribly-dishonest answers. Admissions boards saw right through her and declined her applications.

Finally they found an agency desperate enough to take any help they could get. It was low, menial labor, work few other volunteer enlistees would do. The sort of work that neither Hazel's parents nor Tante Solange would approve of. But it was all they could find.

The work neither assisted victory efforts nor aided soldiers. Allied soldiers, that is.

They took employment working in kitchens, preparing and serving food with a Red Cross agency overseeing the concentration camps in France for German prisoners of war.

HADES

The Pink Room—April 12, 1918

IT WAS THE QUIET that first startled James. The quiet, and the clean.

The bedclothes were crisp and white. His light blue pajamas felt soft against his skin.

I've died, he thought. *This is Heaven.*

A hospital is Heaven?

The sunlit room was modern and spick-and-span. Its walls were pink. At his bedside stood a vase of daisies. There were no sounds of shelling. Only city traffic in the street below.

A nurse entered. She wore a gray dress, a white apron, and a short red cloak. A white armband displayed a large red cross, and a white veil held her hair off her face and neck.

"You're awake," she said. "Would you like some water?"

She poured him a glass, and he gulped it down. When the water hit his tongue, he realized how sandpaper-dry and foul it felt. He held out the empty glass, and she poured him more.

"What day is today?" he asked. His voice cracked. It sounded alien and young.

"It's April twelfth," she told him.

He shook his head. April twelfth. The battle . . . when had that been?

The battle landed on him an avalanche. *No, no, no, no.*

The nurse took his wrist between her cool fingertips. She smoothed hair off his forehead.

"It's all right," she told him. "You're safe here. You'll be back on your feet in no time."

"Where am I?" he croaked.

"You're at Maudsley Military Hospital," she told him. "In Camberwell. South London."

London. Back in Britain. Hazel. Pink walls reminded him of her.

The nurse gave him a plate with chicken and mashed potatoes in a cream sauce, and tinned peas rolling about the plate. After trench fare, it looked like a feast.

"Let's come sit in this nice chair by the window, shall we?"

He let the nurse help him up.

"There we go. That's right." She situated a tray in his lap. "Let's feed you up, and get your strength back. Then you can look out and see the trees. That'll do you good."

The nurse left. He scraped up a dab of potato and placed it on his tongue. His mother made better food, but after bully beef, this was fit for a king. He gulped it down, then dove into the chicken, and chased the peas around with the edge of his knife. The knife barely cut the chicken at all. Then James realized. He must be in a mental ward. Can't give sharp knives to the mental cases.

It explained all the kindness, too. Pink walls and a pretty nurse and jolly pleasantness. Because he needed to be treated gently, as one would a young child. His food soured on his tongue.

Elfin green and lacy blossoms peeped from buds on trees below.

The nurse returned. "Your parents have been by. They'll be back this afternoon."

Golden light on pink walls made James close his eyes and breathe slowly. Just like a day at the seashore, visiting his grandmother in the summertime.

His parents knew he was here in a mental hospital. So the damage was already done. But they would love him anyway. Even in the bruised and bleeding sanctum of his heart, he knew that, and he took comfort in it.

APHRODITE

Cabbage in Compiègne—April–May 1918

THERE'S A FRESH, clean smell to cabbages. Something satisfying about the crunching sound of chopping them up and dropping them with a splash into enormous vats of hard vegetable chunks.

Hazel's job was to slice, daily, three wheelbarrows full of green cabbages. Around two hundred pounds of cabbage per day. Her hands grew red and raw from cabbage juice.

But it was better than onions. Hazel couldn't handle onions. So Colette, who could, spared her friend and chopped the entire thirty-pound bag of onions daily. Even so, she had to wear aviator goggles, lest her eyes weep into the soup.

After cabbages and onions, they scrubbed and cut potatoes. Sometimes there were butcher's bones to boil down into the stock. Then the German prisoners standing in the soup line would cheer. These were the high points of life at Compiègne.

The camp at Compiègne housed eight thousand German combatant prisoners of war. They slept in drafty barracks, breakfasted on rationed bread before dawn, then worked all day. The French government had them rebuilding roads and laying train tracks. At night, the men were famished. Hazel and Colette ladled gray soup into their bowls.

Hazel hated seeing how thin and forlorn they were. Beaten down by war and captivity.

Now that she saw Germans daily, with their bright blue eyes and shaggy beards, hearing their *"Danke,* Fräulein" for the soup, she struggled to understand why they and French and British lads had spent four years killing one another.

Of course she knew about the German atrocities in Belgium. She knew what terrible brutality they had caused in 1914. But surely *these* weren't the ones who had done it. How did one nation produce both humble souls and killers?

They'd had mothers and sisters and sweethearts, jobs and hobbies and pets. Favorite songs and foods and books. Why must they die? Why must our boys die?

For Colette, serving Germans each day was agony. In their faces she saw the eyes that had sighted their pistols upon her father, her brother, her friends. She could never forgive them. But she fed them. *Whatever god wants to wound me more will fail, for I have nothing left to hurt,* she thought. *Whatever god demands forgiveness of us will have to make do with cabbage soup.*

Hazel spoke no German, but Colette did. She understood when they were cursing France and Britain under their breath.

A few could speak English, some sounding British, and others American. They made small talk with her. She did her best to be cheerful for them. She hoped whoever had James now would do the same. She prayed that someone had him in their care. The alternative was unthinkable.

Others ignored her, and a few were rude, or even vulgar in the way they looked at her. She didn't know what they muttered, but it took little imagination to guess.

After the commotion of Saint-Nazaire and the glamor of Paris, Compiègne was dull and dreary. After cleanup, they walked a short distance to the hostel where the Red Cross billeted them. They talked, wrote letters, and played cards. Eight other girls, all French, serving in various roles, nurse and typist and laundress, roomed there. They were friendly.

Only the slow approach of spring brought any uplift. Leaves uncurled, and crocuses began to poke through the frosty ground. The breezes began to smell of rain and fresh green things that weren't cabbage. There would almost be hope in the air, if it wasn't for the utter lack of news of Aubrey or James.

"This job is our penance," Colette said one morning as they'd walked to work. "If we hadn't allowed Aubrey into our hut, we'd be there still."

Hazel looked at her in astonishment. "You're not sorry, are you?"

Colette shook her head. "I'd do it all again. If only to spite Mrs. Davies. But Justice is blind," she said, "and rules are rules. Now we pay. In onions and potatoes."

"If I ever leave this job," Hazel said, "I will never, so long as I live, eat cabbage." She laughed. "It's a shame. I used to like it boiled."

Colette wrinkled her nose. "*Ffaugh.*"

"I miss the piano," Hazel said. "I wonder if I can even play anymore."

Colette looked puzzled. "Don't be silly. Of course you can."

They walked on a while longer, until the kitchen buildings were almost upon them.

"Do you think, Hazel," Colette asked her, "that we just need to learn to forget them, and move on with our lives?"

It frightened her to hear Colette voice the question Hazel had been asking herself.

"Certainly not," she cried. "Until we have firm proof otherwise, we hold out hope."

"For how long?"

Hazel watched her drab shoes crunch the gravel. "Until they're safely home again."

April became May, and May moved resolutely toward June. Hazel did the arithmetic one day and realized that she had chopped up something close to eight tons of cabbages. Her hands looked like her mother's—red and raw and cracked.

One evening, when the dinner line had finished, and all the men were seated or huddled somewhere with their bowls of soup, Colette went back to the washroom to change while Hazel consolidated all the dregs of soup from each vat into one small pan.

"More soup, please?"

A heavy German accent spoke the words. Hazel looked up to see a German prisoner standing in the doorway with his bowl cupped in his hands. She glanced toward the doorway where the armed guards always stood. Without fail, they would tell Germans asking for more food that there were no second helpings. But the guards were gone. Hazel was alone in the kitchen area with the German. And he looked so very hungry.

He hung back from the serving line, so Hazel came out from behind the counter to pour soup directly into his bowl. He dropped the bowl and pinned her against the wall. One hand he pressed into her abdomen, and the other into her neck. The pan fell from her hand, and hot soup soaked into her skirt. Before she could scream, he'd covered her mouth with his.

Hazel was so shocked, she didn't know what to do. She fought, but he was stronger. He licked her lips and teeth with his foul tongue, then forced it inside her mouth.

She struggled and fought, but he was much too strong. Even as he forced his face upon her, he laughed at her, a bitter, hateful sound.

Her brain lurched into full alert, and shock and revulsion

morphed into desperate fear. She could barely breathe. She fought and kicked and struggled. If no one came soon, he might—how *could* this be happening? Where *were* those guards?—when suddenly he let her go.

Two other German prisoners had ripped him off Hazel, leaving her drooping against the wall. One slugged her attacker in the face with his fist, smashing into his eye and then his jaw. The other tackled him to the ground and sat on his chest while the first pinned his legs down.

"Go, Fräulein," said her first rescuer. "We are very sorry."

The commotion had brought the two French guards running through the doorway from wherever they'd been dawdling. Colette appeared, too, and was at Hazel's side in an instant.

"Did this man hurt you, Mademoiselle?" the French guards asked Hazel.

If she said no, he might molest her again, or Colette, or any of the young ladies there. But if she said yes, the guards might take her offender somewhere from whence he might never return. International laws prevented countries holding soldiers as prisoners of war from killing them, but "accidents" happened. Some French soldiers were eager for any excuse.

She scrubbed at her mouth with her wrist. The sight of the man on the floor, watching her through mocking eyes, made her gag. But she wasn't ready to sign his death warrant.

"Or were they just fighting?"

Her heart sank. Now even her rescuers were in danger of punishment.

She longed for hot water. A toothbrush. Something to scrub every trace of him off her.

"He was very rude to me." Her voice was as weak as her answer. "They defended me."

Colette whirled upon the solider guards with a torrent of angry French. Something about *Why was my friend left alone?* and *She is entitled to protection at all times.*

Hazel covered her face as waves of shock and disgust and violation swept over her.

"Get up, you three," demanded the chief guard. "On your feet. *Vite, vite.*"

Her rescuers got off her attacker, and they all rose to their feet. Her attacker leered at her from out the corner of one eye.

"Let's go home, Hazel." Colette slipped an arm around her. When they'd left the camp buildings, Colette added, "Let's leave this dump and go back to Paris."

Hazel was only too glad to agree, until she returned to their room and found a letter there from her mother, featuring a clipping from the newspaper.

HADES

Welcome Home—May 6, 1918

AFTER A FEW weeks at Maudsley Hospital, James was discharged in early May.

The days had blended into a pink blur.

There were stretches of time when he thought of nothing at all. Of the robin perched on his windowsill. Of the flowers in the vase.

The shaking subsided. He never saw the syringe now.

They played a gramophone in the common room, where James took meals. He played checkers with other patients. They would talk together, and sometimes they would cry.

His parents sat on either side of him on the train ride to Chelmsford. His mother threaded her arm through his and held him close. It made him feel like a little boy.

The sight of Maggie and Bob, holding back on the porch, then running to him, brought on tears. Bob was taller, with blemishes on his nose, and Maggie had filled out a bit, with hair frizzier than ever. When they saw him cry, they feared they were the cause. He wanted to tell them, no, no, you've never been so grand, but he couldn't, so he went to his room.

He felt thirteen again, like Bob. A dusty set of tin soldiers arranged on his bookcase was too funny to laugh at.

Beside his bed lay a box containing his army kit, which had been found, by some miracle. The sight of it repulsed him.

On the table beside his bed sat a stack of letters. He opened them, saving Hazel's for last, though whether postponing pleasure or pain, he couldn't say.

The first was from, of all people, Private Billy Nutley.

April 12, 1918, it read. *Dear James, Our new sergeant gave me your address. We've been reassigned to the Third Army under the command of General Byng. We're not much farther up the line than before, but things have quieted down. Jerry gave us a terrible beating, but he ran out of steam, and we're holding. It was a good bit of work, but what a price. I've heard from Chad Browning's family. He's back in Wales and seems like he's mending all right. He'll be scarred. His folks wanted to write to you. I gave them your address. I told the new sergeant what you did, holding off the storm troopers and getting Browning to safety. We all told him to write you up for a medal. Gilchrist died, as I think you know, and Selkirk. Mason's gone missing. The rest of us, what's left of us, are all still here. Get better soon and come back and rejoin the regiment. Meanwhile, think of us while you're putting your feet up. Cheerio, Bill.*

The letter shook in his hand. He quickly opened another.

April 20, 1918. Dear Mr. Alderidge, I write to express my wife's and my utmost gratitude for heroically assisting our poor son, Chad, with his burns, and transporting him to safety. He's still recovering in hospital and has had several skin grafts. We remain hopeful for his recovery. He's still our Chad underneath all the bandages. We don't know how to thank you, but we hope that if there's ever a way that we might assist you, you will not hesitate to ask. Sincerely, Mr. and Mrs. Bowen Browning, Tenby, Wales.

Next was a letter from the army. He'd been awarded a

Distinguished Service Medal. Enclosed was a check for twenty pounds and a notice of when the actual medal would arrive.

The next letter bore a woman's handwriting, and a YMCA insignia in the corner. He read the note from Mrs. Davies, accusing Hazel of immoral carryings-on with soldiers.

Paris whirled before his eyes. Poplar. The trains. The Royal Albert Hall.

It was impossible to believe that his piano girl could be anything like what this woman had said. It had to be a lie. But why would this woman bother to send such a letter, then?

He had no more heart left to break, but in some hidden corner, buried beneath the war, he wept. If Hazel Windicott hadn't been what she appeared to be, then there was nothing left in this world to believe in at all. Honor, Right, Justice—they were already out on the dust heap.

He read the letter one more time.

Some kind Fate made the secretary send it, he thought. To ease his pain of saying goodbye. If his lack of correspondence hadn't already killed whatever affection she once had for him, he must kill it now. He was no more eligible for the love of any girl, good or bad. He was only a shell of a man. A shell of a *boy*, cringing in the small bed in his childhood bedroom in his parents' home. Utterly unfit to be what any girl might want now.

He tried to imagine Hazel here, now. Walking into this room.

His skin grew cold.

Not because the sight of her wouldn't be his dearest desire. Because it *would* be.

There might come a day when he could look back at his life, at the mauve-tinted memory of Hazel, and be glad he'd known her. That once, he'd meant something to a girl like her. That once, he'd kissed her and heard her say she loved him.

The letter from Hazel, forwarded from the Fifth Army's HQ, sat unopened. A large, stiff envelope was all that remained. He opened it and pulled out a black cardboard folio. In the photograph inside, he, Cupid, and Hazel, in the new coat he'd bought her, smiled at the camera.

For the rest of the day, when his family knocked, he didn't answer.

ARES

Spelling the Word "American"—May 14, 1918

THREE AMERICAN REPORTERS searching for stories of dough-boys abroad and visiting regiments of General Pershing's American Expeditionary Forces throughout France arrived in the Champagne sector on May 14, 1918. Their names were Thomas M. Johnson (New York *Evening Sun*), Martin Green (New York *Evening World*) and, most famous of all, Irvin S. Cobb, a popular writer for the *Saturday Evening Post*.

They knew colored soldiers were serving in the war, but believed them to be working as stevedores. They'd heard rumors of a black regiment in action, but had seen no official reports.

Finally word reached their ears of a 369th US Army division, attached to French command, serving in the Champagne sector, so there they hurried to scoop the story. As Fate would have it, they arrived the morning after two privates, Henry Johnson and Needham Roberts, fought off some twenty-four Germans in a raiding party.

Irvin Cobb, a Southerner from Kentucky, was famous for depicting black people as lazy, ignorant "darkies," trading in stereotypes and watermelon jokes. Many black soldiers refused to greet him. But Cobb, learning of Henry Johnson's and Needham

Roberts's heroics, and seeing the spot where the battle occurred strewn with German weapons, and a puddle of congealing blood the size of a washtub, knew a story when he saw one.

All three reporters dispatched articles home. "Young Black Joe," they called both Johnson and Roberts. Later features dubbed it "The Battle of Henry Johnson." The story was a national sensation. They described the battle in vivid detail—how Roberts, shot in numerous places, lay on the ground and hurled grenades at the foe, while Johnson, also shot many times, still fought off the Germans and defended Roberts, first with his rifle, then with the butt of the rifle, then with a bolo knife. The bolo knife would make him a star from coast to coast.

Even Cobb, who had made a living peddling in Jim Crow stereotypes, and knew it, was moved by Johnson's heroics. He put a curious coda on his own article:

. . . *as a result of what our black soldiers are going to do in this war, a word that has been uttered billions of times in our country, sometimes in derision, sometimes in hate, sometimes in all kindliness—but which I am sure never fell on black ears but it left behind a sting for the heart—is going to have a new meaning for all of us, South and North too, and that hereafter n-i-*-*-*-r will merely be another way of spelling the word American.*

APHRODITE

House Call—June 1, 1918

ON SATURDAY, the first of June, on a bright and hazy mid-morning, Hazel knocked on the front door of a large home on Vicarage Road, Old Moulsham, Chelmsford, with her heart in her throat.

A comfortable-looking woman in a calico day dress answered the door.

"Good morning, dearie," she said. "Who might you be?"

"Good morning," Hazel managed to say. "My name is Hazel Windicott. I'm looking for a Mr. James Alderidge." She swallowed. "I'm his friend."

The woman's expression changed. "Are you, now?" she said. "Come right on in, then."

The woman threw a plump arm around her shoulders and steered her through the entryway into a front sitting room. It was dark, paneled with stained oak. It felt more homey than elegant, which relieved Hazel.

"Let me take your jacket. What a pretty pink! Here, make yourself comfortable."

A young woman of fifteen or so with the thickest sandy-brown hair Hazel had ever seen poked her nose into the front sitting room. Maggie.

"Margaret, dear, there's a *friend of James's* here. Fetch us some tea and biscuits, will you?" She layered "friend of James's" with the significance of "Queen of England."

Maggie's eyebrows shot up. She disappeared toward the rear of the house.

Hazel felt rather dizzy. Every aspect of her appearance, she realized, was now being studied. Was her violet-colored skirt too garish? Her Paris shoes too vain?

"Tell me," the woman asked, "how do you know James?"

Is James here? Why won't you tell me?

"We met at a parish dance," Hazel said. "In Poplar. Right before he left for France."

"A parish dance!" the woman said. "Well, isn't he one for not telling his blessed mother anything! Though I suppose most young men are."

Hazel took the plunge. "*Are* you Mrs. Alderidge?"

The woman clapped a hand upon her forehead. "Dearie me, yes! Lost my head along with my youth ages ago, it seems. Yes, I'm Mrs. Alderidge." She chuckled.

"And is James here?"

The woman's face grew still. She opened her mouth, then paused. "You don't know."

Hazel's flesh went cold. God in heaven, please, no.

"Mrs. Alderidge," she pleaded, "what don't I know?"

"Oh, you look so pale," said Mrs. Alderidge. "When did you last hear from James?"

"We had been writing regularly," Hazel said, "but then there was the great battle, where the Fifth Army—well, anyway, after the battle, the letters stopped. And I was so afraid."

Mrs Alderidge's face melted with sympathy.

"And then my mother sent me a clipping she saw in the paper," Hazel's words rushed on, "saying he was receiving the Distinguished Service Medal."

Mrs. Alderidge swelled with pride.

"So I came back from France, where I'd been doing war work, to see if I could learn anything about him."

"You came back from France," echoed Mrs. Alderidge wonderingly. "Where you'd been doing war work. Oh, you dear, dear girl." She closed her eyes, as though the tenderness of the scene was just more than she could bear.

This is James's mother, Hazel told herself. *Don't grab her shoulders and shake her.*

Maggie appeared then in the doorway with a tray laden with a tea service, which she set down upon a table nearby. "Shall I take some, er, upstairs?" she asked her mother.

Who's upstairs? Hazel was desperate to know. Was Maggie trying to tell her something?

"I will in a bit, Margaret," Mrs. Alderidge said.

Maggie retreated slowly from the room. Mrs. Alderidge busied herself with pouring tea and asking Hazel how she took it, cream or no, when Hazel's patience burst.

"Please, Mrs. Alderidge," Hazel implored, "is James still alive?"

A shadow passed across her hostess's face. "He is, thank the Lord." She set down the cup and took both of Hazel's hands in hers. "You poor dear lamb. You feared he was dead?"

Tears pricked Hazel's eyes. She closed her eyelids tight.

"Is he badly wounded, then?"

Mrs. Alderidge released her hands slowly. A new dread settled onto Hazel's shoulders. *It doesn't matter,* she told herself. *Whatever it is, it doesn't matter. As long as it's James.*

James's mother watched her for what felt like an eternity.

"He is well in body," she said at length, "but he's not yet, quite, himself."

In other corners of the house, people moved about, but no sound reached Hazel. *Not. Yet. Quite. Himself.*

"Why don't I pop upstairs," Mrs. Alderidge said, "and just have a little chat with James? Seeing you might do him a world of good."

Hazel soon heard footsteps ascending the stairs.

She tried to compose herself.

He is well in body but he's not yet, quite, himself.

Yet.

"Yet" meant he could become himself. What was wrong could be made right with time.

The footsteps were in the room directly above this one, over-looking the street. She glanced up at the ceiling. There was James. Somewhere above her. Right there.

Shell shock? Was that it? Some of the German prisoners had suffered from it. The more severe cases had been kept in a separate ward. They couldn't work.

Her mind conjured up unspeakable things. Straitjackets. Ravening insanity. Violence. The thought of German prisoners brought back the horrid scene from Compiègne that had haunted her quiet moments and her nightmares. She pressed a fist over her lips.

Stop it.

Why hadn't James come down?

Maybe he was getting dressed. She tucked imaginary stands of hair back into place.

Or maybe he couldn't see her today, but he'd be eager to see her very soon.

That was all right. Of course! Let's see. She could find lodging somewhere, maybe, and stay in the area a couple of days, wire her parents a telegram. Find some respectable older woman who let rooms to boarders, and . . .

A much slower tread sounded on the stairs, coming down.

Hazel braced herself. *James.*

But it wasn't James.

"I am so very sorry, Miss Windicott," Mrs. Alderidge began. "James is not feeling up for company at present."

Hazel willed herself to smile. "That's all right," she said. "I can come back another—"

Mrs. Alderidge shook her head. "James has asked me to give you a message."

Hazel lowered her head. It was all the privacy the moment allowed her.

"He asked me to say," the woman said, "that it's best if your friendship end with the pleasant memories you've shared. He wishes you his very best for your health and happiness."

Mrs. Alderidge had the tact to let Hazel sit a moment.

"Whatever is wrong with him," she whispered to her knees, "I would help him. I would be patient while he got better."

Mrs. Alderidge sighed. "That's very good of you, my dear," she said sadly. "Very, very good."

Hazel dangled, suspended in shock, until she remembered Mrs. Alderidge was watching.

She rose. "Thank you for the tea."

"All the best to you, my dear." Mrs. Alderidge handed Hazel her coat. "I just can't tell you how sorry I am."

Hazel headed down the gravel walk to the garden gate. Everything in her wanted to look up at the front windows and see if James's face would be there, but she felt Mrs. Alderidge's gaze pinned between her shoulder blades and moved quickly down the street.

APHRODITE

Watching Her Go—June 1, 1918

IN THE DOORWAY of the Alderidge home, Maggie stood by her mother.

"James sent a girl like *that* away without so much as a hello?"

Her mother sighed. "It's not his fault, Mags."

Maggie shook her head. "I don't care whose fault it is. It's stupid, and I liked her."

"So does your brother."

"Then why doesn't—"

"Don't you dare meddle in this, Maggie," her mother said. "I've said too much as it is. The poor boy's got enough trouble."

Maggie wandered off to the butler's pantry she'd made into her typing room and pecked at a keyboard exercise, thinking, thinking.

In a second-story window, James stood in shadow and watched her leave. He couldn't help it.

As she turned at the gate, he caught a quick sight of her face in profile. There she was, downcast and perfect.

Her tall posture, her dark hair piled atop her head, her long neck, her head bowed down in sadness, her steps slow. The soft white lace of her collar, wrapped around her throat. That bright coat he'd bought her. She was *right there*. With sunlight casting a halo around her. Growing smaller, though, as each step carried her farther away.

She had come. To see him.

If she were what that woman from the YMCA had said, would she have come?

If she were what he'd believed her to be, how could he watch her leave?

If only he could bolt out there now, and take her in his arms, and die there.

But he was no longer what she'd known him to be. He would never be that James again.

I will never hurt you, Hazel Windicott.

Oh, God.

Better that he hurt her once, now, than prolong her hurt, or even allow her pity and kindness to lock her into a commitment that would pain her for the rest of her life.

If he loved her, he must leave her alone.

He watched her until a bend in the road took her out of sight.

APHRODITE

Spasms—June 1, 1918

THIS WAS THE crucial moment. All my work was about to go up in flames. I lose enough loves to misfortune, stupidity, and selfishness, not to mention disease and deadly war. I couldn't let Hazel get on that London-bound train. I searched desperately. I had only minutes to avert a tragedy.

Her footsteps carried her blindly along, seeing nothing through a film of tears.

Up ahead stood an old vicarage. Knitting on the porch was the vicar's elderly wife.

I'm not proud of what I did next.

In my defense, this sort of thing happened to Mrs. Puxley several times in any given day.

I gave her a back spasm. She cried out in pain. I knew she'd be theatrical about it.

Her cry reached Hazel even through her despair. She hurried up the walk.

I know it wasn't sporting or nice. I never said I was either. But I'm not a monster. The remainder of her week was spasm-free, and her husband kissed her cheek, twice.

May I continue? Thank you.

Mrs. Puxley was so doubled over that when Hazel offered to help, the white-haired lady saw only a violet skirt and a pair of elegant shoes such as Parisian girls can buy off the rack whilst the ladies of Chelmsford only dream of them, and faintly disapprove.

The skirt and the shoes helped Mrs. Puxley indoors and onto a sofa, found cushions for her head and knees, and fetched a drink of water. Despite her pain, she got a good look at Hazel.

"Who are you, my dear?" she asked. "You're not from around here."

"No," replied Hazel. "I'm from London. I came to the neighborhood to visit a friend."

Mrs. Puxley winced as another nerve chose to express itself. "Well, you've been an angel of mercy to me," said she. Mrs. Puxley, that is. Not the nerve.

"Is there anyone I should summon for you?" inquired Hazel.

"It's the maid's day off," moaned Mrs. Puxley, "and my husband is at a funeral in town."

"Shall I get you some aspirin?" asked Hazel.

"Nasty German stuff," answered Mrs. Puxley. "I don't believe in it."

The old lady seemed so frail and pitiable that Hazel didn't know how to leave.

"You keep on glancing at the piano, my dear," observed Mrs. Puxley. "Do you play?"

"I do," Hazel said, "though it's been a while."

"Play something for me," said Mrs. Puxley. "Something gentle, for my poor nerves."

Hazel hesitated. She had no music with her, and it had been months. She had come straight to Chelmsford from France. She hadn't even stopped at home to see her parents. She could go see them to celebrate finding James, she had thought, or to cry on their shoulders if—

If.

So many ifs. Never had she imagined this one—James, alive, refusing to see her.

"My dear?" inquired Mrs. Puxley. "Are you all right?"

"Oh." Hazel tried to smile. "I'm fine."

"There's no need to play if it's upsetting to you," said the vicar's wife.

"No, no." Hazel rose quickly. "I'm happy to."

So she played, for Mrs. Puxley, Beethoven's "Pathétique." The second movement. "Adagio cantabile."

Beethoven's "Pathetic," Aubrey had called it. She sent up a little prayer that he was out there somewhere, safe.

And she understood now, in a way that she never had before, the sorrow and longing wrapped up in Beethoven's Piano Sonata Number 8 in C minor, opus 13. They flowed into her playing from her broken heart. This was what she'd needed. This salve for her wounded soul.

"My dear," Mrs. Puxley whispered breathlessly, after the last notes had reverberated throughout the house, "who are you?"

"My name is Hazel Windicott," said she.

"Are you an accompanist? Do you give lessons?"

Ah. Hazel tried to think how to answer. "I was doing war work," she explained, "but circumstances forced me to leave my position, and I came here." She wished the older lady would stop questioning her and let her play. So brief a taste, after months without music, was agony.

Mrs. Puxley very nearly salivated. "You mean to say," she whispered, "that you are completely unattached at present?"

Her unfortunate choice of words pricked Hazel's heart. She

was very much attached, even if her beloved was no longer.

"I had planned on returning to some other kind of war work, if I could find it," she said, "but my hope, eventually, is to prepare for auditions to a music conservatory."

Her words surprised her. Yes. She *would* apply. Where was her fear of performing for others now? Gone, along with so many other childish things. Whatever else her future held, she would play the piano. Because *she* wanted to. Not because anyone expected it of her.

"I should hope you *do* intend to study at a conservatory," Mrs. Puxley said decisively. "With a talent like yours, it would be a crime not to."

Hazel had played at enough piano competitions to know hers wasn't a legendary talent. But there ought to be a seat for her somewhere, at some reputable music school, if she worked hard.

"You have a beautiful piano," she said. "A lovely tone, and the room has fine acoustics."

Mrs. Puxley saw her opening. "Miss Windicott," she said, "this is rather precipitate of me, but it's just my husband and I, here, in this big old place. Our son is married and gone. We lack a children's pianist right now, for the Sunday school. What could be nicer than to have you stay with us for a spell, practicing for auditions and making this old place a bit brighter?"

Hazel was dumbstruck.

I will not say that I was uninvolved in this rather rash invitation.

"My husband's always asking me, why *do* I go to the expense of keeping that instrument tuned," she went on, "but I tell him, 'Alfred, you never know when you'll need a piano.'" She turned to Hazel. "Obviously, you're a well-brought-up young lady. Have you any luggage?"

Luggage? Had they reached the stage of discussing *luggage?*

Should she do this dreadful thing? To situate herself just down the street from James, after he'd said he didn't wish to see her anymore?

Do it, I told her. *Seize the chance.*

He deserves it, she thought wickedly. Sending her off without even a hello! She'd come all the way from France to make sure he was all right, and she wasn't leaving until she'd done so. Let him tell her to her face that it was over, and then she would go. Meanwhile, she would stay close by and practice on this lovely piano. Why not?

"My luggage is at the station," she told Mrs. Puxley.

"Excellent," said that worthy woman, rising from the sofa and forgetting all about her spasm. "I'll send the neighbor to go claim it for you."

The vicar's wife, having found the piano girl for her lonely hours and her children's Sunday school, was not about to let her walk to the station and change her mind.

ARES

Light Duty—June 3–4, 1918

ON MONDAY, JAMES ventured into town, dressed in a suit coat and tie. His appointment was with the military board of review, whose job it was to determine his rate of recovery, and his readiness to return to military service. If they found him well enough, he'd be back at the trenches, where, in his dulled state, he wouldn't last a week. If they found him unfit, it would be yet another humiliating reminder of his shattered self.

There were three physicians on the board. One seemed to be of the "get back to it, you shirkers" philosophy, while another was full of sympathy for neurasthenic cases, as shell-shocked patients were called, and a third kept his sentiments well guarded. James submitted to an orderly's poking and prodding, then sat and answered questions fired at him by the panel of three. It felt rather like Judgment Day. When the interview was over, he sat numbly until a verdict was announced: he had made progress. Rest had done him good. He was not yet ready to return to combat but likely would be in time. He was to report to the recruiting office in town the next day for "light duty." Paperwork. He could don his uniform and do his bit.

He walked home.

Just the thought of his uniform made him shiver. He didn't want to leave the safety of his room. But maybe it would do him good to get away from his mother's hovering.

The following morning he bathed, dressed in uniform, and headed up Vicarage Road toward the town.

APHRODITE

Hoping It Might Be You—June 4, 1918

"YOU LOVE MY brother, don't you?"

Hazel jumped up. She'd taken a walk at midday through the park around the church, and was kneeling to admire some flowers. Now she rose, nearly colliding with a girl. A girl with frizzy hair.

Margaret.

"You can call me Maggie," the girl said. "So, do you love him?"

Hazel took a step back. "I—"

"Because I could take him a note for you."

Hazel blinked. "Your mother certainly would not approve."

"I wouldn't tell her," said Maggie, as if this were the most obvious solution in the world. "That's why you stayed in Chelmsford, isn't it? For the chance to see him?"

Was Hazel's heart that obvious?

They continued the stroll Hazel had been taking before Maggie appeared.

"Maggie," Hazel said, "how is James? Is he . . . all right?"

Maggie thought about this question. "Mum says he'll be fine, but Dad's not so sure."

A stab in the heart. "And what do you think?"

Maggie walked a bit, then turned to Hazel. "I think he needs something, and he won't get better until he finds it," she said. "Mum, I could tell, was hoping it might be you."

"But now she doesn't think so."

Maggie shook her head. "No. She doesn't."

Hazel walked unseeing. "I guess," she said slowly, "that's what I'd been hoping, too."

APHRODITE

Work—June 4–9, 1918

JAMES WORKED ALL that week. Hazel practiced all week.

The first few days at the recruiting office were misery. They had neither a job nor a desk for him, so he sat on a bench until someone produced a meaningless task. Hours dragged, and his attention roved. *I'll never see Hazel again.*

At the piano, Hazel rebuilt her strength and dexterity. She tried to focus, but one persistent thought derailed her: *what could have happened that James won't see me at all?*

Eventually the recruiting office found something useful for James to do. Sorting through draftee files and updating them with details from casualty lists. It was excruciating. Many of the casualties were lads he'd grown up with, or their older brothers, and in some cases, their fathers. Grief and sorrow everywhere.

Sometimes, walking home, he heard strains of piano music wafting from the vicarage. It reminded him painfully of Hazel.

On Saturday, June 8, 1918, the Germans launched Operation Gneisenau at Noyon-Montdidier, France, the fourth of their five great pushes in their Spring Offensive.

On Sunday, June 9, 1918, James agreed to attend church with

his family, but Hazel, stationed in the children's Sunday school, never saw him, nor he, her.

The gentle, elderly vicar prayed that the war would soon come to an end.

HADES

Let It Be Me—June 14, 1918

JAMES SAT AT dinner with the family now. He smiled sometimes and talked about the day's work.

His sister thought, *I know something nobody else knows.*

On Friday of that week, he went out for a walk in the evening with Bobby. They walked out of town a ways, to a woodsy ramble near a stream that James had always liked when he was young and which Bobby, ardent Boy Scouter, was crazy about. Evenings were long now, and Bobby brought his field glasses. He showed James various birds, and pointed out the names of trees and plants, and which were edible. James was impressed. This juvenile hobby had its uses. In war, if Bobby were separated from his squadron, he'd survive better than most.

The thought of Bobby having to go to war socked James in the gut. He stopped walking. Bobby went on, watching a chipmunk through his glasses. Such a beautiful kid.

James had held Bobby as a baby. Rolled balls to him, read him stories, taught him to walk, steadied the handlebars of his tiny bike. Bobby showed signs of young manhood on the near horizon, but he was still James's baby brother.

He saw Bobby's burnt and blood-soaked body lying in the mud at the bottom of a trench.

Let it be me, he told the sky. *I'm damaged, but he's free. Make me better, and send me back, so I can die instead of Bobby. He has a future. Send me back where I belong.*

APHRODITE

Mangled Up—June 14, 1918

BOBBY WANDERED OFF after the chipmunk. James waited, listening to birds whoop and chatter, then, knowing Bobby would find his way home, James headed back. He knew what he needed to do, and that would give his days purpose until he returned to the Front. He had one other item of business that he must attend to, and soon there would be an end.

He turned toward Vicarage Road, nearly colliding with a young woman.

"I'm sorry . . ." he began.

"Hello, James," said she.

Four startled eyes, two pounding hearts.

He swept off his hat and gazed down into her anxious, pleading eyes. He could barely see for the swirling riot inside his head.

"Why are you here?"

The words bruised. They came out like an attack. James immediately regretted them. He hadn't meant them that way, not the combative tone, but it was too late. She stepped back and looked away. Then she raised her head proudly.

"I came to see if you were alive," she said, "and to be with you, if I could, to help you with your recovery, if you weren't well."

The sight of him frightened her. He looked pale and thinner than in Paris. And he was *changed*. The sound of a distant automobile made him twitch and look over his shoulder.

But he was still her beautiful James.

She had never looked more glorious. He'd never seen her in a summer dress, with bare arms below the elbow, and bare ankles tapering into lightweight shoes. Her cheeks were pink from walking. Strands of hair had fallen loose from her coiffure and swayed in the evening breeze. The lavender sky was just her color. It wanted to wrap itself around her too.

"What if I'd been mangled up?" he blurted out. "Lost an arm or something?"

It stung to know what he was really asking was, *What if you don't love me enough?*

"*Have* you been mangled up?" she asked him.

He covered his mouth with his hand. It was almost funny. Had he been mangled? In brain, but what of it? His hadn't been a legendary brain to begin with. He'd seen true mangling. Laughter, as it so often did these days, flipped quickly into tears. He forced them back.

He could see that he was hurting her, and it frightened him.

"I'm sorry," he told her. "I'm so sorry."

"For what?"

For surviving.

The answer would be pathetic, would sound like a desperate cry, and he had some dignity left, somewhere, so he didn't say it. He replaced his hat, bowed, and walked away, trailing broken bits of himself, like bread crumbs, or blood droplets, in his wake.

APHRODITE

Ride to Lowestoft—June 15, 1918

THE NEXT MORNING, early, Hazel arrived at the Chelmsford railway station. The Puxleys' neighbor had brought her and her suitcase in his wagon. She purchased a ticket for a London train.

James entered the station and boarded a train already in the stable. He didn't see her.

Let him go, she thought bitterly.

But the seed couldn't take root in Hazel's heart. There he was, boarding that train, like One More Chance about to slip away.

She struggled to drag her heavy case back over to the ticket window.

"Can I change my London ticket to one for that train?" she asked the cashier, a balding and slightly oily person, neither through any fault of his own.

"Where are you bound?" asked he.

"Wherever it's bound," was her reply.

The cashier's eyes bulged. This was the most interesting thing to happen at the Chelmsford station for a month of Sundays. He changed her ticket.

"You're not chasing after that young chappie who just got on the train, are you?" he said.

"That's a rather impertinent question, don't you think?" snapped Hazel. "Porter!"

The cashier watched her go. "She's chasing after that chappie," he told his fellow cashier at the adjacent window. "I'd bet my week's wages."

"I would too if I were her," replied the other cashier, a spinster of a certain age. Women, in men's jobs! The war, of course.

Hazel boarded the train. When it pulled out, she rose and worked her way forward until she spotted James. He sat alone in a group of four seats and watched out the window. She barged into his section and sat down in the aisle seat facing his. If he tried to leave, she vowed, she would kick out a leg and trip him.

If she didn't manage to trip him, I would do it myself.

He looked up soon enough, but not instantly, pausing just long enough that she wanted to scream. But discover her he did, and the surprise on his face was worth an extra train fare.

He gazed at her, dumbstruck, for what felt like an eternity, then sank back into his chair, hid his face inside the bell of his hat, and began to laugh.

Hazel didn't know whether to be relieved, or to swat his knees with her handbag.

He said something, but through the felt of his hat, Hazel wasn't sure what.

"How's that?"

He removed his hat. "I said, 'What am I going to do with you?'"

"You're going to talk to me," she said firmly. "I think I deserve that much."

He couldn't help it. He smiled at her, even if his face had forgotten how. She was angry, and so *adorably* angry, that he didn't know what to do. That was undoubtedly a very patronizing thing to think, but it didn't matter. Guilty as charged.

The sight of his smile defrosted something in Hazel.

"What do you want me to say?" James asked her.

What indeed?

"Where are you going?" she asked.

"Where are *you* going?"

"None of that," she said firmly. "I asked you first."

"To Lowestoft," he said.

This was the last thing Hazel had expected to hear, not that she had any expectation at all. "Perfect day for a sunny outing at the beach?" she inquired.

"Don't be sarcastic."

"Just the place to get one's mind off their troubles."

The look that passed across his face made her pause. She tried again in a gentler tone.

"What brings you to Lowestoft?"

He turned to look at her. "To see someone."

"Someone you met in France?" she asked.

He shook his head. "A woman."

To Hazel's credit, she did not become jealous. Baffled, though.

"How long is it to Lowestoft?" she asked.

"Two and a half hours, nearly," he said. "Will you come with me?"

She looked up quickly. "To spend the day with you?"

"It doesn't appear," James said, "that I have any choice in the matter."

"You don't," she agreed. "But I try to seem polite."

He smiled, against his will, and shook his head. "You're quite a girl, Hazel Windicott."

She met his gaze. "So a good friend once told me."

HADES

What Adelaide Needed to Know—June 15, 1918

THE RIDE WAS LONG. James watched out the window. Hazel's attempts at small talk went nowhere. She hid behind a novel. She bought a bag of nuts and offered him some, which he declined.

"You know," she said, "you still notice all the grand buildings, in every town we pass."

He smiled. Just a little, but Hazel saw it. "Do I?"

They settled into silence. At Ipswich, they left the train and waited for another. James helped Hazel with her luggage. Again they sat in a private booth, facing each other.

"How is your friend?" he asked at length. "Colette."

"She's well." Hazel paused. "Well, and not well. You remember me telling you about Aubrey? My friend, the jazz pianist at Saint-Nazaire?"

He nodded.

"He went missing," Hazel said. "The band shipped out, and he wasn't supposed to go with them, but he vanished, and nobody's had any word of him. But there was a murder of a black soldier at the base, and"—she gulped—"Colette is convinced he's the one who was killed."

"Do you think he was murdered?" asked James.

"I hope not," Hazel said. "But if he's alive, and he cared for Colette, why didn't he write?"

She realized her gaffe too late. She wished she could crawl under her seat and hide.

"Perhaps he didn't care as much as your friend thought."

Hazel's face, she was sure, could light kindling wood. She dove back into the novel.

"Was it spending time with Aubrey," asked James, "that got you and Colette in trouble?"

Hazel looked up sharply. "How do you know about that? In my letter, I said we'd quit."

He hadn't read the letter but couldn't admit it. "So you didn't tell me the entire truth?"

"Well, who told you?" she retorted.

He was caught now. "Your supervisor," he said. "Mrs. Davies."

Hazel half rose from her chair. "She *what*?"

James glanced around, embarrassed. "She wrote to me," he whispered, "when my letters piled up after you left. She said you'd been dismissed for entertaining soldiers after hours."

Hazel's anger was no longer exactly adorable. "How *dare* she! Of all the *nerve*!" She whirled upon James. "And you believed her, is that it? Is that why you stopped writing?"

"No," he said simply. "It isn't."

This left her deflated, then stunned. "Are you sure?"

He looked out the window. "Very sure."

Hazel's bitterness of heart was acute. It was almost funny. She'd grown excited, she realized, and hopeful. If Mrs. Davies had sundered them, an explanation could fix all. But if his caring for her had died on its own, nothing could ever fix that. She fished urgently around in her purse for a handkerchief.

James saw the tears and knew he was the cause.

The conductor announced the Lowestoft station, coming up. James gathered his things.

Once more they collected the heavy suitcase and stowed it at baggage claim. James consulted a card in his pocket with an address, then studied a map. Together they set off.

Half of Britain had decided to spend a sunny Saturday at the seashore at Lowestoft. Mothers and children, youths too young for war, and the middle-aged streamed off the train platform with picnic baskets. James and Hazel followed the crowd toward the waterfront until he turned onto a side street.

James found the number he wanted, and Hazel wondered if she ought to stay at the gate. But James held the gate open for her, and as she passed through it, she caught once again that familiar scent of him, of clean, ironed cotton and spicy bay rum aftershave. It was humiliating, really, how much it affected her.

James took a deep breath, approached the door, and knocked.

A woman slowly opened the door.

James knew the face, but the expression was unlike the image he'd seen. She was enormously pregnant, carrying a husky toddler boy on one arm.

The child made James ache. That round, chubby face. He'd need a dad to play catch with and teach him to swim. James wanted to take the tyke in his arms. Or bolt for the train station.

"Mrs. Mason?" he asked.

"Who's asking?"

"My name is James Alderidge," he said. "I served with your husband in France."

She clapped her free hand over her mouth and gasped. "Come in, come in, please."

Hazel absorbed this information in quiet shock. Frank Mason.

The one he often mentioned to her in his letters. His closest friend at the Front. Dead. Gone. He must be.

They followed her into the kitchen. It wasn't tidy, and Mrs. Mason clearly felt ashamed.

"I'm so sorry," Mrs. Mason stammered. "What with the baby on the way, and this one wearing me out, I've been a bit slack. . . ."

"Please don't give it a thought," murmured Hazel. She wished she could help by washing the dirty dishes in the sink, but it would multiply the woman's embarrassment.

"I'm Adelaide." The young mother held out a hand to Hazel. "You're Mrs. Alderidge?"

Hazel blushed. "No, I'm a friend. Hazel Windicott."

"Your lady friend, then," Adelaide told James. "How nice of you both to come." She filled a kettle with water. "I'll just get this heating up, and we'll have tea, all right?" She glanced over at the corner, where the toddler was busy dragging all the pots and pans out of a cupboard. "Here! Frankie. None of that noise now, love. Go play with your blocks."

Little Frankie had no intention of giving up the pots and pans. Hazel sat on the floor and reached for the wooden blocks. She tried to interest him in playing, but the sturdy little lad ignored her, so she built a tower herself. Once she no longer appeared to care about Frankie's attention, she had it in full. Before long they were at work, adding blocks in turn to the tower, and laughing when it fell. She realized James and Adelaide weren't talking. She looked up to see the boy's mother smiling, and James watching her intently, with a look she couldn't place.

Frankie, she thought, *at last I've found you. A lad whose feelings are easy to read.*

"Your turn." She handed him a red one.

Adelaide Mason set out mugs for tea. "It was awfully good of you to come."

"Frank never told me you were expecting," James said gently. "Did he know?"

The poor woman's face grew red. "He did." She found a kerchief in her apron pocket. "Frank always did want a big family. A handful of sons to join him in the fishing business."

She began to cry. Little Frankie toddled to his mother, hid in her skirt, and joined in.

"Poor little tyke." She laughed between sobs. "He's got a mama who cries more nowadays than her own baby does."

James watched little Frankie. The child wandered over to study him.

"Hello, little man." James managed a smile. "Shake hands?"

Frankie wasn't interested. When Mrs. Mason's crying subsided, James addressed her.

"Your husband was in my company, in my squadron," he said. "I was a new recruit. He taught me how to survive in the trenches. I'd be dead a dozen times over if it weren't for him."

They all heard the question percolating in the poor woman's mind. *Then why is he dead?*

"He was the kindest, most thoughtful man."

"He was that, wasn't he?" Adelaide's tears erupted again. "He never treated me like anything but a lady, and never acted like anything but a gentleman." She blew her nose.

Frankie resumed their tower building. Clear spittle ran from his gummy mouth, complete with eight pearly baby teeth of his own. Hazel wiped his chin on his bib and hugged him.

"It gets awfully lonely out there, in the trenches," James said, "and having a friend like Frank made all the difference."

"I'll bet it did," said the widow. "He wrote to me about you, too, you know. Said you were a real fine chap. From Chelmsford, is that right?" She smiled. "He said, when the war was over, we were to have you up here to the seaside to visit." She stuck out her chin. "You can still come." Then she remembered, apparently, that James was a single man, and she, a widow. "Well, when you and this nice young lady make it official, you can both come." She beamed at Hazel. "Frankie's taken a real shine to you!"

"The feeling's mutual." Hazel took a blue block from his sticky hand and set it atop their fourth tower. She waited for James to comment on them "making it official," but he said nothing.

"Tell me," Mrs. Mason asked James, "do you know anything about how he died?"

James's eyes closed.

"The other widows around here, they've gotten letters from commanding officers telling them what happened, and packages containing their husbands' personal effects, but I've had nothing! Nobody seems to know. Is he buried? Where's he buried? I've written and written."

Hazel stacked blocks without seeing them.

"Says in the papers the Fifth Army's disbanded," she went on. "To whom do I write?"

With effort, James sat up straighter and begin to speak.

"I was with Frank when he died," he said gently. "I was there."

The tablecloth bunched up beneath Mrs. Mason's hands.

"It was the twenty-first of March," he said. "The first day of the battle of Saint-Quentin. We were under attack," he said. "The Germans had us hopelessly outnumbered."

"*Bock,*" said Frankie, injecting vocabulary into their building exercise.

"We were guarding a section of trench," he went on, "when German storm troopers invaded it."

This quiet young man, the one who had danced with her in London and in Paris, surrounded by Germans with guns.

"I read about those storm fighters," Adelaide whispered. "Did they get my Frank?"

James shook his head.

"There were two of them, with pistols," James said. "I took out one, then Frank stopped the other from shooting me before I could get him, too. He saved my life."

"And you saved his, sounds like," Adelaide said.

But not for long, said no one.

Hazel's hand shook. James, Germans, guns, and blood. Down came the wooden tower.

"*Boom!*" squealed Frankie.

"One of the storm troops had a flamethrower," James went on. "They got our pal, Chad Browning, pretty bad."

Adelaide sucked in her breath. "Not that funny young kid! Did he die?" James shook his head, and she sagged with relief. "Frank mentioned him, too, in his letters." She nodded in Hazel's direction. "My Frank was a fine one for writing letters."

"Because he missed you," Hazel said, "and he loved you."

Mrs. Mason smiled sadly at the tabletop. "What happened next?"

"I shot the soldier with the flamethrower," James said slowly, "and Frank and another kid dropped on top of Browning to put out the fire. Then we carried him to the Red Cross station, which was a ways off, through the trenches."

"Frank was a hero, wasn't he?" said Adelaide. "I always knew he would be."

Little Frankie got tired of the tower they were on and demolished it with a burst of laughter. Hazel gathered up the blocks and started again.

"Some German soldiers stood atop the parapet, shooting down at us in our trenches," James said slowly. "We were easy targets. So as soon as we'd gotten Chad taken care of, Frank and

I climbed up top to take out the German shooters."

There were those words again: "take out." Like something one does with a sack of rubbish. Hazel looked at the grinning, gummy, chubby-cheeked child at her knees, playing building blocks, and at the sober-faced young man seated at the table. *Once he was you,* she told little Frankie silently. What dread experiences must one face in order to speak so casually of killing?

May you never face them, little one.

But her prayer went unanswered. Frankie is a man now. Private Frank Mason Jr. of the Suffolk Regiment. Stationed in Algeria, bravely fighting the Nazis, just as his father fought the Germans before him.

HADES

James's Answers—June 15, 1918

THE FOG IN James's head and the fog over the trenches blended together. At last the mist parted.

"There was a Jerry with a grenade launcher," he said slowly. "I got him."

Mrs. Mason sat very still now, with her eyes closed.

"And another, taking aim at me. Frank got him."

Mrs. Mason flinched, as if she'd felt the impact of the bullet.

Hazel found herself holding her breath. What was this nightmare her James described? This hell faced by her sweet boy who could cry at the loveliness of a symphony orchestra?

The kettle began to shrill. Little Frankie emitted an ear-piercing imitation. Adelaide poured it, through a cloud of steam, over the tea leaves in the strainer, and into the china teapot.

"The fog was thick," said James. "We were on the ground. A Jerry took aim at Frank."

"The bastard!"

Hazel covered little Frankie's ears.

"But he didn't get him," James explained. "I shot that Jerry, too, before he could."

The kettle clunked back onto the gas stove. "Then who did?"

Hazel's heart bled for Mrs. Mason. She already knew how this sad tale ended. She was just searching to find its villain.

"I don't know," said James faintly. "Some gunner from a couple of miles away."

Adelaide's handkerchief found its use again.

"When I shot the German trying to kill Frank," James said, "Frank was so surprised that he jumped up tall, from where he'd been lying down." He swallowed hard. "Just in time to catch a shell right in the chest."

Silence fell over the kitchen. Adelaide wrapped her arms around her middle, as if to ward off the missile, finding to her surprise that there was a baby there to protect too.

"*Boom!*" squealed Frankie, capsizing another tower.

Adelaide jumped. "Not now, child!" she cried. "Can't you tell Mummy needs to think?"

Frankie blithely ignored the scolding, as well-loved children usually do. Hazel busied herself with a novel creation: a double tower, two blocks wide. Frankie quickly got on board with this plan. Build and destroy, build and destroy. This game never grew old.

"Do you mean to tell me," Adelaide asked James, "that if Frank had stayed down, he might be alive today?"

"I'm so sorry." James's voice cracked. "I told him not to come up top. 'You've got a wife and a kid,' I told him. 'Stay down.' But he wouldn't let me go up alone."

Adelaide seized his hands. "No more would my Frank've done so, and that's the truth."

James's chin drooped. "I'm so sorry." His body shook. "I'm so, so sorry."

Adelaide cast a despairing look at Hazel. *What should I do?*

"I wish it had been me," James said. "He should've come home to you."

Adelaide Mason poured out a mug of tea for James. "Now, don't say that," she said. "It doesn't work that way, and you know it." She winced, and rubbed her pregnant belly. "This one's a boy too, or I'm daft. He's a kicker, just like his big brother." She smiled. "They'll be swimmers, like their dad. He was a fish. Always wondered why he didn't join the navy."

She poured mugs of tea for Hazel and herself, and a tiny cup that was mostly milk and sugar, with a spot of tea, for Frankie.

"Can I ask you, James," she said softly, "whether you think Frank suffered any pain?"

James sat up a little taller. "None," he said. "I'm sure of it. It was so very sudden."

She plied the kerchief and wiped her nose. "That's a blessing, ain't it?" Her voice squeaked as she tried not to cry. "I've had long nights to imagine him in every kind of suffering."

Frankie grew tired of blocks, so Hazel found a dog-eared children's book and began softly reading to him. He plopped his chunky self right down upon her lap.

"Did they bury him, then?" Adelaide asked.

James's body stiffened. "I don't know," he whispered. "After that I . . . lost consciousness for a long time. I spent a good deal of time in hospital. In neurasthenic wards."

Hazel closed her eyes and silently wept. Frankie prodded at her to continue the story. This was why the letters had stopped.

"I think it's likely," James said, softly, "that there wasn't much to bury."

The widow winced and looked away. It was unspeakable.

James reached into his jacket pocket and pulled something out.

"I received a DSM for what happened," he said, "which ought to have been his." He handed the medal, wrapped in wide red and blue ribbon, to Mrs. Mason.

"I can't take this," she protested. "It's yours."

"I want you to have it," insisted James. "And the twenty pounds. Take it for the baby."

Adelaide glanced once again at Hazel, seated on the floor, for guidance. Hazel nodded firmly. *Take it.* Adelaide surrendered, and accepted the money, and finally, the medal.

He then handed her Frank's little singed prayer book. When she saw it, she sobbed.

"Frank showed me your picture, more than once," he said, opening to where it was. "He was very proud of you and your son."

She took the tiny book and pressed it to her heart. "I don't know how to thank you."

Frankie took this moment to twist around on Hazel's lap and fling his chubby arms around her neck.

"I worried so much about my Frank out there, all alone." Adelaide pressed on through her tears. "That was what haunted me. The thought of him, with no one." She wiped her nose. "And when I knew he'd died, I couldn't sleep for thinking of him, dying all by himself, with no one there to care." She took James's hands once more. "To know that he was never alone, that he died helping his good friend . . ." Her eyes overflowed. "It'll be such a comfort to me in the years to come. Such a comfort."

She reached beckoning arms out to Frankie, who forgot about Hazel and toddled to his mama. She took him up fiercely and pressed him close. "His sons will know it about their dad."

Hazel turned to James. How much older he was than when she'd met him, seven, eight months ago. He looked exhausted. Drained and pale and spent.

Even so, there was something in his face she hadn't seen since Paris. Something, she thought, like peace.

ENTR'ACTE

Seaside—June 15, 1918

APHRODITE

THEY LEFT THE little house together, promising to visit again. Hazel wondered if she was lying.

The heel of Hazel's shoe twisted slightly, and she stumbled. James offered her his arm. She blushed but took it all the same.

They reached the corner where they ought to turn right to head back toward town and the train station, but James steered them to the left.

"Aren't we going back to the train station?" she asked.

James shaded his eyes from the sun. "It's a beautiful day," he said. "Seems a shame not to spend a bit of it at the beach, don't you think?"

Hazel didn't know what to think.

They followed the well-worn path down to the waterfront, where dirt gradually became sand, and grass became sparse weeds and then vanished. They took off their shoes and socks or stockings, which was a tricky proposition for Hazel, but she managed it, underneath her skirt. The sight of her bare feet was just about enough to give poor James a stroke there on the spot.

They rolled up their hosiery and stuffed it into their shoes and carried them on down through the sand. The novelty of hot sand between her toes made Hazel forget herself. She ran down to the water, dropped her things in a heap, and charged into the shallow waves, hitching up her skirts almost to her knees. James hung back and watched her.

She almost made him forget the pain. And her legs! He shouldn't look. *Yes, you should. But more discreetly.*

The feel of sea breezes and hot sand, the laughter of children and the cries of seagulls, the smell of popcorn and sizzling sausages, filled him. White-crested waves rolled endlessly in.

He'd gone and seen Frank's widow and son. He'd done it. He'd known from the start that he must do this. All these weeks, the effort of beating back the fear had left him half dead.

And there Hazel was, bending over to pick up a seashell and squint inside it.

HADES

A faint smell of Woodbine caught James's nose. A presence he knew stood beside him, but he must not look. This ought to be alarming, he thought, but it was familiar as morning.

He kept his gaze fixed on the horizon line. "You're a lucky man, Frank."

"Not by half," said Frank.

"That's quite a family you've got."

"I know it."

They both looked out toward Hazel in the water.

"Why should *I* get to—"

"Because you can," said Frank. "Go get her, chum. You're doing me no favors if you don't. You don't think I would?"

James remembered the robust little child in Hazel's arms, and how she had laughed and played with him. Had there ever been a girl so marvelous, and so kind? One who loved children. Would there ever be . . . ? He felt hot all over, and it wasn't the sun. *A child*. He remembered Adelaide's round belly. Another child who would never know its father.

"I'll be watching out for them," Frank said. "I know you will too."

"They'll send me back to the war, you know," said James.

Frank chuckled. "You'll be out of it soon, sonny," he said. "No fear. I think you'll come through the other side. It's not much longer now."

James watched as Hazel kicked at the rolling spray.

"You're not really here, are you?" says James. "This is part of my madness?"

"Does it matter?" asked Frank. "If it's madness telling you to marry that girl and be happy, whose advice would you rather have?"

"We're a bit young, don't you think?"

"I didn't say you had to do it tomorrow," said Frank. "Do you feel young?"

"No," admitted James.

"She'll make you feel young again."

"I don't even know how to make it through a day," James said.

"Nobody does," said Frank. "But that girl, there, will help you."

He felt a firm hand push between his shoulder blades. He stumbled forward in the sand.

APHRODITE

For a terrible moment Hazel thought James had abandoned her. She couldn't see him. Her skirts sank into the waves, soaking up cold water and clinging to her legs. Then, suddenly, there he was, before her, in trousers rolled-up to the knees and sleeves to the elbows, with his shirt open.

She was seized with a desire to inspect these new bits of James now on display.

He took her face in his hands. Her heart caught in her throat at the pain in his expression.

"You know that I can never be the boy you used to know."

She pulled away from his hands. "But that's who I see," she said. "The only boy I see."

He closed his eyes tightly. "What I've done, and what I've seen, will always be with me."

This was the last time she would make this plea. "Let me, too, always be with you."

He stood there, saying nothing, for longer than she could bear to wait.

She turned toward the sand and headed ashore.

James ran to her then and stood in her path. Before she could speak, I sent a little wave pushing her into him, and she fell into his arms. James only barely braced himself in time to keep them both from toppling over.

The feel of her body pressed against his went through him like an electric shock. When she righted herself and pulled away, he pulled her back to him and held her close, spinning her around and around. Her toes drew circles around him in the sunlight on the water.

ACT FIVE

APHRODITE

The Battle of Henry Johnson—June 5, 1918

BACK IN PARIS, Colette picked up shifts at a café. One morning, while swabbing tables, she noticed a newspaper left behind and ringed with coffee. She was about to toss it when a headline caught her eye: "*La Bataille d'Henry Johnson, Héros Nègre Américain! 24 Allemands Tués!*"

She abandoned her customers and devoured the article. It told of the heroics of one Henry Johnson, a black American soldier from New York State, who had bravely fought off a large German raiding party. He was a member of the *369e Régiment d'Infanterie US*, attached to the French Fourth Army, under the command of General Henri Gouraud, and stationed in the Meuse-Argonne sector. This division, the article mentioned, was famous for its remarkable band.

She dropped into a chair. Her heart thumped and her head flooded. Hope, her dread enemy, came pounding at the door.

Colette ignored customers whose coffee had grown cool. She propped her elbows on the dirty table and tried to think. Aubrey had belonged to the 15th New York National Guard. Could it possibly be the same division? Or were there dozens of black divisions in the American army, all with remarkable bands?

But what if it was Aubrey's regiment? He was dead.

His commanding officer, at least, could confirm that to her. She might still spend the rest of her nights lying awake, but it wouldn't be wondering. Not if she knew for sure.

Colette could handle the truth. She knew that much about herself.

The battle had taken place a few weeks prior, in May. It was now mid-June. They might still be there. It was worth a letter to find out.

APHRODITE

Medical Review Board—July 1, 1918

THE MEDICAL REVIEW board in Chelmsford declared James to be improving. A great deal of eating, dancing, and laughing were apparently the tonic he'd needed. He received orders to report for retraining on July 15.

Everything had changed. He had no desire to go back to war and die for Bobby. He wanted to live for Bobby, and for Maggie, and especially for Hazel. Nights became harder again, as scenes from the trenches stalked his sleep. But when morning came, he pulled himself together. Why waste sunny summer days with a lovely girl by your side? Seize the day.

Hazel hated the news, hated it, but it was still two weeks out. They'd had two weeks already. She determined to enjoy these remaining weeks without fear.

After all, the news reports were very hopeful. The Allies had managed to stop all four major German advances thus far this spring. The Germans hadn't reached the Channel, and Britain's naval blockade of Germany still held. The Americans were finally exerting their strength. What the Americans lacked in experience, they made up for triply in morale, in supplies, and in seemingly limitless numbers. The tide was turning. It had to be turning. The rest of the war would be brief, and James would come home safely, and soon.

APHRODITE

Mail Delivery—June 29, 1918

"COLETTE," TANTE SOLANGE called. "Someone here to see you."

It was early morning. Colette stumbled out of bed. Perhaps Papin, the oily manager at the café, had followed her home, the slime. She'd tell him where he could look for another waitress.

"*Un moment*," Colette called to her aunt. She pulled on yesterday's clothes and shoved a few pins into her hair. She wouldn't bother to look too polished for Papin. Should she clean her teeth? *Non*. She'd kept the visitor waiting. If it was Papin, and her breath was foul, *bien*.

She came into the sitting room.

Leaning against the doorway, filling it up, filling the entire room, drawing to himself all the morning light, was Aubrey.

Really and truly and solidly Aubrey.

Her shriek did, I admit, wake the neighbors. She nearly collapsed for crying. She just about buckled in two. She slid down to the floor and wept.

Joy can do that. It can hurt as much as pain.

Aubrey, who'd spent a train ride fretting over what to say, panicked. This was terrible.

"You monster!" she cried. "I thought you were dead."

Yep. He was in huge trouble.

There was that rascal smile she remembered.

"The Boche did their best to kill me," he said, "but I didn't hold still to let 'em."

Colette would not let him charm his way out of this. "What do you have to say for yourself?" she demanded, through tears. "How could you do this to me?" He smelled of soap and peppermint. She remembered, to her horror, that she did not.

(That's not what Aubrey was noticing just then.)

This, he knew, was a moment where he'd better choose his words carefully.

He held out an envelope. "I wrote you a letter," he said. "I wanted to make sure it got here, so I figured I'd better bring it myself."

She eyed the letter suspiciously, then edged away. "Let me get cleaned up . . ." she began, but Aubrey held her hand.

"I promise," he said, "you're the cleanest thing I've seen in months."

Tears crashed over her once more, and her vision blurred. "Are you really here?"

"I am," he said, "but don't tell Colonel Hayward."

She pulled away. "You'll be shot for desertion!" she cried. "You must hurry back!"

He laughed. "I worked out a deal with Captain Fish. I'll go back tonight."

But to leave Colette Fournier behind, now that he'd found her! The Kaiser's armies combined couldn't make him do it.

Poor Colette's emotions besieged her. "I thought you were dead," she repeated. "We heard about a murdered soldier, and— Why didn't you write?" She swallowed. "Those things you said to me. Did you mean none of them?"

"I meant them all." His throat was a lump. "I still do." He held out the envelope once more. "It's all in the letter."

Colette took the envelope uncertainly. She'd waited long enough for an answer, and yet, somehow, being asked to wait for as long as it would take to read the letter felt like one insult too many. *Just tell me!*

But he'd come this far. He was trying to apologize. She should be gracious.

She sat on a couch and heard stirrings from Tante Solange's room.

"Be careful," she whispered to Aubrey. "My aunt will have her hands all over you."

He laughed. "I think I can handle an old lady."

Colette shrugged. "*Bonne chance.* You are on your own."

Ten minutes later, they left the apartment and strolled the streets.

"You weren't kidding," he told her, "about your aunt."

Colette had no time for her aunt's misbehavior just then. "Aubrey," she said, "I am sorry about your friend." She shook her head. "*Quelle horreur!*"

Aubrey said nothing but squeezed her arm. They walked on. Aubrey's eyes saw Paris, its charming streets, its elegant shops, without taking in much.

"I understand why you didn't write," Colette told him. She poked him in the ribs. "That's not to say that I forgive you. Yet."

Aubrey knew he was forgiven and continued.

It was the grin that got her, every time. To think, she realized, she'd never before seen it by morning light. Never even known how this Aubrey of hers glowed in the sunlight.

I wasn't even doing that, I swear. It was pure Aubrey. Other women they passed on the street noticed it, too.

Colette smiled to herself.

Of course, her smile made Aubrey melt. Just like the first time.

"It doesn't seem right," he said at length, "me, here with you, while Joey's in the ground. When it was me, thinking I'm immortal, that they were coming for."

Colette listened. She let Aubrey take his time.

"Why me?" he said aloud. "Why do I get to live when so many die? Why do I get to live when so many black folks get killed just for breathing the same air as angry white folks?"

Colette didn't trust herself to answer then. If she said what was in her heart—"You were spared because I need you"—she would reveal to the treacherous skies that she needed Aubrey, and then, next time, the Fates wouldn't miss the target she'd just painted on his chest.

"If I'd heard them," Aubrey went on. "If I'd gone out with him. If I'd had my pistol."

"Then you might be dead too."

"If he'd just not had to take a leak!"

She leaned her head against his shoulder. "I know."

Aubrey remembered, then, how well she did know.

"He was my friend," he said. "I know that's not the same as losing your family."

She stopped him with a kiss on his cheek. "Grief is not a contest," she said. "What happened was horrible. No one should face it. Especially not from their own countrymen. It's a crime against humanity. Against decency and reason."

"Sometimes it feels like America's short on all of that," Aubrey said bitterly.

"But America produced you," she said. "So it can't be all bad."

"It's not as if," Aubrey said, "this was just a couple of bad guys. Sick in the head, you know? This is all over the place. All over the military. All over the South. And not just the South."

Colette watched him. "Will you go back?" she asked. "Or can you stay here in France?"

His eyes grew large. "Stay here?" He considered the prospect, until his expression fell. "Uncle Sam won't let me," he said. "And I'd miss my family."

She leaned against his arm. "If you have a family," she murmured, "and you can be near them, do."

He kissed the back of her hand. "I can't believe I'm here," he said. "You can't know how much I've missed *you*."

"Yes, I can."

His smile fell. "I'm not who I was before," he said. "I haven't got much to offer you. I'm a soldier now, not a pianist."

Colette laughed. "Yes, and I'm a ballerina."

"You are?"

She rolled her eyes. "You'll always be a pianist, Aubrey. No one can take that from you." She gazed at him with sorrowful eyes and traced a fingertip lightly over the contours of his face. "You're not just mourning Joey," she told him. "It could've been you. You think it should've been. You blame yourself for not being the one in the latrine when killers came looking. You're in shock over your own death."

He stiffened. "You make me sound selfish."

Her eyes narrowed. "*Non.* I make you sound exactly like me."

He watched her curiously.

"I blame myself, every day, for crossing the river that morning to pick apples. For running for the convent as soon as I heard the first guns."

He caressed her hand. God bless apples, and God bless nuns.

"I feel like a monster for surviving the Germans who hunted down my family and shot them in cold blood. I'm a selfish coward— after my mother died of grief, my heart kept on beating. I loved my own life, you see, more than I refused to face a world without those I'd lost."

Pedestrians filed around them on the street.

"You're not a monster for living," he told her. "There's no crime in picking apples."

"And there's no crime in sneaking out at night to see your *petite amie*," she said, then smiled wryly. "Well, the army would say there is, but that's a different matter."

Aubrey watched curls of Colette's hair, escaping from her scarf, dance in the breeze. They'd found each other once, then found each other once more. Here she stood—not a jazz singer, not a glamorous Belgian, but a grieving girl who understood. Who had fought to live, and who filled Aubrey with the will to fight and live beside her.

But what came next? Tonight he had to go back to the Front. If this war ever ended, he'd have to go back to New York.

New York felt so very far away. In New York, he couldn't kiss her in the open air without fear of what onlookers might say.

But in Paris, he could. He could kiss her like he was making up for lost time.

At least for that kiss, death and grief were far away.

Maybe, he thought, he ought to just kiss Colette and never stop.

But even the best kisses end eventually.

"I've missed you so," he whispered. "I never wanted to leave you behind."

They strolled on. A kind of peace filled Aubrey's body. He hadn't realized how heavy a weight it had been, keeping Joey a secret for all those months.

"I wish I could do something for Joey," Aubrey said at length. "Or for his family. Or something to remember him by."

She smiled. "That's a good idea," she said. "Something to preserve his memory."

"But what?" he wondered. "A fancy gravestone?"

They turned a corner. "I have often wished," she said, "that I could do something for my brother, Alexandre. A memorial. But any idea I've ever had felt weak. Insufficient."

"Gravestones are cold," said Aubrey. "Memorials only go so far."

"Get rich," she teased, "and donate a building in Joey's name."

They began to look around and actually see Paris. He realized he was thirsty, so they stopped in a café for lemonades.

"I wrote songs for Joey in the trenches," he told her. "I wrote songs for you, too."

"Let's go to New York, and record them," Colette said.

Aubrey dropped his straw. "Is that an offer?"

Colette flushed. Had she spoken too soon? "Um, is yours an offer?" *I'll go anywhere you are, Aubrey Edwards.*

"It's an offer, mademoiselle," he told her. "You'd better believe it."

DECEMBER 1942

A Possible Ending

"WE CAN END there," Aphrodite tells the other gods. "We can end at this moment, with both our young couples happy at last, after enduring much."

Hades presses his fingertips together and watches the goddess of love thoughtfully.

It's been a long story, but what is time to immortals? Aphrodite can squeeze an epic into the space between second hand clicks of the clock.

Hephaestus strokes his bearded chin. Then he rises and hobbles over to the golden net. At one touch of his hand, it parts, leaving an opening for Aphrodite to pass through.

"Court is adjourned," he says. "The defendant is acquitted." He smiles wryly. "This defendant's arrest is declared unlawful. Forgive me, Goddess, for detaining you."

Aphrodite blinks. For a moment she's too stunned to seize her exit. She draws close to Hephaestus and speaks softly, for his hearing only.

"Do I leave now?" she asks. "You want me to be done?"

He gestures toward the door to show he will not stop her. "You're free to go if you like."

"It's not what you think," she whispers. "Me, with him."

He shakes his head. "Don't," he says. "Let's only deal in truth from now on, you and I."

She bites her lip. "That's not what I mean." She turns to catch Ares craning his neck to try to hear them. "I'm not denying the affair. What I mean is . . ."

Hephaestus would rather hear anything but this right now.

"The pull, for you, is strong, during a big war." Far better for him to voice the words than her. "Too many hearts need you. It's intoxicating, being needed. Is that it?"

Apollo tinkers at his piano and pretends not to eavesdrop. Hades watches out the window at the city street below.

"I'm not what they think." Aphrodite's gaze is on the floor. "I'm not just some tart."

"I know." He does know. No matter what others might say, nor how they might judge.

She steps through the opening he's created for her in the golden net.

"Thanks for the story, anyway," Hephaestus tells her. "I won't forget it. You're good at what you do. And . . . I think I understand what you mean."

Her pensive face breaks into a smile.

Hephaestus can't resist smiling back. "I envy your mortals."

One of her eyebrows rises. "As Ares says, they die, you know."

The god of fires nods. "They do. But the lucky ones live first." He bows slightly. His crippled back makes it hard for him to bend far. "The luckiest ones spend time with you."

Aphrodite blinks in surprise.

Ares has had more than enough of these two whispering. He

tries to dart through the opening Hephaestus has created, but he's unable to pass. "Hey! Let me out of here."

"You can rot in hell," Hephaestus tells his brother.

"Technically, he can't," observes Hades.

Ares calls after his brother. "That isn't the end of the story. She's not telling you everything." A sneer spreads across his lips. "She's *never* told you everything."

The Rest of the Story—
July 15–August 17, 1918

ARES

THE WAR GROUND ON. The Germans' last big push, the Champagne-Marne Offensive, or the Second Battle of the Marne, had ended in crushing defeat for Germany. At a total cost of a quarter million casualties, dead and wounded.

Both James and Aubrey saw combat in the battle, many miles apart on the Western Front. James had been reassigned to Britain's Tenth Army under General Charles Mangin. He was sorry not to be back with his old friends, but that couldn't be helped.

James arrived at the Front just when the battle began. A seasoned veteran, a deadly shooter, he fought like an Aegean warrior. Not because he loved a battle, but because it gave him the best chance of coming home.

I wish I could say that he fought without fear. That he felt impervious to danger, after all he'd been through. But the battle was brutal. Death on every side. If he hadn't had his girl to think of, and his family back home, he never would've have made it.

Aubrey, too, fought like a dragon. This was the worst combat he'd seen by far. All the 369th men were dragons on the battlefield.

Giants. Hoplites. Of them, 171 would receive the Croix de Guerre from the French. "Les Hommes de Bronze," they called them. "Blutlustige Schwarzmänner." German for "bloodthirsty black men."

I don't know about "bloodthirsty," but you didn't want to be a Jerry who fell into a Harlem Rattler's trench. You definitely didn't want to be a Jerry who took a Harlem Hellfighter prisoner. They'd be coming after you, and they always got their man.

They fought as one. They fought how they played in Lieutenant Europe's band. Experience breeds unity; a band of soldiers who have fought the same enemy, the same war, together, for their entire lives, understands unity. As did their parents and grandparents before them.

APHRODITE

I never said I wouldn't tell the rest of the story, Ares.

Colette and Hazel were back chopping cabbage and onions at Compiègne. Hazel had been apprehensive. The German who'd assaulted her stalked her nightmares. She and Colette began their second sojourn at the concentration camp by meeting with the guards and sergeants in charge and putting them on alert that they expected their safety, and that of all workers, to be assured. The camp directors were so understaffed and so grateful that the girls had returned that they accepted all terms without argument. Hazel watched but never saw a sign of her assailant.

Compiègne was close to Soissons, where James was posted. Letters flew back and forth between them almost as fast as telegrams. Though the echo of guns was louder, she had such frequent letters from James that she never wondered for long if he was all right.

When the battle ended, James wrote to let Hazel know that he'd have half a day of rest and relaxation the following Saturday. Was there any way she could come spend it with him? The same day, a letter arrived from Aubrey saying he would have the following Monday off. So the girls concocted a plan. They would don their old YMCA uniforms and travel by troop train to the depot nearest to James's sector. He would meet them there. They'd spend a few marvelous hours together. Then Colette and Hazel would take the spur line back to a main artery that would lead them toward Verdun. They'd travel Sunday and spend Monday with Aubrey.

It was wicked and daring and harmless and so simple. They boarded the train in Compiègne without opposition and sweated their way through the short ride in the August heat to their meeting place. Seeing how no one seemed to care whether they were with the YMCA or with the circus, they peeled off their wool uniform coats. As the train approached the depot near Soissons, Hazel borrowed a mirror and comb from Colette to neaten herself up. She was too excited to feel the heat.

James waited at the depot for their train to arrive. He felt jumpy with anticipation. These few weeks apart felt longer than the entire war.

He mopped the sweat off his brow and searched for anything in this scorched earth that could give a chap some shade.

ARES

The occasional rumble of guns in the distance was as normal now as traffic in the city or birds in the country. James barely noticed it.

The track began vibrating. He saw smoke and heard the engine's song. *Here she comes!*

Inside their passenger car, Hazel looked up.

"Nearly there," she told Colette. "The train's slowing to a stop."

From nowhere, a rush of air knocked James to the ground.

Then came the whine, after the shell itself. From a long-range gun. The Long Max. Thirty-eight centimeters.

The explosion shook the earth beneath him. The geyser of dirt rained down upon train track. Smoke and flames roared upward from what remained of the train.

HADES

The engine and the first two cars were annihilated.

The cars beyond buckled and crashed into one another.

Soldiers and war workers were thrown all about the cars.

Shards of glass from shattered windows flew like shrapnel.

Colette emerged unscathed, for Hazel had thrown her body over her friend's.

James found Colette holding on to Hazel, rocking her like an infant. As though she'd only gone to sleep. As though she could be persuaded to wake up.

"It's my fault," she repeated. "It was wrong of me to love her. I had no right to do it." She gulped and keened. "*La guerre* takes everyone I love from me. She won't even spare me Hazel. I never should have made myself her friend."

James the battle veteran, arriving on the scene, knew what to do. Apply pressure to the bleeding and summon a medic. Clear airflow, release tight clothing.

James the boy from the parish dance was lost in the fog of a dark world, searching everywhere for one who would not be found.

HADES

The Royal Albert Hall

HAZEL ARRIVED. She wore a light summer dress and walked in bare feet through soft grasses. Tiny white flowers glinted like pearls among the deep green.

Her steps led her to an unfamiliar door. She pushed it open and found herself in a vast, dark room, so huge that no walls could be seen. The lack of any echo gave her vertigo.

She wasn't ready to be here.

In a far distance, she thought she saw a glimmer of light. Cautiously, stepping blindly, she made her way forward. A wooden floor felt smooth under her bare feet.

The light grew. A spotlight, in its perfect oval, illuminating a gleaming ebony satin Steinway & Sons nine-foot grand piano. Its opened top beckoned.

A gorgeous instrument. Never in her life had she come near one so deluxe, so pristine.

That, in fact, was still the truth.

Hazel approached the bench and sat down.

Houselights rose to the faintest glimmer. Just enough for her to see where she was. The grand room appeared in solemn majesty.

An empty Royal Albert Hall in the middle of the night.

She touched the keys, playing tentative notes. As each bead of sound rang outward, her hesitation fell away. She began to play. "Pathétique." The second movement of Beethoven's Piano Sonata Number 8 in C minor, opus 13. "Adagio cantabile."

The sound filled the empty hall and rushed back upon her like a revelation. Such purity, such sweetness of tone. Each hammer striking its string like a chiming bell, filling the darkness with beauty.

Tears fell from her eyes. Never, never had she played like this. Never had she had such an instrument nor such an acoustically divine space. Never had she felt such freedom to play as she longed to, without a nervous body getting in the way. No paralyzing fear from an audience—yet now, she saw, what a crime it was that no one else could be there to hear this music.

I sat beside her as Monsieur Guillaume. He wasn't actually dead, but Hazel understood.

"Have I died, monsieur?"

She looked up, still playing, and saw, high in the balconies, right where she and James once sat, a small clump of people. Her parents. Colette, Aubrey. Tante Solange. Georgia Fake and Olivia Jenkins. Father Knightsbridge. Ellen Francis. Reverend and Mrs. Puxley. Maggie.

James.

They were far beyond reach, yet she could see them as clearly as though they were close.

Beside them were other people. Slowly spreading rows upon rows, filling the balcony. People she had yet to meet. People who would have come into her life and graced it, filled it, but now they would not. A young woman with dark curls. A sandy-haired boy.

"Please," she asked me. "Might I go back for a little while longer?"

She waited for my answer while her fingers still played.

I am not unmoved by music. We need not all be you, Apollo, to appreciate it.

Nor am I unmoved by love, no matter how many loves I've been forced to cut short.

Hazel persisted. "Can't you send me back?"

"It's been known to happen," I told her. "Though nothing would ever be quite the same."

"Please," she begged. "When you call me the second time, I'll come willingly."

I rose from the bench and retreated into the shadows. Much as it grieves me, I do understand that my company isn't always welcome. Hazel continued to play, and I was glad to see it. Music was the best thing for her then. Nothing could do more to resign her to this painful transition.

Someone else appeared at my side.

"Why, Aphrodite," I said, if you recall, Goddess. "To what do I owe the rare honor of your visit?"

You bowed. "If it pleases you, my lord," you said. "If I have ever pleased you, I beg you to give Hazel back to me. Let her go."

"Lovely Goddess," I told you, "these are the fortunes of war. If every loved soul were snatched from death simply because she'd be mourned and missed, the universe would fold in upon itself."

"Hazel's not done," Aphrodite insisted. "She has so much more to give and to do."

"I can say the same for each one of war's millions of fallen dead," I said.

Aphrodite, you turned to me then, and fell upon your knees. "Please, give me Hazel," you begged. "Hers is a love I'd only barely begun. James needs her. Her parents need her. Colette needs her. Please, Lord Hades, God of the Underworld, Ruler of All."

I believe, if memory serves me rightly, I needed a handkerchief.

"She's badly injured," I told you.

"Not where it matters most," you countered.

"The Fates will shriek in protest," I warned. "They will dog her steps."

"I'll watch over her, my lord," you said, Goddess. "I will shield her as much as I can."

Though the mortals have long portrayed me thus, and I forgive them for it, mine is not a heart of stone.

I took your hand and raised you to your feet. "Passion, Love, and Beauty," I told you, Aphrodite. "You know she can no longer have them all."

APHRODITE

Lazybones—August 20, 1918

TUBES OF RED blood dangled from jars mounted to a metal frame and ran, Hazel realized, into a needle injected into her arm. It burned where it stuck there, wedged into her flesh like an insult.

She didn't know it, but she was in a field hospital.

Her body ached. Her abdomen—even breathing was agony. Things inside her that she couldn't name cried out in protest. She turned her head from side to side in order to see. That slight movement sent ripples of pain up and down her body.

She tried to sit up, and fell back into her pillow with a gasp.

Colette was at her side in an instant. "Good morning!"

Hazel looked about. "Is it really morning?"

Colette kissed Hazel's cheek. "*Non, ma chère.* It isn't. But you've had a long night's sleep." She pulled up a stool and sat close by. "Does it hurt terribly?"

Hazel breathed slowly. Her head was still somewhere between drugged sleep and wakefulness.

"Never mind," Colette said. "I can see the truth."

"How long have I been here?" Hazel marveled at how scratchy her voice sounded.

Colette's eyes filled with concern. "Three days," she said. "We've been so afraid."

"We?" Hazel gave up the struggle. "Can I have some water?"

Colette slid her arm under Hazel's pillow and eased her upright. She caught the wince of pain and held a glass of water to her lips.

Hazel closed her eyes. Colette took her hand and entwined her fingers through hers.

"I can't tell you how good it is to see you awake."

Hazel smiled and opened her eyes. "It's good to see you, too." She took a measured breath. "Three days?"

"Lazybones."

Hazel laughed for a second, until the pain told her not to.

"Colette," she said, "what happened to me?"

Colette's heart bled. Where to begin? "Do you remember the train ride?"

Hazel nodded once.

"Do you remember the explosion?"

Hazel frowned. "Do I?" She waited. Her mind was still a muddled swirl. "Maybe?"

"A shell hit our train," Colette explained gently. "People died. Many more were hurt."

Hazel studied Colette's face. "You seem to be all right."

Colette gulped. *She doesn't remember what she did.* She opened her mouth to tell her, then paused. Something—it was me—warned her not to do so.

"You know me," Colette said lightly, though it killed her. "Always the lucky one."

"Figures." Hazel grinned. "Well, what hit me?"

"Broken glass," Colette said. "Like shrapnel. Your body was badly cut. You bled a great deal." She pressed Hazel's hand to her lips. "We thought we'd lost you."

Hazel took inventory. She wiggled her fingers. They were there. She wiggled her toes. They were, too. She saw bumps on the bed jostling where feet should be.

"Did we lose any parts of me?"

Colette wanted to laugh but didn't allow it. Apparently they hadn't lost Hazel's humor.

"They operated," Colette said, "to remove the glass and stop your bleeding. The doctors said it's a wonder you pulled through."

Hazel tried to comprehend all this information. What had she known? What did she remember? Something about piano. Something about a concert hall. A presence, there beside her. Not frightening, but not altogether comfortable, either. Just there, watchful.

And while all this had happened, she'd nearly died. She'd been carved open on an operating table. Strangers had examined her insides. She shivered.

"Colette," Hazel said, "do my parents know?"

Colette nodded. "It took time, tracking them down. We expect them in a few hours."

Hazel gestured for more water, and once more her friend assisted her. She spooned a mouthful of stewed apples between her dry, chapped lips. The patient closed her eyes. These sensations of liquid and food were almost more than she could comprehend.

"Colette?"

"Yes, darling?"

"Why can't I see out of my right eye?"

A laugh, or a sob, burst from Colette's lips. "It's all right," she said. "It's covered with a bandage. The eye itself is fine, though. That's what the doctors say."

"But it's covered with a bandage. Why?"

Tears spilled down Colette's cheeks. She remembered the

terrible sight. Red, and white, and bones where her friend's lovely face should be.

"Your cheek was badly cut, *chèrie*," whispered Colette. "And your forehead."

Hazel's mind was blessedly dim just then. She couldn't feel all that she might later feel about this.

"But your eye was unharmed," Colette went on hurriedly. "The doctors say it was a miracle. As if someone had covered it for you."

"Well." Hazel took a ragged breath. "If I can ever figure out who it was, I'll thank them. You can't buy eyeballs at the store."

A shadow fell from the doorway. Colette glanced up, and Hazel, though sluggish, caught on and looked up, too.

Private James Alderidge stood in the door.

"Hello, Miss Windicott," he said. "I've been missing you."

APHRODITE

Scars—August 21–September 1, 1918

COLETTE AND JAMES never told Hazel that she had saved Colette's life. Heroism is much too heavy a burden to carry. James knew it, and Colette agreed. With a little help from me.

Hazel didn't need heroic deeds to reconcile herself to her new face. She was alive. She had everyone she loved close by. Ever since her brush with death, many things that seemed to matter once just didn't anymore.

Only for James's sake did the angry red scars carving up the right side of her face cause her any worry. When the bandages came off, James begged to be there, along with her parents and Colette. Hazel was reluctant to let him, but she agreed.

A nurse gently peeled off the bandages and plaster. Hazel right eye opened and blinked at the unfamiliar light. All the better to see James smiling down at her.

"Look at you," he told her.

"I can't, unless you've brought me a mirror," she told him tartly. "Please do."

He handed her a mirror, and she appraised herself with curiosity.

"These have healed up better than I might've expected," said the surgeon, examining her scars. "No infection. You're very lucky."

Better than he'd expected? "I look quite horrible," she said matter-of-factly.

"Compared to how you looked on the train," said James, "you look remarkably well."

"Thank you," Hazel said. "I think." She glanced at her parents and saw her mother struggle to keep her composure. Poor Mum.

"I'm Frankenstein's monster now," Hazel told the room. "This will be useful any number of ways. Scaring burglars, warding off evil spirits . . ."

Mr. and Mrs. Windicott, huddled close together by Hazel's side, beamed at their girl and poured forth every encouraging word. If they went back to their hostelry that night and wept into their pillows, no one, I believe, will blame them for that.

Aubrey managed to visit one Sunday afternoon. Colette kept his visit a surprise, then paraded him into Hazel's hospital room, where she sat diligently completing her strengthening exercises.

"Whatcha been up to, Lady Hazel de la Windicott?"

Hazel squealed and tried to jump up, but a sharp twinge of pain stopped her. Aubrey swept up the piano girl in an embrace. He knew what she did not about what she'd done on the train, and he would never forget it.

Aubrey and James met at last. I'm certain they would've been friends under any circumstances, but with Hazel and Colette in their lives, they quickly became brothers-in-law, or, if not in law, in truth.

August wore on, and the nights began to cool. Hazel learned she would be dismissed from the hospital the next day.

James's current sergeant was a tenderhearted soul, underneath a great deal of bluster. He let his young private visit his injured volunteer girl whenever he could be spared from duty. With the Second Battle of the Marne well behind them now, a great deal of repair and fortification and cleanup work remained to be done, but if a heroic young lady in love with a soldier in his company didn't deserve comfort and cheer, who did? Private Alderidge wasn't good for much if he hadn't gotten his hospital visit in every couple of days.

That last night in the hospital, after Hazel's parents had returned to their rooms to pack for tomorrow's trip to London, James arrived in Hazel's room and sat beside her.

"You're not really leaving me tomorrow, are you?" he asked her.

Already her scars were flattening a bit, though still crimson and cruel. Her face would never be the same. He knew that; she knew it. Her smile was crooked now, and her right eyebrow was crisscrossed with lines. A wedge of pink lower eyelid intruded upon the view of her right eye. Her cheek would never again be round and smooth.

But she was wholly here, and entirely Hazel.

"They're kicking me out," she said. "I haven't been paying my rent."

"I wish you could stay," James told her, "but I'm glad to have you safe, away from here."

Hazel rolled her eyes. "It's quiet now," she told him. "The papers say the Allies have pushed the Germans back to the Hindenburg Line."

"The tide is turning," he said. "This year, I think we just might be done by Christmas."

Hazel closed her eyes. "Wouldn't that be heaven?"

She turned and watched James. Her heart was brimming, and broken. He'd been so kind, and she, ever since waking in this hospital room, had played along with the charade that all was still right between them. It seemed the kindest thing to do. But the pretense could not continue.

When she first woke up, life felt bundled in sweetness and gratitude. Any life, even a maimed life, was a gift. Her scars, hidden behind bandages, didn't weigh her down.

But with each passing day, the sweetness sloughed off, leaving uncertainty in its place.

At last she made up her mind. It was time; she was going home. The war wasn't over. Any parting could turn out to be a last goodbye. And some things die even when everyone survives. There were words she needed to tell James while she still could.

"Thank you," she said. "For saving my life. And staying close by me, all this time."

He smiled. "You don't need to thank me for that."

"You've been the dearest of friends to me," she said. "Your kindness has meant everything."

James's eyes grew wide. "Hazel," he said quickly, "what are you saying?"

Her heart sank. For days she'd been dreading this. How could she ever put it into words?

"Hazel Windicott," he said, with a waver in his voice. "Are you telling me goodbye?"

She took a step back. How could he sound so shocked, so hurt? And how could she bear to do it? She took a deep breath and steeled herself to what must come next.

"I'll never be the same," she said. "That's plain to us both."

He drew closer. "You can't mean what I think you're about to say," he said. "You can't."

She turned her face so that her right side greeted James in full. Gashed by livid red lines. A mockery of what her face had been.

"Is this the face—"

"It is the face." He cut her off. "The face I want to see." His eyes searched hers. "Do you think scars would matter to me?"

How could he ask such a question? When she looked like this now? "They should matter," she protested. "They'd matter to anyone. That doesn't make you unfaithful or weak."

"Hazel!"

Her hands gripped the back of a chair for strength. "I can't let you yoke your life to this," she said. "I can't let you promise your forever to this out of pity, or noble duty."

His face fell.

Now he would protest, now he would insist, now he would make some declaration that the years would wear away at like water upon sand. He'd be trapped.

Now she would have to argue with him and win, to persuade him to let her go. A horrible treason of the heart against itself.

He reached up and softly, gently, stroked her face with his fingertips. He hovered lightly over the scars to not cause any pain.

Hazel's left eye ran with tears.

James pulled Hazel to him and encircled her in his arms. She couldn't escape, nor had she the will to try. She hid her cheek against his chest.

"I'll never be the same," she said.

He pulled away to look into her eyes.

"You will always be the same," he told her. "You'll always be my lovely Hazel."

Was that still love she saw there? As much as in Lowestoft? Chelmsford, Poplar?

James kissed her scarred cheek. "*I* will never be the same," he reminded her. "You know that."

"You are to me," she protested.

He looked at her pointedly.

"You're doing splendidly," she said. "Your troubles are behind you now."

He was silent for a time.

"I wish," he said at length, "that that were true. That my troubles were behind me."

She wanted to embrace and reassure him. *No, foolish girl,* she reminded herself. *That's what you can no longer do.*

"You're still you," she said. "Still James. Still wonderful. Still clever and kind. Still handsome. Still brave. Still strong."

James paced back and forth like someone desperate. He raked his hands through his hair until it stood on end. "Do you think I sought you out at the Poplar dance for your *face*?" he demanded.

"Watch it there, Charley," she told him. "I suppose now you're going to tell me my old face was horrid?"

He reached his hands toward her, then held them back. "Your face has never been horrid," he said. "It's always been perfect. It still is."

She laughed in bitter disbelief. "You're mad!"

He looked at her pointedly. "Yes," he said. "I am. Now you see. So mad, so mental, I had to sit for weeks in a pink room. After spending weeks doped on morphine. Who knows when I'll need to go back and do it all again?"

Hazel hadn't realized. Not really. *He's still afraid.*

"If you do need to go back," she told him, "that's nothing to be ashamed of. You'll get through it. You'll get better, just like last time. What happened to you isn't your fault."

He looked back at her.

Of course what happened to her wasn't her fault either, but it wasn't the same.

"Why didn't you leave me?" he whispered. "Why didn't you run away from the lad touched in the head?"

Hazel felt tears prick her eyelids once more. "How can you ask me that?" she said. "Why would I ever do such a thing?"

"You think I love you less than you love me," he said softly.

"I never said that!"

"You think I can't see past lines on your face," James said. "Lines that in time will fade."

Hazel wiped her eyes on her sleeve. "But never go away."

"Yet you see past the shadow," he said. "All that's left of a kid who went off to war."

She shook her head angrily. "You're wrong to call yourself a shadow." Her breath came rapidly. "You're everything to me."

He sank into a chair. "Then how can you leave me?" he cried. "How can you try to make me leave you?"

She wiped her eyes on her sleeve, but the tears wouldn't stop. "Because all your life, James," she said, "you'll look at me, and you'll see the scars. You'll see them, and I'll watch you. All your life, if I let you stay, I'll watch you work to reconcile yourself to the face you made a promise to. Even as you come to wish you hadn't." She hid her face, scars and all, behind her hands. "I won't be able to bear it."

"You're wrong to call yourself a face," he said. "Damaged or otherwise." He pulled something from his pocket, pried her hand gently off her face, and placed the thing on her palm.

A slim circlet of gold.

"If you think I can live without you, Miss Windicott," James said, "you don't know me at all."

DECEMBER 1942

Handkerchiefs

IF ONE COULD listen with a god's ear, in that dark hotel room, in the pregnant hour before dawn, one might hear the moist sound of immortal gods holding back tears.

Hades produces a pile of handkerchiefs. Even Ares takes one.

Aphrodite turns her gorgeous eyes to her husband.

"Do you see?" she asks. "Why I envy them?"

Ares stuffs his used hankie behind a cushion. "You mean, you'd trade places with her?"

"It's easy to give an answer for a choice that will never be offered to me," she says. "Yes. In less than a heartbeat, I would."

The god of war shakes his head. "You're the goddess of beauty," he says. "Why would you ever trade your looks—your perfection—for her mortality? Her scars?"

Apollo and Hades exchange a despairing look.

"We see what we're capable of seeing," says Hades.

Ares rolls his eyes. "Don't be cryptic. I've had enough of that."

Hephaestus grips the armrests of his chair and prepares to duck. In case Hades takes issue with Ares's tone.

"Whether you see a scarred face," says Apollo, "or a love for the ages, is up to you."

APHRODITE

Elevens—1918 and Beyond

WEEKS PASSED. Autumn grew colder and grayer, but four young hearts barely noticed.

And then, a miracle: the war ended. The Kaiser abdicated, a new German government formed, and German delegates signed the armistice, at 11 a.m. on November 11: 11/11, 11:00. Most soldiers on either side of the Front just watched the morning pass, and then turned around and left. In some spots, hostilities carried on right until the minute hand struck eleven.

One must be precise about killing, it seems.

It took a long time for the American Expeditionary Force to bury its dead, pack up, and return to the States. While they waited, Aubrey Edwards's 369th Division traveled to Germany, becoming the first Allied division to reach the Rhine—something the Allies had believed they could do before summer's end, 1914. Or by Christmas. Always, always, "by Christmas."

When they weren't busy, Aubrey spent time in a French military hospital, visiting Émile. This *poilu* had lost an arm in the last week of fighting, and he had four years' worth of accumulated curses to fling—not at his wound, but at its timing.

"Where were you, you stupid injury, when I could've used you to get out of this wretched war?" he would roar. "But *non*, you stayed away, leaving me healthy and sound, so the Germans could piss on me with their shells and bullets year after year, and now, now, when it's finally over, *now* you show up?"

He waved his stump at the sky.

"Nurse," Émile would say, "fetch us a bottle of wine, and a piano, so my useless friend here, with all *his* fingers, can put them to some good use and get my mind off my sorrows."

Émile was a great favorite with all the nurses.

"Who are you calling useless?" demanded Aubrey.

"You, you swine," Émile said. "Some of us are working hard here, having our toenails trimmed by the nurses and our buttocks wiped—very pretty nurses they are, too—and you just sit there, like you've got nothing better to do than come laugh at your poor friend Émile, who taught you everything you know."

"Well, you've got me there," Aubrey said. "After a year of fighting, and weeks of rebuilding roads all day long, and playing jazz all over France, I come here just to prove how useless I am."

"I always knew you'd amount to no good," Émile said. "I told my lieutenant, 'Don't pair me with this useless piano player, for God's sake,' but does anybody listen to Émile? Nobody listens to Émile."

Half a dozen nurses stood in the hall, giggling and listening to Émile.

"I'll die a lonely man," roared he, waving his stump around.

"I can see that," said Aubrey.

"Nurse!" bellowed Émile. "Fetch me that piano!"

And one day, the nurses actually did. Émile laughed so hard, he fell off his bed. From that day on, Aubrey's concerts drew patients from the entire hospital, until finally Émile recovered enough to be sent home. One of the nurses, it seemed, had resigned at around the same time and would be traveling home with him.

He seized Aubrey with one hand and one stump and gave him a whiskery kiss on each cheek. "You'll come see us, my friend," he declared. "And we'll come see you in New York. We are brothers, you and me."

"Brothers," said Aubrey.

James made it home long before Aubrey. After a stop in Chelmsford, he went to Poplar and stayed with his uncle to be as near to Hazel as possible. He took her to dinner. To museums and winter festivals and Christmas concerts. To J. Lyons tea shops.

"My mother wants to know," James told her one evening, as they strolled home from a play, "if we would join them for Christmas dinner."

Hazel's eyes grew wide. Christmas dinner, two weeks away, sounded quite official. But nothing was truly official yet. At least, not to anyone but her and James.

"I'd love to," Hazel said. "But I'd feel terrible, leaving my parents all alone."

They crossed a crowded street. "They're invited," James said. "The more, the merrier."

"Perfect!" Hazel grinned. "My mother will spend the rest of the holiday season worrying about what to wear."

"I was thinking," James continued, "that we should invite Colette and Aubrey, too. If he could get some leave, they could come spend Christmas here."

"Oh! I'll write to her immediately," Hazel said. "No. I'll send a telegram."

James wasn't finished. "And then I got to thinking," he said, "that if we're all gathered for Christmas dinner, we ought to kill two birds with one stone."

Hazel paused to notice a woman's garish orange hat. "And celebrate Boxing Day?"

His reply was nonchalant. "And hold a wedding reception."

Gone and forgotten was the hat.

Hazel's jaw dropped. Her feet refused to take another step. "You're not serious."

He nodded. "Like the maggot," he said, "I'm in Dead Ernest."

Hazel couldn't even scold him for the joke. Her mind reeled. On her bureau at home stood a little china trinket dish. Inside, hidden to the world, lay a golden ring. Sometimes, at night, she'd slip it on. But she never wore it openly. Her parents didn't know it existed.

James stood before her, watching, waiting.

Hazel treasured the ring, and the love it represented. But to her mind, it only meant that someday, some far-off someday, they would, if James still felt the same, perhaps, eventually . . . She couldn't even admit to the word. And now—

"*You want to get married,*" she said slowly. "In two weeks."

He nodded. "Only because I can't think of a respectable way to do it sooner."

How is one supposed to behave at such a moment? Not, Hazel was sure, like a beaming idiot. (She was wrong, incidentally.) But someone, she thought, ought to keep a level head.

"Marriage is forever, James," she told him firmly.

"That's the point."

She gulped. "Aren't we rather young?"

A look of worry crossed his face.

"Do you think so?" he asked seriously. "After this war, I feel a hundred and two."

"Me too." She smiled. "Ninety-seven, at any rate."

He wrapped his arms around her, whispering close to her ear.

"I waited once to kiss you," he said, "and almost lost my chance. I waited for the war to end before asking you to marry me, and you nearly died." He kissed her forehead. "If the war's taught me anything at all, it's that life is short. I won't waste any more of it waiting for you."

"I had no idea," she said, "that you were so impatient."

You can imagine, I'm sure, what happened next. I, of course, got to watch.

They took their time about it. But finally speech was once again possible.

He folded his arms across his chest. "You still haven't answered me," he said sternly. "Christmas dinner? Christmas wedding? What will it be, Miss Windicott?"

She must find some way to torment him, just a little longer, first. So she tapped her finger against her chin.

"Now, I wonder *what* I should put in Colette's and Aubrey's Boxing Day boxes," she mused. "We must make it fun. I imagine neither of them have ever celebrated it."

He slipped his arm through hers, and they resumed their progress down the street. "So long as they're there on the twenty-fifth, I don't care a bit about their twenty-sixth." He gave her a meaningful look. "*We* will be otherwise occupied."

Aubrey managed to get leave to travel to London and take Colette to the wedding. He played, and she sang, and James's Chelmsford friends marveled that he had made friends with such jazz luminaries during the war. Those two were going places.

Chelsmford was correct.

Hazel and James ate the cake and threw the flowers, and found a cheap little second-floor London flat. Hazel kept flowerpots in windows. James pulled a muscle wrangling a secondhand spinet piano around a bend in the impossible stairs. To their neighbors' dismay, they adopted a poodle.

Maggie came often on weekend breaks from business training college. Colette came when she could get away, until Aubrey's division sailed for the States.

Hazel taught youth piano lessons, and James found a post at an engineering firm. They burnt their dinner and ran out of money and figured things out as they went along. They invited their parents to come for tea. They took long walks in Hyde Park, remembering.

Three years after they married, Hazel gave birth to a daughter, Rose. Her infatuated parents called her Rosie.

James pulled another muscle relocating the spinet to a larger flat. A year later, Rosie learned to walk by clutching the poodle's hair and toddling beside him.

And then one day, a letter of acceptance reached James from the Bartlett School of Architecture, University College, London. A new flat was needed once again, in a different part of town. Hazel took on more piano students and resumed her studies with Monsieur Guillaume.

There were nights when James woke up sobbing. Freak moments when a flashing light or a car engine backfiring set his body shaking. But Hazel was right there, to comfort and to listen. She urged him to reconnect with one of the doctors at Maudsley. Eventually James joined, and ultimately led, a service fraternity for Great War veterans. Once again, the boys in khaki served together by looking out for one another. Helping others cope, as Colette had learned years before, was a sound prescription.

The same year that James graduated from architecture school, Hazel received a thick envelope in the mail from the Royal Academy of Music in London. She made her way through the degree program, taking a pause for a while when their second child, a son, Robert, was born.

James secured a position as an architect, and the spinet grew overnight into a secondhand baby grand.

Whenever James would ask her, teasingly, if she wanted to play the Royal Albert Hall, Hazel's answer was a firm no. He never understood why. She played at smaller venues to lucky audiences.

Some of her classmates wondered if her scars had hurt her career, or if motherhood had set her back. Hazel didn't care a teaspoon. She had exactly the life she'd begged for.

She never won major prizes or achieved great acclaim. But those who heard her play recognized her love for the music and her gratitude for life.

Her greatest fan was James.

There was a time, in their flat, when the position of the piano meant that while James played with little Rosie and held baby Robby and watched Hazel play, he saw only the left side of her face. She looked just like the girl he'd first seen at the parish dance in Poplar.

But when a furniture rearrangement took place, on a whim, leaving Hazel's right side on display, James decided he liked that view even better. She was his, from every angle. The scars were a reminder that she came back.

Harlem Bound—1919 and Beyond

ARES

THE TRIUMPHANT SURVIVORS of the Harlem Hellfighters marched in a parade up the entire length of Fifth Avenue to a wild homecoming welcome. Never before had black soldiers been given a parade in New York City. Marching in perfect synchrony, in razor-straight formation, holding heads and rifles high, proudly sporting stripes and medals and dozens of Croix de Guerre, they dazzled the city. Families and sweethearts struggled and failed to keep to the sidewalks. They broke ranks and attacked their homecoming heroes with hugs and kisses and babies some fathers had never seen, except in photographs.

They marched all the way to the armory where they'd enlisted to be processed for honorable discharge. The night was dark by the time Aubrey finally left the armory. He couldn't wait to get home.

APHRODITE

But home had come to fetch him. His mother and father, Uncle Ames, Kate, and even sleepy old Lester, ambushed Aubrey as he left better than any German patrol had ever managed to.

Six days later, Aubrey brought a Belgian beauty home for Sunday dinner.

And there she stayed. Aubrey's family loved her. Whenever Colette wasn't auditioning for roles as a backup singer for a nightclub, or a low-budget show, and whenever Aubrey wasn't playing with the 15th New York Army Band—which happened a lot—they practiced and wrote new songs together.

APOLLO

Lieutenant James Reese Europe had big plans. The fame of his music, and the Hellfighters' legendary exploits, had made James Reese Europe a household name. He lined up recording sessions for the band to lay down tracks with Pathé Records. They recorded W. C. Handy's "Memphis Blues," and his own compositions, "Castle House Rag," "Clef Club March," and his biggest war hit, "On Patrol in No Man's Land." Europe scheduled the band for a nationwide tour, starting with the Northeast. The Allies had won the war, and now Europe was determined to win Americans over to his bold new sound. Everywhere they went, they were a sensation. Here was a chance to change not only musical tastes, but attitudes about race in America. Or so Jim Europe hoped.

HADES

But on the night of the Boston concert, just before they were to take the stage, Steven Wright, one of the "Wright twin" drummers, grew angry with Jim Europe for favoring the other drummer, as he saw it. When he protested, Wright, himself a victim of shell shock, stabbed Europe in the neck with a penknife. Europe instructed Noble Sissle to go ahead and conduct the show while he went to the hospital to patch up the wound. But the cut had severed an artery, and Europe died within hours. America had lost a jazz visionary on the cusp of what was sure to become a legendary career.

Aubrey rode the train home from Boston in stunned disbelief. Jim Europe had taught him everything he knew about jazz. He'd picked up where Uncle Ames had left off and made a real musician out of Aubrey. He'd kept him alive at Saint-Nazaire after Joey died. And he'd put his broken pieces back together in Aix-les-Bains. He was going to be the express train that would carry Aubrey on to great heights of achievement. And now he was gone.

James Europe was the first black person to receive a public funeral from the City of New York. Thousands lined up to pay their respects.

APOLLO

Aubrey and Colette auditioned at clubs and restaurants all over New York.

Owners slammed doors in their faces, or blew clouds of cigar smoke at them. A few places let them play sixteen bars of a song, only to determine their customers didn't want Negro music, even if a white gal was singing it. Many proprietors had no use for foreigners or "darkies" at all. Even so, Colette received more than a few lewd offers to come back later on, sans Aubrey, to audition for roles of a different sort, and Aubrey was frequently told that the kitchen was hiring busboys and dishwashers if he wanted to do an honest day's work. He never touched Colette in their presence, but he was warned more than once to keep his hands off her.

The rejection would've been too much for most people. It was almost too much for them. Until, one day, at an audition they went into halfheartedly, certain it was pointless, a café owner told them, "I think I could use you."

I wish I could say it was smooth sailing from there.

They scraped together a band and played a few weeks at that café, then the owner canceled them after a night when two of their horns never showed up. But another club owner had dropped a business card into the tip jar on Aubrey's piano.

Money was slim. Band members quarreled and quit. Audiences loved the music, or they hated it. Colette drew snide comments, and women warned her she wasn't safe with black men.

Aubrey pushed his anger aside and wrote new pieces. The more he performed, the better he composed. The more she sang, the bolder Colette grew, and the more collaborative she became in writing lyrics and arranging songs. She trained with dancers and learned the fox-trot.

It was a hectic, chaotic, crazy, creative time. Aubrey flew high. Colette was the happiest she'd been since Germany invaded Belgium. She missed Hazel, and they wrote each other faithfully, but Colette was far from lonely. She adored Aubrey's mother and his sister, Kate.

Then 1920 rolled around, and Prohibition became law. Restaurants and clubs struggled. Some became speakeasies. The Jazz Age began in earnest.

Aubrey and Colette's band grew, their song list grew, and their reputation grew, and their booking fees rose. They went on a Northeastern tour, and then a Midwestern tour, and even an East Coast tour. That meant Southern cities. It meant the Jim Crow South.

Their booking agent mostly got them gigs in Southern venues where black musicians were welcome. But there were times where managers met them as they tuned their instruments, took one look at them, and sent them packing—unless someone other than Colette would sing.

"Around here," one manager told them, "we like white bands, and we don't mind black bands, but a white lady singing with a black band? You must be out of your minds."

"Play without me," Colette told Aubrey.

"No chance," he said. "We play together, or we don't play."

They lost money on the canceled bookings. At other gigs, they learned to leave the club quickly, and all together, out the front door, despite the owner's protests. The back door was what black musicians should use. Problem was, a handful of drunks—Prohibition or no—often waited for them outside the back door.

"I fought the Huns in France," Aubrey told Colette bitterly. "This is worse. I'd rather fight the Boche than play for bigots. In combat, you know who's your enemy."

They returned to Harlem to studio recordings, albums, and sheet music sales. Soon they had their first radio gig. New York was beginning to know their names.

APHRODITE

"We've got a day off next Saturday," Aubrey told Colette one morning over breakfast.

"I know." She searched for just the right rhyme in an American English dictionary. "That would be a good day to go look for that new suit you've been wanting to buy."

"Already bought one," Aubrey told her. "I need it for Saturday."

She tapped her pencil on the tip of her nose. "*Romance, dance, chance, glance* . . . what else is there?" She jotted down notes. "When did you buy a suit?"

"*Prance.*"

"*Non, merci.*"

"So," Aubrey said, "want to get married Saturday?"

Mrs. Edwards, peeking in through the kitchen, held her breath and squeezed every muscle in her body. She never heard Colette's answer, but she could fairly well imagine it. Not the most elaborately romantic proposal ever concocted, but no less loving for that. Mrs. Edwards immediately started planning a menu. Lordy, if that boy could give a mother a little more notice! The cake alone would take days to plan.

EXIT MUSIC

DECEMBER 1942

Closing Arguments

"YOUR HONOR," Aphrodite says, from her new seat by the fireplace, where she has stretched out her legs before the embers, "the defense rests."

It does, Hephaestus thinks. *Beautifully.*

"Can we leave off with all this sham-courtroom nonsense?" says Ares. "This ceased to be a trial before it even began."

Apollo plays a riff on his piano. "Frog Legs Rag" by James Sylvester Scott. "As if you'd know," he told Ares. "You were the one on trial, War. You've been convicted of being a Class A chump. Or did you never catch on?"

Hephaestus's eyes dart to Aphrodite's.

"All the harm in these two stories," Apollo tells Ares, "was your handiwork. Colette's losses. James's traumas. Hazel's injuries. Even Aubrey's injustices trace back to war." He frowns. "By way of bigotry, prejudice, slavery, and hate. But still."

Ares stands majestically, despite the golden mesh enclosing him. "Is he right, Goddess?" he demands. "Were you playing a trick on me?"

Aphrodite smiles. "It's a nice theory, Apollo," she tells him.

"Don't flatter yourself, Ares. This wasn't all about you. Though Zeus knows you had a finger in every pie."

Ares's relief quickly yields to aggravation. "Look, just let me out of here, all right?"

"If I release you," asks Hephaestus, "how do I know you won't rip my head off?"

Hades's voice reverberates with the authority of the ruler of the Underworld. "Ares will behave," Hades says. "Or he'll have me to answer to."

Hephaestus parts the net. His brother emerges, clenching his fists. Veins ripple along his torso as his unfettered powers return. He drinks in an exultant breath.

"Well, I'm off," he says. "But before I go . . ." He hesitates, and turns to Aphrodite. "Goddess. Your story. After the war ended. What came next?"

She's puzzled. "Next?"

"For James and Hazel." He shrugs like he doesn't really care. "For Aubrey and Colette."

"What do you mean?" inquires Aphrodite. "They got married. Isn't that obvious?"

"Both couples," Apollo says, "happily ever after."

"Well," Hades says, "I wouldn't use those words."

Ares's brow furrows. "Why not?"

"Life's never quite like that," Hades says. "Particularly, there's the war. This one. The current one. It came along just as their sons—both James and Hazel's, and Aubrey and Colette's—would soon reach draft age."

"Really?" Ares looks pleased. "Good. Two generations in battle. I'll keep an eye out for them."

Hades catches Aphrodite wearing a strained look.

"Where to next, Ares?" he inquires.

The God of War considers. "I need to visit the Pacific Theater," he says. "Check on the latest developments. But then, Babycakes, I'll be back at Olympus, waiting for you."

"You do that," calls Aphrodite. Hades eyes her curiously.

Ares disappears with a rolling boom like the firing of a Paris Gun. Hephaestus's face relaxes, almost imperceptibly. His inhale sounds like it's the first he's had in a while.

Aphrodite turns to her other two witnesses. "Thank you both," she tells them, "for being here tonight. And for all that you give to my work."

Apollo bows like a concert pianist. "Don't mention it, Goddess," he tells her. "Wouldn't miss it. Love and Art go together like baritone and alto, paint and canvas, like sunrise and a burning atmosphere. Anytime you want to tell a story, I'll bring the soundtrack."

Aphrodite blows him a kiss. "Thank you, Apollo." She nods toward the window. "Sunrise beckons. You'd better hurry."

"You know, Goddess," Apollo says, shoving his argyle feet into his brown-and-white wing tips, "we should collaborate. Produce something on Broadway, maybe?"

Hephaestus turns to his wife. "You really should."

Aphrodite's jaw drops. "I . . . er . . ."

"I'll be in touch," Apollo says. "We can bounce ideas over lunch sometime." He winks at them both. "Later, you two." With a flash of sunrise, he's gone.

Hades rises and dissolves his severe-looking chair. It vanishes with a faint *pff.*

"You've got me wondering, Lady Aphrodite," Hades says, "whether I was not, myself, perhaps, on trial tonight."

Aphrodite rises to a kneeling posture, a look of dismay written across her lovely face.

"Then I have failed, my Lord Hades," she tells him, "to show fitting gratitude. You are my crown and my glory."

Hephaestus is surprised to see what might—or might not—be a tear in Hades's eye.

"I scrabble in sticks and clay," she says. "You make of my work a temple."

Hades bows to the goddess of love. "For such gracious words," he tells her, "a boon, if it's in my power to grant it. What would you ask of me?"

Aphrodite presses her hands together. "If it pleases you," she tells him, "look after their children, in this war. James and Hazel's. Colette and Aubrey's. Bring them, I beg you, safely home."

Hades nods. "If the Fates allow me," he tells her, "I will." His brow darkens. "If the Fates don't allow, we'll have words, they and I."

Hephaestus would almost worry for the Fates, but they're tough old cookies.

"I promise this," Hades continues. "When anyone from these families finds their way to me, I will make their passing painless. One way or another, I'll bring them safely home."

He disappears, leaving husband and wife alone.

"Not quite what you'd hoped for?" Hephaestus asks Aphrodite.

She gazes into the glimmering coals. "One never gets quite what one hoped for from Death," she muses.

Hephaestus chuckles. "I mean, from the telling of your story."

"Oh." She gazes into the fire. "That remains to be seen."

Oh?

Hephaestus stretches his crooked legs. Divine though he may be, stiffness and aches are his to know. And he's been sitting for a long time.

Why did he do this? What did he hope to accomplish? It all feels so embarrassing. So utterly stupid to think that by confronting Aphrodite and exposing her unfaithfulness, he could make anything change. Had he gone mad? What could've come over him?

And yet, here she sits, beside him. And all through her long tale, her stance toward Ares seemed to be—what? Not what Hephaestus would expect from a goddess to her lover.

"I think you're right," he tells her. "About Olympians being unfit for real love. About death and frailty being essential."

She leans closer to the fire. "We say a building is made of brick," she says, "but it's the mortar, filling in the cracks, that holds it all together. That provides the strength."

"The scarring," he says, "that makes a broken bone harder, stronger than it was before." The one god flung down from Olympus as a child to land in a shattered heap upon the earth knows something about this. His bones are iron.

Aphrodite leans her head against a cushion.

He's a god. He's seen her a trillion times. But her beauty melts him still. Always. No less so for being eternally beyond his reach.

He's been thoroughly beaten down. Shown for the puny, jealous child he is. Humiliated by the web he wove—literally—to humiliate his cheating wife.

And yet, she's still here.

He decides to try one more time.

"You say perfection limits you," he says. "But you're not so perfect as you like to let on."

Her eyebrows arch. "Is that so?"

"Yes, it is." He turns his crooked shoulders toward her. "For one thing, you have terrible taste in men."

The corner of her mouth twitches. "Which one?"

My dumb brother. "All of them," he says. "You've picked a string of winners." He shrugs. "You did marry me, after all, and I'm no prize specimen."

She glances at his form and looks at him as if to say, *And?*

"You're completely soft where mortals are concerned," he tells her. "Heart on your sleeve. Vulnerable to everything. I don't like to say it, but you're a byword on Olympus for it. Way too invested, they call you. Too far down in the weeds with the mortals. It ruins your cool. Warps your judgment."

Her hackles rise. "Who says that?"

"Oh, you know." He shrugs. "Folks."

"Hermes," she says darkly. "He'll be hearing from me."

If this is his attempt at winning her, it's working about as well as his last try.

"All I'm saying," Hephaestus says, with his heart in his throat, "is that, if love demands brokenness, don't count yourself out." He gulps. "And you'd have to search far and wide to find a more broken god than me."

She gazes at him. Her Mona Lisa smile reveals nothing.

"What do you say, Goddess?" he asks her. "How about me?"

She pulls her knees in close and wraps her arms around them. "I say it's about time."

DECEMBER 1942

About Time (Part II)

HEPHAESTUS SCRATCHES HIS shaggy head. "*What* did you just say?"

"You have no idea." Her voice rises to a scolding pitch. "Years, I've been trying to get you to offer me that. To offer me *you*."

He blinks in disbelief.

"How I've suffered through those god-awful meet-ups with your stupid, arrogant brother." She rolls her eyes. "Making sure to strategically pose for Hermes's camera. *Ffaugh*."

Hephaestus thinks the room may have started spinning.

Aphrodite stretches out on the hearth. "He is *so boring*," she says. "I thought I would start chewing my fingernails. And I would *never*."

"You . . . wanted . . . *me*?"

"You never wanted me," Aphrodite tells. "You're the one god who didn't. So Zeus sticks me to you like a postage stamp. Fine, you tell yourself, I'll take a wife if I must. But you never chose *me*. You! The one god with half a brain and a quarter—oh, let's say a third—of your typical Olympian ego."

"Half a brain?" he cries. "One third of a—"

"But you resented me," cries Aphrodite. "I was an embarrassing reminder that you were—what? The Olympian charity case? You were sure I could never love you. So you shut me out."

"How can you say such a thing?" he roars. "All I've wanted—"

"You were willing to have a *wife*," she says, "if Zeus forced you to. But you never got to know *me*." She pokes a log in the fire. "Do you know how hard I worked to make sure you knew Ares and I would be here tonight? This little trial was *months* in the making."

Hephaestus wonders if he's dreaming. Hallucinating. Losing his mind.

"Months in the making?" he cries. "*I* planned this."

She pats his knee. "Yes, dear."

He looks away. He doesn't know whether to laugh or smash a window.

"So it really was me, on trial," he says slowly. "On trial for being incapable of love."

"No, you blooming ass," she cries. "You are charged with *being* capable of love. And of being loved. If you would for once look at me and know who I am."

The god of fires flexes his fingers. Nothing makes sense. This is all an odd dream.

"You must have no idea how much I look at you, Goddess," he tells his wife. "I tell myself, I can stop anytime."

She rises to her feet, an angry goddess in her full wrath, and the chandeliers begin to shake. "Then *why haven't you ever seen?* Don't you see how hard I've been trying to tell you? You could know me, if you tried. I would love you, if you let me."

Not even Poseidon, the Earthshaker, could make Hephaestus feel more wobbly.

The mirror behind Aphrodite shows him his balding head, his bristly beard, his crooked form. His gnarled hands, singed and scarred by an eternity in his volcanic forge.

"Would it make you feel better," she asks, "if I took on a different appearance? Something a bit more—shall we say—average?"

Hephaestus swallows. "That's all right," he tells her quickly. "We should be able to, er, be ourselves with each other."

Aphrodite snorts. She covers her face with a hand and snickers. In spite of himself, Hephaestus starts laughing, too.

The laughter dies away. After all that's been said, poor Hephaestus's head lies in fragments on the floor. He feels shy now, beside his wife. Marriage was simpler, he realizes, when the game plan was "catch her in a net."

"So this was all your doing."

"You said it yourself," she says. "I'm good at what I do."

He shakes his head. "I still don't see how me catching the two of you together would—"

"I needed to show you what love looks like," she tells him. "How you each responded would reveal to anyone with the brain of a goldfish which of the two of you has a loving heart."

"The brain of a goldfish," he echoes.

Between the curtains, rose and gold sunlight bursts forth. Their all-night tale hasn't prevented Apollo from serving up another breathtaking sunrise. Tailor-made, Hephaestus thinks, for a couple in love. He hopes that somewhere the Alderidges and Edwardses see it, too.

"So, what happens next?" he says at length.

She flashes him a wink that, by itself, would melt entire armies. "We could meet up some morning," she says, "for tea and lemon cake."

Hephaestus stands and extends a hand. She takes it and pulls herself up to her feet.

Now? Hephaestus wonders. Is *now* the time? He's waited for this moment, far too long.

Aphrodite helps him out. It's what she does best, what she's famous for.

Kisses by the billions happen every day, even in a lonely world like ours.

But this is a kiss for the ages.

HISTORICAL NOTE

Lovely War is a work of fiction, but several characters are real, and the timeline of Great War events depicted is real. The British Expeditionary Force (B.E.F.) privates and sergeants named are fictional, but the senior officers named are real. For more on the fate of the Fifth Army, see *The Fifth Army in March 1918* by Walter Shaw Sparrow.

James Reese Europe, composer and conductor of the Clef Club Orchestra, and first lieutenant in the 15th New York National Guard (later the 369th US Infantry), helped kindle France's love of jazz, along with other black army band conductors. During his time in Aix-les-Bains, he joked about never sleeping but staying up each night to copy "three million notes" as he arranged new scores. (I thought it would be fun to add Aubrey as his uncredited helper.)

Europe's star rose along with those of Vernon and Irene Castle, white dance-duo super-celebrities of the pre-war years. They danced to Jim Europe's music, using versions of African American dances that he had taught them. They were global phenomena, trend-setters, and style icons, helping bring African American music and dance into the worldwide mainstream.

Europe's boundless creative energy and talent would surely have made James Reese Europe a household name had his life not been cut tragically short on May 9, 1919, by an unprovoked attack from a disgruntled drummer likely suffering from shell shock. For more on his remarkable life, leadership, and music, I suggest *A Life in Ragtime: A Biography of James Reese Europe* by Reid Badger.

Captain Hamilton Fish III, K Company captain, was a Harvard football star and the son of a wealthy family with deep roots in American history and politics. Following the Great War, Hamilton Fish III was elected to the US House of Representatives, where he served for decades, a staunch advocate for veterans and soldiers, and for peace.

I used several Army Band members' real names, including Pinkhead Parker (saxophone), Alex Jackson (tuba), and Luckey Roberts (piano). Jesús Hernandez (clarinet) was one of several horn players from Puerto Rico recruited by Jim Europe to round out his orchestra. Noble Sissle (drum major, vocals) went on to lead a band. His talent and charm are captured in footage available online. Sissle was one of Europe's close friends, along with legendary jazz and ragtime piano composer Eubie Blake. (Blake claims it was Europe who coined the term "gig" to describe an event that a musician is hired to perform at.)

Events involving the Clef Club orchestra and the Harlem Hellfighters are all drawn from historical sources, starting with the Carnegie Hall "Concert of Negro Music," and through to the victory parade marching up Fifth Avenue. Their experiences of persecution at Camp Dix, Camp Wadsworth, Saint-Nazaire, and Aix-les-Bains are all taken from the historical record. (A light postscript on the Carnegie Hall concert: some of my sources said ten upright pianos were used in the orchestra. Others claimed *fourteen*. I went with the smaller number, though this may be the only book in print that asserts ten pianos on a stage to be "the smaller number.")

BLACK SERVICEMEN IN THE GREAT WAR

The story of America's contribution to the final year of World War I is one of sacrifice, valor, and honor. But it's not a story of unalloyed white heroism. The shameful truth of how black servicemen who risked all for their country suffered widespread hatred, betrayal, and violence *from their country* is a crucial part of the story.

The US 369th infantry wasn't the only black regiment to see combat in the Great War. Of nearly 400,000 black American soldiers who served, 200,000 were sent to Europe, and of them, approximately 42,000 fought. The rest worked as dockworkers, gravediggers, road and railroad builders, and other heavy laborers, in the military branch known as SOS (Service of Supply). Black SOS soldiers were cruelly misused, worked from morning till night seven days a week, often given minimal food, clothing, or housing. They faced brutality, humiliation, and violent reminders that they were to bow to white authority; and that restaurants, shops, train cars, and most of all, white society, particularly, white women, were off-limits. One SOS soldier described their treatment as being "in the spirit of slavery."[1]

THE LONG DARK NIGHT

As the Great War broke, white supremacy in America was having its post–Civil War heyday. White America, long scarred by the bitterness and divisions of the Civil War, was tired of remaining adversarial, North versus South. The political, economic, and cultural opportunities possible in healing the breach between North and

---

1. Lentz-Smith, *Freedom Struggles*, page 94.

South were too tempting to pass up. Segregation, whether eagerly embraced or quietly overlooked, became the compromise that lubricated a nationwide reunification of northern and southern political and economic interests, at the expense of black Americans' legal, civil, and human rights.

Black activists described the period between 1890 and the Great War as "the long dark night." With the 1896 ruling in *Plessy v. Ferguson* that legalized "separate but equal" facilities, segregation, now legally blessed, soon infiltrated American life. Schools, trains, buses, restaurants, theaters, workplaces, churches, and civic spaces were segregated on both sides of the Mason-Dixon line.

White supremacy wasn't the view of just a narrow, hateful fringe; it was ubiquitous, enshrined in the White House with the 1912 election of Woodrow Wilson, the first Southern Democrat elected since James Polk in 1844. As president of Princeton, Wilson had blocked all black applications to the university. As President of the United States, Wilson staffed his administration with Southern Democrats who dismissed and demoted black workers, segregating the postal service and the Department of the Treasury. Such policies helped residential segregation laws pass in southern state legislatures.

White supremacy rested—and still rests—on greed, specifically, the desire to enrich oneself with free or cheap labor or stolen resources, or to reduce competition for jobs and privileges by suppressing other groups' eligibility; on fears of black political power at the polls; on fears of the strength of armed black resistance; and especially, on fears of contaminating the "purity" of the white race through interbreeding. It rested, therefore, upon sex as much as on dollars, laws, votes, and guns. "Degenerate" blacks had to be kept far from white women, and from circumstances that would display their intellect, capacity, character, strength, resolve, bravery, and ambition.

Where better to demonstrate these admirable qualities than through military service? Black Americans, eager to prove that black America could produce exemplary citizens and soldiers, flocked to the Great War, seeing it as a major opportunity. By contrast, white supremacist America—the America in full control of the reins of political power—saw armed black men trained in effective combat as their worst nightmare.

EXPORTING JIM CROW

Military white supremacists watched with alarm as the relatively egalitarian French embraced black soldiers as brothers-in-arms, fearing it would "spoil" them and further destabilize the "race problem" in America. The US Army forbade black soldiers from interacting with white women overseas, yet local women welcomed their company.

Finally, in desperation, US Army officials induced French counterparts to distribute a memorandum to French military officials titled "Secret Information Concerning Black American Troops." W. E. B. du Bois published it in the NAACP magazine, *Crisis*, in 1919. Below are a few illustrative excerpts.

. . . the French public has become accustomed to treating the Negro with familiarity and indulgence.

Americans . . . are afraid that contact with the French will inspire in black Americans aspirations which to them [the whites] appear intolerable. . . .

Although a citizen of the United States, the black man is regarded by the white American as an inferior being with whom relations of business or service only are possible. The black is constantly being censured for his want of intelligence . . .

The vices of the Negro are a constant menace to the American who has to repress them sternly. For instance, the black American troops in France have, by themselves, given rise to as many complaints for attempted rape as all the rest of the army. . . .[2]

The slanderous accusations regarding rape were utterly false.

To their credit, when higher French military command learned of the memo, they ordered that it be gathered and burned. At the war's end, the French Army lavishly honored the contributions of black American servicemen, and the 369th's in particular.

THE HEROES' WELCOME

When the war ended in 1918, and black servicemen returned home, their evident pride, self-respect, and confidence infuriated southern white supremacists. Lynchings spiked in 1919. Black Great War veterans were frequent targets, and many more were beaten, threatened, and abused. Some faced violence simply for publicly appearing in uniform.

Conditions did not materially improve for most black Americans who served; for many, the aggressive backlash made things unbearable. But for better and for worse, black servicemen

....

2 From "Secret Information Concerning Black Troops," dated August 7, 1918, reprinted in *Crisis Magazine*, May 1919 edition, volume 18, number 1 (whole number 103). Edited by William Edward Burghardt du Bois. The Crisis Publishing Company, a publication of the National Association for the Advancement of Colored People.

returning from the war were idealistic no more. They came home confident, angry, and determined; ready to organize and demand legal and civic rights. When World War II came along twenty-five years later, a million black soldiers served. Within twenty-five years of the Second World War's end, the Civil Rights Act (1964), Voting Rights Act (1965), and Civil Rights Act of 1968, known as the Fair Housing Act, had passed. Fighting for freedom despite violence and oppression became part of the generational context from which civil rights heroes emerged.

For more on black servicemen during and after the war, I recommend the extraordinary work *Freedom Struggles: African Americans and World War I*, by Adriane Lentz-Smith. For a closer look at the Harlem Hellfighters, see *A More Unbending Battle: The Harlem Hellfighters' Struggle for Freedom in WWI and Equality at Home*, by Peter N. Nelson; and *Harlem's Hell Fighters: The African-American 369th Infantry in World War I*, by Stephen L. Harris.

A 1977 documentary film, *Men of Bronze: The Black American Heroes of World War I*, directed by William Miles, then the official historian of the US 369th, features original footage of the Harlem Hellfighters, along with interviews with Captain Hamilton Fish III and other survivors from the regiment. The murders at Saint-Nazaire of men of the 15th New York National Guard (as they were then called) by marines, followed by retaliatory killing, are described in those interviews.

Many accounts chronicle the ugly reality of how all black Americans, Northern and Southern, were treated by white America during the early part of the twentieth century. I found *Black Boy: A Record of Childhood and Youth*, the autobiography of Richard Wright (also the author of *Native Son*), to be a riveting account of the chokehold racial hatred had during the war years and the decades that followed.

WOMEN AND WORLD WAR I

The Great War had a reverberating impact on women, particularly in the United Kingdom, where such a large percentage of men were pulled into the service of the war effort. Prior to the war, stringent laws and attitudes kept middle and upper-class British women within constrained, largely domestic spheres. Working-class women were chiefly employed as household servants, earning meager pay. Some women worked in factories, under appalling conditions, with wages they could scarcely live on.

When war broke out in Europe, millions of British men went overseas. Every industry now faced a dire labor crisis: farming, preaching, teaching, clerical work, entertainment, professional athletics, manufacturing, medicine, transportation, and more. Suddenly women were operating trains, driving trucks and ambulances, working in factories, assisting in hospitals, and even performing surgery. Women from every rung of the socioeconomic ladder stepped up to "do their bit." Wealthy women organized charities and relief organizations for Belgian refugees, for war wounded, for widows and orphans. They opened hospitals and hired women doctors and nurses to staff them. Young women joined the Women's Land Army and moved to the countryside to grow urgently needed food. The Red Cross employed thousands of nurses and nursing assistants. The Young Men's Christian Association (YMCA) enlisted volunteers and secretaries at relief huts. Countless thousands of women left domestic servitude and took better-paying war production jobs in factories, turning out millions of artillery shells. For an engaging, thoughtful, and at times, hilarious account of how women stepped up to "do their bit" across all aspects of British life, I recommend *Fighting on the Home Front: The Legacy of Women in World War One* by Kate Adie.

Much of society was aghast to see women in the workplace, exposed to worldly vices. An anxious traditionalist element of society insisted that this "unnatural" state of affairs was temporary; as soon as the war ended, women would give up their jobs and return to domestic life, yielding jobs to the men. In large measure, this is what happened.

But women's capacity had been proven, exposing the fallacy in the belief that women were too fragile, emotional, or unintelligent for political life. When the war ended, the British Parliament passed the "Representation of the People Act 1918," granting suffrage (voting rights) to all men, regardless of property, and to all women over the age of thirty, with minimum property ownership requirements. In 1920, the Nineteenth Amendment to the United States Constitution granted American women the right to vote. In 1928, Parliament extended the Representation of the People Act, granting suffrage to all women over the age of twenty-one, on equal footing with men. (It took the Second World War drawing to a close for France to grant the vote to women in 1944.)

For a moving account of one young war nurse who became an activist for peace and women's rights, I recommend *Testament of Youth* by Vera Brittain. This beloved memoir stands as one of the greatest women's accounts of the First World War. A 2014 BBC/Heyday Films feature film adaptation starring Alicia Vikander and Kit Harington beautifully depicts the book's essence.

American women volunteered in large numbers as well, including African American women. *Two Colored Women with the American Expeditionary Forces*, by Addie W. Hunton and Kathryn Magnolia Johnson, is a firsthand account that provides a frank look at the persecution faced, and the inspiring work done, by women who served as YMCA volunteers at the Camp Lusitania "Negro hut" at Saint-Nazaire.

IMPACT OF WORLD WAR I

World War I was the first war to use aircraft for surveillance and combat in any significant way, and the first war in which submarines were used to great effect. Tanks were invented during the Great War—a project directed by Winston Churchill—in hopes of bursting through the craters and barbed wire of no-man's-land to penetrate enemy lines. By land, by sea, and by air, an entirely new form of war was waged, using heavy artillery field guns capable of bombing targets scores of miles away. Although nuclear weapons and smart missiles were yet to appear, World War I gave us modern warfare as we now know it.

Medical advances emerged from the treatment of the war's millions of casualties. Modern weaponry created ghastly, debilitating injuries, but innovations in prosthetics and reconstructive surgery brought many an increased quality of life. Prosthetic facial masks, if eerie-looking, concealed gruesome facial injuries and lent their wearers dignity and privacy.

Injuries less likely to be seen, but no less debilitating for many, were mental and emotional. It wasn't until later in the war that the concussive impact upon the brain of nearby explosions was better understood. It took longer still for the psychological devastation of trench warfare to be seen as a war injury and not mere cowardice or weakness. Manifestations of "shell shock" varied from uncontrollable shaking, to refusal to return to combat, to erratic behavior, suicide, nightmares, screaming, depression, anxiety, and violent behavior. Hospitals like the one in Maudsley grew in number and expanded their mental health facilities, designing them with comfort, therapy, rehabilitation, and medication management in mind. Pink walls and friendly, cheerful treatment were innovations. Though the world had, and still has, a long way to go in understanding, treating, and destigmatizing mental illness, it's inspiring to see what gains were made in the name of compassion and sympathy for those who suffered in ways that, not long prior, would have been scorned as cowardly or "unmanly."

A WAR OF THE OLD UPON THE YOUNG

Older men made the decisions that thrust the world into war in the summer of 1914, but it was chiefly the young who bore the war's burden. Countless youth lied about their age and enlisted as young teens.

Throughout the war, soldiers who saw lives wasted in endless, futile carnage for no perceptible gain grew increasingly disillusioned with the middle-aged leaders who poured out young blood like water from the safety of their leather-backed chairs. The disparity between the gore and filth of the trenches and the image of heroic honor conjured by war propaganda caused a crisis of faith—both religious and patriotic—for millions.

Poets and artists in the trenches used art to lambaste this war apparently waged by the old upon the young. The works of Wilfred Owen, Siegfried Sassoon, Robert Graves, Ivor Gurney, Alan Seeger, and Edward Thomas, and even the idealistic early war poetry of Rupert Brooke, stand as memorials to youth and innocence lost forever, alongside works by well-known writers and poets such as Thomas Hardy, Ezra Pound, Rudyard Kipling, William Butler Yeats, Carl Sandburg, Ernest Hemingway, and Gertrude Stein. Women working at the Front, among them Vera Brittain, the author of *Testament of Youth*, contributed stunning poetry to the war canon. The Poetry Foundation has compiled an outstanding collection of World War I poetry on its website. It's brilliant, bitter, and heartbreaking.

For memoirs and fictional accounts of life at the Front from soldiers who fought there, I recommend the perennial classics *All Quiet on the Western Front,* by Erich Maria Remarque, and *Goodbye to All That,* by Robert Graves.

The causes and provocations that led the world into such a devastating war aren't easily distilled; perhaps for that reason, the First World War remains less understood than the Second. For eminently readable accounts of how we got into such a global mess, I recommend the highly acclaimed works *The Guns of August,* by Barbara W. Tuchman, and *The War That Ended Peace,* by Margaret MacMillan.

IN MEMORIAM

Researching and writing *Lovely War* made me love these soldiers, these Tommys and Poilus and Doughboys and Anzacs and Jerrys who fought and died along the Western Front because they had no choice. But it wasn't until I traveled to France and Belgium, visiting preserved trenches and underground tunnels, still-hollowed shell craters, breathtaking monuments, war museums, and row after row of pristine gravestones—witnessing Europe's fidelity to their memory—that I began to glimpse the true cost of this war. I have never seen anything like it. Lovingly tended graves marked "Welsh Soldier, Known Only to God," broke my heart.

A frequent theme in the writings of men at the Front was their marveling at how, over the shell-blasted wasteland of the killing fields, a glorious sunset could still paint the sky, or the freshness of dew and birdsong could still make morning sweet. Even in the trenches. For all its horror and despair, for many, the Great War sharpened life, showing it for the brief and fleeting gift it was, and revealing home, freedom, safety, family, beauty, and love to be precious beyond price.

Many never returned from the war. Others returned but were never the same. Still others returned to bigotry and hatred that history has yet to leave firmly in the past. They paid a price.

Their children paid a similar price in the global war that followed.

We owe a debt.

How might the twentieth century have gone if nineteen-year-old Gavrilo Princip had failed to assassinate Austria-Hungary's Archduke Franz Ferdinand at a June parade in Sarajevo in 1914? Possibly some other spark would have lit the same fuse. Possibly not. We can't know.

But we can choose to use whatever means lie in our own power to be agents of healing, hope, justice, plenty, and peace.

SELECTED BIBLIOGRAPHY

Adie, Kate. *Fighting on the Home Front: The Legacy of Women in World War One.* London: Hodder & Stoughton, 2013.

Badger, Reid. *A Life in Ragtime: A Biography of James Reese Europe.* New York: Oxford University Press, 1995.

Brittain, Vera. *Testament of Youth: An Autobiographical Study of the Years 1900–1925.* New York: Penguin Books, 2005. First published in Great Britain in 1933 by Victor Gollancz Limited.

Graves, Robert. *Good-bye to All That: An Autobiography.* London: Penguin Books, 2008. First published in the United Kingdom in 1929 by Anchor.

Harris, Stephen L. *Harlem's Hell Fighters: The African-American 369th Infantry in World War I.* Washington, DC: Potomac Books Inc., 2003.

Hunton, Addie W., and Kathryn Magnolia Johnson. *Two Colored Women with the American Expeditionary Forces.* Brooklyn: Brooklyn Eagle Press, 1920.

Lentz-Smith, Adriane. *Freedom Struggles: African Americans and World War I.* Cambridge: Harvard University Press, 2009.

MacMillan, Margaret. *The War That Ended Peace: The Road to 1914.* New York: Random House, 2013.

Miles, William (director). *Men of Bronze: The Black American Heroes of World War I.* 1977.

Nelson, Peter N. *A More Unbending Battle: The Harlem Hellfighters' Struggle for Freedom in WWI and Equality at Home.* New York: Basic Civitas, a member of the Perseus Books Group, 2009.

Remarque, Erich Maria. *All Quiet on the Western Front.* Toronto: Little, Brown & Company, 1929.

Sparrow, Walter Shaw. *The Fifth Army in March 1918.* London: John Lane, 1921.

Tuchman, Barbara W. *The Guns of August: The Outbreak of World War I.* New York: Random House, 2014. Originally published by Macmillan, 1962.

Wright, Richard. *Black Boy (American Hunger): A Record of Childhood and Youth.* New York: Harper Perennial, 2006. Originally published 1945 by Harper & Brothers.

ACKNOWLEDGMENTS

THE WAR TO END ALL WARS failed to live up to expectations. It didn't end in a month. It wasn't over by Christmas. It wasn't glorious, and it most certainly did not halt future war.

Those who supported me in writing this book, however, exceeded all expectations.

My first draft was supposed to be over by Christmas. It wasn't. But when it finally appeared, my editor, Kendra Levin, climbed fearlessly over the parapet into the no-man's-land of those early drafts, time after thankless time. There ought to be a Distinguished Service Medal for editorial valor. I'd go further and lobby for Kendra's nomination for the Victoria Cross.

My agent, Alyssa Henkin, and my publisher, Ken Wright, have championed this project from its inception. I hope always to live up to their faith in me.

The entire team at Penguin Young Readers embraced *Lovely War*. Regina Hayes and Dana Leydig provided superb insight into early drafts. I could do nothing without Janet Pascal. Special thanks to Kaitlin Severini for her painstaking efforts. Kim Ryan has taken my work around the globe. Marisa Russell brings my work into the sun, and Carmela Iaria puts it in just the right hands. Samira Iravani and Jim Hoover make my books gorgeous, and Jocelyn Schmidt and Jennifer Loja make all of this possible.

I'm lucky to have early readers who shared their time and

insights so generously. To Nancy Werlin, Debbie Kovacs, Kelly Anderson, Alison Brumwell, Kyle Hiller, Hannah Gómez, Herb Boyd, and Luisa Perkins, thank you for leaving your mark upon this story.

I prayed my way through every page, and that which has carried me aloft thus far never forgot me. Divine help gave life to this project, including but not limited to Aphrodite's contributions.

The pace and process of researching and writing this book was unusually intense, and my family had to live with a Julie who was present but not. They cheerfully carried on, gave me a wide berth to do what I needed to do, and celebrated each milestone with love and takeout. Thanks especially to Daniel, for always believing. It really is the Berry family who brings these books into the world.

At the vanguard of the Berry army stands my glorious Phil, my best-beloved, and *Lovely War*'s subject, theme, and inspiration.

JULIE BERRY is the author of the 2017 Printz Honor and *Los Angeles Times* Book Prize shortlisted novel *The Passion of Dolssa*, the Carnegie and Edgar shortlisted *All the Truth That's in Me*, and many other acclaimed middle grade novels and picture books. She holds a BS from Rensselaer in communication and an MFA from Vermont College. She lives in Southern California with her family.